CLOUD-CASTLES

DAVE FREER

MAGIC ISLE PRESS

Copyright 2021 Dave Freer

A Magic Isle Press book

E-book ISBN:978-0-9925490-4-6

Pring ISBN: 978-0-9925490-5-3

Cover art: Mark Baldwin

Cover design: SanderlyStudios

Proofs by R.B. Knott and K.J. Knott

WELCOME TO CLOUD-CASTLES

Get off my lawn... Oh sorry. Um. Welcome! I'm not really the grumpy old man of writing... yet. I'm just practicing. I'm only at 24 or so novels, and I believe 30 is the minimum requirement. A couple of my books scraped onto bestseller lists, and one got to be a finalist in Dragon Awards, in two categories – up against Sir Terry Pratchett in one and Larry Correia in the other. It didn't win, but it did mix with the right books.

To stop myself from turning into the grumpy old man of writing, I don't stick to any one genre or series, so I have written everything from murder-mysteries to hard sf – from rural fantasy to military sf and every possible combination of genres. They tend long on satire and dry humor, problem-solving, and action, rather than introspection. I get bored reading three hundred pages of angst for twenty pages of story, and assume I am not alone in feeling this way.

If your tastes run in a similar direction, and you enjoy my books, you can find and follow me on Facebook (https://www.facebook.com/Freer.Dave) and MeWe. Just tell me you're one of my readers to get onto the friends list. You can sign up for my newsletter (https://www.davefreer.com/), which will come out when there is something to tell you, and have notifications of new books and special offers. There's also my website (https://www.davefreer.com/) and Coalfired Cuttlefish (https://coalfiredcuttlefish.wordpress.com/), and I am a regular Monday contributor to Mad Genius Club. (https://madgeniusclub.com/)

To the memory of the men and women of the Eureka Rebellion

Acknowledgments

My greatest thanks go, as always, to my wife, Barbara, first reader and dearest friend. It's been a tough book to write while trying to build a home for ourselves. That was hard enough without the Augean stable of modern, urban-shaped Australian bureaucracy, so very different to the aspirations of the brave men and women who built my country. It did shape the book, somewhat! My thanks also go to the friends who have rallied around my little Eureka Stockade, keeping us going, and kept me writing under difficult circumstances. My thanks also go to my first readers, and advisors on particularly the medical matters, Dr Alex John, Dr Mark Baldwin, and Intensive Care Paramedic Jon Purtell. Any errors are mine in misunderstanding their sage advice. To my proof-readers, official and unofficial, Larry Bauer and Katie and Richard Knott, thank you for your help and patience.

GLOSSARY OF TERMS

Arvo - afternoon.

Battler - someone struggling their way up, a person who gets up and tries again, no matter how often knocked down. A great compliment.

Blood's worth bottling - someone rare and precious, they're worth preserving.

Bludger – a lazy parasite.

Bottle-o – a place for buying alcohol.

Brass Razoo – a tiny amount of money.

Butcher – seven fluid ounces of beer.

Bush-pig – an unattractive prostitute.

Cobber – a compliment. A comrade.

Cop a serve – get told off.

Daks – underwear.

Dead dog's eye – meat pie.

Dinkum – really, truly, genuine.

Drongo – a fool.

Flat out like a lizard drinking – working hard.

Full as a goog – can't eat any more. A 'goog' is an egg.

Lammo – lamington – sponge cake, coated in jam and dipped in desiccated coconut flakes... or something.

Mystery bag – sausage.

Middy – half a pint of beer.

Nong – simpleton.

Rack off – get lost.

Raw prawn – something difficult to swallow.

Root – to have sex.

Shout me, or my shout – to pay for the drinks or food of whoever you're 'shouting'.

Schooner – 15 fluid oz of beer. Don't ask me. I have no idea where this comes from.

Snot block – custard slice.

Sook – soft, soppy.

Tea – the main meal, eaten before bed.

Yakka – work.

Wowser – a strait-laced puritan, usually one who doesn't drink.

Wouldn't be dead for quids – having a great time.

Zack – five cents.

AUTHOR'S NOTE
ON SYBIL III, CLOUD-CASTLES AND THE CHARACTERS I POPULATED IT WITH.

The idea for this book came out of reading astronomer John S. Lewis's WORLDS WITHOUT END (1999) where he posited that a gas-giant with no true solid core might have a 'life zone', where conditions of pressure & temperature allow liquid water and a breathable atmosphere to exist. He posits that convection currents would make the evolution of life there unlikely.

However, there is no reason why such a zone could not be 'colonized' with tailored lifeforms that never touched ground. It would be a strange world to live on... or in... but a very large one.

Sybil III was just such a world. An ancient meeting place between two rival alien empires (now both largely destroyed by an internecine war) – the one piece of real-estate neither wanted. Humans have expanded into the ruins of both empires now deserted worlds – and, quite by accident onto Sybil III – where the surviving trading magnates of the Thrymi and Zell Empires still live in their decaying Cloud-Castles, drifting in an endless sea of sky.

The human 'colonists' were being transported to a new colony as convicts, that their home wanted to be rid of – rather like the colonists who were once sent to Australia. In fact, these ones were from a future Australia.

Now, because I believe in the pendulum nature of human society, I suspect we're already on a backswing away from a 'world society' to one of smaller regional or tribal insularity. Australia, like many isolated societies, developed its own variant of English, its own traditions, legends, its own way of life. They were profoundly proud of these, and for generations, fostered them. Then the pendulum (particularly in the cities, which, like any crowded places, require more conformity) swung the other way, and while many of these speech-patterns and traditions were considered to be fine for old people and country bumpkins, imitation of the speech and ways of the coastal cities of the US and London was far cooler.

I believe this pendulum swing has passed its apogee and we're heading back – and that's where Sybil III's involuntary colonists (many of the characters) come from.

CHAPTER

ONE

The castle -- an ethereal mixture of faerie frailty and an acid-fueled dream of someone madder and more romantic than Mad King Ludwig -- floated among the roil of red-lit clouds. The fragile hanging turrets, spires and battlements dangled over the hungry emptiness of the thousand-mile void below.

"Thrymi," said the second mate to the passenger who was staring out at it. "The Zell Cloud-castles are more solid-looking."

"I've never seen anything quite as beautiful in all my life," said the slim young man -- all knees, elbows, and an eager puppy expression - who clung to the rail of the tiny observation deck, the knuckles of his outsized hands white with hanging on through the buffeting.

The mate nodded. "The castles are pretty. Unlike the Thrymi." She stood easily, riding the turbulence with the confidence born of experience.

The young passenger shook his head. "They're just misunderstood. Really. It's a very different and complex culture..." he said enthusiastically.

"They're just murdering bastards," she interrupted. "Actually, the whole place is full of murdering, thieving, evil bastards who'd sell their own mothers for half a dollar. It's a good thing that there isn't much standing space for them, or there'd be more of them."

Young Augustus StJohn Thistlewood III looked sorrowfully at the second mate of the SS Star of Space. He knew better than to argue with such a closed mind. It was a shame that the person that carried it had to be so physically attractive. He struggled to talk to women at all, and this had been a rare chance to do so.

"Anyway," said the second mate, "I came to tell you that you need to go and strap in, Sir. We'll be landing at the trade plate soon. Landing can be a bit bumpy."

Augustus nodded. "A pity. I'd like to have seen the plate from above."

"Above is fine, Sir," she said dryly. "It's seeing it from below that's a problem."

"I'd love to see the gravity repulsors! I didn't know that there were any flights below it!" exclaimed Augustus, enthusiastically.

"There aren't. Most people see them briefly in passing," said the second mate, cryptically. "About three minutes to touch-down, Sir. I'll have them put external video through to your stateroom."

"Thank you. Just one question -- what is that?" Augustus pointed at a drift of purple-red scrubby spikiness coming up on the starboard side of the little starship.

"Floating vegetation. The Zell normally keep it cleared around the plate. It can be really thick in other places. I'd better go and tell the skipper. Excuse me, Sir." She hurried off.

Augustus swayed and bounced his way to his euphemistically named stateroom. When selling tickets for passages to Sybil, the Star of Space's agent could hardly admit that it was actually a broom cupboard.

Looking at the screen-feed he could see the great trading plate coming into view. From above it appeared to be a solid four square-mile chaos of varicolored roofs. As it grew closer, he tried to work out just where they could land. That, in part, was the issue. Sybil III just had no land. None. Or none that any human could survive on. It was

2

a gas dwarf world, and its solid core lay somewhere many, many miles down below at enormous temperatures and pressures. The lifezone, such as it was, was up in the outer atmosphere. It was a vast lifezone, just resource-poor, and short of solid landing platforms. Life would probably never have evolved here by itself, but Sybil III had been the only point with a breathable oxygen atmosphere that neither the alien Zell nor the Thrymi empires wanted. On this neutral territory they'd built the anti-grav trading plate, with now lost technology, and the merchant houses had built their cloud-castles - palaces for rich merchants of yesteryear. They'd introduced the genetically engineered airborne lifeforms too, including the floating plants he'd read about, seen pictures of, and failed to recognize when he saw them in reality for the first time.

Of course, that had been long ago, before humans discovered FTL, and before the Thrymi - Zell War had catastrophically destroyed both their empires.

And before the human colonist ship Botany Bay had made a crash landing onto the trading plate.

Augustus had to admit there was an element of guilt in the way most of the people of his world regarded Sybil III. The old first-generation FTL Botany Bay had been lumbering along towards Azure and would have got there a full half-century before Great grandfather Thistlewood, and the other first settlers, if it hadn't been for an engineering malfunction. There, but for fortune... Well, for the next year, Augustus was here to dedicate himself to improving the lot of the Sybilians.

The ship was closing in fast now... he could see that most of the roof area supported trays of plants on racks. The airbrakes were roaring. They were going to overshoot! Miss the plate... Augustus fumbled frantically for the buckle... although what good being free would do, was something that he'd not quite worked out. Then the screen showed a narrow sliver of metal -- like a diving board out over the edge of the void. They were going to hit it! Augustus frantically buckled up again.

And with a bounce, they landed. The engines were still. It was apparent why -- in spite of the drifting faerie-like castles, no large tourist ships came to Sybil III. The splinter of metal which - like most of the building material here -- must have come from the wreck of the Botany Bay, was barely wide enough for the little Star of Space's landing struts. Already a friendly, waving crowd was lining up on the other side of the barrier. Looking at them on the video input, Augustus could see that cloth must be in desperately short supply here too. The ladies all seemed to be wearing very little of it, poor things. The loose weave on the stockings under their short skirts could hardly keep them warm! They needed some good solid sensible Azure woolens! He would have to write to various charitable societies back home. He could see that his university texts on the customs and traditions of the Botany Bay survivors was lacking in many details. Why did the ladies, so eager to welcome them to this friendly backwater, wave with their legs? He blushed, glad that the pretty second mate wasn't here to see him looking at the display.

He unbuckled and busied himself with packing the last few of his possessions into his travel bag. Toothbrush, razor, shaving cream -- on Earth, apparently, various nano-depilatory treatments were available -- but with Earth under blockade, the colonies had to fend for themselves -- which had meant a return to the razor. For Augustus shaving was a daily adventure, which so often seemed to end in disaster.

Then, from his bedside he packed up his copies of Melkinthorpe's *Suffering the Human Condition*, Belcher's *Philanthropy and Uplift*, and, of course, his secret vice, an antique copy of *On Human Self-Sufficiency*. He always tucked it under the other books, as he was rather embarrassed by Kabongo's rather forthright and unfashionable views. But it did have some fascinating ideas even if he had discovered that many tasks were not quite as simple as the author had made them out to be. Augustus picked up the bag and headed out to help the people of Sybil.

The other passengers were also waiting to disembark. Augustus had to admit that he really hadn't gelled with either of them. He'd tried -- it had been a two-week journey. Ionno Low was a legal practitioner. A man that should know and appreciate Melkinthorpe's writing. But he'd been quite insulting about it! As for Jay Wynand, why the man was a professional pornographer! Augustus had been horrified to find out that he was sharing a ship with such a person. The man had left his scurrilous publication on the mess-table, and Augustus had been shocked to see the crew of the Star looking at the pictures in it. Doubtless he was here to take shameless advantage of the quaint customs and innocence of the local people. The other two passengers had become fast friends on the journey, showing just how unfit Low was to be part of the legal profession. Where would society be if lawyers chose to associate with people like that? Augustus had done his best to ignore them both, which as they were continually sniggering between themselves and ignoring him, was not difficult.

The hatch dropped open. Humid, warm, oddly scented air rushed in. The other two passengers rushed out. Augustus was about to leave too, when the second mate tapped his shoulder. "I've organized for your trunk to be sent on to the Hotel Hyaton, Sir. We've got some safe transport for our cargo. You can't trust the locals..."

"I believe that trust begets trust," said Augustus gently.

She nodded. "Right, and any begetting around here starts with the bastards trying to screw you. Do you want me to arrange a guide for you? They probably won't try to kill you. Not since Admiral Halberd got the Capo's, and their local Zell and Thrymi bosses together and told them that if just one Azure citizen got done in, he'd wipe all the life off a quarter of the plate. He demonstrated on the place we now use for cargo landing, where two of his marines had got beaten up."

"That's barbaric!" Augustus was horrified.

She shrugged. "That's about all they understand around here. Anyway, we have an arrangement with the Bondi-boyz. I can sort it out for you..."

"I have a map. I've come here to help these people. The sooner I get to know them, and all the different neighborhoods, the better. I'm not going to stay in the Hyaton for very long. I'm going to find myself a lodging among the wonderful people of Sybil. Various anthropological sources testify as to how friendly they are, once you get to know them. I can't wait!"

She shook her head. "I reckon you're right, Sir. The sooner you get to know them the better."

Augustus had the feeling that she might be being sarcastic, but he was not sure why. He would get a guide -- he suspected the map might be a little out of date, as it seemed to show all sorts of fortifications. But he wasn't quite ready to admit that to the second mate. One of the friendly young ladies who was welcoming the incoming ship would be perfect, except he was rather nervous about strange women, but if that was what he had to do, he would cope. He could practice his Sybil dialect on them.

But when he got to the fenced gate the welcoming ladies had all vanished. He saw several of them in the distance, surrounding the tall figures of Low and Wynand. He hoped that those two would remember their duty as members of an advanced society, and not lead those innocents into any form of vice.

At the gate a scruffy man wearing what could once have been a braided peaked cap stuck out his hand and said: "Passport."

Augustus put down his bag to take his passport out of his pocket. A little urchin darted forward to help him with it, but the passport control official kicked him back. "Briz, yer gutter rat. Keep off my patch."

The urchin, from a safe distance off, made a fascinating traditional noise -- just as Pearl Honeybeere had described in her seminal anthropological study *Female and Male*.

"You blow bleeding raspberries at me and I'll kill yer, yer hell-spawned brat. That'll be a hundred and fifty Azure dollars, Mister. And you keep a grip on that bag, see."

"A hundred and fifty..." Augustus began reaching for his pocket.

That would make quite a hole in the living expenses allowance Papa had given him. He had to live on that until next month. The Thistlewood genes were horrified by the sheer profligate spendthrift waste of such expensive bureaucracy, and it almost moved him to protest. But given the desperate needs here, the government must raise revenue somehow...

"He means a dollar fifty cents," said the second mate, from behind him. "Don't you Sharkey?"

The customs officer looked sulky. "What's it got to do with you, Maira? He's gonna get skinned. I might as well get my cut first."

She put a hand on the customs officer's shoulder, although he tried to squirm away from the friendly gesture. "He's come to help you. To uplift you from your poverty and squalor," said the second mate.

The customs officer looked at her incredulously. "You're pulling my chain aren't yer? Ow. Yer didn't have to squeeze so hard. I got the message. It'll be a dollar fifty."

"Is this lady worrying you, officer?" asked Augustus, relieved but feeling guilty at the possibility that something untoward was happening. "I could ask her to leave."

The grubby customs official winced suddenly. "No, no. It's a fair go," he said hastily. "Maira and I are old friends."

"Ever since I persuaded you that it would be good for your health." She looked at Augustus. "You bring out the worst mother-hen aspect in me. It's a pity I'm on duty or I'd like to watch your progress and education in this cesspit. Keep one hand on your wallet and one hand on your bag at all times. The Hyaton is about 300 yards straight along that lane," she pointed. "The whores and their pimps have gone with the others, and if you move your skinny little butt you can be inside the doors before they realize there is more fresh meat out here. We're flying out again tomorrow and your return fare is already paid. I reckon that you should have done any uplifting that you're going to do by then." She made a strange gesture with her hand and forearm quite like Pearl Honeybeere's description of the ritual greeting of the Bankawanna. "Mind you, with you it really is hard to be sure."

"I reckon he won't make it past the first block," said the customs agent.

Augustus felt their eyes on him as he picked up his case. He walked, as nonchalantly as he could towards the narrow, eave-hung lane.

"Holy shit! Not that one," yelled the Second Mate.

The ragged, baggy-clothed, and bright blue-eyed urchin that had received such undeserved rough treatment at the hands of the customs official appeared, as if by magic, from behind a pile of rubbish. "Need a guide, Mister?" he asked in a gruff voice.

Augustus felt that it had been rather his fault that the poor fellow had been so rudely treated. "Yes," he said. "Can you take me to the Hyaton, please?"

"Sure. No worries. Those blokes were telling yer to take the long bloody way around. Dangerous too. Lemme take your bag."

For a moment Augustus hesitated, their warnings ringing in his ears. But one had to begin with trust somewhere, and this poor young man was obviously making a cry for that trust. The others had allowed themselves to be biased.

So, although he felt such labor might be demeaning, he handed over the grip. "I trust you."

The young man's eyes widened at the compliment. "Too bloody right, I'm honored, Sir. Now if yer'll just follow me..."

And the young man set off at a terrific pace down a narrow side alley, with a one-fingered gesture that must mean 'follow me' in this culture. It was strange how a deadly insult on one planet could become a gesture of welcome in another culture.

Ten minutes later, Augustus had to admit that he'd lost his guide, despite his all but superhuman efforts to follow the little ragamuffin. He was also completely and utterly lost. The map he'd been so proud of having was completely useless, as he had no point of reference and no idea where he was. All the buildings with their roofs of scrap metal and shredded plant material were so tightly packed that he was in virtual twilight in this noisome alley. This seemed to be an even poorer quarter of the plate than where they'd landed, although decay and disrepair seemed to be the norm here on Sybil.

He had to sorrowfully admit that he'd made an error of judgement. He had to understand, though. Given the poverty of the environment, it was hardly surprising that the temptation had been too much for the boy.

Also, he had the uncomfortable feeling that he was being watched.

CHAPTER
TWO

Charles Anson Roberto Thistlewood IV, universally known as Charlie, except by his grandmother when he was in dire trouble, calmly faced the assembled family. "I didn't know about it either. Augustus pulled the wool over my eyes as much as yours." He smiled. "And good for him. I didn't think he had it in him."

His grandmother addressed him by his full slew of names. "Unlike you, Augustus has never given us a moment's worry."

"Except the paragliding incident," said his father.

"Which we promptly put a stop to," said his grandfather.

"Maybe," said Charlie, "That's why he didn't tell you until it was too late. Anyway, I've done some checking. It's much safer than paragliding."

His grandfather snorted. "It's another planet. And full of the offspring of convicts. It's a world full of criminals."

"It's a fraction over four square miles, and it has one important statistical anomaly in favor of you not worrying too much about Augustus," said Charlie.

"And what is that, pray?" asked his grandfather, stiffly, but not quite as stiffly as he might have. Numbers were grandfather's obsession.

"In terms of violent crime committed by those 'criminals' of Sybil III on the persons of tourists and visitors from Azure, you would be surprised to know that Augustus is safer there, than here. There hasn't been a serious incident for more than thirty years, and there hasn't been a death in more than seventy. They have a substantial number of visitors from here, it appears." What Charlie didn't say was that there was petty crime aplenty.

His grandmother sniffed. "It's a loose, immoral place. I looked it up. I don't know why he has to go there."

Charlie held himself back from saying that his younger brother had to go there because it was a loose immoral place. He was fond of his grandmother; she'd done her best to mother them when their mother had died. He knew she loved them dearly, but she was not exactly maternal. It was a bit of a mystery how she'd ever managed to conceive his father. He set about soothing her. "Whatever company he finds himself in could hardly be worse than the Sociology Department at Azure College, which it takes him away from."

"Er," said his father. "Would you care to explain, Charlie? I'm, to be honest, not quite sure what Sociology is. Or what they do."

"I don't think anyone knows. It's where the upper-class and upper middle-class girls go in cheerful and good-looking, and come out miserable with funny haircuts. I looked into it myself because the female to male ratio is the highest in the college, but decided there were better places to go fishing. As for what they do, I think they either stay at Uni and teach it, or go into HR."

The family looked at him, wide-eyed and open-mouthed. Thistlewood Mechanical Industries had had one brush with having a 'human resources' section. The horror stories were still told around the dinner table.

The first to break the silence was his grandmother. "There are no... attachments, there, that we need to be aware of?" she asked in steely tones.

For a moment Charlie was tempted to invent one, but that might have consequences, not the least an inquisition about his own failure to marry suitably and produce offspring. "No. Neither male nor female. In fact, in the little bit of asking I did, the women claimed he made them uncomfortable."

His grandmother stiffened. "Augustus is a perfect gentleman. He would never say or do anything untoward, unlike you, Charles Anson Roberto Thistlewood IV."

"I think that was the problem, grandmother. That and the fact that Augustus is far too bright, far too logical, and dresses funny."

His grandmother sniffed, and looked at Charlie's clothes. "He dressed like a Thistlewood. I always saw to it that he had good, solid clothing of the best quality."

"Which looked nothing much like anyone else's clothing. Anyway, you can set your mind at ease, and be happy he's out of there. Hopefully he'll learn a few things while he's away."

"We worry, Charlie," said his grandfather.

"I would have a word with your contacts in government, Grandpa. Tell the embassy there to keep an eye on him. By the sounds of it they must have lots of experience in dealing with Azurians going a bit off the rails." He saw the warning signs in his grandmother's eyes. "Not that Augustus is likely to go wild. But he does rather blunder into things, you have to admit."

"Usually," said his father, wryly, "Without him even noticing. And sometimes with him getting lost in the process, as we all remember. Anyway, I've put an activatable tracker into the heel of his shoes. It has an eight mile range on it, so we should be able to activate it and triangulate on his position if need be."

"The whole place is only four square-miles," said Charlie. "We should be able to find him easily enough. But honestly, I suspect we're all worrying too much."

"I just hope he gets it all out of his system and comes home soon," said his grandfather, heavily.

CHAPTER

THREE

In her nest, Briz put down the case, still incredulous. No one could possibly be that bloody much of a drongo. It just couldn't be true. She looked at the case with suspicion. Suppose it had some kind of tracker on it? It just had to be a trap. Was it going to explode when she opened it?

She sat and looked at it for a full minute, trying to figure it out. There had to be something that she hadn't spotted. Had to be. One thing Briz had learned young, like anyone else who survived here: if it seemed too good to be true, it was.

It looked just like an ordinary -- if slightly elderly and solid – brown leather valise. She took her lock-picks out of her pocket, then realized that there was no lock. Just her luck! It must be a personal finger-print job. She could try a hammer and chisel, or perhaps it would need explosives... those came expensive. She poked at the latch button with an irritated finger.

The latch popped open. Briz backed away suspiciously.

No way was this possible! After watching it for a full minute she used a piece of dried skyfrond to push the lid open as she crouched, ready to run.

There was no explosion. No ear-piercing shriek of an alarm. She sniffed suspiciously. No gas. Or at least not one with a smell that she recognized. Was there something nasty and toxic that smelled slightly of socks? Beside socks? She peered cautiously, then smiled gleefully, if a trifle unbelievingly. The old booksafe trick! Briz could read. She'd been apprenticed to a forger for a while, and he'd beaten the knowledge into her, until she'd been able to push his drunken body over the edge, one night. No real book could ever be titled '*Philanthropy and Uplift*' by G.A. Septimus Belcher. If it had been *101 Nights of Sodom* or *Orgasmic Lulu*, she might have believed that it was just a book in the luggage of the typical visitor to the Big Syd.

Cautiously, Briz picked up the book. Excitement filled her as she felt the weight of it.

The book opened.

Inside was a wealth... of paper. And more paper. There weren't even any pictures! Well, with a title like that... it had to be something really salacious and thoroughly perverted. Briz read well, by local standards. This was not the local standard, nor like anything she'd ever encountered. She strained over the text, her lips moving... "The... pseudo-ambivalent... relationship between the donor and the end-recipient of charitable end...endeavour is in the neo-Jungian sense a..."

Briz shook her head. "And" and "the" made quite a lot of sense. Possibly end-recipient... maybe he'd come for the boys in Claggs back-alley. There were only two reasons to come to this place. And he just didn't look like a drug-buyer.

She had to admit to herself that he didn't look much like a man in search of a good time, either.

There weren't any pictures in the next book. The third one had pictures, and diagrams. Lots of them... but not of strange sexual positions. No, instead, there were pictures of how to make bricks. Of basket weaving. Of cheese making... Briz put it down in disgust. The next item was a pair of what could possibly have been pyjamas. They were blue, made of a thick felt-like material and had pictures on them. Alien creatures of some sort. And then at the bottom of bag was a plain brown envelope. By now Briz was inured to disappointment. She still had the lining of bag to search, and the covers of the books, but she had begun to suspect that somehow, someone had set her up with this patsy.

She opened the envelope. It was marked "Private, Confidential, Ambassador Porcatrip" and sealed, so she had to read it.

She read it. And then read it again, her eyes wide. And then put it back into its envelope. Very, very carefully. She lit the stub of a candle and dug out a tiny bit of sealing wax. And very carefully resealed the envelope. A little work with the finest pick of her lock-tools and the seal was good enough to pass a cursory glance. Now she had to go and find the man before anyone else did. This was not the sort of luck that landed in her lap every day.

She didn't care what he'd done to be made a remittance man here. It wasn't something that she needed to know. There were a quite a few men and women that no one wanted back home, going to hell in their own way on the plate here on Sybil. What was important was that he, and the three hundred dollars a month to be delivered via the embassy, was hers. Hers, hers, hers!

She'd found him first!

She looked at the bag. Selected the book with the pictures. Changed her mind and took the next one. And then she closed up the bag, and crept out of the tiny eaves-room. Then she was off over the roof, between the growing racks, heading back to Dog-End alley, where she'd left him.

FOUR

Augustus felt the loss of his grandfather's case keenly. It was true that it had been inclined to spring open at the most inopportune moments, but, as his father had pointed out, other than that, there was still plenty of good use in the solid dire-bull hide. That was the Thistlewood way, after all. Yes, the new plastics from the factory in New Detroit were pretty and fashionable. But would they outlast a solid Dire-bull hide valise? No. Thistlewood possessions were occasionally in fashion. Sometimes several times in their lifetimes, as fashion followed a pattern of circular repetition every twenty or thirty years or so. He would miss that case. Well, doubtless the youngster's need had been greater than his own, and the poor boy would have to live with his conscience. At least the books would be a valuable and informative addition to this society, however much Augustus knew he would regret losing them. Looking up at the eaves here... Kabongo had such an effective guttering and hydroelectric system which could have been applied to provide light here. Augustus knew most of the book off by heart, but he would still have appreciated being able to refer to the diagrams. Well... there was no use in crying over spilt milk... Augustus stepped closer to the dripping eave for a closer look.

Something whistled past his ear, and there was a loud thump. He turned. A man was standing behind him, clutching the side of his head with one hand. He had a most unfunctional walking stick in the other. Barely a foot long, thick, and full of protrusions, it made a poor thing to lean on. Augustus blinked. That was blood oozing from between the man's fingers... and the young ragamuffin, who Augustus had mistakenly thought had run off and left him, was holding the dire-bull case at the ready, ready to hit the stranger again. The ragamuffin was perched on the opposite eave, holding on with his toes. "Rack off, yer hairy-legged bludger," said the youth. "And yer can drop the truncheon before I splatter your brains properly."

The man looked up, warily.

Augustus was horrified by the blood and the violence, and puzzled by what seemed like might be abusive language. He'd have to look it up, but in the meanwhile, he must render what help he could. "Oh, I say," he exclaimed. "Can I..." and began to reach out to assist the poor man. The fellow must have misinterpreted the gesture, because he spun on his heel and ran, staggering a little, and dropping his stick.

Augustus picked the stick up and ran after him, yelling and waving the stick, so that the fellow would see what he'd dropped, and could return to claim it.

The poor man must have been concussed into confusion because he found an extra burst of speed and disappeared around the next corner.

When Augustus arrived at the corner, panting, he was nowhere to be seen.

Then his young guide caught up with him. "You hurt that man," said Augustus, sternly.

The ragamuffin-boy nodded. "Yeah, even though I couldn't get a good swing in. Yer pretty handy with that truncheon of his," he said admiringly.

"I would have liked to return it to him," said Augustus.

The ragamuffin nodded. "Too right. Exactly where he was going to give it to yer. On the back of the head."

"He was trying to assault me?" Augustus shook his head, trying to absorb the absurd idea. "I don't understand! I came here to help you all!"

The youth nodded. "I reckon that he just thought that he'd help himself first. Let's get you along to the Hyaton. Stick close by me this time, see. I don't want yer getting lost again."

Augustus knew that this was the lad's way of apologizing. The youngster was not going to admit that he'd run away, but at least his conscience had brought him back. Maybe the boy was still redeemable. "Lead on, McDuff. I'm staying at the Hyaton today. But I'll be looking for accommodation with a family in this fine city of yours, from tomorrow. I want to absorb your culture and learn as much as possible about your people. Belcher says that any philanthropic efforts are usually doomed to fail if the donors and the fieldworkers do not have a firm grasp of local conditions and do not take local partners on board. And of course, there is the endemic problem of corruption and extortion. Local partners are what I need!"

"Too right!" said the boy. "Now we'll just cut along this alley to avoid Bondi turf see. I'm paid up with the Cronulla skegs." He pointed at a splash of paint on a corner. "That's their turf mark, see. And my name's not McDuff. You c'n call me Briz. I reckon I'm yer local partner." He spat on a skinny, grubby hand and held it out.

Determinedly, Augustus spat on his hand too, and shook. The lad had a firm grip. Augustus felt that he'd at least set a good and valuable example to the boy. "Augustus StJohn Thistlewood III. I'm here to spend a year in charitable and philanthropic work."

The boy blinked. "You're pulling me a raw prawn, aren't you? I wish I'd thought of that. When the Bacon try and spell that break-teeth mouthful, they'll just figure it's easier to go and write a charge on someone else. Neat! Anyway. Yer just come out and call when yer need me, see. I'll be watching."

The Hyaton was a display of unnecessary ostentation which must inflame the locals. The hotel chain had obviously flown in materials to build the place. It must really cause great resentment!

"Bunch of Ned-bloody-Kellys," said Briz pointing at the place -- which had enough space around it for a small patch of greenery.

If Augustus hadn't known that Ned Kelly had been an infamous highwayman, he might almost have thought that there was admiration in young Briz's voice.

The boy handed him his bag. "Here yer go, mate. They won't let me in without a strip search see. And rhino. I haven't got a brass razoo." Briz looked meaningfully at him.

Augustus blinked. And then caught on. "Well, the workman is worthy of his hire. I really can't afford very much, Mr Briz. I only have a month's allowance from home, and I'm hoping to start some projects with that. And I'll need a guide later today again."

"Five dollars a day," said Briz promptly, "and cheap at twice the price. And I'm not Mister Briz. Just Briz, see."

"Well, I don't want to exploit you..."

Briz waved largely. "Too true. It's a mate's rate, but yer a good bloke. We'll talk about rates for any extra..." his voice dropped, "services. Introducing you to the right people. Stopping yer head from getting beaten in. Seeing that you don't end up with no bush-pigs." The lad looked meaningfully at the odd stick that Augustus had continued to carry along. "You won't be needing that in there. They don't even let Palm Beach skegs in with weapons."

"Oh. Well, could you see that it gets back to its rightful owner?" asked Augustus, handing it over awkwardly. He wondered if there was some wildlife in this place after all. Bush-pigs? Perhaps there was some livestock that had gone feral, but it was hard to imagine what they would live on here, and how they could avoid being caught.

"Well," said Briz, seeing Augustus feeling in his pockets. "Yer better have these, I suppose." And the young Sybilian reached into the front of his baggy trousers and produced Augustus's wallet and passport. "You'll need to get yourself a pocket with a zip in the front of your daks. Otherwise you'll lose 'em. Yer need to learn to be careful with loose money around here, see, or the Lebs will take it off yer. They've got a safe in the hotel that I hear even a Zell master couldn't open. Yer better put most of it in there."

Augustus felt his jaw drop, but he was powerless to prevent it doing so, or to say anything. So instead, he dug out five Azure dollars.

"And another ten for getting your property back," said Briz, with a hand out.

Augustus felt that there was some justice in that, so he paid up. It did cut across the Thistlewood grain, but it was -- as the locals would say, according to his dialect guide -- "a fair go."

The interior of the Hyaton was everything that the city on the plate outside was not. It was modern, clean, and spacious. It also -- even from the foyer -- had a spectacular view over an endless vista of clouds. Augustus could see the edge of a dark blocky castle drifting amongst them. When he produced his passport the bulky concierge inside the thick-glass-walled cubby had let him though the inner electric door. Inside the air was crisp, dry, and cool. Augustus realized then how he'd been perspiring outside. The receptionist smiled at him. "Mr Thistlewood? Your trunk has arrived. Will you be making a long stay with us, Sir?"

Her accent lacked the Sybil twang. In fact, hearing it, Augustus was sure that she came from Azure. But why would the Hyaton import staff? Surely, they would use local labor and create much needed employment opportunities? "I am just here for tonight," he smiled politely. "I've come to spend a year here on Sybil, to do some charitable work."

"A year!" she exclaimed. "Well, I hope they are giving you serious danger pay, Sir. We only have to cope with this dump for three months at a spell. The poor embassy people have to do six. And at least I don't have to go outside."

Augustus could hardly believe his ears. "But it is so beautiful! And it has such a fascinating culture, and the people are so generous and friendly."

She rolled her eyes. "Your keys, Sir," she said sweetly. "Room 12, just up the corridor to your right. Do enjoy your stay here at the Sybil Hyaton. Luncheon will be served at 12.30 in the Marvel Room."

Augustus made his way to his bedroom. With the exception of a cloudscape that couldn't be beaten, it was another generic air-conditioned Hyaton room. How could anyone choose this over the exciting wonderful world out there? True, this did have the view. There were two castles visible right now, the Zell one he'd seen earlier and a Thrymi one. As he marveled at them, a jagged bolt of violet shot out of one of the Thrymi castle turrets and was met by a green shower of coruscating sparks from the Zell cloud-castle. The Zell fired a howling projectile -- howling so loudly that it made Augustus -- who was at least two miles off, and behind glass -- clutch his ears. An outer hanging balcony on the Thrymi castle was struck and shattered. The Thrymi fired two more of the purple bolts -- which were met with yet more green scintilla, as both Castles moved off in opposite directions. Soon the view just consisted of tranquil red-shaded clouds and a distant rainstorm. A flight of fluffy creatures flapped across an opening in the cloud on batlike wings.

Augustus shook himself from his reverie. What a planet this was! He had to make the best use of the year that Papa had finally agreed that he could spend here "to get this philanthropy nonsense out of your system, boy" to see as much of it as possible, before he went to follow the family tradition by starting on the shop floor at Thistlewood Mechanical Industries. He looked at his watch. Well, he would have looked at his watch if it had still been on his wrist. He must have mislaid it somewhere. Anyway, his stomach thought that it was lunch time. So, he went in search of the Marvel Room.

It was indeed a marvel -- and a rather insubstantial place to eat. It hung out beneath the plate and the floor and walls were pieces of thick glass, which were held in place by very thin girders. The tables were also glass topped. The entire effect was heightened by a drift of cool mist cascading off a central fountain and pouring slowly across the floor.

It literally felt as if he was dining in the clouds.

The prices on the menu brought Augustus down to earth with a bump. He looked at them again, sure that he'd misplaced a decimal point. Even if that had been the case they were still outrageous! The Thistlewood clan seldom dined out back on Azure. Great grand-mother Agatha would have frowned on such a prodigal waste of money, and her dictums still held true, generations later. Augustus beckoned at the hovering waiter. "Surely," he said, acutely embarrassed, but rigidly determined, "There must be a printing error on this page. A fillet steak cannot cost... 40 Azure Dollars."

The waiter lifted his nose, something which was guaranteed to get up Augustus's own nose. "I am afraid so, Sir. Our food is all flown in from Azure. It does put the prices up, rather."

That had started to bring Augustus's temperature down, despite the fact that no one looks down their nose at a Thistlewood. Food must be scarce here. "I quite understand. You can't deprive the locals. It would be wrong to strain their scarce food resources further."

"Oh, local food's plentiful enough, Sir. It's just not up to the standard we require for the Hyaton's discerning guests," said the waiter.

Augustus StJohn Thistlewood unfolded himself from the chair and stood up. "I think," he said stiffly. "That I am not refined enough. I find that I am not hungry." He stalked out with as much dignity as he could muster, carefully not looking at the modest portions on the glass plates of the diners. He went to the front desk. "I am going out," he said, still fuming. "I would like to deposit some items in the hotel safe."

"Certainly, Sir. Are you not staying for lunch? It's a fresh shipment in from Azure today." The receptionist slid a safe tray toward him, and Augustus counted out some of his money, and put that into his breast pocket. He put his wallet into the tray. "No," he said firmly. "I am going to try the local food. Can I leave my passport here too?"

She nodded. "Retinal and fingerprint ID are registered on the house computer, Sir. Like the safe tray. I would advise you to leave it here. You can't trust the locals. They'll rob you blind. And you can't eat their food. They eat eyeballs."

"I would rather eat an eyeball than pay forty dollars for five dollars' worth of steak," said Augustus, walking away.

A number of well-dressed people were coming in. He had to wonder where they had come from, and if they were going to spend forty dollars on a steak. They seemed to be very keen on displaying large diamonds in their teeth, and chunky gold chains on their necks, as his grandmother said, very under-bred people were wont to do. It was quite uncalled for. Such a display of wealth could only offend the poor local people.

He'd no sooner stepped out when Briz appeared.

"Finished yer tucker already?" asked Briz cheerfully.

Poor mite. He was so very undersized. He probably had never had a square meal, let alone a fillet steak. "No. I decided that I'd better start as I intend to go on. Take me to a local hostelry, some place where I can buy a meal. I should imagine that you are hungry?"

"Too bloody right I am. You gunna shout me tea?"

"What? Tea?" Ah. That was what they called an evening meal. "Oh, yes. I will buy you tea too."

"In that case it's the Black Stump. Two bob and all the jumbuck tripe you can eat. If you were gunna eat with the flies I'd have taken you the Galah. They do tour groups from the Hyaton." The boy sniggered. "They sell 'em a five bloody dollar plate of jumbuck eyeballs. They sell us local folk tickets to watch 'em. They've got this one-way glass. I been a few times. It's a bloody good laugh."

The Black Stump was literally that. The half-melted remains of a huge girder, it stuck out like a bowsprit from the wall of the plate. It was strung with a web of rigging over the void. The locals had improvised their own Marvel room, not for the view, but to make up for the lack of space. It was no restaurant, however. It was a market place. Briz led him along a swaying, narrow, plank walkway between stalls hung with greens, racks of small, winged things, or strung with huge glistening flasks, or full of metal scraps and other industrial debris. The air was smoky and full of the smell of frying and the sounds of noisy barter.

There were any number of stalls with bubbling pots over little braziers, and although he looked into several of them, Augustus did not see any eyeballs. Some of them looked and smelled of things he'd rather not think about, but there were no eyeballs. He began to feel quite superior to the poor people stuck in the Hyaton. Fortunately, he wasn't scared of heights and had a good sense of balance. Near the outer edge they came to a stall that was rather more smelly than usual, with a small crowd hanging about.

A man was flensing out one of the fluffy batwinged creatures Augustus had seen flying earlier. "What is that?" he asked, as the fellow heaved the steaming guts into a wood-staved bucket.

"Yer dinner. Jumbuck with its tripes coming out."

Augustus wished that he hadn't asked.

"Gimme half a dollar, and I'll get us a couple of bowls," offered his guide, blithely unconcerned by the smelly, bloody slaughter.

What was it that his grandfather had always said? "When in Rome, eat spaghetti." It was a little too apt, but Augustus dug a dollar note out of his top pocket, and then looked determinedly out into the cloudy vista. Very shortly it wasn't going to be much of vista, as the leading edge of the nearest cloud would envelop them soon.

They sat on the rigging -- dangling their feet over the edge into the mist -- with roughly carved bowls of spicy, fragrant... food. Augustus had decided he'd better just eat and not think about it. The fiery spices in it should kill anything but the most robust germ anyway. There were no eyeballs in the bowl, but Augustus wondered if his own were steaming. He was grateful for the cool cloud-mist. It meant he could not see the endless drop his guide was so happy to dangle his feet over.

The ragamuffin boy ate as if it had indeed been a while since he had last seen food. Augustus felt a warm glow at this, but it could just have been the spiciness burning all the way through his intestines. Steamed fish with a parsley butter sauce was considered a good Thistlewood dinner, if a little exotic and adventurous. He wondered what his father would say if he could see him now.

Briz belched. It was obviously not a social solecism here. It might even be polite. So, Augustus tried. The resultant explosive roar turned heads at the stall.

"Bloody hell!" said Briz. "Have to take yer everywhere twice, the second time to apologize and to pay for the furniture. Well, they do say that yer poor bastards from Azure got no bloody manners. So, where do yer want to go next, 'cause I think we're about to get asked to leave here." He pointed at the void. "And yer really don't want to be thrown out of this place."

"Well," said Augustus. "I need to make contact with the civic authorities."

"Who?" said Briz, looking puzzled.

"The people who run the social services on the plate," explained Augustus.

That got another: "What?"

Augustus tried for a third time. "The bosses."

"Are you bloody mad?" demanded Briz, staring at him. "The Thrymi'll kill yer as soon as look at yer. And the Zell ain't much better."

"But... this is a humanitarian matter," said Augustus. "I'm here to set up some uplift projects."

Briz pulled a face. "That's just it, Mister. They don't care much about humans. They say that any humani-whatsits are our problem. They leave us to the Capo's."

"The Capo's?" asked Augustus, searching his memory of the slim book of Sybillian terms.

28

"They sorta run the various operations for the Zell or the Thrymi. Spike side is Thrymi turf. This side's Zell Capo's," Briz explained.

"I suppose I could start there," said Augustus. "How do I make an appointment to see them?"

Briz looked doubtful. "They ain't people yer bother. Yer kinda hope they don't want to see you. Yer don't go and see them."

"I need to, I'm afraid," said Augustus apologetically, but firmly.

That made an impression which his earlier statements hadn't. "Well, I guess if yer afraid, I could take yer to the Capo of the Cronulla skegs. Get yer some protection. Mind you, yer could o' talked to him yourself, at the hotel. He went into the Hyaton just before yer came out. Feller with a big diamond in his tooth and a fat gold chain."

"Oh," said Augustus, remembering the man, and his entourage of large companions. "I thought he was just a tourist going into the hotel."

"Nah," said Briz. "All the big shots like to eat there. Kind of shows that they've made it, see. I hear the food sucks. But if yer can afford to go there, well, you're the man."

"Vainglory and folly. Well. I suppose I don't know the man and I ought not to condemn him without speaking to him first," said Augustus, knowing that it would be hard. Vulgar ostentation always annoyed him.

"If you got it, flaunt it," said Briz. "Look, I'll take yer there. But I ain't going in. Those goons of his can be rough, too right they can. You take it easy, see. Mostly he controls the slags, but he's into other stuff too. Can be dangerous."

"What are slags? Foundry waste?" asked Augustus, faint but pursuing.

"Nah. That bunch of bush-pigs of his."

Ah, at last it made a little sense. This place plainly needed a pig-hunter, the way more civilized parts needed a dog catcher. Well, the city dog catcher was one place to start dealing with civil authority. 'Capo' must be the local term for the job.

Briz led him along several alleyways until they came to a walled building -- which had distinct crenellations in its metal walls. There was a narrow gate with heavy bars. "In there," said Briz nervously. "Don't yer tell Capo Kasagolis that I brought you, see."

Poor child, thought Augustus, as he walked up to the steel gates. The gates were the most solidly constructed things he'd seen outside of the Hyaton. They obviously must need them to keep the pigs they trapped inside. Augustus's mind was perhaps on other things when he rang the bell. He really knew very little about pork.

"Watcha want?" demanded a voice from a grilled box on the outer wall.

"I'm from Azure. I would like to speak to Capo Kasagolis."

"He don't see no visitors," said the voice.

"It is a matter of some importance," said Augustus, doing his best to project Thistlewood certainty into his voice. Normally, he was utterly useless at it. Being firm and authoritarian was something his brother Charlie or father or grandfather did easily and naturally. They made it sound as if one ought to be apologizing for bad service. Augustus always felt he should be apologizing for giving it.

This time, however, it seemed to have worked, at least in part. "Bout what?" said the voice.

Augustus thought about what young Briz had said. He was sure that some of the traps described in *On Human Self-Sufficiency* would work on bush-pigs. "About bush-pigs and the possibility for marketing the product on Azure." There was a silence from the metal grill. "And other.... er stuff," said Augustus, lamely.

The gate creaked open on elderly servos.

Augustus walked in. The house hidden behind the wall was very spacious and smart for the equivalent of the local dog catcher, thought Augustus. Still, in a society like this they could probably sell the meat. He walked up to the front door. It opened silently as he got there. "Step into the scan chamber," said another disembodied voice.

He did. And then walked through into a further room. A neat and luxuriously furnished room. There was only one man in it. He was a big baldheaded fellow with tattooed arms. Augustus examined the tattoos with interest. He'd always had a daydream about getting one. It was not the sort of thing a Thistlewood would do, but he found it fascinating. His examination seemed to disconcert the man, who cracked his knuckles. "Don't do that," said Augustus. "You'll give yourself arthritis in your old age, and we don't want that, do we?"

The tattooed man must have agreed. Anyway, he did look a little discomforted. "How did you find your way here?" he demanded.

"I have my contacts," said Augustus, mindful of his instructions. He'd heard the phrase once, somewhere, and had never had the chance to use it before.

He obviously should have done so years ago, because it plainly opened doors. The tattooed man let him into the next room. Clearly the bush-pigs were in need of culling, and they were about to go on a hunting expedition, because the men sitting there had an array of weapons of various vintages. Unbelievably, there was even a Holland and Holland 50:50. Augustus could not contain his excitement. Such a magnificent antique piece! Grandpapa had quite a collection, and Augustus had always loved the craftsmanship of old weaponry.

"Oh, I say! Mind if I have a look?" He plucked the weapon from the man's hands, and felt the weight of it.

For some reason the other four men in the room dropped their weapons. Looking at them Augustus saw that a couple had magazines in place, and the safeties were off. He was shocked. Such carelessness! Grandad would have tanned his hide for that. Augustus's wrath must have been visible despite his best intentions; he didn't say anything but the fellows all crowded back into the corner. It later occurred to him that he might have been guilty of waving the 50:50 around indiscriminately, but at the time he was just angry. The beautiful old 50:50 had a strap, so he put it on his shoulder and knelt next to the weapons. Really. Firearms-care among these pig hunters was terrible! Working the actions -- they all had live rounds up the spout. He put the magazines and the loose rounds into his pocket. "I'll keep these," he said crossly. "You're not fit to be trusted with firearms! They all need cleaning." He swung the 50:50 off his shoulder again, just as the far door opened to reveal the man with the diamond tooth and thick gold chain. He was rather too plump, and his eyes looked as if they belonged on one of his own bush-pigs.

The plump man stared at the 50:50. At his pig-culling team. "What the hell?" he said, edging back.

"Capo Kasagolis?" asked Augustus.

"Uh..."

"My name is Augustus StJohn Thistlewood III. I'm from Azure. I wanted to talk to you about... bush-pigs and... stuff."

The diamond toothed man paused his retreat. Looked at the hunters. "I guess... you might be someone we can deal with. Can you stop pointing that elephant gun at me?"

So, Augustus did. He shucked the cartridges from it and put it down. "Fine weapon," he said. "But those hunters of yours are not fit to be trusted with a firearm."

The Capo scowled at them. "Don't worry. They won't be again. Better come into my office, Mister Thistlewood. You say that you're from Azure?"

The office of the head bush-pig hunter was more like something out of a plush fashion design magazine than that of a civil official. It was also a bit odd that he locked the door behind them. Augustus was taken aback, but determined to try to be polite. "Yes, I am here to speak to you in my capacity as the field officer for the Azure Charitable Outreach and Rehabilitation Society. They call us the Blue men."

"Neat front!" said the Capo admiringly. "Wish that I had thought of it." He took a cigar from the box on the desk and put it between his fat lips. "So wazza deal? We c'n get you anything them Palm Beach skegs can, but at a better price. We'll need a bit o' hardware, tho'. Some decent gats. Maybe a few heavies..."

"Oh, I wasn't offering a deal," said Augustus. "I want your co-operation. I want to uplift your poor. I want to make them all as rich and comfortable as you are."

Augustus wondered why the man was so red in the face. It must be guilt making him blush as he did. "If I can have your help, there will be no need for Capos. Just wealthy happy citizens!" said Augustus, hoping to carry him along with this wonderful vision.

It didn't seem to be working very well. The man looked unwell. It must be the cigar smoke, thought Augustus. It was really making him feel quite queasy himself. "You need some fresh air. To be at one with nature instead of cooped up in here."

The fellow was turning puce, fumbling at his jacket. "Let me loosen that for you," said Augustus kindly, reaching over to pull it open, seeing as he seemed to be having trouble.

A large pistol fell onto the floor in the process. The poor man's eyes bulged, and his face went white. Augustus pushed him down into a chair before he fell over. He put the Capo's head between his legs to avert a faint.

He realized he should have taken the cigar out of the man's mouth first, as the Capo leaped upright, frantically beating at his trousers, which were not of a sensible flame-retardant tweed like Augustus's. Augustus tried to step in to help, grabbing a flask of water off the table and dashing it onto the flames...

It... probably wasn't water, Augustus realized a few seconds too late, as it too caught fire. As per the Blue Men standard First Aid and rescue training, Augustus tackled the burning man to the ground and rolled him, to put it out. That was very successful, but the Capo didn't seem to appreciate it.

Perhaps it was the screaming, but as the Capo hit the door, frantically clawing at the lock, it broke open with two of his hunters falling into the room and him falling over them. "Fire! Fire!" yelled someone above the struggling fighting knot of men. Several of the hunters obviously misunderstood, and did, adding to the chaos.

There was a lot of smoke – but not much fire by now. Augustus tried to tell them as he stomped out the burning carpet. No one – it seemed, was listening. There was a lot of shooting and yelling going on.

Augustus took his courage in both hands and went out to try and calm the situation. It did seem he was making a terrible first impression amongst the very people he had come to help. He really had to admit he wasn't much good with crowds and angry people, or in taking control of situations. Taking control was what Thistlewoods did, and thus, growing up surrounded by them, he'd never had to, or had a chance to try. His older brother Charlie would have had no trouble. His father would have had them marching around in neatly dressed ranks by now. His grandfather... that didn't bear thinking of. Well, he was none of them. So, he went out and said, tentatively: "Er. Excuse me..."

To no-one.

It was hard to tell quite what had happened, but the furniture had suffered. His first thought seeing the chairs tumbled and torn, fabric ripped, foam cushion shredded, was that it wasn't like Thistlewood furniture, solid ironwood, which would be unmoved by a charge of rampaging dire-beasts, and had never met a cushion, foam or otherwise. His second look at the room told him that it was in fact Thistlewood furniture... well, made by Thistlewood Mechanical Industries. His grandfather might disparage it as modern junk that wouldn't last, but if that was what people wanted to buy, Thistlewoods would make it.

Augustus had discovered – once he went to college -- that he actually did like cushions, even if, like these, they didn't last well through being shot up.

He felt he ought to apologize, but despite searching, he couldn't find anyone to apologize to, so eventually, feeling it hadn't gone particularly well, he left to look for his local guide.

A few yards down the road the lad dropped off a gutter with sinuous ease... and part of the gutter came with him

Briz scowled. "Don't make nothing to last,' he said as he turfed the piece of spouting into the ooze of an alley. "Seemed like yer had a bit of strife with them skegs. I chucked a few of Old Barnsey's tomatoes at them to make a distraction like. They come out shooting. I was worried about yer."

"It was all a terrible misunderstanding," said Augustus. "However, I think I might have to start with someone else. We seem to have got off on the wrong foot."

CHAPTER

FIVE

When Augustus had knocked at the gate to the Capo's compound, Briz had scooted up a creaking drainpipe and into the roof-garden opposite. It was unlikely that even one of the Capos would actually do her meal ticket any harm, even if he was a real drongo. You didn't go too far with Azure citizens. But... they might steal him, if they figured out there was money to be made off him.

The roof-garden, with its beds of produce, was guarded of course – but only when there was no-one working there, because no one would be daft enough to rob it when there was. Briz had figured this out some time back, and just nicked enough to not make it obvious. Old Barnsey was supremely unaware of her little raids while he was tending plants on the far side of the roof, and she wanted to keep it that way.

Then the shooting started in the compound.

She decided that a few tomatoes a week were worth less than keeping her meal-ticket alive. So, she started flinging tomatoes, and then a few melons, as high as she could so she could hear them splattering as they hit the roof and the walled garden. Of course, those inside weren't to know just what was hitting the roof, and came out shooting – and getting the hell out of there. Naturally, in these parts, a few people shot back. By the yelling, the assumption was that it was the Bondi Boyz again and a counterattack was needed.

Briz was beginning to wonder if she dared go and look for her meal-ticket when he wandered out, looking a little puzzled -- as seemed usual for him, and a bit upset. Perhaps the Jumbuck's tripes hadn't agreed with him. That could happen. So, she suggested taking him back to the Hyaton. He nodded abstractedly. "I really need to digest all this. It's... a little different from what my Anthropology and Sociology lecturers led me to believe. I'll have to talk with them when I get back home."

The only part of that that made whole lot of sense to Briz was 'digest'. So maybe it was the tripes, she thought. And the 'going home' part. She wouldn't want him to do that in a hurry.

So, she led him back to the Hyaton.

It seemed like other people had different ideas about his leaving. Later that day, two of the skegs from the Cronullas and another couple of heavies – one of them was definitely a Clovelley boy, and the other sounded like one of the Palm Beach Galahs cornered her on the way to the Stump, where she thought she might drink some of her profit. "Yer gunna come along with us. Capos wanna talk with you," said the Palm Beach skeg, in his mamby-pamby accent. Like he was from King's bloody Cross or something. For a brief second, Briz considered kicking him in the nuts and running. But you couldn't run... not far, on the Big Syd. The plate wasn't big enough to hide for long. If one gang was after you, you could run to someone else's turf, but this looked as if it wasn't just one gang. Briz knew she was in deep strife.

She was right about that. Story of her life, but she'd not really guessed quite how much.

It had all started a few hours before, when after a few nasty street fights between the Cronulla Boyz and the Bondi's, Capo Kasagolis had recovered from being knocked senseless by one of his own mob and was now dealing with having burned thighs, and a singed undercarriage, as well as a few other injuries. The worst of those was his to dignity, and his position. He sorted the latter pretty quick by shooting a few people. The former... was more difficult. He was suitably wary about just shooting Augustus Thistlewood. Admiral Halberd's example had put the frighteners on all the Capos, and worse, onto the Zell and Thrymi bosses. You didn't want word getting back to the Zell or Thrymi that you'd caused a problem. The Capo worked a Thrymi district. They were a lot worse than the Zell for sheer nastiness. The Zell made up for it by being more efficient.

But... there were a fair number of expat Azure residents here, that no-one, not even their government or admiral, would notice or care if they just disappeared. If that was the case... someone would be seeing the bottom of the Trading plate soon.

He sent a message to Senior Undersecretary Camelthrob-Princhbut. The Undersecretary had certain... weaknesses. The Cronulla skegs saw to it that he could indulge in those... and ship a few things to Azure with his effects. Princhbut could find out just who this Augustus StJohn Thistlewood III was, and if he'd be missed.

The Undersecretary didn't send him an answer. He came in person. His face was a sort of waxy grey, and his forehead beaded with sweat. He wasted no time on beating about the bush either: "Don't tell me you've hurt, or, heaven help us, killed, young Thistlewood? Because if so you'd better get offworld. I'm booking a passage on the Star of Space..."

"My boys say he was seen going back into the Hyaton about an hour ago," said the Capo. "We're watching until he comes out. Don't want to cause trouble in there."

"You don't want to cause trouble with Thistlewood anywhere, you fool. Just leave him alone," said Princhbut.

"Fool? Whaddya mean, fool? You... "

"I mean if you touch a hair on his head, you might as well kill yourself," said Princhbut tersely. "The Embassy didn't realize who he was... no one in the Ministry saw fit to tell the staff. The Ambassador is having fits."

"Who the hell is he?" asked the Capo.

"Old Man Thistlewood's youngest grandson."

That hadn't meant much to the Capo. But it plainly meant something to the Undersecretary. So, the Capo asked again: "So who is he and why do I need to worry? He comes here and tells me he wants to make everyone as rich as a Capo."

"He probably could," said Princhbut, sourly. "Or his grandfather could, if he ever decided to spend money. TMI."

"Whaddya mean 'Too much information'?"

"I mean Thistlewood Mechanical Industries. It's one of, if not the biggest and most powerful company on Azure," said Princhbut.

"But... he don't look rich. I mean, I hear he complained about the price of steak at the Hyaton."

"He doesn't HAVE to look it. He IS it. And Thistlewoods don't spend money," said the Undersecretary.

"Whatsa point in having money, in that case?" said the Capo, genuinely puzzled. You had to let people see wealth...

The Undersecretary shrugged. "I have no idea. But they're known for it. I wish he'd get off Sybil III. We're going to have to have staff watching him all the time. You'd better let the other Capos know."

The Capo scowled. "Them Bondi Boyz and us ain't talking. But I'll put out the word. You think he wants ta get rid of us? And we can't do nothing?"

The Undersecretary sighed. "Look. If the Ambassador found it necessary to remove him for good reason, 'good reason' being that it would please the Thistlewoods, not you, then I think at least he'd be out of here."

The Capo nodded. "And outta our business. I'll call a meeting of some of my... associates."

Which was how a nervous Briz found herself being dragged in front of a whole mob of powerful people she'd rather not be in front of, people that she'd prefer didn't even know that she was alive.

40

They did though. They knew she was alive and what company she was keeping. And they had plans for him. Plans that did not include making his monthly allowance hers.

Plans they expected her to help them with. She had little choice, but she didn't have to like it. But, she thought to herself, she wasn't goin' to make it easy for the bastards, not if she could get away with it.

While the Capos were grilling Briz for what she knew about Augustus and his possible weaknesses, Augustus was asleep in his flannel pajamas. As grandmother had never come to accept that her youngest grandson was no longer four years old, but nearer to twenty-four, the flannel was printed with pictures of Pooh Bear. Augustus had often wondered how he would cope with these and marriage. He really wouldn't have wanted to hurt grandmother Thistlewood's feelings and not wear the pajamas she made for him, but he was uncertain quite how women would feel about it. He was uncertain how women would feel about anything. Or would feel, for that matter. Being a Thistlewood had rather isolated him from them.

He had imagined that it might be different once he left his tutors and went to college. Instead, he found that reality was even stranger. Thistlewoods being, well, Thistlewoods, no-one had realized the oddly-dressed, awkward and shy young man was quite who he was. That, after all, was the Thistlewood way, or so grandfather frequently said. Of course, he had enrolled to take a degree in Engineering. No Thistlewood would ever do otherwise! It had been quite by accident, and because he had the wrong building and the wrong day (a problem he often had) that he'd walked in and sat down and found himself in his first Anthropology class. There were a number of young women there, which was an improvement on his structural engineering class. The structural engineering... well, the problem was that he was a long way advanced on the lecturer, let alone the class. But Anthropology and Sociology... why, that was like a fantasy world, full of things he'd never even heard of.

He eagerly drank it all in. And discovered he could do a large number of Arts Courses, and easily keep up with the requirements for his Engineering Degree. And no-one at home had the least idea. No one at the college seemed to have any idea either. One of the Physics Lecturers had once asked if he was related to his brother, Charlie, who had been something of a legend there. He'd been able to truthfully say 'less closely than I'd like to be." He was very fond of his older brother, even if the two of them could hardly be less alike.

The Arts still hadn't helped with the girls. He still stammered and turned red if they spoke to him. Eventually it got better. But not better enough to really talk to them or venture on a date. So, he threw himself deeper into his studies. He'd never been athletic like his brother, so sport had interested him not at all. His only venture into adventure outside of academia, was signing up for a paragliding course with the college club, which had not ended well. So: it had been academia.

He'd absorbed a lot of study like a sponge.

A silent sponge, chock-full of everything from Math to Socio-political theory. It was only after graduating, that the subject of his future had come up at all, at home. "Well, son," said his father, after dinner – serious discussions were always saved for after dinner. "Your grandfather and I have been discussing which of the units you'd best be suited to for your apprenticeship..."

"I want to go and spend a year helping the less fortunate," he informed them.

Father had blinked: "Everyone is less fortunate."

"Less fortunate business units," said grandfather. "Good idea! The foundry in Tarkastadt..."

"I mean philanthropy," explained Augustus.

"Didn't know we had a unit called that. Humph. I pride myself on knowing them all," said grandfather.

"I mean doing good to poor people. Helping them to raise their standards of living."

The rest of the family had looked at him in some puzzlement. None of them said 'why?' Plainly that thought had never occurred to them. Eventually his father broke the silence. "We do that. We provide them with jobs. And your grandmother personally deals with the Christmas parties and the gifts for the employees' children."

"Good, sensible and educational," said his grandmother. "Very hard to find, you know."

"I've already signed up with the Azure Charitable Outreach and Rehabilitation Society. The Blue Men. They looked at my qualifications... and they're sending me to Sybil III, for a year."

A shocked silence settled across the table. Finally, his father found his voice. "Sybil III... but it's a gas-dwarf, son. With nothing. No land, no prospects, no... industry. It's... it's..." he shook his head, unable to think of anything more horrifying than no industry.

"It's only for a year. And I have made the commitment," said Augustus. He knew that that was enough. A Thistlewood, he'd been told virtually since birth, always honored his commitments.

So, here he was, looking out at a cloudy vista of a late Sybil III afternoon. It was, effectively always late afternoon on the Trading Plate. That was the time of day that the air in the exosphere was most stable, so the Trading Plate kept up with the slow turning of the planet far, far below.

It felt... wrong. Decadent and immoral to be waking in the late afternoon, but he'd have to get used to it. So, he got up and went in search of a late afternoon breakfast. He had commitments to honor, and work to be done.

CHAPTER
SIX

Augustus thought that Briz's dirty little face looked a little pinched, when, as usual, the urchin appeared as he left the Hyaton. Today he was determined to actually make some progress. To move out of the Hyaton, and to start living among and getting to know and to be trusted by the people. The boy didn't sound his cheerful self either, in his greeting. Perhaps he too was depressed by their lack of progress with the pig hunters. "Today is a new and better day!" he said, brightly. "Today I want to get cracking on uplifting the masses."

Briz was plainly translating this into the odd vernacular of the trading plate. "Cracking...?"

"Get started," explained Augustus.

"Oh." The boy looked faintly relieved. "Thought yer meant something else. Yer want to start upliftin' massas?" he looked rather critically at Augustus. "It's hard yakka."

"Er. Yakka?"

"Work," explained the dark blue-eyed ragamuffin in baggy clothes.

"Nothing a Thistlewood loves more!" said Augustus, eagerly.

Briz shrugged. "We better get along to Zell-dock then. Follow me."

So, Augustus did his best. Briz had to stop a few times – but after a good half an hour of threading through various noisome alleys and crooked streets, they came to the edge of the plate and a sort of dockyard. The wind was stiff here, without much to break it. There was a big blocky cloudcastle moored there – not one of the delicate Thrymi ones, but something that looked even less likely to float around the clouds. Several large men were unhitching its moorings, and smoke... or perhaps, steam, roiled out of various cracks and orifices. From close up the cloud-castle looked... old. A little grimy, and in need of some maintenance. No Thistlewood machine or vehicle ever looked thus. Not that they weren't old. They usually were. It was just that they were greased and polished and cared for. Augustus found himself a bit shocked. The trading plate was of course grubby and ramshackle – but that was because it had several hundred thousand people living on it.

That was what he'd thought: but maybe it was also old age, and neglect. Both the Thrymi and the Zell had actively blocked any attempt by the scientists of Azure to get a closer look at their areas, or their machinery. There were archaeologists braving the radioactive and toxic ruins of their cities on several of their former colonies, but on those there was little left that functioned. Somewhere, perhaps, both or either alien species survived on worlds other than on Sybill III. But humanity had not encountered them yet. The Thrymi-Zell war had bypassed Sybill III, leaving the traders cut off from their homeworlds, trapped here. It seemed anyway, that neither alien group living there had any contact with their homeworlds. They still hated each other with a passion. It was known that their respective cloud-castles would still dock at absolute opposite ends of the Plate.

Trade of some kind continued. But, in the research papers and books Augustus had read, no one was really sure what they traded in.

It seemed no one had actually been to look.

The Zell, anyway, traded Massas for whatever it was that they wanted. Sweating human stevedores carried great sacks of it into a warehouse.

"Yer left it a bit late," said Briz. "They're nearly done uplifting it."

"Er. What is it?" asked Augustus, fascinated, despite the fact that it wasn't quite how he'd thought he might help the poor of Sybill III.

"Massas. What you wanted," said Briz, patiently.

"Er. Yes." Augustus wasn't quite sure how to explain that it hadn't been at all what he meant. "But just what is it?"

Briz shrugged. "Dunno. The stuff yer make bread from. The Zell sell it."

"Flour?" asked Augustus, faint, but pursuing.

"Nah. Yer can buy flowers, dunno what for meself, but never heard of no-one making bread from 'em." Briz pointed a grubby finger at the toiling men. "You goin' to go and work?"

Augustus looked at the sweating stevedores and, feeling a bit guilty, shook his head. The gravity of the Plate was a little lower than that of Azure, but he knew he was not particularly strong. His brother Charlie had rejoiced in all the physical sports that a Thistle-wood should excel in at college. Augustus had either studied, read, or made models. That was hardly the training he felt he needed for this. He'd barely scraped the Blue Men's physical as it was. "I don't think so. It er, looks like hard yakka." Augustus was quite proud of his foray into the local language.

"Too right, and not much moolah, neither. It barely pays for the tucker yer burn off."

That reminded Augustus: "I didn't have breakfast this morning. That seems to be a hostelry just there, by the sign. That's what a green bush means, doesn't it?"

Briz blinked. "It means it's a pub."

"Ah," said Augustus trawling his memories of the vernacular. A public house, presumably a house that served the public. It had a jaunty sign next to the green bush, proclaiming it to be 'The Queen's Legs' which was rather puzzling. "Do they serve food?" he asked.

"Uh. Free lunch," said Briz.

"A charitable organization!" exclaimed Augustus. "I must make their acquaintance! What a lucky chance."

"The beer ain't free," said Briz. "And the food is salty."

"Oh, that is all right, I don't really drink anyway," said Augustus. "I'd far rather have water or fruit juice."

"Uh. If yer drink the water, something like fruit juice will be comin' out of you pretty quick," said Briz.

"What? I don't understand."

"Yer really, really, really don't want to drink the water. And that'll be ten dollars, 'cause I just saved your life, mister," the ragamuffin stuck out his hand.

Augustus worked it out. "Sanitation does seem to be a problem," he admitted, and I suppose alcohol would kill some of the bacteria. It's something that would be worth working on, making beer un-necessary."

"Yer really don't want to say that to them neither," said Briz. "And just don't touch the gin."

"Ah. I'm not familiar with gin," admitted Augustus.

"Trust me Mister, yer don't get familiar with it. It gets familiar with you, and you end up blind."

"I'll keep that in mind," promised Augustus.

So, they went in. The place was fairly well populated, mostly by large, muscular men dressed in the black singlets that the stevedores had seemed to regard as safety garb, and by some of the friendly ladies who had welcomed the Star of Space. Judging by the smell, many of them seemed in need of Briz's advice. The honest truth was that most of the trading plate – outside of the Hyaton -- smelled a bit like a faulty septic tank. This place had a twist on that – it smelled of beer, and urine, and fried food. Part of Augustus's stomach wanted to rebel, and another, more primitive part, said the fried food smelled good. Frying would surely kill most bacteria? But the scrum of big men around the bar and the noise did take some braving. "Perhaps we should try elsewhere?" said Augustus, peering at the crowd in the smoky haze.

"Now, yer wouldn't be turning down me tucker? Me horsepistality?" said a huge, fat man in an apron, putting a hand on Briz's shoulder. "I got told special to help yous out, eh, Briz," he said with a voice that sounded like gravel being crushed.

That wasn't a friendly look that Briz returned, Augustus decided. But the boy didn't say anything. "I was just hoping to buy a meal for myself and my young assistant."

"It's on the house," said the enormous man. "Free lunch! And let me shout yer a drink."

Half the bar turned and looked at them. Acutely embarrassed under this stare, Augustus said hastily, "No, I can't do that."

"Yer won't have a drink with me?" asked the big man, loudly, thrusting his bullet head forward.

The bar was now deathly silent. Plainly he had committed some terrible social solecism. "He means it's his shout, first," said Briz.

"Exactly!" said Augustus. "Only good manners."

"I thought yer thought yer was too good ter drink with us," said the fat man. "Gin. I'll have gin. You'll have gin too." He walked up to the bar which magically cleared to make space. "Davo. We'll have two trebles. One special."

The barman nodded. "Sure, boss," he said. He took down a bottle of clear fluid. Augustus couldn't see him pour because his body obscured the glasses, but he turned around and put a tumbler on the bar in front of each of them. One, the one in front of Augustus, seemed rather fuller than the other.

Augustus knew he should say he'd rather have beer. But just then he felt he'd already overstepped the social norms, and very nearly caused bad feeling. The fat man was plainly the proprietor of this establishment. So, he just smiled weakly at the barman. The smell was fairly powerful, even from here. "That'll be half a dollar," said the barman.

"Um. I am sure my assistant and guide would like something, but not gin. He's too young," said Augustus, trying to recapture his confidence.

"Beer," said Briz.

Augustus might have said something about that, because really, the ragamuffin boy was quite small. It was hard to tell his age, but then he remembered what Briz said about the water, and said, "Yes, Beer."

Beer it seemed was more expensive than gin because that was also half a dollar. And, as the fat man turned to look at the barman drawing the frothy brew from the tap, Briz switched the glass in front of Augustus, for that in front of the proprietor.

Augustus picked it up, cautiously, and took a tiny sip. It was all he could do, not to choke. "It's er, strong," he said.

"Yer supposed to throw it back. And chase it with a beer," said the barman, drawing two more beers.

"Like this," said the proprietor and showed him how it was done.

"Oh. Well, could we have some food too? I, um am not really used to alcohol." The barman looked condescendingly at him. "Yer pulling me a raw prawn. Yer was drinkin' gin since the day that yer was born."

"Um. No." Augustus was instinctively truthful. "I've never had it before. And, um, you did mention food. I... er feel I need it."

The barman laughed. "What a drongo. Yer don't know Burke Street from Chrismas do yer?" He turned to a door off to the side that plainly led to the smoky kitchen. "Give us a feed of whitebait, Maurie!"

Moments later a wizened, short little woman with her hair coiled around her head came out and plonked a steaming plate in between them. "Er. Thank you," said Augustus. "Very kind of you. Um. What is it?"

"Bleedin' whitebait."

There seemed to be no blood involved, but plenty of batter. "But... I thought whitebait were fish?" said Augustus.

The cook-woman nodded. "Yeah."

"Er. But there are no oceans. Or... rivers. Or even streams. Do you import them?"

"Nah. They comes from the panflowers," said the woman. "Yer buy 'em from the outbackers. A quart o' gin for a bucket full."

By the time that the history of the tiny fish which hatched and lived hasty lives in the pools of water that a certain kind of floating plant collected in its flowers and their airborne eggs had been explained, and the other patrons had distracted the host with demands for more beer, Augustus was amazed to find that his glass of gin was empty. He hadn't drunk it, surely? Grandmother's sherry trifle at Christmas was normally his alcohol tolerance. He had a mouthful of beer. It did explain what the proprietor meant by horsepistality. But it was better than the gin. Well, at least the gin was gone, and he didn't remember drinking it. Maybe it was the saltiness of the whitebait.

"Ish my shout," said the proprietor, swaying slightly. "Gin! Trebelsh!"

"Uh. Boss," said the barman.

"Ish my blooming shout! I'm shouting all of yers," he said, pointing a swaying finger at Augustus and points to left and right. "It's my shout! How did there sumn... suddd...ing get to be three of yous drongos what I got told to get blind on the lash? Ish MY SHOUT. Yer all going drink wiv me. Yous think yer too good to drink wi' me?"

"BOSS," said the barman, into the sudden silence.

"The boss just shouted gin for the whole bar," said Briz. "It's your shout, boss."

"My SHOUT!" bellowed the fat man, and fell off his chair.

Augustus found the next few minutes a confusing descent into pandemonium. Because the bar's patrons, large stevedores and scantily dressed women had heard the proprietor offer them all treble gins. It didn't matter what the barman said. And when several of them hauled the boss onto a stool, and he shouted them all more gin before falling forward onto the bar and breaking it.

The barman tried not serving them...

That was a mistake, even before someone threw a plate of hot whitebait at him.

"Yer know how to make an impression," said Briz. "But I think we better skedaddle."

"If that means leave, I think you are dead right," said Augustus as someone punched the barman.

"This way, then," said Briz and led him into the kitchen, and out of a back door, while Maurie was still protesting about their intrusion into her domain. The little yard beyond was full of rubbish in various bags and woven baskets– which Briz made into a convenient staircase for them to walk up to the glass-studded wall, and jump over.

"Oh, I say. Should we be leaving this way?"

"Yer right. Maybe we should go out the front door. Only, it seems like they're having a bit of a blue in there," said Briz, jumping down into the alley, somehow not spilling the mug of beer or the plate of fried whitebait the ragamuffin had snagged on the way through. They walked out of the alley, and onto the road beyond. "Couple of your embassy galahs in there," said Briz, cheerfully, offering him some of the plate of whitebait.

Augustus, despite his reservations, took a handful. He was hungry, and what didn't kill, as his grandmother said, made you fat. They were salty, fishy, and rather tasty, in spite of it. There was a sound of breaking glass and yelling from the pub behind them. "Oh dear. I do hope the embassy people are all right. I have to go and present some papers there later."

"Holy dooley! Yer leave them dropkicks to look after themselves," said Briz. "They're a bunch of bastards, always up to some sort of rort."

Translating, Augustus worked out that his guide had a low opinion of the ambassadorial staff. It was, from what he'd gathered, not surprisingly, a dead-end posting. There was hardly any point in having an embassy here, except to deal with Azure visitors who got themselves into trouble.

Augustus rather wondered who had got themselves into difficulties this time. Still, it was none of his business. He ate some more of the whitebait and actually wished he hadn't left the beer behind. He said so.

Briz brighted perceptibly. "There's a bottle-o one over. We can get a couple o' stubbies. And yer owe me ten bucks for saving yer life, or at least yer liver, besides today's wages."

"Er...what? I mean, yes, I owe you the day's wages. But the rest didn't make a lot of sense. And I have a very small budget that I have to live on."

"I swapped yer glass. It had a Mickey Finn in it that would have sent you on a bender where yer didn't know yer mother from yer own ear-hole. Yer saw what it did to the fat bastard. He was as pissed as a newt, and he can put it away, my oath he can. Saved yer a fortune. And I poured yer gin out onto the floor. I told yer not to drink it. Stick to beer or bundy."

Faint but pursuing, Augustus worked it out as best as possible. "You mean... that drink was drugged? We ought to tell the authorities."

"I think what yer call the 'authorities' already know." Briz looked around, warily. "They're tryin' to set you up. But don't let on I told yer."

Augustus felt fury bubble within him as he absorbed this. "I suppose the powers-that-be have an interest in seeing this venal criminality persists. They don't want the people uplifted. Well! I will not be stopped. There have to be ways around this web of corruption! I will have words at the embassy. Send messages to the Blue Men. Briz, take me back to the Hyaton. I will collect my documents and then I will need you to show me the way to the embassy! But first, here is your fifteen dollars. Well-earned, indeed," he said, taking out his wallet, and giving Briz the money.

"So... now you don't want to go to the Bottle-o?" asked Briz, making the money vanish into the rags. "His grog is good. Even the Bundy is the real thing."

But even the thirst caused by the whitebait could not overcome Augustus's sudden flood of both guilt at his own lack of success, and determination to right this corruption. "No, I must seize the day. Carpe diem!"

"Carpay? Only the Zell and Thrymi got cars, Mister. And yer can't pay enough. But a rickshaw I can get yer... We'd have time for a butcher then."

Rather than explain, or find out why he needed a butcher, Augustus said: "Let's just walk. Rickshaws are degrading."

"Yeah, most of them are pretty broken down. Let's leg it then."

So, they did, and in what felt as if might have been half an hour – it was hard to tell – because Augustus decided, reluctantly, that his missing watch might possibly have been stolen -- they were back at the Hyaton.

Briz promised to be waiting when Augustus returned from its precincts, and was. The Embassy was some distance away, in the center of the plate, and Briz once again suggested a rickshaw. Augustus almost weakened, but held out, so they walked again through the winding streets, Briz showing him what he considered things of interest like turf marks, bottle-os and various hostelries. Admittedly, away from the edge and the magnificent skies, much of the plate was little more than a vast shanty-town, made with scrap from the crash of the Botany Bay, and dried native vegetation. Skyfrond, Briz called it. It was used for thatch. It was woven into walls, it was even laminated into planks. It was still rather scruffy, a far cry from the vast landing deck with Zell halls along the one edge and Thrymi palaces along the other that had apparently been there originally.

The exception was the ambassadorial district, where five worlds kept up some sort of presence. These were real buildings, of brick and mortar. Now that he'd spent a day – even if it was always one long late afternoon on Sybil, Augustus had to wonder why there were even that many.

Briz left him at the impressive stone gate. It might well be the only stone that wasn't somewhere down near the hot core of Sybil. The studies he'd read suggested there was at least semi-solid material down in the gravity well, and that was hot and had spectacular eruptions, material from which actually reached up into the outer atmosphere the trading plate drifted in. This gate, however, had to have been brought in from Azure. There was a very precisely uniformed Azure Marine on guard, who demanded to know his business.

"I'm an Azure citizen," said Augustus stiffly, producing his passport. "And I have a letter to hand-deliver to the Ambassador."

"You'll have to make an appointment, Sir," said the soldier. "You could see one of the junior attaches and arrange it. The Ambassador only sees people every second Tuesday. I'll get someone to escort you. May I know your name, Sir?"

"It's on my passport," said Augustus, handing it to him. The marine stepped back into his guardhouse and called someone. And then stepped out, saluted respectfully, and handed back the passport. "They're sending someone down right away, Sir. It seems the Ambassador will see you after all." He looked Augustus up and down. And then said, in a wondering under-voice: "Who are you? God?"

"I'm here as one of the Blue Men, doing my best for poor people in need. Maybe they feel that's important. I know I do."

"Be the first sign I saw of it, Sir. They're a right bunch of rogues," said the Marine.

"They're just misunderstood. It's a different culture. Or are you talking about the embassy staff?" asked Augustus, hackles rising.

The soldier plainly missed Augustus's change in tone. He laughed. "Both, I reckon, Sir. But don't tell the nobs inside I said that. The outbackers are all right. I've met a few that wouldn't steal you blind. The locals though... Ah. Good grief. It's the Senior Undersecretary!"

The diplomat – who introduced himself as Senior Undersecretary Phillip Camelthrob-Princhbut had plainly come as fast as he could, but he was walking with some difficulty. He also had a black eye. "Mister Thistlewood. We're honored to have you here. I was just about to go to the Hyaton to look for you again."

As the soldier was now behind the diplomat, the diplomat could not see the marine's jaw fall open. But Augustus did. It hardened his suspicions. But nothing could have been more affable than Ambassador Porcatrip. "My dear boy, you must allow us to help you as much as possible! Nothing could be better than for the Blue Men to be sending someone of your stature here."

"I'm a Blue Man class 003.5, sir," said Augustus, acutely embarrassed, as he always was about family... and he suspected that this was about that. "That's about as low as you can get for field staff."

"Ah, but it is a noble effort, uplifting the poor. I'm sure we can help you, make you suitable contacts. You must come and stay in the diplomatic guest chalet. So much less impersonal than the Hyaton," said the ambassador. "I've asked them to send your trunk directly."

"I was hoping to find lodgings among the people. To live and eat and sleep among them. To learn how they live and to understand their culture and needs. To make bonds," said Augustus.

Now it was the Ambassador's turn to have his mouth fall open. But he was quick to recover. "Excellent, my boy. Excellent. But finding something suitable will take a little time. So, until then, eh. We have very good cold storage and our food is all from Azure. None of these bowls of eyeballs that the locals eat. Their food will make you gag, I'm afraid."

Augustus wondered if he should explain to the Ambassador that the locals paid to watch Azure tourists gag on the eyeballs but decided against it. "I really wanted to speak to you sir. I've done some exploring and it would seem that there is some resistance to my being here among the officialdom. Corruption seems to be endemic. They seem to want to keep their own people in poverty!"

"Shocking, isn't it! But there are some forward-looking people. Mr Kasagolis..."

"I've met him," said Augustus, stiffly. "It's my belief that the pork he deals in would contravene health standards, hunted like that."

"Pork?"

"He apparently deals with the bush-pigs that scavenge a living here. Where they live, and under what conditions I cannot imagine, and his hunters are extremely badly trained."

"Uh, quite so," said the Ambassador, sticking a finger into his collar. "I'm sure my staff... Senior Undersecretary Camelthrob-Princhbut has made quite a study of local customs. I'm sure he'll be of great help to you. He's unfortunately suffered a minor injury. Got caught on the periphery of a brawl, I gather. But he'll be happy to consult and make local arrangements. Serve as a local guide, as it were."

"I've already hired one of those, Sir. A local boy."

The ambassador looked at him as if he'd sprouted two heads. "They're just not reliable, my good chap."

"He's proved very trustworthy so far, reliable and glad to have employment. I'll be happy to talk to Mr Camelthrob-Princhbut, but I really need to make my own contacts as well," said Augustus firmly. The more he thought about it, the more he was sure that he'd seen Camelthrob-Princhbut before, even if he couldn't place quite where. But his instincts said that the less he had to do with the embassy, the better. On the other hand, he was spending rather more than he'd planned, staying at the Hyaton, and so far, Briz had hedged off on his suggestions of finding accommodation elsewhere. It would be easier once he got to know a few more people, he hoped. "I would be very much obliged if I could stay in your chalet for a few days until I can arrange a billet with a local family. But I will have to go back to the Hyaton and collect my things from the safe, pay my bill and collect my personal belongings."

"Oh, certainly. I'll have one of the staff call you a rickshaw."

"I prefer to walk. It will give me an opportunity to speak to my guide, and explain that I will still be employing him."

The Ambassador looked a little less than pleased about that, but did invite Augustus to join him for dinner that evening. "Just a cozy pot-luck, eh."

Camelthrob-Princhbut was waiting to see him out, being all affability and light, despite limping. Augustus asked something that had piqued his curiosity as they tramped down the long corridors of the ornate building. Most of it seemed un-occupied. "Why is the Embassy so big?"

"Because it has to be bigger than the Roptor Embassy and the Sinopese Consulate put together," said Camelthrob-Princhbut, without a hint of irony.

"Oh... but the trading plate is so crowded."

The front gate spared the diplomat having to comment on that. Briz was hovering just out of bayonet reach, amusing himself by making faces at the Marine. "I see yer brought the dunny-budgie back with yer," said Briz jerking a distainful thumb at the Senior Undersecretary, as they started to walk away from the ornate pillars and cornices of the embassy. "He was one of the blokes at the Queen's Legs, just after we left. Musta got his daily kick in the fork, and a poke in the eye too." Briz sounded quite pleased about that, whatever it meant. "Nasty piece 'o work. You watch him, Mister."

"You know him?"

"No. He likes Claggs alley. Not my kind. But word gets around, see."

Like so much of what Briz said, about half of that was incomprehensible. Like the suggestion they stop for a dog's eye and a butcher – which proved to be a pie and small mug of beer. But it all served to confirm his misgivings about the embassy.

Back at the Hyaton, he took time to pen two brief letters, one to the Blue Men, and the other to his father, telling them both about the situation and the fact that it seemed there might be corruption afoot, before going out to settle his bill and clock out. When he saw the bill, he was rather glad he'd be staying at the embassy's chalet!

"I hope you enjoyed your stay at the Hyaton, Sir," said the young woman with a fake smile.

Briz was even more worried about being in the presence of various Capos and their representatives than she would have been otherwise – which was to say she was near shitting herself. If they knew she'd mucked up their plan to get her mark off his face and into strife at the Queen's legs... but it seemed they didn't. They wanted to know what he was planning to do next, and they were less than pleased that Augustus was moving out of the Hyaton and into the Embassy Chalet.

"I don't trust that Pinchbut. I mean we got the black on him good, but he's as smart as a dunny rat," scowled Kasagolis. "All right. You keep with him, you little guttersnipe. Does this rich kid like to gamble?"

Briz shrugged her shoulders. "He did say 'I bet' once. But I don't understand his fancy talk a lot of the time."

"We know he don't like the girls. Take him to Claggs."

Briz felt herself flush, to her own surprise. "He don't like boys. He thinks I am one."

That made the Capos laugh. "If he's half as rich as Princhbut says, we may as well make a profit from him," said one of the gambling skegs.

"He hasn't got a lot of cash," said Briz. Why was she defending him?

"We have ways of collecting on IOU's," said the gambler-boss with a sharkish grin. "Besides, just having a bunch of them might send him scurrying back to Azure. We got contacts there too. But I won't bring no trouble down on myself. I'll just let a couple of the big players fleece him, all straight and legal. That way if there's a problem with this family of his, it's their problem. You bring the mark to Straight Jonnies. We'll deal with him."

"But how?" asked Briz.

"You tell him Jonnie has some rooms to rent. You said he don't want to stay in the embassy. They probably crimp his style. Now scram. We got other business to talk."

Briz was glad to get out of there. But, she had to admit to herself, she wasn't too happy at setting up the patsy from Azure to get fleeced. In a world that had been set to do her over, if she didn't get them first, it was odd to deal with another human who seemed to really have no interest in doing so. She was getting quite protective about him. Protective, but not a dill. She took him to Straight Jonnies, telling him their story.

Ambassador Porcatrip sent for Phillip Camelthrob-Princhbut just as soon as the Senior Undersecretary had seen Augustus on his way. "Is that boy mad?" he said, irritably. "He was going on about pork exports!"

"Pork? Unless that's some new name for an exotic drug I haven't come across," said Camelthrob-Princhbut rather hopefully.

"He said our friend Kasagolis was hunting feral bushpigs."

Camelthrob-Princhbut gave a snort of laughter, and then winced as that hurt his bruised ribs. "He's a confused innocent. 'Bushpig' is a derogatory term for an unattractive prostitute."

"Oh." The ambassador steepled his fingers. "I don't think there is any need to enlighten him. We really need the fellow out of here. I've too much riding on this business, and my retirement is coming up. It is a sleepy backwater no one back home cares about, let's keep it that way, eh?"

"Absolutely, Ambassador."

"I have to put up with him at dinner," said the Ambassador, sourly. "So, the sooner he goes the better."

I f he had known about the Ambassador's desire to see the back of him, Augustus would have said the feeling was mutual. The dinner was long, and the food expensive, ornate, and matched with suitable wines, most of which Augustus really didn't like much. Neither, to be honest, did he like the company. So, he did what he'd always done when he felt out of place: shut up and said as little as possible. And listened. It didn't take long as the wine went down, to work out that the Ambassador loathed his posting only slightly less than he loathed the people of Sybil, and peculiarly most of the people back on Azure. In fact, the only thing the Ambassador didn't loathe was his food and drink and the rather pretty charge d'affaires that was serving as his hostess. She had a smile that reminded Augustus of the clerk at the Hyaton when he checked out.

Augustus really was up for anywhere else by the end of it all. But rain was hissing down – perhaps furious that it had such a long way to fall to the ground and the plate was in its way, or perhaps just because a world of clouds and high water-vapor also had lots of rain. He commented about it to the young marine who had been on the gate earlier and was now detailed to escort him to the chalet, as they waited beneath the eave for the rain to ease off.

"Oh, this is nothing, Sir. The plate stays in the best and most stable weather. I went with the Geographical mapping expedition as one of the guards – before the Thrymi complained to old puff-guts... uh. Well, you know who I mean, sir. Anyway, we got called back, but I saw a couple of storms that made this look like drizzle."

"I had no idea that there'd been any attempts to explore... I mean, the habitable zone is just air. Much the same, isn't it?"

The marine laughed. "Not really, no, sir. Ah. It's slacking off. Better make a bolt for it, Sir."

So, they did. But Augustus was left wondering what could be so different. It would have made a far more interesting subject for dinner conversation than vapid observations on fashions in New Paris or the excellence of Azure beef and how hard it was to get decent servants. It was as irritating as discovering his copy of Belcher missing. That would take another trip to the Hyaton, where they would doubtless deny everything and blame the locals. He was determined that, in the morning – well, when he got up, he would take steps to get out of there. To engage with the people of Sybil, no matter how intimidating he found it. So, when Briz suggested taking him to someone called Straight Jonny about somewhere to rent, he was enthusiastic about the idea, and even willing to take a rickshaw, because it had come on to rain again. He apologized to the poor man drawing it, to have him out in the rain. "Good weather for this sort of yakka," said the Rickshaw-man trotting along with ease. "Good moolah to be made in a bit o' rain. I'm right glad of it!"

Things so often turned out to be quite the opposite of what you thought they were, reflected Augustus as they got down at the door of 'Straight Jonny's'. It looked quite sleazy... but as he had just determined not to let his preconceptions rule, he went in with Briz. There was a bar, not well occupied, and several booths with tables in them, but Briz led him over to the bar. There was noise coming from beyond that suggested several other rooms. It was actually much better on the inside than out, thought Augustus. "Come to see Jon," Briz said. She jerked a thumb at him. "He wants to hire a cubby."

The Barman nodded slowly. "You just take a seat. I'll let the boss know. You want some'ting to drink?"

"Give us a couple of middies," said Briz. And then to Augustus's surprise, said: "My shout."

"Oh, I think I ought to pay," he said, feeling for his wallet.

"Yer said yer wanted to learn the local customs," said Briz catching his arm with a skinny hand. "It's not done, see."

Briz paid for the two mugs of beer. It was a lot cheaper than it had been at the Queen's Legs, to Augustus's surprise. And, although he still wasn't sure about beer, this was very much more drinkable too.

"Yeah," said Briz, tersely, leading him toward a table in a booth.

"Yer need to think about why it's cheap and good, Mister," Briz said quietly.

Augustus worked that out. Reluctantly, he had to admit to himself it probably wasn't because they were fair and generous. But, perhaps he was mistaken. It was best to give the benefit of the doubt, to treat others as you wanted to be treated, as his grandmother always said.

They had barely sat down when two men and an elegant lady drifted to their booth, drinks in hand. "Mind if we join yous? The other tables are full," said the first of them, a mustachioed man in a rather better-looking coat than most Sybilians seemed to own. He didn't wait for permission but handed the woman into the seat next to Augustus.

They all sat down. "You must be from off-world," said the woman, favoring him with a smile and a view of her ample cleavage in her low-cut blouse.

Augustus blushed, just faced with it. "Er. Yes. I'm from Azure. Uh. I am with the Blue Men... I've, um, come to do charitable work here," he said, awkwardly. "We're just waiting to see... Jon."

"He'll be a little while," said the second man. "Gone to visit his sick old mother."

"We could come back later," said Augustus. "I don't want to intrude."

"Sit. It's raining out and you can never get a rickshaw when you need one," said the mustachioed man, easily. "We'll have a little game to pass the time," he said producing a deck of cards. "Just a friendly game."

"Oh. I can't. I've never played cards. I've only ever played board games." Augustus held off saying his grandmother called cards 'tickets to the devil,' and frowned on their existence, let alone having them in the house.

"It's an easy game. Libby will help you with the first couple of hands."

Which was how Augustus found himself being taught to play a

form of poker. Having the rules explained to him by the ample breasted Libby, and having several more men join the game. It was rather entertaining. And then they started betting.

"Oh, I can't do that. I don't gamble," said Augustus, looking at Briz... Who had somehow evaded playing, and wondering how he could get out of this politely. "We're just here to see Mr. Jon."

One of the other men laughed, but the mustachioed man said soothingly. "It's a way of keeping score. Here: I'll stake you. That way it's not your money."

"Unless he wins, of course," said Libby, roguishly. "He seems to have learned the game really well."

He had. He had learned far harder things, and he was already calculating the probabilities. And he was actually enjoying the game. And, as it went on, it seemed it he was either lucky or really good at it. His enthusiastic comments seemed to take them a bit by surprise. "You're not actually supposed to tell everyone you've got a good hand," said Libby. By this stage he had a very large pile of money in front of him to show his score.

"But why not?" asked Augustus. "I mean there is a 0.378 probability of anyone having better hand."

"What?" said one of the other card-players warily.

"What what?" said Augustus.

"What are the numbers you just said?"

"The probability of my hand being beaten."

The man's eyes narrowed. "I thought you said you'd never played the game? How the hell did I fall for that one!? Straight Jonnie," he said, pointing a finger at the man with the mustache, "You said he was a dipstick. That it'd be a joke fleecing him. We've been set up, boys!"

The man looked remarkably angry. "I say!" said Augustus. "It's just a game. If you're going to get upset about it, I won't play."

Suddenly the light above the table exploded. So did a lot of other things. Tempers, and it seemed, fire-arms. The table went over, and Augustus found himself under several sprawling, fighting people. He struggled out from the scrimmage, and a small hand found his arm and pulled him under a bench seat. It was Briz, and in the noise and chaos, Augustus let himself be led, crawling, away. Briz whispered: "We gotta do the Harold Holt."

Augustus had no idea what that meant, except something to do with leaving. It seemed a good idea.

Briz had been quite down when she'd delivered the poor drongo for plucking. Straight Jonnie himself, and half the high-rollers and card-merchants on the plate had been either involved or looking on. Straight Jonnie must have told them her Mister was worth a lot of money... They'd started by giving him easy coups. Letting him get sucked in. Letting the grog flow, too... except he wasn't drinking. His attention was entirely on the game.

These were gamblers who worked the odds, made their living out of reading people's faces... they could read the faintest trace of nervousness or excitement at a good card or hand. Reading their opponents was what they did. Briz knew perfectly well she'd have had no chance of fooling them, if she had good cards or bad. They kept their own masks perfectly... for a while.

But even that had started to slip as Mister Drongo... walked away from the traps and got them to fold when he had almost nothing. She understood their problem. He wasn't in the least tense... about anything. He was just as excited about a pair of twos as a full house. He cheerfully told them when he had a great hand... Several of them bet big on that. And he had.

It had come to her like a slap about the head. They were all assuming he'd try to play the game the way they would – to deceive, and to not reveal unless that revealing tricked their opponent into a rash move. Their mindset dictated that their opponent had to care whether he won or lost – and that would change the way he behaved. The drongo didn't. He was genuinely delighted when someone else won a hand. It was like he didn't realize that there was a small fortune on the table, more money than Briz had ever seen in her life. When Straight Jonnie had told him that it was a friendly game to pass the time, and that money was just a way of keeping score... He'd believed them, and was having fun.

It couldn't end well. They would figure it out, sooner or later. But she'd spent a lot more time with him than they had. So, she'd been ready to throw her glass at the light. She hadn't been ready for the shooting, but should have been. What she was ready for right now was getting the hell out of there. And she'd be doing exactly what the capos said – keeping the drongo healthy. So long as they didn't find out that some of the money on that table had somehow fallen into her pockets.

She figured the best way out was probably the front door, and she was right, seeing as the bouncers had run in to deal with the fight. She had him out of there and into a rickshaw and heading away before anyone had a chance to stop them, and before he could ask what happened.

"Straight Jonnie got shot. He's dead," she explained.

"What! I mean... shouldn't we go back and help with witness statements to the police? The Blue Men advise us to stay away from local police, but..."

"Too right," she interrupted. "And they won't be asking no questions anyway. Now I was thinkin' yer might want to do what a few of the tourists do: go for a closer look at the Thrymi quarter. Only you can't go too close, see. They don't like it."

"Oh yes! Well, really, I feel it would be wasting time... I should be working on uplift, but I'd love to see it. But I still need to find some lodging. I... um, don't feel that was the right neighborhood."

"And Straight Jonnie is dead. Yeah. Sorry. Look, I'll... have a word with some people. It'll just take a little time. Yer just come and take a sticky-beak at the Thrymi palaces." She had a moment of inspiration. "It'll help yer understand the culture." Culture seemed to be a magic word. She wasn't sure what it meant, but had heard that they used it in making some kind of cheese.

And it worked this time too. Augustus stared in amazement at the slim, elegant Thrymi towers. From a distance, because that was how you looked at the Thrymi quarter. "They're so unlike the buildings in the rest of the plate. I don't see why people don't all build like that," he said, marveling. "Maybe not the same choice of colors. They seem fond of that chartreuse shade, but the sheer elegance and delicate lines would be worthy of imitation. So why not?"

"'Cause we hate the Figjams. Also 'cause how do you build something like that out 'o scrap, cheap tin, and skyfrond?"

"I suppose there are some architectural limits to the materials," conceded Augustus. "But what do they use?"

Briz shrugged. "Could be spit and ear-wax for all we know. We ain't allowed to go no closer. And they don't build nothing. Not now, anyway."

"It's actually quite a small area. There can't be more than twenty buildings."

"Yeah. Zell-side is bigger, but most of them live in the skycastles. They just come in to the Big Syd every now and again, when they feel like it, I been told."

"Oh. Why do they do that?" asked Augustus.

"Struth, I dunno. Yer can't guess what goes on in their pointy heads. I mean why would yer ever want ter live anywhere but here? There's nothing out there."

"There must be something," said Augustus, with a smile.

Briz shook her head. "Miles and miles and miles of nothing. All the way, up and down. Now, yer want to see the Zell quarter? It's a bit bigger but it's not so pretty. An it's gonna rain again. We need to find a rickshaw."

So, they found one, and headed across the width of the plate.

Augustus found they had to change rickshaws several times, not because it was tiring out the poor men used as human motive power – they seemed remarkably strong and did the work without even raising much of a sweat, but because they crossed several 'territories'. Augustus found this fact had been entirely left out of his map – which actually did have some vague semblance to reality – including fortifications. "What are those?" he asked Briz.

"Bacon shop. Where the filth hang out. Yer stay as far as possible from 'em."

A bit of further inquiry did lead Augustus to discover that they didn't actually sell bacon, and were not particularly dirty... but you still stayed as far as possible from them.

The local argot, while follow-able in general terms, Augustus found exhausting to try to understand. It was nearly as illogical as sociology, in which black could be white and male could be female, except when it suited itself to be what someone might naturally think it was. In a way the Zell side of the plate was similar... in that it was just... not the way any human would build anything. It was quite blocky. Often black to dark green... with sudden stark bits of maroon. And a lot of it started narrow and grew bigger, upwards. Humans could go into the Zell quarter, so it was possible to get a closer look.

Other than signs of old age and lack of maintenance, Augustus couldn't see a great deal more than he had of the Thrymi buildings viewed at long range. The doors were too low for humans.

They were the right size for the alien Zell, however. Two of them emerged from one of the doorways standing on some sort of hover-plate. Briz pushed him back. "Stay back and out of the way!" The two Zell, short, wide, blue skinned and with oddly pointed heads, clad in some shimmery grey fabric, paid them – and others on the street -- as much mind as people did to microbes.

The hover-plate shot off in the opposite direction and left Augustus with nothing to see but the odd buildings, made of dark green-grey slick-looking material. It could be metal or ceramic, thought Augustus. He reached out to feel it. "Don't yer touch it," Briz warned him grabbing his arm.

By now he'd learned to take Briz's warning seriously. But he asked why?

"They're watchin'. They'll know and they don't like it. Blasted a good few fellows on the prig to ash." There didn't seem to be any windows to watch from, but Augustus was willing to defer to Briz's superior knowledge, or possibly experience. He was learning a fair bit from his scruffy guide's casual talk. One of the things he'd learned was that despite appearing relatively young under the dirt, Briz had accumulated a great deal of experience that hadn't come Augustus's way. Augustus, to his sadness, realized some of it had to be criminal, although Briz seemed wholly unaware of the heinous nature of petty theft or casual mayhem.

Augustus was determined to set a good example rather than lecture. It wasn't easy. But there was much to be learned. When – very proud of his knowledge of the local slang – he suggested they get a dead dog and a butcher, he got rolled eyes. "Yer don't want to eat that. Not in this part o' town. And whatever yer do, don't eat the mystery bags. They might have yer cousin Freddie in 'em."

Mystery bags, it turned out, were sausages. And people disappeared in these parts. Briz loftily informed him it was the kind of thing that the Bondiboyz would do, but he wouldn't say it too loud in this part of town, and maybe they should be getting out of it, so he could do some finding out about somewhere for Augustus to stay.

"I'd also better get back to the Hyaton. I need to ask about one of my books. It's missing," said Augustus.

There was a moment's silence. Then Briz said, gruffly. "Yer don't need to do that. I'll get it back for yer. This arvo."

Arvo... afternoon. It was always afternoon here. But by now Augustus had figured it meant 'later'. He also figured that this meant Briz had taken his Belcher. Augustus took a while to digest this. At first, he was a little hurt. But then he realized that Briz hadn't needed to do or say anything. "You are welcome to read any of my books,

Briz. Just ask," he said quietly. Books must be a rarity here. And Briz could read, he'd discovered.

For the first time in their acquaintance, Briz managed a look of discomfort on his skinny little pinched face. He must be very young as there was no sign of a beard.

"How old are you, Briz?" he asked.

"Dunno," Briz said with a shrug.

That was in itself an issue here. You couldn't even measure days by the passage of night and day, as the gas giant turned slowly and the trading plate remained in the temperate zone, in the late afternoon.

Days and indeed years passed here, but there was little sign of their passage, with daylight more or less the same, depending on cloud thickness, or rain, and certainly no change in season.

At a later time, which was not night, but during which Augustus was asleep:

"Strewth, Capo. Why don't yer just let him be? He's harmless," said Briz, in spite of her best intention to keep her mouth shut.

Briz thought her last moment had come. "Harmless? Harmless?" shouted the Capo, spittle flecked beard inches from her face. "He just killed Straight Jonny, wiped out his club, left the place a burned-out ruin... and he goes orf sightseeing! He gets into a brawl in the Queen's Legs that wrecks the place and breaks big Adam's arm, and destroys all the grog in the place... and doesn't get a bruise. He comes into my place and sets the joint and me on fire, steals our guns... and you tell me he's 'harmless'?

"But he wasn't trying to do nothing..."

"What the hell is he going to do when he does try then?" said the Capo, angrily.

"He is something of an innocent," said Camelthrob-Princhbut. "But don't worry, Capo. We'll fix it. You know those investigators looking into counterfeit Azure dollars? The fellows who have been at the Hyaton for three weeks now?"

They all laughed. "I'll let them know we've had a tip-off. That the young man is the courier."

"Stashing it in his gear in the Embassy is a bit close to home," said the Capo.

"Exactly. Which is why you're going to provide Briz here, with a suitable place for him to rent. Respectable, affordable... and a long way from us. Then we'll set things up so he gets a large bundle of notes – and we'll have these Azure policemen waiting for him. We'll watch him the whole way into their arms so he can't go anywhere else with it. Besides Briz will be watching, won't she?"

"Yeah," said Briz, uncomfortably.

"But... won't this bloke's family get him off?" asked the Capo.

Princhbut shrugged. "Almost certainly. But the people used for the Azure Interplanetary Criminal Investigation Unit have a... a certain reputation for probity and incorruptibility, which is, unfortunately fairly accurate. People trust them, back home, and it won't do him, or his family any good to get him arrested by them. He'll spend a few nights locked up at the embassy until they can ship him off to Azure for the trial. And while they might get the charges dismissed... he won't be coming back."

"I want worse than that for him," said the Capo, sulkily.

"Yes. But it gets rid of him. And shames him and the family. And, who knows, the arrest process might be a bit rough, eh. I shall tell the investigators he's using dangerous drugs that make him violent."

They worked out the details and Briz listened with a sinking heart. Beggars lane was no place for her to intervene without being seen. And some of those beggars would be the Capo's men. The crib they had arranged was good, she had to admit. And he'd be better off back home on Azure. She couldn't get him out of every jam he got into. The only downside was the packet of Scopo-powder they gave her to put in it. It made you see things and totally wrecked some people.

These Jacks might catch him with the fake money, but they weren't going to catch him with that. The Capo would never know.

So, she went to find a lurk outside the embassy compound to wait his coming out. She had his patterns of comings and goings pretty pat by now. And she had her thoughts to occupy her. Mostly they were thoughts about how she'd like to toss that Pinchbut and Capo Kasagolis over the edge to see if they could fly.

Then of course it got more complicated. Because it always did. She took the poor drongo to see his crib, he paid for it – a month in advance! Which peeved Briz – rip-off artists. She had to fight the price down for him. Then he thought he'd take a rickshaw to help with his trunk and case. "I thought you said they was degrading. I mean some of them are. They're falling apart. Can be dangerous," she said.

"I've had to rethink that in the light of talking to the gentleman who pulled the rickshaw the other night. He seemed genuinely proud of his work. It is honest labor, and worth supporting."

"At the rate you get ripped off by them, I reckon you better let me do the dickering," said Briz, crossly. If anyone was going to rip him off it should be her. Especially as she didn't have long to do it in. That scratched her up raw inside, for some reason. What call had these bastards to interfere? It wasn't like he was doing any harm... she thought about the last few days. Well, it wasn't like he set out to do any harm. They brought it on themselves, messing with the big sook.

But she still had him walking down Beggars Lane at the appointed time – after a trip back to the Embassy guest-house to collect the things he'd left behind. He sighed as they approached it. "The Blue Men training specifically forbids giving your cash to beggars. I... understand their reasoning. But I find just walking past people in such distress very hard. It's the only thing I can fault about the lodgings you have found me. Why are there so many distressed people begging just here? I mean, I have seen these unfortunates elsewhere, but not in these numbers."

"Casino at the end of the road. Three bars, and the bread-works," explained Briz.

"You mean they rely on the generosity of winners and drunks and the bread-works?" asked Augustus.

"Nah. Mostly they're losers and don't want to be far from the bar..."

Then, from above, a fat wad of $100 notes landed straight in front of Augustus.

And he failed to notice. Nearly stepped right over them. Briz was obliged to say: "What's that?"

Augustus looked down and blinked. "Goodness! It is someone's money! Oh dear! Did you see who could have dropped it? We must find them at once. They will be upset and anxious." He picked up the bills. "Has anybody lost..." he started to call out.

Briz was obliged to shove her hand in front of his mouth. "They'll all claim it!" she said.

"Oh. I suppose some people might be that dishonest. Well... my research last night says there are some form of police here. We must turn it over to them immediately."

Briz looked at him in horror. "Yer can't give that to the Jacks!"

"What? Oh. I suppose that means police."

"Yeah! And it has to be stolen money or drug money, see," said Briz, hastily. "And they'll just nick it and claim it was the proceeds o' crime. Might toss you inside to keep yer quiet."

Augustus looked grave. "The research I did, did suggest they weren't known for probity. What can I do with it then? I could take it straight to the embassy," he said starting to turn.

"What would those jokers do with it?" said Briz, desperately pulling at his arm. "Look, it's gotta be stolen money, or drug money or something." Failing to find another argument she said: "Just think what yer could do with it instead!"

Augustus stopped. "You know... you are right. That doesn't

contravene the Blue Men guidelines! It's not my money. And we're encouraged to help with redistributive programs. Plainly anyone with this many notes to drop, is not in need." And he walked up to the nearest beggar... pulled off the rubber band, and dropped several thousand into the man's hat. "Make a new start for yourself. And stay away from gambling and liquor." And with rapid strides he walked on to the next, to do the same, all the way down Beggars Lane, beaming while happily handing out bunches of notes. Briz tried to stop him. So did a few of the Capo's men... it was hard to get anywhere because the alley had turned into a melee of running men and women, with flying notes and fleeing crippled beggars – many of whom had had instant cures.

Briz would have been fighting for her own share, if she hadn't known they were dud notes. Instead, she fought her way through to him as Augustus tossed the last notes over his head. He smiled at her. "There, I hope I have changed a few lives. Very satisfying!" Then he looked at her, with some dismay. "I suppose I could have given you some, my little guide. I just never thought of it. But at least you've honestly earned your money. That makes it a more valuable thing."

And while Briz's jaw hung open in disbelief, he unlocked the door to his little apartment, and walked in.

The two Jacks stepped out, one from next to the closet and the other from behind the door. Another man and a burly woman stepped up from outside and closed the door. Briz got the feeling she should maybe have stayed out there with the fight on Beggar's Lane.

"I say! What are you all doing in my room?" asked Augustus. To her surprise Briz discovered he could sound like something other than a drongo. His voice was sharp enough to make even the Jacks pause and hold back slightly.

"We're acting on the basis of information received, Sir. I am Chief Inspector Peleton of the Azure Interplanetary Criminal Investigation Unit. I must advise you to take no rash actions and to co-operate fully with my officers. We need to search you, Sir."

"I'll need to see some form of identity first," said Augustus. "But, if you can prove you are who you claim to be, I will certainly co-operate. You will have to do a 'please explain' to your seniors about just what you're doing inside my apartment. It's a clear breach of Azure Law."

Briz found herself wondering if, somehow, the drongo had a double and they'd done a switcheroo. Because this guy sounded like he was used to giving orders. And he was coldly angry, and the four strangers were in trouble, not him. A thought occurred to her. Maybe that roach Pinchbut had done him a favor. They thought he was dangerous. It might have been funny, if it wasn't so full of things that could go wrong. But, although they were treating him warily, threats were enough to tell these Jacks they were onto a sure thing. They were carefully moving to box him.

Their leader, however did reach into his jacket with calm confidence... which evaporated. He felt frantically in his pockets. "I... I've been robbed!"

That was enough to give the other Jacks a stopper. "What, Chief?"

"My wallet has gone! It must have been that fellow who jostled me just outside the Hyaton!"

Briz took the opportunity -- as all of them checked their pockets -- to drop the Jack's wallet down behind the sofa cushions. That'd show these blow-in Jacks to push her out the way like she wasn't there. And as luck would have it... one of the others had had his wallet nicked too. Briz would have been laughing her head off, if there was somewhere to run. Teach them to come and do their dirty on her turf.

The few seconds of chaos gave Augustus time to cool down... a little. To realize he'd been, for the first time in his life, acting like his grandfather at the experience of finding them in what had already become his sanctum. They were, by their accents anyway, definitely from Azure, and quite upset. The latter, he had to admit, pleased him. It was rather ignoble, but he really hadn't liked finding his room invaded without as much as a knock. It cooled him down to the point of – also for the first time in his life -- merely acting like his father. "I see some of you at least have retained your wallets. Perhaps they could provide their identity," he said in a voice of calm hauteur. "And then we can address this situation more civilly." He pointed at one of the two who actually holding his wallet, not just patting his pockets frantically. "May I see your ID please?"

The young man looked rather startled by this, but opened his wallet to expose an embossed Identity card, which he handed to Augustus. It revealed him to be Detective-Inspector Carlson, of the Azure Interplanetary Criminal Investigation Unit. Augustus handed it back. "Well, Inspector. Could you please tell me what this intrusion is all about?"

"Uh. Yessir. We're acting on a tip-off. I am afraid we have to search you, Sir."

"Certainly. I have nothing to hide." He looked at the room, and his open trunk. "I see you have already searched my room." Ice formed on the words.

"We have a warrant from the local Police Commander," said the one who had called himself Chief Inspector Peleton.

"Well, let me see it," snapped Augustus, feeling his grandfather's attitudes rising. Even he knew you presented the warrant first, and searched after.

"I'm afraid it was in my wallet. I will obtain a copy," said the policeman, actually flushing a little.

"Indeed, you will. I find this all very irregular. But, should you wish to search me, I suggest you do. What are you looking for?"

"Uh. Thank you for your co-operation, Sir. I am afraid we can't tell you, Sir."

They searched him. They found his wallet. They found everything else he had in his pockets, pen-knife, handkerchief, even the rubber band which had been around the bundle of notes. They made him take his shoes off. And then they opened his wallet... which had fifty-three Azure dollars in it, seeing as he had paid the rent. They seemed taken aback at that. One of the men looked at every note with a small magnifier. "They're all clean, Chief."

The four policemen were all looking very uncomfortable by now. Their large Chief hit on the possible missing link – Briz. "Search the local," he snapped.

"Is that on your warrant?" asked Augustus, dryly.

"Aw, 'strewth," said Briz cheerfully. "Yer welcome. I got nothing to hide. But she's gotta do it. I ain't having yous lot sticking yer hands all over me."

"That seems reasonable," said Augustus.

The woman shrugged and said: "That all right by you, Chief?"

"It had better be," said Augustus, his voice chilly. "Briz works for me. I'll not have him mistreated."

"We're only doing our jobs, Sir," said the policeman.

"Without a warrant, ID or the proper procedural protocol," said Augustus dryly. "But you have Briz's co-operation. Let us clear this matter up."

So Briz was searched. They found nothing, not even a wallet, and no money at all. Augustus found that a little odd. And they found it a little awkward. The Chief obviously decided that it was best faced up to. "Well, Sir. It seems we... were given the wrong information. I must apologize."

"Who told yer?" asked Briz.

"I can't reveal that information. Confidentiality..."

"Yeah. Well, you take a long, hard look at who sent yer here to give my mister a hard time, and five gets yer ten... he's who yer lookin' for. Me money's on that Pinchbut fellow."

The startled look on the face of the policeman said that Briz had struck the bulls-eye. "You mean... Undersecretary Camelthrob-Princhbut? Er. Do you have any information?"

"Do I look like I'd bleedin' grass to the Jacks if I did?" said Briz.

"Word on the street, see. Drugs." She nodded and tapped the side of her nose knowlingly.

The policeman looked for all the world like a terrier, who just caught a hint of movement in a rat-hole. "Right," he said slowly. "Well, thank you for that... and our apologies. We're only doing our job. We have to act on information received. I'll see a copy of the warrant is sent to you, and thank you for your co-operation despite that." He sighed. "Now I will have to deal with a mountain of paper-work to account for my missing ID."

"Before you go, I would like to know just how you got in here? I was assured this was quite a secure little place," asked Augustus.

"The landlord let us in. We were told you would be coming in at this time, and would have the... goods on you." He grimaced. "Our informant called us just before you got here to let us know you had it and would be here with...the goods. He said you'd just picked them up and would be here within five minutes."

"I disapprove deeply of drugs," said Augustus, stiffly. "I'm here as one of the Blue Men to spend a year on projects to help uplift the poor of Sybill. Drugs appear to be one of the problems."

The policeman blinked. "I was told you were a remittance man with a drug problem. I did... wonder, looking at the contents of your case and trunk."

"Who told you that?" Augustus was more than a little indignant.

"Sorry, Sir. I really can't say. But I think we have been misled. I'm going to investigate the matter. If you'll excuse us, Sir, we'd better be on our way. My apologies again."

"I'll see yer out and into some rickshaws. It don't look like yer can look after yerselves too well," said Briz, shooing them in front of him.

"Your boss is, er, quite forceful," said the boss Jack, once they were well outside. "I thought he was going to make me stand to attention any minute. Not... quite what we were expecting. Still, we'll be watching him."

"Good-o," said Briz. "He needs looking after. Look", Briz said, in a quiet and confidential voice, "Just between you and me, that Pinchbut was very upset that my mister was ignoring his...advances, see. I don't think my Mister noticed... he's so fixed on this uplifting. But Pinchbut was real put out that he was moving out of the Embassy guest lodge."

"Ah. When did he do that? Move out, I mean."

"Moved his stuff in a couple hours back. But he organized it earlier," said Briz.

"Ah. I was not informed that it had only just happened," said the policeman with a bit of a snap to his voice.

"He's only been here a couple of days. Look," said Briz, bending down to the gutter. "It's me lucky day! A wallet."

She picked it up, opening it. "Looks like your picture, mate." And held it out to him.

He took it. "Well! The cash is gone... but the cards are there! That's a relief." He raised an eyebrow at Briz. "How convenient you finding it just there."

"Too right," said Briz innocently. "Yer lucky day. Could have been lost forever."

"You have a point. And your fingerprints are on it, because you just picked it up," he said. There was just a hint of a dry smile there. "So, what's your game, youngster? Like everyone in this cesspit, you have one."

The question took Briz rather by surprise. She didn't actually have an answer. She hadn't really thought about it, recently. Just known she was pissed at the Capos and Pinchbut trying to nobble the drongo. Why should she care? They'd nobble their own mothers. Mind you, she'd have nobbled hers if she'd had any idea what had happened to her. "I don't know," she said, irritated by a question she couldn't even answer to herself. "Noffink to do with yer, anyway. But yer keep an eye on 'im." She looked around, warily. "They're out to get rid of him, see."

The big cop looked at her, askance. "I didn't go this far in the force without learning to tell the truth when it was spoken to me. And rather obviously, that young gentleman was not even trying to lie. You lie by habit, but this time I suspect you're telling me the truth. I'm just not sure why." He opened his wallet, took out a card. "He's an Azure citizen. If you need help... come to the Hyaton and give them that card. I'll let them know at the desk to call me. And I'm going to be looking hard into what we know about the embassy staff." He raised an eyebrow. "And into your 'Mister'."

"I don't think he knows how to hide anything," said Briz. "And I'm no grass, see. I didn't tell yer nothing and I won't tell yer nothing. And there's a rickshaw. Yer can trust 'im – once I tell 'im not to take yer the long way."

So, she did. Pulled up a second one, because they had money and the blokes were big. Even that woman who felt her up. And then she went back into the apartment.

"I must say," said Augustus. "I feel quite upset by those policemen invading my space."

"'s what they do," said Briz counting the money she'd taken from the copper's wallet. "They should pay them better, maybe they'd have something else to do with their time."

"But why would they be informed I had drugs? And why would the Embassy people be involved? I mean, I can't say I took to Camelthrob-Princhbut, but why would he say such a terrible thing about me? Especially when he was going to be proved wrong."

"He's a piece of work, that feller,' said Briz, not mentioning that it was the money that Augustus had been tossing away that they'd been looking for. It didn't seem to have occurred to him. Beggars Lane had been unusually empty when she'd got there with the Jacks. They didn't notice either, but then they hadn't noticed much. Azure must be a soft place, to judge by its policemen. She'd heard it was fairly horrible, with too much sun, and weird un-natural things called hills and mountains and seas, that she wasn't entirely sure what were. Besides, apparently you were just heavier there. Maybe that slowed their brains or something. "So: what are your plans now? Some tucker? A bit of rest? A big blue?"

"A what?"

Briz explained. Augustus shook his head. "I really was never much good at socializing, especially in large groups. I must admit to finding the crowded nature of the Trading Plate a little claustropho-bic. It was an aspect of the Black Stump I found appealing – looking out at all that space. If it is not going to rain, I wonder if we could go and eat there again. But I feel somewhat insecure leaving my trunk and valise here."

"No worries, Mister. I'll get someone to keep an eye on the crib. Yer can trust them, not like that Ned Kelly landlord."

"I really do have to watch my finances, Briz."

Briz had to laugh. "Yer were chucking away money earlier."

"Ah, but that wasn't mine. I couldn't have kept it! That would just have been wrong... If I'd known those policemen were going to be here, I could have given it to them. I should have told them about it! I was just so...angered by finding them here that it went clean out of my mind," said Augustus. "I wonder if I should send them a message?"

"Nah. Got nothing to do with them," said Briz. "They ain't the local Bacon. And those will know all about it, see. I'll sort out a watchman for yer. Cost yer half a dollar a day. Gimme a few minutes."

"I suppose I can afford that," said Augustus.

"Yer can't afford not to afford it."

———

Augustus did enjoy the fact that the beggars all seemed to have moved off. A rickshaw, a watchman, eating at the Black Stump... He was truly learning to be like one of the locals, he supposed. He enjoyed his meal, although he could not identify the meat, and went back to enjoy his first sleep in his new home-for-the-year, quite content that at least he was making a little progress.

* * *

To Briz the town was like a tank full of nasty, bitey things that had been stirred up with a big stick. You could hear the fights coming out of a lot of money tossed around right across the bars and brothels. It was going to get worse when the word got out that it wasn't real money. She enjoyed the jumbuck ribs at the Black Stump, even if they were pricy. It might be her last meal. She had spotted one of Capo Kasagolis' goons just as they went into the market-place. But not even the Capos would cause too much strife here. Too much of the trade and food for the plate moved through it.

But, as she expected, she'd barely dropped the drongo safe in his little nest when she got hauled off to a meeting she'd much rather have avoided.

If she hadn't been scared she might just be killed, she would have been laughing her arse off though. Four of the Capo's top enforcers looked like they'd been through a meat-grinder. And some were just missing. Maybe they did go through the meat-grinder. That was kind of a satisfying thought. If she lived through this lot she'd have to watch out for what might be in the mystery bags.

If she didn't live through this, she might end up as mince in them herself.

"What the hell happened there?" demanded the Capo. "We've lost thousands of dollars. And they're good fakes, dammit. You were supposed to see him safe to those Jacks. You only had to see him down a hundred yards!"

"He was going to take it to the Azure Embassy, or give it to the Bacon. I told him he couldn't do that, and he just started giving it away. I couldn't stop him, they was as thick as flies around a dunny, between me and him. Yer boys didn't help me none!"

There was a moment's silence. "He was going to do what?" said the Capo in disbelief.

"Said it wasn't his money. He couldn't keep it. That it would be wrong," said Briz, out of lies to tell. "And I saw at least one of yer boys running of with yer money. I didn't take none of it, or them Jacks would have arrested me!"

The Capo slammed his fist onto the table in frustration. "And what happened there?"

"Seems they didn't find nothing, 'cause he didn't have nothing. They're having a close look at him... and Pinchbut for leading 'em on. Checking out the embassy."

The Capo clenched his teeth. "What! That's our best operation!" he hissed between those bared teeth. He ground them in rage, and the diamond tooth bounced out and skittered across the floor under a chair and into a crack in the floorboards. "My toof! My bloody toof!" yelled the Capo, scrabbling after it.

Briz took this as a great time to leave, as it appeared they were going to have to get the floor up to look for it, and no-one was paying her a blind bit of notice.

Besides, she had to get out of there or bust herself laughing. Keeping a straight face was killing her.

The upside – and it was a big upside, was she'd got out of there alive. The downside was she had no idea what they planning next, or how to get the drongo to avoid it. No doubt she'd find out, probably the hard way. In the meanwhile, sleep – somewhere that wasn't her own crib, and stashing a few bits of money, were wiser than going out on the firecracker-town. It was not often that Briz opted for wise above 'seemed like a good idea at the time'. This time was different.

CHAPTER

SEVEN

"It seems," said Charles Anson Roberto Thistlewood IV's father, Charles Anson Roberto III, to the family who were sitting and sipping their pre-dinner sherry – a very small glass of dry sherry, "That Charlie may be right."

"I suppose," said his grandfather, dryly, "that has to happen eventually. What is Charlie right about, besides it being dinner time?"

"I have had another letter from Augustus. Less full of description and more outraged by civic corruption," said their father, holding it up.

"Isn't that the definition of government: corrupt by default, when it isn't incompetent, or both," said his grandfather. "We've always told the boys so."

"Being told and experiencing it firsthand are two different things. Charlie said he might learn a few things, and, as I said, it seems he was right. Augustus has also acquired a reliable local guide, and holds no high opinion of our embassy staff."

"A reliable local guide seems a bit unlikely," said Charlie, wishing he'd found some reason not to come to dinner. He wasn't fond of dry

Amontillo sherry, even if it did come all the way from Earth, from pre-blockade stocks. "According to a few people I have talked to the place only has an ambassadorial post because Roptor and the Sinopese do. The population size doesn't warrant it, and the aliens they're supposed to represent us to, disregard their existence and never attend any of the functions."

"They have a function?" asked his grandfather.

"Not as we would mean it," said Charlie, who understood perfectly what the old man meant. He was, after all, also an engineer. "Still, I bet Augustus is getting an education and his eyes opened a bit. I wish I was there to see it."

"Drink up," said his grandmother. "We have some lovely steamed fish with parsley butter. It won't do for it to get cold."

Charlie wondered what Augustus would be having for his dinner. It had to be more appealing. He wondered about the trusty native guide. Hopefully she was more appealing too. Although, knowing his brother, she probably wouldn't be.

"So, what do yer want to see next?" asked Briz – having shown up the next 'day'. Augustus was a little puzzled as to how he knew what 'day' was – it seemed human circadian rhythms still operated. The plate had distinct groups of people on the streets, and apparently, working, during the different times. Many of the locals had time-pieces... something he'd been somewhat saddened to discover he didn't have any more.

Augustus sighed. The 'guidelines' the Blue Men supplied, had 'seek co-operation with civic authorities' as its first point. Unfortunately, no one seemed to have any idea, back on Azure, just who these might be. The locals seemed to have the same problem! Really, starting with the equivalent of the local dog-catcher had been folly. Maybe the aliens ran things – and they had certainly made it clear they wanted no human intervention in their affairs. So what next?

"Er. Education? Perhaps there is a government school I could volunteer my services at?"

Briz looked at him in puzzlement again. "I thought yer Azurians came here to get an education. Or that's what one of them blokes off the Star said. He said we were an education."

Despite himself, Augustus had to ask: "What did he learn?"

"How to get yer pocket picked, and yer watch nicked," said Briz. "He learned real fast too."

"I've learned that too," said Augustus, looking sadly at his wrist. "I miss my great grandfather's time-piece."

"Oh, well if it's old it can't be worth nothing. I'll see if I can get it back for yer," said Briz generously. "For a small fee."

"I would appreciate that. But I don't want you to have to consort with criminals."

"I don't do no consorting. I ain't got the looks for it," said Briz, obliquely. "I'll get it back for yer. I reckon I know who would have done you the dirty."

"So. Er, tell me about schools. Who runs them?"

"I dunno. What's a school?" They were walking as they talked, moving through the colorful but rather dirty streets, and passing the people of the Plate on their various forms of business as they talked. Some of that business seemed to be holding the ramshackle buildings up, by leaning on them. One of the leaners detached himself from the wall – and Briz, who mysteriously managed to repel too close a proximity by the rest of the Plate's foot-traffic, suddenly stepped well clear, to let the stranger talk. "I overheard your mention of education and schooling," said the rather slick-looking fellow. "As it happens I am... one of the governors of a select, exclusive... seminary. We have young ladies of quality. I could take you there for some lessons."

The man sounded at least educated himself, even if he had been leaning against a shabby building a few moments back. Actually, he sounded as if he'd been educated on Azure by his speech. Augustus was eager to seize any opportunity, however. "I was really hoping to help those in educational establishments that were non-exclusionary."

"Oh, believe me, they'll take anyone. Now, I'll go ahead and arrange things. My associates here," He pointed at a large man, and a smaller ratty-looking sharp-eyed one, who had somehow, mysteriously, come from somewhere to join them. "We will escort you to our establishment. I'm sure this will be a great day for our young ladies. You do like young ladies, don't you?"

Augustus beamed. "I like children. Young ones especially. And you have to start teaching them young to give them the full benefit of learning."

"Oh..." said Briz.

"Oh what, Briz?" asked Augustus. His guide looked uncomfortable, particularly with the large man leaning so close to him.

"Nothin'," said Briz, stony-faced.

Something plainly had upset the boy. But Augustus was excited by the possibility of teaching. Yes, it would take time for the skills to permeate through, but education was key. He should have seen that earlier. And he really was more at ease talking to the young.

The 'school' seemed quite an odd building. It didn't say 'school' on the façade. It was called 'Madame Lolita.' And it was quite heavily barred, even by the local standards. Briz started to turn aside as they reached the door. "Could you come with me, Briz," said Augustus. "I find too many people don't understand me, and you're more familiar with my speech."

The stormy look on Briz's face lightened. "Yer going to talk to them?"

"Well, I should think I will have to. How else does one teach children? My real fields of expertise are mathematics and physics, and numbers of course, are an international language. But I must assess their educational needs first. I hope I can be useful. I feel I haven't achieved much uplift yet."

His guide shook his head. "I ain't wanted in there."

"I insist," said Augustus. Something was making Briz unhappy, and Augustus felt he ought to keep an eye on his young guide.

"Briz can wait out here," said the small sharp-faced one.

"No," said Augustus firmly. He'd taken a dislike to the furtive-faced man for some reason.

He was led into a large room, rather garishly decorated for a school, which had some six young girls sitting in various postures on a long red settle. They were extremely underdressed for schoolgirls, Augustus thought. "Which girl do you want?" said the sharp-faced man with a wink. "Some young beauties there, eh. Nice and fresh."

Personally, Augustus thought they all looked underslept. "All of them I should think. They seem much of an age. Where is the school room? Hello, young ladies. I'm here to help with teaching. How is your mathematics?"

"What?" said a little blonde in a skimpy blouse.

At this point the slick-looking fellow with the Azure accent bustled in: "My dear sir. Is everything to your liking?"

"He wants all of them, Boss."

"What he wants he must have," said the fellow expansively. "What else can we do for you, Mr Thistlewood?"

"I was hoping for a school-room. Or at least a table and some chairs. And if possible a blackboard. I'm a little surprised by their dress for class, Mr... I am sorry we are not formally introduced. You seem to know who I am, sir, but I don't know your name."

"You want them in school uniform? A common request from our Azure clients. Girls. Wardrobe. Bodmin. See that a table is brought in. I believe there is a blackboard somewhere. I will see to it. Take a seat, Mr Thistlewood. The girls will be right back. Can I get you any other requirements? A cane, perhaps?" He licked his lips.

"Good gracious no. I doubt if there is any need for that. No, chalk and a blackboard, and I am good to go. I am not precisely experienced at teaching, but I have been told that it is very hard..."

"Oh, yes."

"To find good math teachers," Augustus continued. "Mathematics is the foundation of everything! The key to a brighter future."

"Uh. What?"

They did seem to say that a lot in this exclusive seminary. Augustus noticed that Briz was doing a peculiar little dance. "Do you need the bathroom, Briz?" he asked, distracted from the unnamed philanthropist so involved in running this establishment.

"What?"

"Your little dance," explained Augustus.

"Oh," said Briz, looking a little awkward. "No, it was just me excitement that yer was going to be teaching... mathematics to these little bushpigs. I wish I could be that lucky."

"I'm sure you can join them," said Augustus, smiling, as two men carried in a table and another a blackboard and an easel. Someone had left some rather disgusting images on it! Augustus was shocked. "Clean that off immediately! It is not the sort of thing I expect to ever see here again," he said to the man who had just set it down. "Good gracious! I am shocked. What if the young ladies had seen that? Are you all right, Briz?"

"Just swallowed something the wrong way," said Briz, as two other men brought in a selection of chairs.

A few moments later the girls filed in, now dressed in school-dresses, and looking, Augustus thought, much more like school-children. "That's much better! A neat appearance is the first step towards a tidy mind, as my grandmother would say." Then he looked at them in puzzlement. "But where are your notebooks?"

"What?"

"I can't expect you to remember everything. You will need your notebooks and pencil cases," he explained, patiently.

The girls looked at each other in puzzlement. "We was told we got to do anything yer like. But we ain't got no pencil cases or notebooks."

"Good gracious!" said Augustus. "What a situation! Well,

perhaps we can find eight pencils and some paper." He took out his wallet. "Will five dollars be enough for that, Briz?"

"Yeah. Plenty," said Briz. "Yer want me to go away and fetch it for yer?" Briz looked... disappointed.

"Oh no. I am sure this gentleman," he pointed at the fellow scrubbing the blackboard, "could get it for us, now he has finished that job. Now, all of you sit down..."

"Yer want me to sit on yer knee, Mister?" asked one of the girls.

"Good gracious, no. That would be most improper. I am afraid I must insist on decorous behavior, or I will have to ask you to leave, young lady. In future if you want to talk, please raise your hand and wait until you are asked to speak. Now sit down. I will ask each of you to introduce yourself, and I'll ask a few basic questions to ascertain what level your mathematics is at."

Augustus was somewhat dismayed to find that rather than calculus, he was going to have to teach absolute basic arithmetic to girls who he guessed to be in their early teens. But... without arithmetic there could be no maths. And to his surprise the street-urchin Briz was comfortably ahead of the young refined ladies, at basic arithmetic, and very quick at mental arithmetic, while some of the others did not appear to even grasp simple addition without resorting to using their fingers.

Admittedly, Briz probably didn't help by calling them dumb slags. Augustus had to frown sternly and tell him not to interrupt. They were not an easy class, and several of them tried to interrupt and distract him with various feminine wiles. They were far too young for that sort of thing, and he told them so. Perhaps he was too strict. Some of the young women showed promise, particularly after Briz had said something about being able to work out when they were being done over by that pos. Perhaps that was short for 'Possum', which, his books led him to believe, was a legendary creature among the plate's peoples. Like much of what Briz said, it was still something of a mystery to him.

It was hard going, but he at least had them reciting the times table with him, even if he was not sure they understood it.

Perhaps he could use reward as a teaching method. "I think we should all take a break. Let me arrange some tea and... do you have cream cakes here, Briz?"

"We got lots of creams," said one of the less bright girls.

"Shut up, yer silly little bushpig," said Briz. "Dunno what that means, mister. Some kind of tucker, right?"

"Ah. There probably isn't any cream here. Um. I meant a sweet cake. A treat. I need a large one. Big enough for eight."

"Ah. Gotcha. I reckon someone out there might be able to run to Gunters and pick up a beesting for yer. Or a big slab of snotblocks," Briz informed him.

Several of the girls squealed. Plainly 'snotblock' was not the horrific thing it sounded like, but a word for some delicacy. "That sounds very appealing," said Augustus. "Can we order one?"

"Yer mean yer want eight?"

"No, the point of the exercise is to divide it. I need one large treat, big enough for eight."

"Yer gunna have a fun time getting' that. Tell 'em yer need it for a bit of fun with the girls," said Briz.

The poor boy must be cold. He was shaking. Augustus wondered if he was feeling well, as it was quite warm in here. He went to the door. "I'll get someone to go out and get it. How much would such a thing cost?"

"Yer get an ordinary one for 50 cents. Dunno what one eight times as big would cost," said Lily, one of the girls.

That enabled him to explain the use of the five times table. He thought he saw a couple of lights coming on... dimly. Briz was the only one who arrived at four dollars without effort. But he could see some of the others reciting the new taught times table. Several, however, were just looking puzzled or bored.

He went to the door, and found someone right there. "Just didn't want to interrupt," said the sharp-faced man, peering around the door. "You ain't a fast mover, are you? They're still all dressed."

Now it was Augustus's turn to be puzzled. "What?

"Uh. Nothing. Boss said yer was to do what you liked, see. The girls know that."

"Well, what I'd like now is a large four dollar uncut slab of snot-block from somewhere called 'Gunters', and also some tea."

The sharp faced man looked a little nonplussed by that request. "Wow... never heard of that kink. I'll get it for you real quick."

And indeed, he was. The girls were still arguing about whether four dollars was right, when the sharp-faced one and the blackboard easel carrier arrived with a large slab covered in sticky white icing, with a thick yellow filling between sheets of pastry. It was surrounded by peculiar pink spiky blocks. "Lammos!" squealed one of the blondes who had been determinedly arguing that four dollars was too much. To Augustus's surprise and dismay, she tried to hug him. Fortunately, Briz took her by the collar. "Looks like it works," said the sharp-faced man. "That's more enthusiasm than I seen her show before."

The noise was quite overpowering. Augustus had to bellow to try and quell it. "Sit down! Be quiet!"

It had half the desired effect. But then Briz added a loud: "Or yer get chucked out."

That ensured a sudden absolute silence, such as Augustus had been unable to achieve in the previous teaching session. The facto-tums were allowed to set the snotblock and lammos down, and a matronly woman followed with a large kettle, on a tiny burner-stand to keep it hot and a tray of miscellaneous mugs, and a look of disbe-lief. They all left and the door was closed. "I should have asked for a knife," said Augustus, "And perhaps plates."

"Got a knife," said Briz, producing one. "And no worries, we got hands," he said, sticking out a slim-fingered grubby hand. "Right, girls?"

"Too right!" said Lily. "I got a knife too."

So, it seemed, had the others.

Augustus was rather taken-aback by this, but... well, in Rome, eat spaghetti. At least – on closer examination the snotblock looked rather like a vanilla slice back home. Except those were never as big or sticky or surrounded by pink cubes. The spikes on the 'lammos' could be desiccated coconut... or something like it, he supposed. "Well, first we'll have to work out how to divide it. How would we do that, Cynthia?

"Fast," said the blonde who had tried to kiss him.

"No. I mean cut it up into shares. How do we do that?"

"Cut it in half," said Briz.

"Very good," said Augustus. "Then you have two halves. Now you have divided it in two what is next?"

"I grab half and this bunch of little bush-pigs scrimmage over the other half," said Briz reaching out with his knife.

"Not so fast, Briz" said Augustus, sternly. "I mean equitably. That means everyone gets a fair equal share. Think about it. There are eight of us. If it is cut in half, how many is half of us here?"

They arrived at four. And then Augustus measured it out, took Briz's knife and cut it in half. "Now if you cut each of those halves in half, what do you get?

"Smaller pieces?"

With patience, he led them to quarters and then eighths... and then gave each a piece.

It gave him some minutes of silence to think. The girls and Briz ate every last flake of pastry with obvious relish and appreciation. Licked their fingers clean and... "Are yer going to give us them Lammos too," said Cynthia, fluttering her eyelashes and looking as if she was a starved puppy, with a sticky face.

"Yes, but I am going to show you a few more calculations first. Maybe you would pour tea first?

"I reckon you're the best john we ever had, but... don't yer want to do nothing else?"

"So many things!" said Augustus enthusiastically. "Geometry, trigonometry, Algebra, Calculus! The delights of fractals..." he saw the puzzlement. "I want to teach you to love numbers."

"Uh, why? They don't pay for nothing."

"Yer dumb bushpig," said Briz, scornfully. "I bet if yer get five roots a session yer johns pay two dollars a time, about dollar ninety too much for yer, yer don't know how much yer cut is."

"I gets fifty cents for a sailor's holiday," said Cynthia, defensively.

"Yeah. Still forty cents too much, but how much is that for four roots?"

It obviously made sense to them. Augustus had to wonder what these root-crops were and where they were grown. Perhaps in the roof-top gardens. The class turned into a rather free discussion – but as calculation of the value and share of roots, if not square roots seemed to be central to it, Augustus was happy to let it run. It rapidly evolved into Briz using Lammos as symbols for the roots. "Yer can't." protested Lily. "They's nothing like roots"

"They're pink, ain't they? Look, they're like using yer fingers... ter count, yer dumb bushpig," he said when she sniggered. And Briz proceeded to demonstrate division. It took a while. But as it went on a strange almost quiet developed – with a disturbed background of mutters and lots of finger counting... and finally an angry outburst from Lily. "We're being done!"

"Tell me something I don't know," said Briz, promptly shoving two thirds of a Lammo in his face, and chewing.

"Ah. Do tuck in, girls," said Augustus rather weakly.

But their interest in the pink spiky rectangles had vanished. "I'm gunna tell the other girls," said Cynthia.

"Er. What about some tea?" asked Augustus as the girls all got up and headed towards the door in a militant phalanx.

"I'll give 'em bloody tea!" said Lily, and snagged the kettle. The door burst open and the man from Azure who had claimed to be one of the directors with his henchmen, the little one and the big one and the fellow who carried the easel all just behind him. "You little slags are all due a good beating!" he said savagely, his hands reaching for his belt-buckle.

To his shock, Augustus saw Lily also grab his belt, pull it towards her, and pour boiling tea down the gap she'd created in the front of his trousers.

He screamed and clutched himself frantically and fell back into his henchmen, knocking them backwards. Lily followed up with an arc of hot tea in their faces, before hitting the Easel-bearer with the teapot. Then all the girls in a mob were on top of the men, screaming, kicking and punching. The words 'cheat!' and 'thief!' were being yelled a lot, along with a lot of words that Augustus never expected from delicately reared young ladies in an exclusive seminary. More girls arrived – some wearing less than the class had been at first, and... instead of getting them to stop, they seemed inflamed by what they heard and some kind of explanation by Cynthia – who stopped kicking for long enough to tell them.

Briz sat on the table with a broad grin on his little face and watched, and slowly ate another Lammo.

"How do we stop this?" asked Augustus, who had tried shouting a few times. He might as well have kept his mouth shut.

"Like tryin' to stop the wind," said Briz cheerfully, belching. "Yer taught them they was being robbed. This 'mathematic' stuff is real hot. Like that tea was."

Briz had had her own reasons for being uncomfortable about the latest trap for the drongo. She could have been there herself. Nearly had been. Only it had hurt a lot. In the Big Syd, pretty well anything went. But Madame Lolita's had been close to pushing the edge of that. Heh. She should have guessed her drongo would push it right over the edge. He seemed to have a gift for that. Still. It all had to come to a messy end sometime soon. "Come on," she said.

"Let's get out of here. I don't think yer want to explain this lot when the bacon gets here. That creep gives them a lot of backhanders."

"I don't think you mean a slap," said Augustus, following her through the door. "Not that I approve of violence."

"Too right, but it approves of yer. Now, I'll take yer back. I gotta see a man about that watch o' yours. I didn't know it was just some old thing."

They stopped for a butcher and a mystery-bag in a piece of massass-damper. She'd be turning into a porker if she kept eating like this. Snot-block, lammos and more tucker, all in one day. There'd been times when she'd been lucky to see that in a week.

Still, a full stomach didn't stop her noticing – when she headed back from her crib with his watch, that she hadn't got around to selling yet – a watcher on the drongo... one that shouldn't be there. She slipped away down an alley and up onto a roof, and away as fast as she could, to the Hyaton... where she discovered that no matter how magical the Azure Jack thought his card might be, the bimbo at the reception desk did not think it was. "Get out before I call security!

Briz held up the magic card again. "The Jack said I was to show this to yer, and he'd let yer know he was to be called. That Azure drongo is in real strife!"

"Security!" said the fake blonde into the microphone at the side of her desk.

"Look, you gotta tell him. I'll go straight off, no trouble. Just give Chief Inspector Peleton a message..."

A large man in a neat suit arrived and reached for her. Briz dodged his hand and ducked under his arm. "Look, all I gotta do is give this Jack," she held up the card at the bouncer, "A message. He told me to come here. He said he'd tell the front desk."

"They do that, kid. They let us chuck you out, instead of telling you to get lost," said the bouncer closing on her.

He wasn't that fast. She sidestepped, and jinked around him the other way. "He's a copper. The bacon, you nong. There are four of 'em, all cops. I'm the grass." She felt disgusted at herself admitting it.

Something about that must have got through to the bouncer. He peered at the card. "Susie... we got any police here?"

"It's wot it says on the card, see," said Briz. "I ain't here to cause no trouble. I just got information for him. I can write it down."

"I don't know about police... Peleton?" She looked at her screen. "Oh. There is a note here. He did leave a message saying he was to be called."

That was just as well, because the bouncer had grabbed her arm. It took all the control Briz had not to stick him with her knife. She didn't like no-one putting their hands on her. But at least she'd be able to get the drongo back to safety. "I told yer."

"Yes. Unfortunately, he's not in right now," she said, checking her screen. "Room status is locked from the outside."

"You said there were four of them, all cops," said the bouncer, not letting go.

"Yeah. Yer can call one of the others then," Briz dredged her memory. "I think one was called Carlson."

"Ah. I thought he looked like a busy," said the bouncer. "Yeah, all four of them went out. Got me to arrange a couple of rickshaws for them. To meet a ship that's coming in, and then to the embassy."

Briz swore. It was descriptive enough to impress the bouncer and to make Susie-the-fake-blonde looke shocked and say: "You can't say that!"

"I just did," said Briz, puzzled. "It ain't hard."

"They're coming back," said the bouncer. "They haven't checked out yet, have they, Susie?"

She looked at her screen again. "No. And their passports are still in the safe. I didn't know the Star of Space was coming in today. She's not due for another four days."

"Can't be her then. Wonder which other ship," said the bouncer, tightening his grip, just when Briz thought she'd squirm free. "Look, kid. You can wait. But not here. We have guests in and out. We can't leave you on the loose in the lobby. We have a reputation for keeping your kind out."

"I can't wait. Yer can shove yer lobby. I gotta get back to my Mister," said Briz. To her annoyance she felt a tear in one eye. She rubbed it angrily and scowled at them both. "Lemme go. Get yer hand off me."

But something – maybe even the tear – did get through to Susie. "Look, I can give them a message when they come in. I'm on duty until after dinner." She grimaced. "Another six deadly hours of smiling at guests."

It wasn't much, but it was something. "Kay. I c'n write it on this card. You got a pen?"

She produced a long stylus with 'Hotel Hyaton" on the side of it, in gold ink. Normally, something that flash, and Briz would have tried to prig it. Now she just wrote on the paper Susie offered her.

'Come qik. To Crooked Mac Beggar's lane, the place what you searched. Augustus's got big strife. Bondi boyz. Bring guns.'

Susie looked at the note. She could plainly read upside down. "Augustus... I remember that name. Checked out a few days ago." She looked at Briz. "Are you a boy or a girl?"

"What do you fink? Mister Drongo don't know," said Briz crossly. "Anyway. I got to go," and pulled her arm free, and bolted for the door.

Once outside, she had a chance to think. Where did she go now? There was no place she could hide forever on the plate, but the mess this was likely to cause might mean that if she just kept low for a few weeks... Might. But with the Bondi-boyz operating on Cronulla turf... and right in the open like that. Either Cronulla got trashed... or Kasagolis had been desperate enough to bring them in. And something made them willing. Might have been there was something in that rumor about that mangy bastard at Madame Lolita's. They said he had ties to those ratbags. Whatever it was, it wasn't good. They made people disappear. Maybe into mystery bags. Or worse. She wasn't sure what worse was, but that was the story.

On the other hand... he was just such a mug. Maybe these offworld jacks would get there in time. Against her better judgement Briz made her way to Beggars lane. And there the Bondi-boyz were watching, thick as dags on a jumbuck's butt. This had to be the dumbest thing she'd ever done.

"Got yer watch," she said, pulling it out and handing it to him. "And we better bug out or fort up. There's big strife coming."

Augustus took his watch, not even commenting on the cut band, just putting it in his pocket. "I've been thinking, Briz," he said, heavily. "I've been naïve. Those... those weren't really schoolgirls, were they?" his voice sounded a lot more like when he'd been telling those Jacks what-for. Like someone was going to get hurt.

"Uh. Nope," admitted Briz.

"Right," said Augustus, his big hands clenching. "And what civic authorities you do have – these Capos – they turn a blind eye to this heinous behavior?"

"Mostly they makes a profit off it."

"The Blue men are not supposed to interfere in local customs and traditions. I am going to have to resign. I am no longer prepared to be code 0035. I can't tolerate that. They're children!"

"That Cynthia is nearly as old as me..." said Briz, feeling, for some reason, strangely giddy.

"You're a child too, Briz."

"No, I ain't..." she said, as her legs folded under her.

The last thing she remembered was him trying to catch her as she fell over.

CHAPTER

EIGHT

Augustus woke slowly, reluctantly... and exceptionally uncomfortably. This bed was really hard, and rather cold.

It took a while for his fuzzy mind to realize that it wasn't a bed. And that he hadn't been asleep, or at least not in the usual sense of the word. He was still holding the scruffy waif he'd taken on as a guide. The little pinched face was oddly different with those sharp blue eyes closed, the fine-boned pale features at rest. Was the boy dead? No... that was a faint breath. But he seemed deeply unconscious. Attempting to keep the boy's head supported, Augustus tried to work out where he was and just what had happened.

Where he was, was an oddly shaped but not very large room. Well, it wasn't very large sideways. But the roof, which had a single skylight, was quite high. The light from that showed that the walls, and floor he was lying on, and the roof that wasn't skylight were all a shade of sickly yellowish chartreuse. Where had he seen that color? It came to him: The Thrymi buildings they'd observed at a distance at the Thrymi enclave quarter on the plate. It seemed, that he and Briz were inside a Thrymi palace. They must, somehow, have been drugged and transported there.

It was either his head, or the place was throbbing – as if there was some distant heavy machinery running, and it needed maintenance and tuning.

Briz woke. Not the way that Augustus had but with a sudden wary rigidity and tension of the muscles... and absolutely no movement. Like a frightened feral thing ready to fight or flee at an instant, but giving no betraying signs – if Augustus hadn't been holding the lad, and felt the muscles tense up. He let go. Briz opened his eyes a tiny crack. "Why was yer holding me?" Briz asked in a low voice – a menacing one, surprisingly.

"Because I caught you when you fell over. Then I think I must have fallen over. I woke up a few moments ago myself. We... seem to have been drugged or tranquilized."

"Gas. Them Bondi Boyz use gas," Briz hissed.

"I suppose that could be the case," said Augustus. "I think I may have to interfere in local politics no matter what the Blue Men think. How do we get out of here?"

Briz looked around the small room. "To think I was worried about yer getting butchered, minced up and put into a mystery bag. We're in strife. I mean real strife."

Augustus had learned enough by now to know what that term meant, and Briz's fear was apparent in the youngster's tone. "Er. What sort of strife? I mean, this appears to be a Thrymi palace, but I thought Admiral Halberd had... um, persuaded them to leave Azure citizens on the Plate alone. I thought it was very harsh when I heard about it, but I am beginning to realize I was not as well-informed as I might be. But I will not allow you to be hurt."

"Mister, we ain't on the Plate," said Briz in odd voice. "Not in the Big Syd anymore. And I reckon they don't care what they think you'll allow. Thrymi..."

"You mean... we're in a cloud-castle? A Thrymi cloud-castle?" said Augustus, excitedly.

"Too right we are. And we'd be better off dead," said Briz. "Mister... on the Plate they was scared of killing yer. Out here, no-one will ever know, and them Thrymi like killing things. Yer just keep your head down an' yer mouth shut, see."

Augustus stood up. It took quite an effort, and leaning against the wall to do it, but he managed. "How do we get back to the Plate?"

Briz shrugged. "Yer can't. Not unless the cloud-castle goes there. And they'll lock us in then, I reckon. If we're still alive. That's what yer hear, anyway."

Augustus looked thoughtful. "How would they know, if no-one ever got away from them?"

"Stories from out beyond the black stump," said Briz. "I reckon they're furphys, half the time. But not about the Thrymi. Everyone knows they go real feral."

"Er. Who tells them?" he asked.

"Outbackers," said Briz, dismissively.

"Who are they?" asked Augustus. He'd heard the term, but it wasn't in any of his lexicons of Sybill III terms – most of which seemed wrong anyway. Hadn't that woman said they gathered the whitebait?

"Them what lives out here," said Briz. "They ain't got nuffink. They blow into the plate sometimes. Don't last long, mostly."

"You mean... there are people just living out... in the clouds? What do they live on?" Despite their situation, Augustus's curiosity was piqued.

"Patches of sky-frond. Or do yer mean what do they eat? There's jumbucks and other stuff," she said vaguely. Briz was an encyclopedia about the plate. Anything off it, was plainly barely worth even acknowledging the existence of.

"Could we escape to among them, perhaps? If stories got back, it must happen."

"Blooming heck. Yer dead set on going from bad to worse. How do yer ever get back to civilization? They just goes where the drift takes them."

Civilization to Briz was plainly the Plate and nothing else. But Augustus's head was full of a sudden realization: from Sybil III being, in his head, a tiny, isolated but crowded human settlement of a few square miles in the midst of millions of square miles of miles of nothing... It plainly wasn't. He started to calculate the possible size of a habitable zone of a gas dwarf with perhaps a kilometer depth of exosphere within the tolerance of human physiology, if you didn't need a solid place to stand... and ran out of zeros. Azure made the Plate seem like the head of a pin. And that calculation made Azure about the same size. Of course, the skyfronds were surely far apart and surely it couldn't carry much weight...

His head was still whirling with these ideas when the door to the room they were imprisoned in slid open. Well, slid part way open and stuck, to open the rest of the way with a kick and a curse, by a human. He was almost certainly human, Augustus decided, despite the scarring that deformed his face. He wasn't wearing very much – rags and scraps of fur and leather. But he carried a whip, which he slashed at both of them. "Yer slaves now, and I'm yer boss. Get that quick-smart and I don't have ter hit yer much."

"Yes, boss," said Briz, nudging Augustus.

"What?" said Augustus, looking to see what Briz wanted, and getting a slash from the whip, the black lash winding around his arm. He jerked his arm away in startled pain. The scar-faced man had the whip in a good firm hold and got pulled forward to trip over the door-sill, and fall headlong into the wall with a resounding metallic 'bong'.

"Crikey. Now yer gone and done it," said Briz. "And we can't run nowhere neither."

"I think he's just stunned," said Augustus, kneeling next to him, feeling for a pulse, and gently rolling the man over. "I didn't mean to do that."

"Yer Azure people are stronger than yer look."

"Well, we have a slightly higher gravity on Azure," said Augustus picking the man up in his arms. "We better find someone to help him."

"He's gunna be real crook when he wakes up. You don't think we should just do a runner?"

"I feel responsible," said Augustus, firmly. "He may have intended to hurt me, but I did not intend to harm him." He paused. "I don't think I could have if I'd tried."

"Yer just go right on not trying," said Briz. "Maybe even don't try to get me back to me crib in the Big Syd."

They walked down the passage-way, their erstwhile captor limp in Augustus' arms. He was startled to find it opening onto a walkway between two small hanging turrets, with the spiky bulk of the Thrymi cloud-castle off to one side, and the endless drop on the other. It was not a very wide walkway, and it had no rails.

"Do we have to cross that?!" exclaimed Augustus.

"I don't see no other way," said Briz wandering cheerfully onto it.

So, Augustus, bearing his burden, edged his way along the path. Of course, about half-way across the scar-faced man groaned and opened an unfocused eye.

"Keep still. I don't want to drop you," said Augustus, wishing the structure didn't sway slightly underfoot.

The man struggled... blinked his eyes, and suddenly was very still in Augustus's arms. "Yer throw me over an' I'll pull yer with me!" The tone did not match the threat.

"I am not planning to throw you over. I am trying to take you to get medical assistance. You fell over and concussed yourself," said Augustus, walking on as steadily as he could. "I'll put you down as soon as we're across, I promise."

The scar-faced man blinked again. "Yer pulling me a raw prawn ain't yer? Don't drop me!" he squealed as Augustus stumbled and had to take a few hasty steps to catch his balance.

"Then hold still. I'm doing my best."

The man closed his eyes tightly. That was fine, Augustus thought. At least he held still. Rigidly still. They continued until they got to the next turret door. Once inside that, Augustus put him down on the floor with some relief. "I'm glad you're feeling better, but I ought to check your pupils for even dilation. And you need to get professional medical help, or at the very least you should go and lie down somewhere for a few hours. You need to treat concussion with care."

The man edged away from him, without standing up.

"You're bleeding crazy! I'm gunna... where's me whip?"

"I think I left it on the floor back in the other turret," said Augustus. "I am sorry."

"They'll kill me if I lose me whip," said the scar-faced man getting to his feet and swaying, and trying to head for the doorway.

"Sit down!" said Augustus, crossly, his voice, sounding, even in his own ears, like his grandfather. The man's mouth dropped open. "You'll kill yourself if you try to walk across there. Briz, could I ask you to fetch it for him?"

Briz looked at him. Nodded. He looked at the scar-faced man. "Boss," he said. "Yer better do what he says. You ain't seen noffink yet. I been there, when 'e gets going," and the urchin trotted out onto the walkway as if there was no drop.

The scar-faced man, still leaning against the wall peered at him... with wary eyes. "Yer got kangaroos loose in yer top paddock," he announced.

Plainly he was hallucinating. "Sit down," said Augustus, firmly.

"I'm the boss," the scarfaced man informed him.

"Right. You're the boss," agreed Augustus. "Now sit down before you fall down."

"I give the orders."

"Well, tell yourself to sit down!" said Augustus, getting little impatient. "You had a nasty bang on the head."

"I means I give the orders to you!" said the scarfaced man a little querulously.

"Then tell me, to tell you to sit down, before I make you lie down. You're being very foolish," said Augustus, a stern voice like his grandfather's coming from somewhere. The man finally did as he was told, looking uneasy and shaking his head, slightly. Augustus did his best to calm him down. "Briz has gone to fetch your whip for you. You should be more careful with it. Now, I want to look at your pupils. Cover your right eye with one hand."

"Yer gunna gouge me eye out," said the scar-faced man, trying to push himself into the wall.

"What a lurid imagination you have. As if I would do such a thing! Now, look at the light. Right. Look away. Good. Now cover the other eye and we'll do that again." Augustus decided that the dilatation of the two pupils was not quite even, but he wasn't too sure what to do about it.

Briz came back, idly swinging the black whip. The scar-faced man looked at it, and the lad, looked at the doorway, his mouth half open, eyes narrowed. "Yer crossed the skybridge. Slaves don't cross the skybridges. That's for the masters, the Thrymi lords!"

"If yer don't tell them, I won't. Anyway, yer drongo, yer just crossed it. How do yer think yer got here?" Briz said, tossing the whip from hand to hand.

The scar-faced man looked around and closed his eyes in horror. "We can't be here!"

"Well, we are," said Augustus apologetically. "I'm sorry, I carried you over here, to look for some medical help for you. Where should we be? Briz, give the man his property."

Briz tossed it to him, and he slashed it at Augustus, as he tried to stand up. But, perhaps because he was a little concussed, he fell over again. It was that, or Briz ankle-tapping him.

Augustus, who had been slightly distracted by suddenly noticing a small control panel low on the wall, ornate, with several strange holes in it, and had bent down to look at it, turned to see him sprawled on the floor. "Tch. You are concussed," he said, sitting the man up. "What is this? An intercom? He stuck a finger into a hole on the panel.

The floor began to slide noisily downwards. Briz clung to him. The scarfaced man moaned in terror. Perhaps because he'd been in elevators before, Augustus was not quite as startled. Admittedly this one seemed a little badly maintained, and rattled and creaked and jerked a bit on its way down the tower. It stopped at a passage dimly lit – because half the lights weren't working, by elongated greenish globes. From down the passage came the sound of machinery.

The scarfaced man looked at the passage and closed his eyes and slumped into a dead faint. Briz – who had stopped clinging to Augustus when the elevator stopped, walked out into it with an insouciant air, such as might be worn by a young fellow who would never let the thought of clinging to someone cross their mind. "Doesn't half pong down here, don't it?" he commented cheerfully, in a voice perhaps just a little higher pitched than usual.

It did indeed, thought Augustus, gathering the scarfaced man into his arms, and managing to bring his whip along too, seeing as the fellow seemed so attached to it, but it was a familiar smell: hot machinery, oil. It smelled faintly as if something was running a bearing. Sounded like it too. Augustus walked towards the sounds and scents of his childhood... although Thistlewood machinery was always better maintained than this! It was fascinating stuff, though. Plainly not made by humans, and certainly not by TMI!

Augustus put down the scarfaced man and began a loving exploration of alien machinery. Some of the devices were a mystery as to their purpose, but... well, obviously machines were machines. Some mathematical and mechanical laws held good. A cog was a cog, a bearing, a bearing. That was a somewhat different design to a grease-nipple and the long-unused grease gun was not built for human hands, but it worked. And the machinery needed it. Such neglect burned every inch of the Thistlewood soul, and Augustus could no more have resisted the need to do the job than he could have not patted a dog. He would have been happily lost in it for days had Briz not come and tugged at his sleeve. "Oi. Mister. Me stomach thinks me throat's been cut. And that bloke's no help."

Now that she mentioned it, Augustus realized he too was both hungry and thirsty. It was... annoying. He just felt he was getting some kind of grasp on what the first few of the vast array of machinery did. The principles of various things were dancing in numbers around his mind. That was definitely a gyroscope... He forcibly dragged himself from the study of the workings of alien machinery, to the realities of where he was, and the problems of food and drink. The scarfaced man was lying in a catatonic ball on the floor, where Augustus had left him. He walked over to him. "I say. We need to get to food and water."

"The masters will kill us all in terrible ways," whimpered the scarfaced man, not uncurling. "We will all die slow horrible deaths over weeks. You touched the machines."

"Someone had to. Several of them are now running better," said Augustus. "They are all in need of maintenance! Someone should be ashamed of themselves."

"Humans may not touch the machines! Not even touch!"

Augustus realized he was a little greasy in places. He looked around for the essential accoutrements of any machine-shop, hand-cleaner and rags, and maybe even a tap and an old towel. He was reluctant to wipe his hands on his trousers. There had to be something...

Alien cupboards were rather different in that they too were hidden in the bulkhead, marked with the sort of little holes that had made the elevator work. By the dust on the bulkhead, no one had been down here, and touched them for many years. But they opened reluctantly to a prod from what was probably a screwdriver, even if it had five little points. The first one revealed various liquids in oddly shaped containers, the second a huge stack of slightly greasy thin metal sheets covered in tiny but varied indents... and diagrams. Diagrams stayed diagrams. Augustus was nearly distracted again, when Briz cleared his throat. The third 'cupboard' proved the charm, with fur of some kind and a bowl of goop that might be hand-cleaner... or acid. Or suited to rather different skin. But that was definitely a faucet, and a drain below. It also had the hole arrangement for opening it, and at first that gave him nothing but an asthmatic gurgle, and then a reluctant yellow-red trickle, and then a gout of steam, and then it began to run. Augustus smelled it, tested it on a fingertip. It seemed to be water. It was a little warmer than pleasant, but it helped shift the grease. So did the fur. It was remarkably good at cleaning one's fingers. "Well, I suppose we should go and face the music, if we're in trouble," he said, determinedly. "Maybe we can find some tucker on the way."

"A butcher and a pie floater," said Briz, with what could have been sarcasm.

"That would be nice," said Augustus, abstractedly, part of his mind taken up with thinking about those metallic sheets. Were they... workshop manuals? TMI was all computer interface. They'd had to step back a long way, with contact from Earth severed, but not that far. But... well TMI still had printed manuals at the plants. Maybe the only company on Azure to still have them, but sometimes it paid off. He must get back and study those.

The scarfaced man had unwound himself. "Look," he said, brokenly. "If yer can get us back up from here... I ain't going to rat you out. Get you on an easy shift on the flensing. You just keep quiet about this. Don't say nothing to no-one."

"Oh, I could never do anything dishonest," said Augustus.

"He means if they don't ask, he won't say, said Briz. "And I found some more of those, what-did-yer-call-ems, elevators. Along this way."

Briz had found three different sets of alien elevators. The one, the central one, was the largest and looked as if the dust had been disturbed in recent years. The other two, not so. They chose one of those. It was plainly the wrong one, as it made a few grinding noises and didn't go anywhere.

The other, however lifted them up to another level in the cloud-castle. If the level below had been the engine-room, this plainly was the store room. The scar-faced man breathed a huge sigh of relief. "Right-o. We can get up to the processing deck from here. We have had ter carry the carcasses from the air-car from here since the lifter packed in.

He led them along – past a wide-open ramp into the cloud they happened to be passing through. The reason for this was soon apparent – a row of long, elegant-looking vessels with stubby little wings were parked there. There were a number of obviously recently vacated slots, free of dust -- and some of the vessels had plainly sat unused – some with parts lying around them, for some time.

They passed another central elevator, and came to a steep stair-well, leading up. "Yer walk ahead. Slaves is always in front."

"So long as yer remember what happened to yer. It'll happen again, if yer try a fast one," said Briz. "And don't think we won't sing about where you've been. I reckon the Thrymi might go look, and the dust down there tells a story."

"Just shut up about it, and walk," said the slave-supervisor.

So, they did. The elevator would have involved less stair-climbing. At the top of the stairs was pandemonium, or possibly part of Dante's Inferno...

Well, a huge meat-packing plant, anyway. It was a place of blood and guts and the corpses of various creatures, of noise and smells that killed Augustus's hunger.

CHAPTER

NINE

For Briz, meat was an expensive and not too frequent part of food. Lots of it was dodgy and of uncertain origin. You didn't ask too many questions about what went into a mystery bag or a meat pie. You wouldn't like the answers so it was best not to know. Here... she couldn't help but know. Yes, there was some butchery at the black stump. But not on this scale. It didn't worry her much. Not as much as whatever he might get up to next!

But it appeared that whatever that was involved large knives. The slave-boss herded them to a cubicle, where they were handed two knives by a bored-looking blade sharpener. The boss pushed them along to a long conveyer belt full of Yesters- the red-furred fanged flyers that occasionally made the market at the Black Stump. "Yours, Marty," said the slave-boss to the line supervisor. "Newbies."

The man looked at him. "Why not on loading?"

The boss flicked his whip. "Because. Now teach them."

The man shrugged. "If yer says so, Pelous. You," he pointed at Briz. "Yer do feet." He snagged a yester off the line. "What's yer name?"

"Briz."

"Well see Briz, yer bend them like this, cut through the joint, pull, twist, cut. Chuck the feet in the bucket, toss the bird back on belt."

The conveyor belt promptly made a screeching mechanical noise, jerked a few times and stopped. Their instructor covered his eyes and groaned. "Bleeding 'eck. Just my blooming luck. We'll have to carry the birds to the wash-deck. You. New boy. Bernie..."

But Augustus had disappeared. It took Briz a few seconds to find him... by spotting his feet. He was under the conveyor. For a horrified moment she thought it had killed him. But then she saw him fumble in his pocket and pull out a little red penknife. By now her staring had attracted the attention of most of the slaves on that line, and the instructor. The all stood horrified, and then the instructor rushed forward and grabbed Augustus's feet. "Leave him alone!" said Briz, prodding him in the ribs with the knife she held. He stopped, and she wondered what the hell had come over her. There was a sudden loud click and a clank, the belt started moving again. Augustus wriggled out smiling like nothing was wrong, dusting himself off.

"Did... you do that?" demanded Marty, the line supervisor.

"What?" asked Augustus.

"Touch the machine. We're not allowed to touch the machine."

"It had a build-up of debris in the reciprocator sprocket," explained Augustus. "Don't worry, I didn't touch it. I just flicked it out with the knife. If you put your hand in there you'll lose it."

"We are not allowed to touch the machines," moaned the man fearfully, looking around.

"She'll be right," said Briz comfortingly. "He's from Azure. He's a blue man. They're allowed to do stuff."

"A blue man... He don't look blue like the Zell. The Zell used to fix the machines. But the last one died, before I got caught."

"I reckon he just looks different because he's from offworld. They've got... hills and stuff. Probably affects them."

"What's hills?"

Briz wrinkled her forehead. "A bit like bumps but bigger," was the best she could do.

"Bumps on the head, I think, eh," said Marty. "Hey, hills-on-the-brain, what's yer name?"

Augustus blinked, and then worked out that he was being addressed. "Oh. Augustus StJohn Thistlewood the third." He stuck out his hand to the oddly dressed fellow who was plainly some kind of slave-supervisor. He realized that, perhaps doing so after putting the knife aside might have been a good idea. The man jumped back, eyed him warily. "I just asked yer name. Yer didn't have to swear at me, and try to stick me."

"I really meant no harm. I do apologize. My name is Augustus StJohn Thistlewood the third. You could call me Augustus, I suppose. Seeing as we are to be workmates. I hope you'll allow me to help with uplift and moving this towards an enlightened society."

"What?" The supervisor shook his head. "Look, Gus. You get busy fetching yesters for the sorters over there. We're behind. We'll be lucky not to get a good whipping."

Augustus wondered what made a whipping good instead of bad, but he went across to the sorters and started carrying handfuls of the birds along. He saw that other carriers had the knife hooked to their belts so he did the same. He carried, and wondered when they got to eat or drink. Several hours later he was still wondering, and still carrying. It seemed needlessly inefficient, as there was a fan of belts from the sorting area. But they were stationary. He wondered if he could have a look, but decided, for now, against it. Maybe later, when they took a break or something.

By the time a loud whistle blew and they stopped, his arms ached and he decided that had been a mistake. He followed the rest of the workers down a smoky gallery and into an even smokier hall.

Briz, as if by magic, appeared at his side. "Hard yakka, this, Mister. Hope the tucker ain't too rubbish."

Augustus hoped so too, but he was hungry enough by this stage to eat it anyway. And actually, it wasn't bad. If you liked lots of meat, that was. If you believed vegetables were good, or even existed, you were out of luck.

And then... they went back to work. By the time they stopped again, Augustus was almost too tired to eat. Any ideas he'd had about fixing the problem with the conveyor system had disappeared into arms that felt like jelly and a general exhaustion, which left him too tired to think. After they'd eaten, and a small measure of recovery had taken place, Augustus found.... They were back at work.

The trouble, Briz reflected, with her drongo, was that he was bleedin' clueless. Half the slaughter-deck was watching him, wondering when he was gonna fall over. He seemed to think 'work' was not hard yakka to be avoided or done as slow and easy as you could get away with, but attacked it like a thirsty man takes a schooner of beer, chugging it so fast it spilled out of the sides of his mouth. And she just had no chance to tell him. Well, by the time the knock-off whistle blew, he was down to about doing three men's work. Some of the women were already discussing his potential. "Reckon he can root for five too," said one thoughtfully.

"Hey," said Briz, waving her knife under the woman's nose. "Keep off him, yer filthy slag."

"You think he's yours, do yer? Well, I'll split yer tripes..."

"See who brought us here, yer bushpig. Nice and respectful-like. Not using his whip. Yer watch yer mouth, otherwise..." Briz hit the woman's elbow, and the knife flew out of a numbed hand, and Briz caught it... "I might give yer knife back to yer where it fits best."

"Keep yer catfight for after work-time," snarled their overseer. "Give her her knife back, Briz. Properly, without cutting her. And Kayla, button yer lip. We're ahead thanks to Gus. Best worker I ever got given. Kangaroos loose in his top paddock, but he's flat out like a lizard drinking."

Which got Briz out of a situation she didn't know how she got herself into. But she resolved to watch him, and that slag. She didn't know why she was doing this...

And later when they had been fed, turned their work-knives in, and the dormitory was opened, she didn't know why she'd bothered. She was close enough to hear the slag say "hey big boy, you want a good root?"

And to hear him say: "Thank you, Ma'am, but I am far too tired to eat."

"I mean do yer want to go to bed?"

"Oh yes! Lead me to it," said her drongo, as Briz pushed her way forward. The bushpig led him to her pallet amid a few wolf-whistles... and he lay down... there was just a little snore before he even quite got down flat.

The woman was still standing there with her mouth open when Briz kicked her legs out from under her, and was on top of her, with Briz's little knife at her throat. "I warned yer." Briz knew, well enough, she had just one chance in this place, to make herself top of the heap, fast, or she'd be at the bottom of it. And she'd done that. Wasn't going back.

"You ain't allowed no knives back here," protested the woman querulously. "Pelous will..."

"He won't do Jack," said Briz scornfully. "You saw him bring us in, you dumb bushpig. You seen him act like that before?" By listening in to what was being said, Briz knew new slaves were given a beating first, to get them in line. There'd been some wonderment among the slaves about it. She had also gathered that Marty's line was the soft option, a perk for those who kissed up right. It never got new slaves.

"I didn't do nothing," said the woman. "He fell asleep, see."

"If I cut yer nose off, yer won't be doing nothing either," said Briz savagely. "Yer will look like a shonk. And no one wants to root a shonk."

"I'll leave him alone, honest," said the woman.

"Yer wouldn't know honest if it bit yer on the leg. I'll give yer a little nick on the tip of yer nose so you remember, cause yer didn't want to learn, yer gotta feel." And she did. The woman squealed – despite the fact that it wasn't much of a cut. "Now yer crawl off to somewhere else. And you stay off my patch. He's mine, see."

"Yer can have him," said the woman sulkily. "He'll do yer no bloody good."

"That's my look out. Now," said Briz, "get lost."

"But that's me bed."

"It was," said Briz, as various onlookers laughed. "Gowan. Go look at yer nose."

Briz lay down next to the drongo. What the hell was she doing? She had some time to think about it all. She wasn't as tired, by a long shot, as the poor drongo. She hadn't worked herself half to blooming death. She'd matched her pace to the rest, who all worked just like slaves do... real hard when the supervisor was watching, real, real hard when Pelous-the-boss passed by, flicking his whip. She kept her ears and eyes open and, mostly, hard though it was, her mouth shut.

There'd been about thirty slaves on the butchering and processing deck. A few more had come in for the meal. By what they said, they worked at the cleaning of the Thrymi quarters and producing the food. That might be a better option, Briz thought. But looking at the cleaners... she thought not. They were all as scarred as Pelous, and had that look of permanent fear. Well, most of the slaves had a bit of that, and it wasn't surprising really. Those pretty-boy Thrymi had a reputation of being out-and-out bastards. Maybe the cooks... Anyway, her attention had been hard focused on how to get out of here and back to the Big Syd. That – from what she'd gathered, was where the meat was going. That was also where – judging by the accents, and comments, at least two thirds of the slaves came from. A couple of them had the tell-tale slower speech and broader twang of outbackers. That would have given it away, even if they hadn't been the only ones wearing manacles.

Briz had asked one of her co-workers why. "Cause the dumb

drongos will jump if they sees some skyfrond, 'n go feral," said the fellow Big Syd slave, derisively. "I'd rather be dead."

Briz could see that. Apparently, they'd all just come out of days of lock-up while the Thrymi cloud-castle had been off-loading at the Big Syd. The Big Syd-born slaves would jump then, if they could. She slept, as she always had, lightly. It was the habit of a lifetime on the Plate, where if you slept too deeply, you'd get cleaned up, if not cleaned out. Lightly enough to see that the slave dormitory was not locked. Slaves came and went, presumably to relieve themselves at the tube-hole just outside. Eventually, she went and checked that out. It seemed there was nothing to stop her going for a walk around. She'd have to find out why, before she did. The Thrymi were a nasty lot. There had to be a catch.

It was odd, sleeping next to someone. It woke her up a lot. But she reckoned you'd get used to anything. There was a fair bit of bed-swapping going on. Briz wondered about that. Wondered about the results of it. Women outnumbered the male slaves a fair bit. She'd have needed a few lammos to work out by how much. Her mouth fairly watered at the thought.

Augustus woke the next morning with someone sticking a toe in his ribs. On moving, he discovered that there were very few muscles that didn't hurt. Briz poked him with a toe, again. "Get up, Mister. They'll flog yer otherwise."

Augustus struggled to his feet. One thing about sleeping fully clothed... it saved dressing. That was the only positive he could see in it. He very soon found out that the day was going downhill from there. Today they had to offload the cargo from the air-cars down the stairwell... and back up the stairwell. And these were not the strange birds of the previous day, but mostly something called shonks, and a number of jumbuck. Today was a shonk day for their line. And shonks were a lot heavier – than the yesters. They were also spiky with sharp scales. All of them had to be carried up the flight of stairs to the processing deck, and then onto the belts.

Augustus soon found himself longing for yester-day. The work was harder than anything he'd ever done in his life before. Still, he had to do his bit. He wanted to fit in, to help the oppressed and downtrodden of Sybil's Plate. This wasn't the Plate, but they certainly were downtrodden and oppressed. As soon as he was less tired he would have to do something about it.

Looking back, Augustus found the first week of his enslavement disappeared into a blur of utter exhaustion. He had never done much physical labor before, and his body ached in places he had no idea could ache. And every day they seemed to give him more to do. It couldn't be true, of course. But it seemed that way. Perhaps he was sick, and that was the source of the pain. After what might have been a week – he didn't think of recording days until a few of them had passed – slowly, by imperceptible degrees, he began to recover... well, his mind did. Parts of his body had been affected by the illness – like his shoulders and forearms, and had become rather swollen. There was nothing he could do but hope that this too would pass.

But his less tired mind started dealing with the situation, the awful lot of his fellow slaves – and himself, for that matter. One of the things that he had realized was that a great deal of the labor was because the machinery of the cloud-castle was in a sorry state of disrepair. So that meant jobs which would once have been done mechanically were now done by slaves.

The second thing that soon became obvious to Augustus was that the cloud-castle – and their fear the Thrymi – made this a prison for most of the slaves – a prison they did not try to escape from, because most of the slaves would rather die than try. That took some understanding. After all, there were no old slaves and no children – that was a puzzle, because, to his embarrassment, they were certainly doing things that should have resulted in children. But surely some would plan to escape? Or even rebel?

The 'plan' part revealed its flaws with him discovering that some prisoners were manacled and locked in: people the rest of the slaves barely spoke to and treated with disdain. Outbackers. He still did not know much about them, because they tended to be worked separately, and everyone else seemed to know already. Some instinct told him not to ask questions or to reveal his ignorance to his fellow slaves. So: when he got a chance, he asked Briz... who he suspected might know even less.

Briz, of course, didn't know less. "Escape?" said Briz, incredulously. "Where to?"

"Away seems a good option," said Augustus.

Briz shook his head. "Look, Mister. We don't even know where the Big Syd is. How would we get back there? I mean, yer could jump onto a piece of sky-frond. That's why they lock them outbackers up. They'd want to. But for the rest of us, it's just a slow death, lost and starving, prey for anything from a herbeen to a shonk. Better to be here with a quick death and good tucker."

"But does this castle not return to the Plate?"

"Yeah. When the meat freezers are full, or the Thrymi feel like it. But we get shoved into the lockup for that."

Augustus digested all of this. "And um," he asked cautiously when he was sure they couldn't be overheard, "Why don't the slaves rebel?"

Briz rolled her eyes. "You don't try to fight a Thrymi. They'd like that. Why do yer figure there are so few men?"

"I hadn't really thought. Do they resist capture better?"

"'Cause when the hunting is slow, or they're bored those bastards will take the strongest slave to chase around and have fun with. The women-Thrymi especially. That's how you end up scarred and messed-up like Pelous."

Bit by bit, Augustus figured it out, or most of it. The slaves – like most humans on Sybil III –were not very mechanically minded, and even if they had over-run the twenty or so Thrymi living in the towers of the cloud-castle, they could not direct it, use the machinery, or keep it running – not that the Thrymi did well at that – nor steer it, or operate the navigational system. And the idea of making a Thrymi overlord do it for you was apparently a ridiculous one. The lockup was locked when not occupied, and the passages of the lower decks flooded with a toxic gas to prevent runaways hiding.

Added to all of this was the information that the slave dormitories were locked when the slaves were working, and open when occupied. Briz had already been on several 'expeditions', he told him.

"Where have you been?" asked Augustus, curiously.

The lad looked faintly guilty. "Around. Just checking things out, see. Not been to get a butcher and a mystery bag at the pub." The lad bit his lip. "See, I figured you might have problems getting us back home. And if I could hide out somewhere when the others got locked up, maybe I could get away."

"Oh. I have been very tired. I think I may have developed some sort of allergic reaction to the food. I have had aches all over and my arms seem to be rather swollen. Although the pain has largely gone."

Briz looked at him askance. "Yer tired because yer doing enough work for a whole shearing gang. Look out, the boss is coming this way," which was the end of that conversation. But it gave Augustus much to think about as he carried carcasses. When work was finished he told Briz that he would like to go exploring sometime during the sleep period. Briz woke him from the depths of slumber much later, and he followed his guide out. The red-lit sky was of course much the same tumult of clouds and drifting skyfrond as ever. Briz waited until a cloud enveloped them in a dense mist, and led him across the flensing deck. "Where'd yer want to go?" she asked quietly. "Up ain't safe."

They spent some time down on the lower decks, which were eerily empty and silent except for the machines that kept the castle aloft, that kept the power on.

They looked at the fliers. The controls seemed simple enough – a steering triangle, and a few levers, and a well-worn set of buttons. Several little screens, that were a dull grey at the moment.

"Can you fly it, Mister Gus?" asked Briz. The lad had taken to calling him 'Gus' as had the other slaves. It was that, or 'drongo' which he suspected wasn't polite.

"I have no idea," said Augustus, eternally truthful, despite the look of disappointment that earned him from Briz. "I've flown an aircar, of course. But this is plainly somewhat different."

"Why?" asked Briz, as Augustus peered underneath the flier that was sitting up on props, a part of the cowling peeled back. "They both fly, don't they?"

"Well, these don't have lift fans. The wings seem far too stubby to provide sufficient lift, unless they have some incredibly powerful form of thrust. And there don't seem to be jet outputs or lift fans..." He looked at Briz's face. "I might as well be speaking Greek. Look, yesters, jumbucks and shonks all fly, but not, by the looks of them, the same way. I might be able to work it out..."

"Working it out while yer falling don't seem a good idea."

"That is quite true," admitted Augustus. So, they walked on, going to the section of the castle that held massive freezers, an area they'd been to before, carrying carcasses. Then on into a largely empty storage hold, and then back to the machine-rooms, which housed the two bits of machinery that fascinated Augustus most. One, he was sure, was the anti-gravity generator – simply by virtue of the way it was massively bracketed to the entire structure. He was beginning to get some inclination of what might happen there, just looking at it. Part of it was a massive gyroscope – one of the bearings of which he'd lubricated. That in turn had several smaller gyroscopes within it. The other structure that was past his engineering experience was the toroid shape which had the cables snaking from it, plainly the source of the cloud-castle's power. Had the aliens somehow solved the problem of cold-fusion and on such a scale as to make it small enough to power this? Augustus wanted to be back in the engineering workshop of TMI with it. He wanted to understand these devices desperately. He wanted to examine what he was now sure were workshop manuals.

Briz broke his intent study. "Mister Gus. We gotta get back. Our shift will start soon," said Briz, tugging at his sleeve.

So, they did. But never had work seemed so tedious and

mundane. Lift and carry, heave and sort... it did not take much brain-power. His mind was taken up by the world of possibilities of what could be done with antigrav units and power units in those sizes, and how to make them. That reverie however was shattered by a shrieking noise, a terrible caterwauling racket. Looking up and around Augustus saw that one of the manacled slaves had somehow ascended onto the wall of the courtyard – or rather was pulling up onto it. Thrymi appeared from various doorways and onto the ramparts as the slave scrambled up. The Thrymi started firing some sort of weapon, but the slave dived over the edge.

Thrymi came swarming out, running for the ramp that led to the fliers. Augustus, who was carrying Shonks up the stairway –which had an excellent view up to the wall the slave had jumped from, and the fliers below, barely managed to get himself out of the way of their headlong rush. There was no mistaking the eagerness, even if the language was alien. He could see right into the cockpit of the nearest flier as the Thrymi pilot thrust at a button, and the flier began to vibrate and whine and bump off the deck. The Thrymi pilot hauled at a lever. With a sudden high-pitched shriek and wobble the flier hurtled out of the launch bay followed by the next and the next. Fourteen fliers in all flew out, plainly hunting.

"Right, yer bunch of drongos," shouted Pelous. "Quit gawping. If they get her, they'll be in a good mood when they get back, but if they doesn't they'll be looking to make an example of some of us."

The slaves worked with an unusual degree of silence, and, even Augustus noticed, more energy than usual, as well as plain fear.

A little later the Thrymi fliers came back. The slim, elegant Thrymi were chattering away in their language, but you could see by the gestures and posture that they were quite pleased with them-selves, or so Augustus thought. Marty confirmed it. "Got her. But she must have given them a run." He looked relieved.

Augustus felt both horrified and somewhat nauseated by it all. It was just wrong, no matter if it was local custom, no matter what Honeybeere had said about not applying Azurian standards and assuming the moral standards of Azure were superior. In this case Azurian standards were! It was odd to feel a faint stir of unease at realizing that maybe... some of the statements he had read and trusted in sociology were... not living up to Sybil III and reality. Maybe Admiral Halberd hadn't been entirely wrong in his actions. It was a pity that it had been applied to Azure citizens on the Plate, and not to humans in general, and to the Plate, and not to the cloud-castles.

Well... he was going to have to do something about it. That was all there was to it. Non-interference in local custom was all very well... in theory.

The first and most obvious target had to be the alarm system, Augustus decided. If it had not been for that the slave might have made it over the wall undetected... but where had they been going?

The answer was visible out of the launch portals: they were obviously moving through a dense drift of sky-frond. The escapee must have jumped, manacles and all, onto some of it. It... must be possible to support the weight of a person on the plant. That seemed bizarre, but it was a bizarre place.

He brought up the subject of the alarm with Briz the first chance he got – when they had knocked off work and made their way to the sleeping pallets. Briz, somewhat to his surprise was in fervent support of the idea – but not for the sake of giving escaping outbackers a chance. "Could have caught me! That was my plan for a way out when we got back to the plate, over the courtyard wall. Them portals is closed. See, the Thrymi always dock in their port area, and that's tighter than a duck's bum, but yer got to take yer chances when yer get them."

"Well," said Augustus. "I am not making any promises, but I will see what I can work out. Will you wake me?"

"Too right I will!" promised Briz.

It proved almost ridiculously easy to identify the alarm system – every slave accessible upper wall or walkway had a simple infrared-light-beam. So too did the flier-portals. Augustus was fairly sure that meant if interrupted, it would sound the alarm. "The skyway on the outside turret didn't have it though. "You could get there, Briz. It seems they do not guard the elevators, as the rest of the slaves do not know how to use them."

"Yeah, but that's a long jump down. The courtyard wall is only maybe six times my height..." said Briz, thoughtfully.

That still seemed very high to Augustus. The only time he'd jumped from that high was in his one experiment with paragliding, before his grandmother had found out and put a rigid stop to it. He still regretted that, slightly. He'd rather enjoyed it despite the less than perfect landing that had ended up with a broken ankle and his grandmother aware of the escapade.

"Well, I have not found the control unit itself. It is possibly up in the Thrymi quarters. I could cut the wiring, but that would probably set it off, rather than stop it. But the noise... did it come from one point, or more than one point?"

"A couple, I reckon," said Briz. "We could muffle 'em, I suppose. Meat or fur might work."

"Let see if we can find those and I will see what can possibly be done."

That too proved relatively easy. The human slaves might not know what a speaker looked like, but Augustus did, and how to disconnect one. "Strewth! You're a regular Ned Kelly," said Briz, admiringly. "And there I thought you was a straight drongo, dinky-die."

Augustus had to admit that he still wasn't too sure what Briz was saying, all the time. But the lad was plainly pleased. They hunted and found – now they knew where to look, and what to look for, another three speakers, and then it was time to go back to the slave quarters. There was no guarantee, of course, that that was all of them, and no way to test it unless someone tried to escape again.

CHAPTER

TEN

Charles Anson Roberto Thistlewood IV looked at the assembled family, hastily convened as soon as he'd got the news. He wasn't looking forward to this. Not at all. Besides, he was worried stiff, himself. He was actually very fond of his little brother. "What is it, Charlie?" demanded his grandfather, still in workshop overalls – an unheard of thing for inside the house.

"Augustus may have got himself into some kind of trouble," said Charlie, not trying to break it gently. "I, um, sent someone to Sybil III four weeks ago. I... sent them to find my brother. Quietly. Just to check on how he was doing, without making a fuss."

"Tell us the worst," said his father quietly.

"Well, he couldn't find him. He's a private investigator, one of the best. Harding – we used him for that industrial espionage problem we had a couple of years ago. He got doors slammed on him and utter-clam up. Eventually he tried the Embassy. And he actually got physically manhandled off the premises..."

"What?" snapped his grandfather. "I have assurances from the vice-premier himself that the Ambassador has been briefed..."

"That's just it. That particular ambassador has, it seems, been arrested. It's not public knowledge yet because they're trying to round up the rest of the network, to some criminal enterprise he was involved in here on Azure. They have replaced the whole lot of them – with the old staff – those not in prison, shipped out to the mission on Novogord, the slow way – to keep it all quiet for as long as possible. New embassy staff have been shipped in, but whatever they're doing, it does not include keeping tabs on Augustus."

"I'll get onto the vice-premier straight away," said his grandfather heading for the door.

"Wait," said Charlie. "Harding found out a bit more from the staff at the Hyaton. Apparently, the day all of this happened – the staff at the Hyaton know something happened, not the details, someone brought in a note about Augustus being in trouble, and asking for some Azure policeman called Peleton to come immediately. Armed. Harding got no further, nor could he find the messenger. The policeman did get the message, but left the Hyaton with his luggage and passport just after. We'll need you, grandfather, to lean on the vice-premier to get us access to this policeman."

His grandfather nodded. "If I have to get onto the Premier herself, it'll happen," he said crisply. "And some heads are going to roll."

Grandmother followed him. "I'll need to watch his blood-pressure," she said, darkly.

"Treat it in advance," said her father after her.

When they had gone and the door had safely closed, Charlie's father said, "Right, Charles. Tell me the rest."

Charlie, despite the circumstances, managed a slight smile. "My little brother seems to have been raising Cain. He's got involved in several brawls and destroyed a brothel."

His father gawped at him. "Augustus? That can't be true."

"That was my thought, too, Papa. But Harding is thorough. He did say some of it sounded like tall stories, but he'd been to the ruins of the bar where one of the fights happened. It's ruined all right, he had pictures. And Augustus was definitely there. But the witnesses clammed up. They've had the frighteners put on them."

"I'll get onto security. I'll have a ship chartered, get them there and have them activate that transmitter, and track him down. We may need some more muscle..."

Charlie nodded. "A few special services boys. Templeton – runs company security down in Tarkastadt -- he was a Sergeant-Major."

"Get him here. Charter a flier," said his father. "And Charlie..."

"Yes, Papa."

"Thanks for sending that investigator. See he gets a bonus, and I'll want to interview him as well. Preferably before your grand-mother does."

Charlie wished he'd been privy to his grandfather's call, but whatever was said had immediate effect. It was not half an hour later that a high-speed military flier landed on the front lawn, and discharged two suspiciously bulky, suited men, with a rather alarmed looking Chief Inspector Peleton of the Azure Interplanetary Criminal Investigation Unit between them. They effectively frog-marched him into the drawing-room. "Mr Thistlewood, this is the man you were looking to speak to, Sir."

"Good," said grandfather. "The housekeeper will see to some refreshments for you. I shall call you when you are needed."

"But..." said one of the two men.

"We..." said the other.

"Go. Now," said grandfather. He turned to the butler – who was also chief of the house security. "Mr. Argo. See these gentlemen out, to the kitchens. They are not to return without my calling for them." He shooed them out, like hens.

The Chief Inspector looked at the assembled Thistlewoods. "Do you mind," he said, "telling me exactly what is going on. And... just who you are and why the Premier's personal security detail have brought me here?"

"My name is Charles Anson Roberto Thistlewood II. This is my wife, Sylvania Aria Thistlewood, my son Charles Anson Roberto

Thistlewood III and this is my grandson Charles Anson Roberto Thistlewood IV. We need to ask you some questions."

The Chief Inspector looked at them. Swallowed. "It didn't occur to me," he said, weakly, "That he was related to that Thistlewood. I promise you, Sir, we were acting on information received, and really..." he trailed off.

"Really what?" snapped grandfather.

"Really, he sounded just like you, Sir."

The family looked at him in some surprise. Charlie was first to find his tongue. "Augustus?"

"Yes sir. I, um was unaware of the relationship, sir. Actually, I was really unaware of who you are, or that you existed. I mean Thistlewood is not that uncommon a name on Azure."

"That is the way we like it and intend to keep it. Now, you clearly met Augustus. I believe you got a message that he was in some danger."

Peleton nodded. "Yes. While the operation to arrest the Ambassador was ongoing... a message was sent. Unfortunately, we only got it some two hours later, when we returned to collect our luggage from the Hyaton. We had to escort the prisoners back. But sir, I did take it seriously, and Carlson and Samuels and I proceeded directly to Mr Thistlewood's lodgings. We... um took it upon ourselves to force the door. But he was not there, nor were there any signs of struggle. His luggage and personal effects were still there. We, um, assumed he was out. We did have his possessions moved to safe-keeping in the embassy. Sir... We had a spacecraft to catch, sir, with a major criminal investigation still underway. I did leave strict instructions with the new senior charge-d'affair's Ms. Latham – who is um, working for the Azure Interplanetary Criminal Investigation Unit, that they were to follow up and check on Mr Augustus Thistlewood's welfare and whereabouts. I mean, after all, we only broke this ring as a result of his... involvement."

"Are you implying," said Charlie's father, "That my son Augustus, of all people, was involved in some form of criminal activity?"

Peleton shook his head, hastily. "No Sir. Definitely not, Sir. We were given false information in an attempt to implicate him. Um. We were told he was a drug addict involved in a counterfeiting ring. Needless to say, it proved entirely false, and, um, his er... local assistant, provided us with a lead, which led to the arrest of our informant... I am not at liberty to reveal his name sir.

"We'll get it," said grandfather tersely. "Tell us about this... local assistant."

"Yes Sir. Her name appears to be Briz. A local. She's also the one who sent us the message saying we should come immediately. I had, er, primed her to inform us of developments."

"Her? Augustus said he had a local boy as a guide," said Charlie.

"One of my officers did the body search. Definitely female, sir. Although wearing baggy boy's clothing and with her hair cut short. Possibly passing for a boy."

"Tell us more about this message. I want every detail you can remember. Why didn't it get to you sooner? Didn't you take the call?"

"She wrote it down, Sir. She attempted to get the Hyaton to call us, to speak to us, apparently. There is no mobile service. But... we were out making the arrests. Obviously, we hadn't told the Hyaton staff where we were going to be, as the embassy people ate and drank there a lot, and we didn't want our hand tipped. I have the message, Sir. She wrote it on the card I had given her to contact me with." He dug in his pocket, produced his wallet, and pulled out the card and handed it to the first reaching hand.

'*Come qik. To Crooked Mac Beggar's lane, the place what you searched. Augustus's got big strife. Bondi boyz. Bring guns.*'

"Remarkable neat handwriting," commented grandmother, speaking for the first time. "Atrocious spelling and grammar. Worse that Charlie's. What exactly does it mean?"

"Well," said Peleton. "The Bondi Boyz are one of the gangs. A rather bad one, I am afraid. 'Strife' is trouble. The rest is an address. I can only assume that meant that Mr Thistlewood had run afoul of the gang in his philanthropic efforts. He was very serious about them, you know. But... it's very unlikely that they'd dare to kill an Azure citizen. The aliens that rule the various human factions utterly forbid it."

"We are going to need to know as much as you can tell us about these 'Bondi Boyz'," said grandfather.

"And I am going to need to know about this young woman," said grandmother. "What sort of person is she?"

"We'll need a description and any clues to her associates."

Peleton sighed. "She's somewhere between fifteen and twenty-five I would guess. Hard to tell. Slight, about five foot three or four. Blue eyes, black hair. I can do a sketch. She looks a typical Big Syd street brat, and dressed in ragged trousers and a large scruffy blue shirt and a few layers of other rags. A pick-pocket – she stole my wallet... and gave it back."

"A thief!"

"It's relatively hard to find anyone in the Big Syd – as they call the Plate, who isn't at least involved in petty crime, ma'am," said Peleton. "It's a venal pest hole. But... for what it is worth, she did give my wallet back, of her own accord, and she also gave us the lead on Camel... uh the major criminal we were looking for. And she did seem genuinely loyal to Mr.Thistlewood... And he to her. Frankly, he seemed a good man to work for, and he stood up for her. That's... probably almost unheard of, there." He paused. "He, um, seemed quite unaware that she was female."

"I think," said grandfather, "That this gentleman has much to tell us. I think we'll need a glass of sherry.

"Whiskey," said grandmother. "I need whiskey, and so does everyone else, I suspect. Ring for it, Charles."

Charlie hadn't known his grandmother to drink whiskey, or, in fact, anything but tea or her evening sherry, and small distasteful sips of wine at important social events. But it seemed the butler did know where to find it. And, as they learned more from Peleton of the environment and people of 'the Big Syd' he was glad not to have sherry. And if he hadn't been rather worried about his little brother, he'd have been both amused and impressed. His grandmother gave the poor man the fifth degree about Augustus's assistant and guide. "Is such handwriting typical of the locals?" she demanded, staring intently at the small, neat letters.

"Well, no," admitted Peleton. "A lot of them can't read, let alone write. I... didn't give it a thought. It's very neat. She sounded and behaved like a local though."

They learned a lot about 'the Big Syd', about its people, about the various gangs and criminal enerprises. Enough, thought Charlie, to worry him immensely that nearly a month had to pass before the security teams searching could report back. He nearly simply decided to go himself, then and there.

CHAPTER

ELEVEN

The next work-day brought another surprise to Augustus. The aircars had gone out – in a hurry. Augustus had not heard an alarm so it wasn't another escaping outbacker, but plainly something had the Thrymi excited. They didn't have to wait long to find out what it was. Later, working on the animal, Augustus had to wish he hadn't had to learn. The fliers had come in towing the thing, visible above the courtyard wall as they maneovered. It was far too big to load onto their catch beds.

It was also far too big for the courtyard that acted as the castle's abattoir. That was only partially open to the sky – and the clouds. And the rain. Sometimes the Thrymi would raise the castle out of a downpour, and on other occasions they didn't bother. It was only slaves working in the rain, so why should they? But this time... the creature they had killed was simply too big.

It was a garish purple, mottled with green. At that size it probably didn't have to worry too much about being seen... except by Thrymi. Augustus wondered what they could possibly plan to do with such a thing.

The answer, as he soon found out, was to sling it under the

cloud-castle and cut it up. Well, not cut it up themselves, the slaves cut it up.

There was a fair amount of meat on the creature. Not nearly as much as its size would suggest, but still a lot.

They got to it by jumping down from the castle gates, opened for the occasion, and down onto the slippery hulk, armed with knives and bags and ropes. The green proved to be some sort of slimy vegetation, that some of his fellow slaves cut and shoved into their pockets or shirts. Augustus did the same, because they were. Pelous yelled at them to get a move on. Augustus was still able to observe that the enormous structure under the cloud-castle was remarkably like that which supported the aircars.

When they were directly under the structure, Pelous pointed two of the larger slaves to a spot which they attacked with axes. The hide of the creature was plainly – by the number of blows required, tough. And then, suddenly, they were through, and then... Augustus wasn't quite prepared for this – a bubble popped out. Well, it looked like a bubble. It came out with venting gas and then more bubbles, about the size of two men. One of the slaves poked one with his knife and it hissed and whizzed away. Pelous hit him with the whip. "Stop that! We don't want to start no fires, you fool. We'll all die."

Ah. So, they were full of hydrogen? Thought Augustus. This skywhale was a kind of living dirigible, then. A potentially very explosive one!

He filed that information away in his head, marvelling at the biological wonder of it. They continued to cut, slowly in through the hide... which, as Augustus found, taking his turn, was indeed incredibly tough. Slowly, they cut a cross into it, allowing the filmy gasbags to escape in greater numbers. And then they slithered down into the body of the beast.... which there wasn't a lot of.

The whole thing was a vast gasbag, with a series of muscular double sphincters around the lateral margin, and gut and a mouth. They had to wade through hundreds of slimy nodules three times the size of a fist, that littered the gut-snaked cavity. His task took him to a huge, almost papery protrusible mouth, the muscles of which Augustus found himself designated to cut out. He wondered what his father or grandfather would have said about this pastime. His grandmother would have been horrified at the state of his clothes, and he suspected his father would have been designing machines to do the flensing, and his grandfather organizing the people and the machinery. And his older brother Charlie? Charlie would have been making comments about 'what a gasbag' and wondering if he could increase the creature's speed of travel with a diet of baked beans.

Augustus instead found himself wondering if the creatures could be harnessed and used to fly the slaves back to the Trading Plate... or at least, away from the Thrymi. He was aware of the statistical improbability of getting back to the Trading Plate with no form of navigational aid. They could, possibly, see it from some miles away. Or they could lose it in a drift of cloud when it was close enough to touch. Even seen from miles off, the sheer vastness of Sybil's skyscape made the oceans of Azure seem tiny. And on Azure... at least you had the stars and sun to navigate by, and the problem was largely one of two dimensions. Here... it was a reference-less three. Yet... it seemed outbackers survived out here, with nothing but drifts of skyfrond. He could see how the skywhale worked, staying aloft, and at a guess, the skyfrond must operate in a similar fashion. He'd like to understand precisely how, though. How did they maintain a level, even, more or less?

That still remained a mystery. A mystery he was to have several days to think over, as once the muscle meat from the skywhale was cut away, and the remains freed from the harpoons and allowed to fall into the abyss, there was lttle else to do. The cloud-castle seemed to drift into an area in which – although the Thrymi still flew out hunting, game was sparse. The slaves cleaned the slaughter deck. Scrubbed equipment... and got, it seemed, increasingly nervous. Oh, and Augustus found out that the green slimy plant cut off the skywhale was an abortificant, and the women slaves were very puzzled as to why he'd collected it. "Cause they're sure you're not a

Sheila, 'cause you've got a beard, see," said Briz, who was plainly still too young to grow one. Briz seemed to find the entire matter hilarious. Augustus hadn't precisely planned to grow a beard himself, but his razor was still back in his Dire-bull hide case, along with his flannel pajamas. He missed the pajamas. Now that the beard was established, it had stopped itching, and it meant an end to his fights with razor-rash. That was one of the few aspects of this part of his expedition to Sybil that wasn't a little chafing at the moment.

The slaves seemed to draw apart from him. He didn't understand it. Yes, the language was a bit different and still somewhat incomprehensible. And yes, he wasn't... yet, doing much to uplift them, let alone liberate them, which he had decided by now, was really what needed doing. But it would be quite a task, without any support... and they would barely speak to him. It hadn't got better... as the Blue Men tutorial had said it would. Instead it had got worse. He was working so hard to do his share and a bit more, too.

He resolved to ask Briz just what he was doing wrong, the next chance he got on their evening expeditions. He'd spent most of the last two studying what he was now sure were workshop manuals. The diagrams had terms, and at least some of those he recognized... but oh, what he'd do for a decent workshop and tools and testing equipment! Even a decent multimeter... he was thinking of how to make do, when things came to a head, suddenly. The fliers had just come in, and the hunt had obviously been dismal, by the scant four Jumbuck, five shonk and a Yester offloaded. Most of the fliers had nothing at all in their load-beds.

Briz had told him the Thrymi got bad-natured... well, even worse natured, when the hunting was bad. Then they would take it out on the strongest slave. But of course, that wouldn't be him. He wanted to help whoever it was.

CHAPTER

TWELVE

Briz had been bracing herself for trouble. She knew the rest of the slaves were aware of the danger, but she was even more than most. They were all as jumpy as fleas... if the Thrymi ran out of things to kill and hunt... she'd heard what happened next. Her Mister Gus, though, he didn't have a clue. She didn't know how to tell him. She didn't even know why she still thought he was hers... she'd never see a penny of that sweet remittance money from Azure. She'd be lucky if she saw the Big Syd again. And most of the women thought they sneaked out of the dorm to root, and that the whale-sludge was for her. Huh. He still called her 'lad' all the time.

He was blinder than blind Freddy. Didn't even know that he'd put on muscle. And he was taller and bigger than the others were. He still hadn't worked out that no-one else flung themselves at the hard yakka like a mad bunyip on crazyweed. It was making the other slaves pissed, because maybe one of the Thrymi would notice, and demand they worked just as hard. The slaves were expecting trouble, and hoping for it. It would get rid of him.

And now the Thrymi bastards were going to kill him, slow. The way they liked it. And there was bugger-nothing she could do about it. You didn't fight Thrymi. That just made them even meaner. It wasn't like you were going to win. Not even the Zell did.

So, when it all went pear-shaped, she wasn't going to do nothing, because there was nothing she could do. She had the slaves buffaloed thinking she was on top, but without getting the Thrymi to think so. Pelous was still keeping a long way away from beating either of them. She just had to keep her head down, and maybe escape when they got back to the Big Syd.

Yeah. Planning. It always worked so well with Mister Drongo around.

They came down in a bunch of five. The females, who were from what Briz knew, the nastiest of the Thrymi. Slim, elegant, in the form-fitting shimmery clothes the Thrymi loved, walking like they owned the place and were going to kill someone. They had the last part right, thought Briz, backing quietly into the shadows next to the rope the carcasses were being hung on to bleed out as much as still possible. Mister Gus was lifting a shonk up, alone, when the lead female of Thrymi strutted up to him and said, in fluting human. "Strong slave. I take you. See if you strong enough for Thrymi woman."

The others sniggered. Mister Drongo, still holding up the shonk... didn't run. Or cower. He just said: "No, thank you."

Briz had the satisfaction of seeing the Thrymi woman's mouth fall open. "You say no!" she slashed out a thin-clawed hand, "I cut..."

Gus pulled away, which kind of wasn't going to help... unless he dropped the shonk. Which he did. On top of her. She fell over like... like someone skinny who got a shonk twice their size dropped on them.

There was a moment's silence, and then a gasp of horror from the slaves, and a hiss of rage from the other Thrymi females.

"Oh. I am so sorry," said the drongo, pulling the shonk off her. Her shimmery clothes were a mess of shonk-blood and cutting floor debris. She sat up, looking dazed, and the drongo moved to give her a hand up. He was totally unaware that the other four Thrymi were stalking towards him. Without knowing quite why she did it, Briz reached up and cut the rope.

That did an even better job of knocking Thrymi over with a shower of carcasses. Well, three of them. The rope was tied pretty high to allow for sag under a lot of weight, so when it fell, it swung. What the carcasses didn't get, the rope slung between them sent sprawling.

The first Thrymi female lunged up off the ground at Gus, reaching towards him, and fell over the shonk, and slithered past on her face, shrieking. Meanwhile one of the four had pulled out a sidearm and fired... completely missing because Briz threw her gutting knife. It wasn't balanced very well, and it hit the Thrymi hilt first, on the side of the head. She pitched forward and the discharge of the weapon wasted itself in a mauve flare, turning the shonk into a mass of smoke. That made two of the remaining Thrymi, struggling free of the carcasses and rope, turn on her. The third was still under the shonk.

She dived right as one fired. That left her in the corner, with no place to run, and the second taking a bead on her, while the first reloaded. That, it seemed, was a mistake on their part. One of them should have watched her Mister. Because even a drongo who can lift a whole shonk above his head, can pick up two little Thrymi by the scruff of the neck and throw them. And not just throw them, but fling them at the offal chute, which was good and slimy with shonk guts. "You leave Briz alone, you bullies!" he shouted.

He pulled the Shonk carcass off the remaining downed Thrymi.

"Behind you!" yelled Briz as the blood and offal-drenched screaming bushpig of a Thrymi that had started it all charged at him. Augustus spun on his heel, still holding the shonk.

That swung too, the carcass hitting the still groggy-but-raging-for-the-kill Thrymi pack leader like a heavy bat hitting a ball, and bunted her into the offal chute too.

Looking up she saw that the outbackers had taken the chance and were scrambling up the wall as best they could, in manacles. The alarm had not sounded. The rest of the Plate-born slaves were huddled, terrified, screaming, in a corner of the courtyard. Two Thrymi were down, unconscious if not dead. Three were stuck down the offal chute. That, thought Briz, sadly didn't lead straight out into the sky. The outbacker slaves might have taken a chance on that. Instead, two levels down there was a grid that couldn't be opened from the inside.

Briz wondered where the rest of the Thrymi were, and why they hadn't come down. They had to have heard the screaming. Then she got it. They'd be coming down if the screaming stopped for too long, because Thrymi having fun with the slaves involved a lot of scream-ing. Fortunately, the bunch in the chute were doing well. You couldn't hear what they were yelling, but they were doing a lot of it. She tossed the yester carcass at the chute, to give them something new to yowl about and trotted over to her Mister. He was examining the downed Thymi. Not cutting their throats, which was what Briz thought would be a good idea. She scooped up a handful of knives from the sharpening bay, and, on the way, a Thymi pistol. She had no idea how it worked or if it did... but it might be useful. "Mister Gus. We gotta get out of here."

He looked at the fallen Thrymi. "I think this one may be dead. I didn't mean it! You don't think we can just explain?"

"Not in a bleeding million years. And too right they meant it, even if you didn't. They were going to kill you."

The silly drongo blinked. "Oh! I suppose they were. I really am unsure about what I should do now."

"Get out of here, before the rest of them come down," she said briskly.

"But... the other slaves. Do you think I should lead them to over-throw the rest of the Thrymi?" he asked, like it was possible.

"Look at them, Mister. They're frightened spitless. They couldn't fight their way out of a paper bag. And we got lucky, 'cause them Thrymi wasn't expecting trouble. We got to get away."

"Well... do we try and take the other slaves with us?"

"The outbackers have gone, and as for this lot... Yer can ask 'em." She spat. "They won't do nothing."

He did. And she was wrong. They did do something. They ran away, back into the dormitory. Screaming. Someone slammed the door. "I reckon," said Briz, "We better scram."

"Er. How... or where?" he asked.

"Yer said that the place to learn to fly one of the fliers wasn't while they was falling," said Briz.

"Yes."

"I kind of think it might be the only place we're going to get a chance."

He nodded. "Let's go, then."

So: they ran below, down the flights of stairs that took them to the flier deck and its launch-portals. She expected him to jump into the first one, but instead he fiddled with a piece of its undercarriage. The cowling dropped open just like on the one up on the stand – just not as far because it wasn't on its stand. "Give me a knife please," he said, so she did. She had seven. Six would have to be enough. She thought he was going to cut something, but he threw the knife instead. He couldn't throw for toffee, but it made a bang and sparks, before it fell to the ground, a chunk burned out of the blade. Maybe six wasn't enough... but he used the same knife on the next, and the next. By the time he got to the fourteenth, the knife was more like a metal stick, and was pretty hot –he was using a scrap of rag to hold it. And then the Thrymi came clattering down the stairs, yelling. "Up into this one, Briz," said Mister Gus. "Let's hope I can make it fly." And he hurled the remains of the knife at the first Thrymi down the stair, and jumped up into the seat next to her, and pulled the canopy down, as the Thrymi boiled onto the flight-deck, running towards them.

"I think it is this button." He pressed one of the more worn buttons. With a bang, a harpoon shot out. The running Thrymi came closer, and an incandescent purple bolt hit the next flyer. "Try this one..." The machine began to hum and vibrate. Then he pulled a lever, and it began to wobble forward. That was when Briz decided that maybe just running around the castle until they got shot was a good idea. Well, as the little flier lurched over the edge, and fell like a bag of guts dropped from the Black Stump. It wasn't flying unless you counted straight down as flying.

Briz panicked. Could she jump? She clawed at the transparent cover to the cockpit. Looking out, she was too late for that. Curiously, the drongo wasn't panicking. He was experimenting with the buttons and levers. He pulled and prodded, and suddenly the flier gave a rushing leap forward.

The next few moments —which seemed like a long time to Briz, but couldn't have been, were spent in a wild twisting, whirling series of bounces and plummets, loop-the-loops and falling spirals as the drongo worked at it. They'd fallen a long way, but now he was slowly and mostly in control, wobbling upwards in a slow curve.

Her Mister Gus had somehow done it!

Her relief was short-lived. The man from Azure was too busy working out how to fly the Thrymi craft to be paying much attention to anything else – like the cloud-castle that appeared through a mist of cloud-shreds off to her right. The castle's Thrymi might have been just as surprised to see them, but Thrymi were used to thinking fast and shooting faster.

"They're shooting at us," yelled Briz.

He yanked the steering triangle and a patch of Skyfrond burst into explosive puffs of flame a few yards from where they would have been in a blast of purple incandescence. The little flier leapt like a stunned jumbuck having a knife stuck into it.

They zoomed upwards as violet rays streaked all around them.

For a brief moment Briz actually thought they might get away. Then the flier shuddered as one of the stubby wings flared into molten slag.

They kept flying. Sort of. If spinning counted – but they were getting further away into dense cloud and then... into dense skyfrond. That didn't help, but they did spin out the other side of it.

Briz got a brief glance down through a cloud-gap at the castle – now distant and far below them, when they smashed into another thick drift of skyfrond. The last thing Briz remembered was that her head hit something.

Augustus had the steering triangle to cling to – and it wasn't so much a sudden high-speed dead stop, as an elastic loss of forward momentum. He still gave himself a few nasty bruises, and lost contact with the drive lever. That was probably a good thing because they came to a stop in the tangle of skyfrond. The flier was on its side, making odd crackling noises.

They were falling, along with it, down into denser cloud. Briz was unconscious, bleeding from a head wound. Like all head wounds it bled generously. Not knowing quite what to do next, Augustus tried to examine it, to see if he could do anything. They were falling to a gravity-crushing death, but... he couldn't just do nothing. None of the controls responded. The little flier hung, dead, in the skyfrond.

So: he thought he might as well try first-aid. He wasn't sure why, but that was all he could do, so he did it. He used one of the knives that Briz was still clutching wrapped in a bundle in a piece of shonk-hide, to cut away some of the fine straight black hair. It was less of a wound than he had feared, and the lad groaned as he held a pad made from a piece of his shirt to it. The little cabin was plainly pres-surized – which would keep them safe for a while, until the external pressure got too much, but the air in it already felt a little stale. He sighed: So much for his ambition of helping the people of Sybil's Plate to a better life. All he had done was to bring one of them to their death.

By now the atmosphere out there would be crushing. Well, no one really knew much about what the surface of Sybil looked like or even was made of. All he'd been able to read about it was theoretical. That theory held that there was serious volcanism down there, sending material up into the stratospheric cloud, to provide the minerals that the airborne plants needed. He wondered if the cockpit of the doomed little flier would hold out long enough for him to see it. Mind you, under all the cloud it would be very dark – unless the lava glowed red... at least the vegetation seemed to have stopped the whirling plummet of their first fall from being repeated. It had got relatively dark by the end of that.

It occurred to him that it wasn't actually getting any darker. It was sort of like late twilight – but fronds might have caused that. Briz opened an eye. "What's happening? Me head..."

"You may as well keep it still, Briz. We crashed. We're falling."

"Don't feel like I am. What's gonna happen?"

"The cockpit will cave in and we'll die."

"Oh." The lad cautiously felt at his head. "In that case, any chance of a butcher and a mystery bag? Seeing as we got nothing to lose."

That attitude kicked Augustus out of his shock. "Well, not here. Let me see if this craft can be restarted." He tried the various buttons and levers, again getting no response. "I am going to have to go outside. I don't know if we'll be able to breathe out there. I don't think I can close the cockpit fast enough to make any difference. So... um, Briz. It's been an honor to have known you."

Briz looked at him. "Me? Yer as daft as a brush, Mister Gus. Come on... let's see what we can do."

It proved a great deal harder than either of them thought, because the mass of skyfrond was tangled around the flier. Once they cracked the seal on the cockpit some air did rush in. It was thick and moist but not unbreathable. But that was as far as they could get right now. They had to stick a knife-blade out and cut frond by frond to make enough of a gap to climb out of. Looking at the fronds closely – there was little choice, they were that tightly tangled— Augustus could see it was like a string of huge beads, little tough bladders strung together. The stuff was remarkably strong and hard to cut – but trapped in the tangle their choice was to cut or stay put.

It was his plan to open the undercarriage panel and see if he could spot anything wrong. Getting there was going to take some cutting. Was it worth the effort, as they fell? Well, one had to do something, he supposed. And the air, while noticeably thicker than in the cloud-castle, was still breathable. Obviously, the buoyancy of the tangle of sky-frond was slowing their fall. But the reality of the gas laws said the extra weight of the crashed flier – and his weight and Briz's weight, would have started a process, where, with extra pressure, the lift from the little bladders would be reduced, which in turn would lead to the frond sinking into a deeper pressure well, which in turn...

He knew he didn't have much time. Once he'd managed to force open the panel he also knew that didn't matter. Even in the dimness he could see the mess in there was going to take far more than a knife to fix. A workshop, a full set of tools, and a workshop manual might still be too little. He turned to break the grim news to Briz.

Briz wasn't there. There was a cut tunnel of fronds though, so Augustus followed it upward. The vegetation soon got thinner and there were fewer cut fronds to follow – but it was distinctly lighter. The vegetation wasn't all the same either – obviously different plants competing for the light, cheerfully using each other as ladders to get there. Climbing a bit more on the bending fronds Augustus heard Briz... only it wasn't Briz. It was three or four small scampering creatures, happily foraging. They darted off through the fronds, seemingly unworried by the fact that this drift of skyfrond was going to fall. They didn't like Augustus's sudden appearance, and neither did Briz, who had been trying to creep up on them. "I thought we could at least have some tucker," said Briz. "Them potamroos are good eating. I had a couple at the Black Stump, one time."

"I can't fix the flier. I'm afraid we're in trouble."

Briz shrugged. "Mister, yer been in trouble since yer got here. We just seem to get deeper into it. So... I figure we better eat. Let's see if we can find them potamaroos again." So, wanting any other course, they did. It was quite difficult, but by the time they had snagged one

– and Augustus had been bitten by it, he had started to make plans on how to do it more easily, next time. And he'd come to the conclusion that there might even be a next time, because as they were hunting, the skyfrond tangle rose slowly out of a cloud. Either the clouds were sinking or the skyfrond was rising.

Then came the problem of what to do with a potamaroo once they'd caught it and dispatched it. "Eat it," said Briz, when Augustus asked.

"Er. Raw?"

Even Briz looked a little taken aback at that. "Must be some way o' cooking it, Mister Gus."

Augustus had worked out by now that when Briz called him 'Mr Gus' he was supposed to solve problems. This, on the damp drift of frond was going to be as much of a challenge as getting the flier going. And even supposing he could make a fire – those bladders on the plants must be full of hydrogen – not ideal for having naked flames too close to. "Let's go back to the flier and see what we can find," said Augustus.

That proved harder than either had guessed. The floating plant tangle had no real distinguishing landmarks and all looked very much the same. Yes, there were different plant-types – including broad, flat leaves which had little ponds in them – and little fish in those ponds, as Augustus found out when he tried drinking from them. Drinking live whitebait was less appealing than eating it fried.

Eventually they stumbled on the cut tunnel and made their way back to the flier. Augustus began to review his options for fire-making... rubbing two sticks together worked best if one was a match. A flint and steel and striking sparks was another challenge best undertaken with either a flint or steel. A fire-bow might be do-able, if they could find something dry enough to burn, a cord and a bow... The basic building block of civilization –fire—was more complicated than he'd realized, here, drifting around the sky of Sybil.

Still, it had not been attacked by a Thistlewood before! Several hours later he had contrived a bow from bound thicker stems of skyfrond, and, with a harpoon rope, now had enough cord for a hundred, and a stout barbed spear. Dry kindling came from under the pond-plant leaves, hardwood from the ornamental trim in the flier, and softwood from a piece of rotten frond, and the panel-cover as a fire plinth... and from an impatient Briz, slivers of raw potama-roo. It wasn't – once he got past the idea – too bad. He had all the requisites to make a fire. What he didn't have was fire. But he kept working at it.

The tangle of frond was definitely still rising, and they spent some time in thick cloud... and then eventually came out above it into the full glare of Sybil's sun, only dimmed by the thin exosphere veil. The air was thinner and cooler up here, but the sun, hot. Looking across the clouds Augustus could see other drifts of skyfrond , almost like hazy green-red clouds themselves, spreading across to the far horizons. And in the far distance, a cloud-castle – not a spiky, ethereal Thrymi one, but the squatter shape of a Zell castle. There was a flight of yesters, and a solitary shonk and – feeding on the edges of the next skyfrond drift, a large mob of jumbuck.

Patience and repeated trying eventually got a curl of smoke from the firebow. And where there was smoke, there was fire... which promptly went out, but at least with proof of concept, it was worth doing twice. The whole idea of fire on a hydrogen lifted structure still made him nervous... but surviving without fire seemed unlikely. Besides, Briz said she'd never heard of drifts of skyfrond burning up – which might or might not be relevant.

Now they had fire, but nothing much to cook on it. "Yer should have got it going sooner," said Briz. "And it is hot enough up here in the sun to cook without it anyway."

That was true. The Plate was high in the cloud-layer, and did see some sun, but it was fleeting. Here, above the cloud, the air might be thinner, but the sun was fierce. "We're going to need hats at this rate. And I need something to drink. I'm going to find one of those ponds and try not to drink any whitebait. I just need to make sure I can find my way back here. Then we'll have to go hunting again."

"Better take the harpoon. If yer meet a shonk you'll need it. And a lot of luck. Maybe I should come with yer..."

"Someone has to tend the fire. And this way I can call out to you for directions if I get lost."

Augustus knew he was making excuses, but he wanted time alone to think. The trouble was there was just so much he did not know. The drift of skyfrond was a couple of dozen acres in extent. Could they survive here? Why hadn't it continued to plunge into the pressure well below them? Could he ever return Briz to the Plate? Would he ever see Azure again?

Soon he realized that he had a more immediate problem: and not just how to avoid drinking whitebait. There were no whitebait to be seen. There was no water in the little leaf-ponds either. The bottom surface of them was spongy... but dry. Of the transparent little fish there was no sign. He did frighten several other small creatures – some into flight, and some into scurrying into the undergrowth of skyfrond. There was certainly a fair amount of life here, but was it enough to sustain them, even if they could find water?

Searching brought him no closer to finding the water, but did let him catch another potamaroo – mostly because when he sat down, it crawled under him and started to try and eat him. He had to hope the bite wasn't toxic, as he took it back to Briz.

Briz was asleep, but the little fire still had some warm coals and Augustus coaxed it back to life, and then set about dealing with the problem of how to cook the potamaroo, with no pan or grid or any way of supporting it while it cooked. So far he had found no type of skyfrond that was rigid enough on its own to be a stick to hold the weight. Besides, the idea of sticking hydrogen bladders in the meat above an open flame might not work well.

Civilization from next to nothing was a great deal harder than Kabongo's SELF-SUFFICIENCY had made it sound. The theoretical requirements – depending on the environment, were water first, food next, and then shelter... and tools and workshop manuals a little further down the list – and an awful lot of the most ingenious solutions in Kabongo's book depended on being able to get things like ten-penny nails or resin or a pot. Well, he had some knives, thanks to Briz, and a harpoon and some strong cord. That was what he had, so would have to do. The harpoon made an adequate spit. While it was cooking, Augustus set about weaving himself a hat from some of the thin, flexible strands of skyfrond. Or maybe he thought looking at it critically, a basket. It was hard to tell, and depended on which way up it was, and whether he put it on his head. He made a slightly better one for Briz, with the benefit of a little more practice, and kept turning the potamaroo. He'd better start keeping the skins, he thought. He wondered whether tanning would be possible.

The smell of the roasting potamaroo woke Briz. "Like the hat, Mister Gus. That smells good enough to eat. We got tucker. Yer find a beer-tree too?"

"No. Actually, all I found is that we have a serious water problem... Look out!"

It appeared that Briz wasn't the only one who thought that the roasting Potamaroo smelt good enough to eat. The shonk did too.

It might have been a better idea if the creature had not tried to swallow the entire thing on the harpoon. Or if it had tried to take it side on, or even from the butt end of the harpoon that Augustus was holding. But it bit down on the potamaroo on the metal shaft – with the blade and point already half way into its throat.

Augustus's first unthinking reaction was to try and pull the harpoon back – but the barbs and the shonk's bite stopped that. Then, perhaps the heat of the meat, or the cutting of the barbs from the pullback made it open its mouth.

Augustus thrust as hard as he could. The next few minutes were a time of confusion, and a lot more excitement and danger than he'd wanted. It did end up with a dead shonk and a live Augustus and Briz, even if they were bruised, shaken up and with added abrasions and no cooked potamaroo, or fire.

In a way it did confirm that unless the skyfrond was dry and dead, it was not flammable. That was the good thing, Augustus had to admit. And they had a shonk. It was, by the carcasses he'd handled, only a little one. It was still a lot of meat, and, potentially, a lot of materials for their survival.

The only downside Augustus could see with that was that they did not have a cloud-castle's freezer-space, or any other way of preserving it. No salt, no smoke in those volumes, and no pressure canning, and certainly no way of air-drying in this humidity. And nothing to drink, right now, and the adrenalin had left his mouth as dry as a desert.

In his indecision, Briz stepped up with down-to earth practical-ity. "Yer best get that spear out, in case its pimp comes looking for it." Briz cut its throat. "Let's see if we can bleed it out anyway. The meat's better for it."

The blood too was something that they might be able to use, but right now, Augustus saw no way of keeping it. He wondered about drinking it. But before he could put that thought to trial, something else came to do it instead. A potamaroo and then another. And then another. And then several more.

"They'll have our tucker if we let them," said Briz. "We'd better flense out what we want, quick."

So they did. It was fortunate, Augustus reflected, that they'd learned how to do that quickly and efficiently as slaves on the Thrymi castle or they would never have beaten the potamaroos to more than a mouthful. The noise too was terrific. Augustus soon realized the little creatures shrieked out their cry after finding the food – which seemed to draw the others in. And the potamaroo's ate – and drank the blood until – they were so belly-bulging they couldn't move.

They carried slabs of shonk down to the crashed aircar and stashed them in the rear locker. They had to do this one at a time so the other one could keep the potamaroos off the rest of the carcass. They'd skinned it all, cutting the hide as little as possible, as the

Shonk hide was hard on the knives. The skin itself seemed a bit too tough for the small creatures' teeth, but they gnawed the meat off the inside of it.

Augustus wondered what they'd do with all the meat – or what they'd do about water. The skin however gave him ideas. So did the gut, but he had no idea how to clean it, without water. Sausages – or as Briz put it, 'mystery bags' or 'snags', would just have to wait. Water – if they could find it – could be stored in the bladder – little though the idea appealed. Perhaps he could find something in the skyfrond to make do instead... if they could stand the thirst and blazing sun long enough. As he thought this, a patch of shade moved across them. Grabbing the harpoon, he looked up warily. It was not a flying predator. It was just a cloud barely above them. Would it rain? And then it occurred to him: earlier they had been above the clouds, looking down on them. Now the brightness of Sybil's sun was faintly obscured. It took Augustus a few moments to work out that the patch of floating skyfrond must slowly be losing height. Not knowing why it was doing that was a little worrying, but it did improve their chances of getting some rain.

Briz noticed too. "We're going down in the world, Mister Gus."

And so they were, but at least not fast.

They set about taking stock of what they had, because while being lost out here for the rest of their time seemed inevitable, death at least did not seem immediate. The engine had a fair amount of wiring, some of which was a melted mess. That, it appeared, was mostly from the main anti-grav drive. Augustus was reluctant to cut or damage any of it until he'd at least worked out how it all worked and what was usable. There were various panel covers, several more harpoons and several net-flingers... and a cabinet that held a number of things which had to be guns of an alien kind, and heavily orna-mented knives – obviously far too good to be used by mere slaves gutting the prey, but to be appreciated by the discerning Thrymi. The cabinet also held three flasks of what must have been the Thrymi's idea of a refreshing drink. Briz, on finding it, immediately snagged one, and opened it, tasted it and spat. "Bleedin' heck. I reckon someone peed in this." She spat again. "I thought at the least there'd be a bit o' gin."

Augustus's approach was a little more cautious, but he had to admit the smell was ammoniacal. He was reluctant to pour it out, in case it was useful, but they were containers at least. They were drifting through the cloud, which was clammy, if not raining. If it did rain, well, they could catch some of it. There were some kind of plasticized cover-cloth, for the transport bin of the fliers, and these they arranged into a catchment-bowl with some of the skyfrond to be a frame.

Augustus came up with the idea of tying up a half-dozen of the potamaroos before they managed to digest enough of their shonk-feast to stagger off into the undergrowth. By the time they'd done that – to the protests and attempts to bite from the captives, it started to rain, and Augustus was left to regret not spending the time on gathering dry fuel.

Over the next while, Augustus worked out just how the skyfrond tangles worked. The masses of frond rose and fell – as the plants needed water. Lower down, below the cloud-base, rain was almost a certainty. When everything was utterly sodden, it would start to rise again, going to the sun – unless of course the frond got caught in a storm. Then, while the plants did compensate, the winds and air currents took the plant mass where it would, and both tore the mass of fronds apart – and pushed them together

CHAPTER
THIRTEEN

B riz was beginning to wonder if she should, just maybe, have paid a little more attention to the drongos and losers who drifted into civilization from the skies beyond the black stump. As a Plate-born Big Syd kid she thought of them as the stuff you scraped off your shoes after walking down the back alley behind the pub. And there, maybe they were. Out here it was a bit different. Still, maybe Mister Gus's luck would continue. It was hard to see how, seeing as there wasn't anyone trying to put one over him here, and assuming he'd think and behave like they did. Huh. She never knew quite what he'd do next, except it wouldn't be what they expected, or what she expected.

He'd been burrowing around in the engine of the flier... she still half-expected him to get it going again and fly them back to the Plate – which, given that he never did what she thought he would, probably wasn't going to happen. So far, he'd made a cage for the potomaroos, a rain cover for the cut skyfrond he kept dry and a flagpole so they could find the aircar easily. He'd also lashed the aircar in place, around a lot of skyfrond, after the first storm had made it shift around.

The inside of the pilot's cab they'd adapted somewhat to make for a comfortable place to catch a bit of shut-eye – after the second shonk. There were worse things out there, like herbeens, but that incident had put the fighteners up them. That had been after they'd had a hard session of making a roof to keep the rain off, and had been working on weaving walls. They'd eaten, and settled in to sleep, and Mister Gus had been out like a light, when the shonk came through that 'wall' like it wasn't there.

Its first rush had, luckily, broken through the wall between them, and not onto either of their pallets. That was where the luck stopped. The shonk had turned and slashed at them with its huge tusks. Briz had woken up and had her little knife out, which was a mistake. It should have been at the very least the big knife or the harpoon, or one of the Thrymi guns. Her instinctive slash did little more than make it mad. The thrust of the harpoon from Mister Gus had saved her life. It didn't kill the shonk, and the shonk shook itself furiously, and sent Mister Gus flying through his own wall. The shonk decided that this was too high a price for a dinner, and went out through the third wall. The roof fell down.

Mister Gus had said it was a tribute to their building skills that it had stayed up that long. He hadn't been under it when it fell. She felt the best tribute would have been 'light'. She was still bruised from that. He'd come out with bruises, several cuts and abrasions, torn clothes and a missing harpoon that he was really angry about. One thing Briz had worked out by now was that on the rare occasions he got angry, Mister Gus was not the same guy as when he wasn't. Practice with the Thrymi guns had happened, right then. And now, they were always armed, and never both slept. One thing about Mister Gus, he didn't know much, didn't see what was in his face, easy, but when he did, he did learn.

"Coo-ee!"

Briz spent a few seconds thinking what kind of animal that was, before realizing it came from a human, if you could call an outbacker that.

There were a mob of five of them, and they didn't look happy to see her, and Mister Gus was back under the flier. The leader was a solid, hairy ocker with stick-out teeth and an expression that could curdle beer. "What are you swaggies doin' on my station? Get yer gear and get out of me paddock. We don't need no thieving swagmen on this place."

"We ain't thieving swagmen. We're..."

"Hello, gentlemen," said Mister Gus coming up behind her. "What seems to be the problem?"

"Yer the bloody problem. Bloody swaggies keep nicking me jumbucks," said the broad-shouldered man.

"Your bleeding jumbucks?" Briz demanded. "Ain't seen you about."

"'s my paddock. My jumbuck. Yer better not have touched 'em or I'll hang the pair of you. Search 'em and tie 'em up, boys."

"I don't think so," said Mister Gus, calmly lifting the Thrymi weapon to his shoulder. "I'll not have Briz tied up, or myself for that matter. We haven't touched your jumbuck – not because we didn't want to, but because we had not, as yet needed to. And were unaware they were yours. You're welcome to have a look."

"Bruce! That's one of them bastard Thrymi's guns. Back off, mate!" said one of them.

Then one of the blokes at the back of the mob, yelled. "My bloody oath! It's him! The bloke what we told yer about, Bruce. The one that was tossing Thrymi around like it was shearing time and he was getting through 'em in a hurry." He pushed forward. "I'd like to shake yer hand, big feller. I never seen anythink like it. We would never have got out of there without yer. Me name's Tiger." He stuck a callused hand out.

After this they got positively matey. Briz wasn't too sure she liked it. Bloody outbackers. Thinking about it, what she really didn't like was that this was their place, and she knew about as much about things out here as her Mister Gus had known when he blundered onto the Plate. It also seemed they didn't have a lot of respect or liking for the Big Syd. The drongos felt pretty much about them the way people from the Big Syd felt about outbackers.

Augustus had come up from the wiring, hearing voices, and, frankly, expecting trouble. Throughout his journey to Sybil III he had not expected trouble but kept finding it. He'd come to realize that he'd been a little naïve. So, this time he'd expected trouble and instead found a welcome. Found fascination with the idea that he'd come from Azure, interest in places that weren't the outback. None of them had ever seen the Plate, but they knew Zell and Thrymi skycastles, and loathed them. They were keen to explain their way of life to an equally fascinated Augustus.

"See, the station is these seven paddicks. This is the littlest one. We raise about three hundred jumbuck," explained Bruce, proudly. "'course there is lots more wild stock, and we rope a few for tucker. Hell to shear them though."

"So, are all the drifts of skyfrond... stations?" asked Augustus, doing a quick mental calculation on the size of Sybill, and running out of zeros.

"My bloody oath no!" said Bruce, laughing. "See, there's always paddicks being cleaned up by them Zell bastards, and new ones forming, and little 'uns not worth working, and the paddicks keep moving around in storms. Yer lose one every now and again, like this one. Seven's about all a feller can manage, and that'll take five-six jackaroos and a couple more at shearing time. I mean yer always got a few cockie-farmers with one maybe two paddicks cleared and more potamaroos than jumbucks. And yer always got bloody swaggies, moving around. Easier to nick a few tame jumbuck than to catch a wild one."

"You tame the jumbuck?" he asked.

"Too right. Yer lucky if you get within a half-paddick of a mob of wild ones. They fly off. Fly faster than we can drift. Yer got to get the little 'uns and hand-rear them. Now, we got to muster this mob and take them to long paddock. You gonna give us a hand and then come over for tea at the station?"

"We'd love to," said Augustus, enthusiastically. "But I have no idea of how to do any of this. I'm absolutely willing to try."

That made all of them laugh. "Had some joker from the Big Syd, once. Thought he'd show us how it was done! Well, yer can give it a go."

"Lead me to it!"

"Good-o, follow us. We can get the job done and get back to the station for tea."

"What do we do with our stuff, Mister Gus?" asked Briz.

"Aw, bring it with yer."

"Can't exactly do that, mate," said Briz. "It's a bit big."

"We have a Thrymi aircar," said Augustus.

"You've got what!?" said Bruce.

"A Thrymi aircar. Only it doesn't go anymore. I think I've just sorted the battery circuit, so we have lights and air-recirc. I could perhaps fix it if you have a full engineering workshop. I'll have to rebuild parts of it."

Bruce looked at him, looked at his men, looked at the two of them. Augustus noticed that Briz had quietly brought her Thrymi gun to bear on the group.

"Well, I'll be dipped in rancid skywhale shit!" said Bruce. "An aircar. In me paddock. Yer lucky that I'm an honest man, Gus."

"I'm sorry about your paddock. We didn't mean to damage it. We got shot by the Thrymi when we escaped in it. I couldn't fly it very well, it's a bit different to the aircars on Azure. It may never go again," admitted Augustus.

"Aw," said Bruce, expansively. "The paddock will grow again. And if you can't fly it, the boys and me don't have much hope, see. But it's a lot of metal, Gus. That's worth a bloody fortune, mate. I'll make you a good deal on parking it in me paddock. Unless yer want to move it over to me home paddock?" he said hopefully.

Briz laughed. "Yer let me dicker with this bastard, Mister Gus."

"Well, Briz..." said Augustus, slowly. "It's not strictly speaking my property. I mean it belongs to the Thrymi."

"Wages, Mister Gus. They owe us for all the hard yakka we done there. Besides the thieving, slaving bastards were out ter kill yer. And possession is nine tenths of the law, see. Those bastards think we ended up takin' the long fall. It's gone as far as they know."

"True, Briz. But anyway, I want to work with these gentlemen. It's great wealth for them out here."

"Be worth a lot back in the Big Syd too. If the bosses didn't get to hear about it. They'd kill yer, sure. They don't want their secrets or their weapons getting back to humans."

"Out here, they won't know. And I could perhaps do what I came here to do, lad. But that means I need to work on getting you back home to the Plate."

"Yer mean the Big Syd, Mister?" said one of Bruce's men. "Crook place that. We come close enough ter drop in a few years ago, and I thought I'd go and visit the big smoke. Bunch of Ned Kelly's, all of 'em. Lost me bleedin' shirt, and couldn't wait ter get out. Was lucky it got hooked up in some dense paddocks and I jumped off before the Zell cleared it all."

"I have a duty of care to my young assistant. It's Briz's home," explained Augustus. "It's an interesting place, but it is rather crowded and corrupt, I must admit. However, Briz wants to get back there. And Briz looked after me very well, there."

"Drift gets around there, every now and again. Yer see the spaceships coming in."

Augustus hadn't thought of that. From the cloud top that would indeed be visible a long way off. If nothing else it would give you an idea of direction. Plainly the outbackers had some way of moving between their 'paddocks'. So, he and Briz could move closer, paddock by paddock. It might take a long time, Augustus calculated. Then Briz surprised him. "I ain't in that big a hurry to get back there, Mister Gus."

B riz had surprised herself, when she said that. What would anyone want or do, out here beyond the black stump? It was all very well for outbackers, losers and drongos. Not for someone from the Big Syd! But they'd... take advantage of him. He needed looking after. She was a big sook. What good would it do her? On one hand she wanted to get back to civilization. On the other hand... maybe it would be a good idea to let the capos forget about her, and him, for a little while.

"Well, if you're sure," said Mister Gus. "I'd appreciate your help, Briz. You're a great help in understanding local custom."

"I ain't so sure about local custom here," said Briz. "Who do they sell to? But there's nothing someone from the Big Syd can't do better than anyone else."

That made the bloody outbackers laugh. "We'll see how yer go at drafting Jumbuck then, youngster."

Briz wondered what she'd got herself into. But all she said was: "Too right. Let's see what you jokers can do and we'll see if we can do better than yer." Backing down would be a sign of weakness.

She wasn't going to let these drongos show her up.

Some time later, bruised, kicked and dead tired, she wondered if stepping up was not a sign of being soft in the head. Mind you, she was doing better at it than Mister Gus, but he on the other hand, was having the time of his life. If the capos had to ask her if he liked girls or boys, she could tell them the bastard liked bleeding jumbuck. She was getting to the point of thinking the only good jumbuck was one with its tripes out and being roasted.

A ugustus had of course handled a fair number of silky-furred jumbuck carcasses since he'd seen one having its intestines hauled out at the black stump. Live ones, however, were another matter. The big difference with live ones was that they weren't keen to let you get your hands on them. They came close – right into the trap-funnel of nets that the jackaroos had set up when Big Bruce called on his whistle – a sort of trumpet-like device made of a shonk-spike. The boys pulled the closing net over, and then it was all in and catch the jumbuck and push them into the float – a cage of net over withies of fresh skyfrond with narrow channels in it – too narrow for the jumbuck to spread their wings.

It was something the old hands made look ridiculously easy. It wasn't. But he was, to his surprise, not too terrible at it. Yes, the outbackers were laughing at him, but they were cheering him on too. It was hard, but oddly, in a good way. And then it came to him: everyone was working just as hard. They might laugh at his ineptitude, and more when a jumbuck knocked him head over heels, but they respected hard work, and they expected hard work.

At the end of it, Augustus found the crew slapping his back and telling him he did good for a new boy. They seemed genuinely proud of his achievement, especially Tiger, who had plainly told the story about Augustus and the Thrymi females a few times, and been accused of pulling a raw prawn. The fact that Augustus and Briz were here, and had got away with a Thrymi aircar and weapons, he obviously felt proved his story.

The crew sat down and to Briz's delight – produced skin bags of beer. To Augustus's surprise he found he enjoyed it. He'd not done a lot of beer-drinking before coming to Sybil – none, really – but it was very much a part of life here. He was rather mystified as to why the bag was 'a stubby', but it was called that, and quite refreshing and cool it was too. They needed that, because work was not over for them yet. The next step was to pack up the nets they'd used to make the loading chute and move the cage which they called a float to the edge of the paddock. They couldn't have carried the sixty jumbuck in the float, but by lifting the edges and shaking they got the complaining animals to put their feet through the net-holes and waddle along, while the drafting crew carried the withy edges of the cage.

Bruce looked over the edge, clinging to a few skyfronds with with the casual attitude of someone who had done this all his life. "Reckon the paddock is close enough lads. Let's get them battens out, and we can get her over and down, and then we'll come back to see about the aircar. Sorry, but me Jumbuck come first."

"Er. Just what are you going to do now?" asked Augustus.

"Fly this mob over to the new paddock," said one of the crew. "See, the oatweed's all grazed up on this one. We need to sow again, get this paddock sorted, and ready for the weaners. Shearing time is coming up and we're gunna be flat out like a lizard drinking, soon.

"How do they fly... do we let them out again?" asked Briz.

They laughed at this. "Yer reckon on getting a stubby every time, do yer? Na, we just pulls the battens out and they flies inside the float. Not very well, but well enough not to hurt 'em landing. We just steer it along."

"Bruce," said Tiger, suddenly. "I just thought..."

"Don't do that, Tige, yer brain'll catch fire. What deep insight have yer got?"

"Well, see, them from the Big Syd don't jump fronds. Do yer Azure people do that?"

Bruce turned to Augustus. "Well, do yer? Or do yer just stay put like them Syd folk? Never go jumpabout?"

"Er. I have no idea what jumpabout means. Do you, Briz?"

Briz shrugged. "Them outbackers come to the Big Syd for a bit, and then go jumpabout."

"What does it mean?" asked Augustus.

"I dunno. Maybe they jump onto a bit of skyfrond. Like the outbacker-slaves on the Skycastle did to try and escape."

"More or less," said Tiger, with a grin. "Never understood how those drongos in the Big Syd stayed put like that."

"If yer haven't done it before, it's going to take a bit of getting used to. Kids here start young," said Big Bruce. "Yer better hang onto the float. Right boys, let's get them battens out."

The battens were double walls of net that kept the jumbuck from spreading their wings. As soon as those were out, the jumbuck were trying to fly and the float started bumping and jumping with their effort as they strained against the roof-net. Bruce yelled: "Grab hold! Hang on tight."

To Augustus's surprise, each of the men sprouted a bubble from their backs – a personal balloon as it were. And then grabbing the sides of the float, they shoved it over the edge. It fell, like a stone... but a stone in low gravity. And the clinging men steered it, using their bodies as airfoils. The distance to the next rising drift of skyfrond was not particularly great and they crash-landed on it. The surface tangle gave beneath them, and then slowly rebounded. Bruce and the crew were deflating their bubbles. "Welcome to me station, Gus, Briz," said the outbacker with a broad, proud smile. "She's a bonza place, eh?"

It was visibly quite different from the wilderness they'd left, in terms of vegetation at least. There were rows of wiry pale green vegetation, plainly planted, interspersed with tall lines of woven skyfrond – still living, and growing with more layers of a purple-leafed frond – which Augustus had seen growing along the edges of the drift of skyfrond-tangle. Over the top was more netting. One of the men pulled the ties holding closed the Jumbuck in, and instead of making a dash to escape, the fliers scrambled into the nearest aisle to get to the purple fronds. Once they were in, a wicker gate was closed on them.

"Well, that's done," said Big Bruce. "Now, a bit of tucker, and we can talk about getting yer ship to the station."

They followed along to what Big Bruce called 'the station'.

It was worthy of a train, Augustus decided. The inverse of the buildings on the Plate, this sprawled – a single story, with broad verandahs all made of skyfrond – as much of the Plate that wasn't made of metal scrap was – but this was neat and fresh with patterns plaited into it. The station rang with cheerful voices, ran with children and smelled of cooking.

Augustus felt like he'd come home... to a place he'd never been, but had always been looking for, without knowing he was looking for it.

CHAPTER

FOURTEEN

Briz's first reaction to the station was that she'd never seen an easier crib to crack. Her second thought was that that would do you a fat lot of good. Where would you go with anything you prigged? And her third thought was that the food smelled even better than the Black Stump. Maybe it was just a long time since she'd had any decent tucker.

It was decent tucker. She'd never thought she'd appreciate a meal that wasn't entirely meat, and this was long on that, but it'd been a while since she'd last had a pie. Maybe she'd had better pastry. But this was good, and in the Big Syd, there was a lot more gravy than meat and the meat was something you didn't want to ask too many questions about. This was a lot of meat, stuck together with a little gravy, and you could taste and identify the meat. And there was beer – which had to improve any meal, as far as she was concerned. And the people were friendly, and curious.

The other thing that took her aback was they gave her... respect? She was just Briz, petty thief, pick-pocket and, back in the Big Syd... not the bottom of the pile, but fighting her way not to be. Here... she was someone. Someone who had been further than most – people knew of the existence of the Big Syd. One or two people had even been there, or so they claimed. But few had been – and escaped alive – Thrymi prisoners, let alone made the bastards suffer. She was getting quite a lot of the reflected glory from Mister Gus's exploits. They even had – thanks to Mister Gus telling them, as well as what Tiger had seen, some idea of exactly what she'd done. He made out like she'd done most of it. She had to tell them he was pulling a raw prawn on them.

Back in the Big Syd, people kind of accepted the Thrymi and Zell. Didn't love the bastards, but they were the bosses of the place. Yer had to live with them, because yer couldn't really get away from them. Out here... they loathed the bastards, and, a fair amount of the time, from what she could gather, did get away from them. They kept track of the sky-castles as best they could, and avoided them, as best they could, which was better than anyone in the Big Syd could say.

As for this 'station': Some bits of the place were as rough as guts, but to be honest it was a lot more comfortable than her crib, and not what she'd expected at all. It wasn't as good as the Big Syd for entertainment or variety of booze... but compared to being slaves, or even trying to make a go on their own, luxury.

But... she had to admit she'd kind of liked having Mister Gus to herself. That, it seemed wasn't going to be true anymore. The outbackers wanted him. Not wanted him gone, like the Capos and that nasty piece of work Pinchbutt, and his mates. That all seemed... very far away. In another world, almost. Not real, out here.

The oddest thing, to her, was the idea that, if she learned how these blokes went jumpabout, she could spot a starship and blooming walk home... or not. If she wanted to. That was how outbackers drifted in and out the Big Syd, other than the poor blokes the Zell caught and dropped there. They cut them so they'd never breed, before they let them go. The others though – they'd get there more often, if the Zell hadn't kept most of the skyfrond away.

Augustus was supremely happy. This was why he had joined the

Blue Men in the first place. Yes, he had discovered that many of the basic premises of the sociology and anthropology were, as far as he was concerned, intrinsically wrong. But these people... well, they took problems... and solved them. They were his kind of people.

"See," said Big Bruce. "It ain't like the Big Syd where someone else collects the massas, and most of yer meat comes in with the Thrymi. Out here we mostly have to do it ourselves. And if we can't do it, we have to make some kind of plan to make do. Now, about that Thrymi aircar. I reckon yer gunna need a few more men than I have got. Yer up for hiring a few? There's a few young fellers about the district."

Augustus opened his mouth to speak, and Briz put in, "Depends on the rate, see."

"Well, now," said Big Bruce with a grin. "Normal pay around here is for bed and tucker thrown in. You'll have to dicker with me for a good price, young 'un."

"Er. I don't have very much..."

"Shut up, Mister Gus," said Briz, equally cheerfully. "I got a brass razoo or two to lend yer."

So, Augustus found himself with three young jackroos and a jillaroo as employees for the interesting task of moving the wreck. "It's a big deal," said Bruce. "Somewhere up north there's a Thrymi castle that stopped being able to move, see. It just stays put. The Thrymi left in the aircars, and some fellers found it. Richest find ever, and they didn't get no guns or anything, just a place that's floating up in the sun – hot as, and the metal it's made of. We keep pretty quiet about it see, we don't want news getting back to the Thrymi that people are living there. It's not as big as the Big Syd, but yer can buy metal blades and the like from 'em. Now, this aircar, it's still a lot of materials. Things people want, even if they don't need. I'll get a good few more jumbuck, and the labor I need to improve me paddocks. So long as we don't get hit by Thrymi hunters or a Zell harvester we're good. Farming: It's hard yakka, but I wouldn't be dead for quids."

Augustus's understanding of the local argot had got better. These days he understood about half of what they said. But the important thing he had got was that somewhere there was a skycastle with a working – if faulty, antigrav. It might have tools too, if they hadn't all been sold or destroyed. Even similar manuals to those that he'd found on the other castle...

The effort to extract the aircar, and transport it, actually taught him a lot more about the society he'd landed in, what they had, and how they worked. Everyone, down to the young kids had come across to the paddock. He and Briz had been sold the strange 'bubble' backpacks that the outbackers used, along with a couple of the hard nodules of hydrogen from the skyfrond-bases. These could be twisted off to inflate the stretchy 'balloon' they blew into the bubble. It didn't make you lighter than air – they'd have had to be a lot bigger – but they did make 'skydiving' with the cloak membrane, spread over the arms and legs, that they all used – made of the light but very strong jumbuck wool – a task that wasn't just suicide and did allow some control of direction. Landing on the generally springy and quite yielding drifts of skyfrond, timing, distance and the relative rise and fall of the drifts made movement across the world of air possible. Enough of the stretchy balloons – which were yet another plant-product – could lift you, and one could travel as the clouds drifted at the mercy of the wind.

There was a lot more going on in the apparently simple life of these farmers than an outsider might guess. Kabongo's self-sufficiency didn't know half of it. That was still geared around the farmer being able to buy a nail. Here... they had to make the nail, and they didn't have metal, or a forge or a lot of hard surfaces or implements. Bone, and skin and plant material, and generations of learning and making do had evolved a whole society. They weren't needing his help as much as he needed theirs... but they still wanted his.

The hydrogen balloons were attached to the aircar and Augustus's painstaking tie-downs undone. The aircar had to be partly cut out of the fronds which were growing around it – and onto it, plainly trying to leach something from the metal with a sprawl of little tendrils. There must be something there that the plants needed or wanted. The shears they used were bone – with cutting teeth from yesters. Briz provided knives from their stock – to the delight and amazement of their new employees. "I want them bloody back, see," growled Briz. "And don't yer try telling me yer dropped 'em or nothink." Augustus noticed they handled them like holy relics – and used their own bone and tooth blades, when they had to do tough work. It took time, but gradually, the aircar was hauled up using pulleys and woven ropes, and pulled onto a net. More ropes, and then more ropes, were added. It looked like it had been trussed up by a very determined and large spider.

The timing was everything in this – the station had 'fooled' the plants into binding their hydrogen again by pouring out the water in all the water-pool pads, so having jumped one way, they were now ready to jump the other way. Every rope that could be spared had been thrown across and tied onto the station float.

"Why not just attach more balloons?" asked Augustus, as they emptied everything from the aircar that could be taken out.

"Wind," explained Tiger. "Yer can blow anywhere, real easy. Yer don't want to take that chance with this lot, Gus."

One wasn't really aware of the wind here on the skyfrond drifts, because they were moving at more or less the same speed as the wind, although one did feel gusts – but Augustus knew the winds were a major factor in the thermoregulation out here. One gust or stray updraft could catch the load and tear it away, and, although the 'balloons' were tough – it was apparently possible to have them rupture or explode. Augustus could see ways for things to go wrong – and in his life here, it seemed that usually happened.

Only, this time, it didn't. Even the bags loaded with the contents of the aircar arrived safe and sound.

The next few weeks were exciting and busy ones for Augustus or 'Gus' as everyone called him, and he eventually came to think of himself by that name. Briz had persuaded him into keeping the 'likely lads' on as assistants. Briz saw them as guards, even though Big Bruce said 'Bush-Rangers' were rare as, these days. Briz was not the trusting kind. "Look, yer want to teach 'em. Uplift them, like you say?"

"That's why I came here, Briz," said Augustus.

"Well, see, yer want them to stick around, yer have to make it worth their while, see. Just like yer pay me, see," Briz explained.

"Um. I don't know that I can, Briz. Pay you or them."

"Oh, yer good for it," said Briz expansively. "I'll wait. And I knows yer just want to just give it all away, but yer catch more potamaroos with bait than nothink. They'll come, they'll learn, they'll use what they earn to go and build their own stations, see. Those that don't waste it on a big blue. That's why Big Bruce has his son and bleeding daughter working for yer. 'cause he sees it a good go for them. Even if I think that sheila's just angling for yer," said Briz darkly.

It was odd to be popular and eagerly listened to – maybe actually sought-after, but the outbacker girls were... getting him quite used to women. He was beginning to wonder if maybe Briz not being such a constant companion might not have occasional advantages. Briz seemed determined not to let him find out though. The result was Briz becoming a better technician and learning more than the rest of the lads put together – not that they were doing badly, mind you. And he was learning a lot from them. They knew how to do things with the local materials. He didn't, but when shown... understood what could be done. And understanding why it worked, as well as just how, was a powerful lever. The Zell genetic engineers who had made the floating plant life were a long way past human achievement – they had made some kind of plant-grown membrane that wasn't easily crossed by hydrogen molecules, a plant that split, absorbed and bound and re-split hydrogen out of water – That alone was a treasure which would be worth a vast fortune, back on Azure. It would take a lot of chemists, biologists and electron microscopes to unlock that – and Augustus didn't have as much as a magnifying glass.

The biggest problem of the process of dealing with the aircar had been a sheer lack of tools — at least tools fit to work metal. A multi-meter would also have been golden too, but some parts of the electrical system were understandable — and he could work on those. The battery system had been as simple as any he'd encountered and had been what Augustus had banked on shorting out in the Thrymi aircars to stop them being pursued. That had provided great excitement when Augustus demonstrated it working — but short term he had no way of recharging it. Still, that gave him the material to make an electromagnet. And from there it was no big step to using some of the steel he had to make magnets. And from there a simple hand cranked generator...

The annoying thing is he could have made a fortune selling copper wire as jewelry in the same time it took to make a simple power generator. He did have some of the lads sawing away with the hardest thing they had — teeth from the various animals — at the sheet-metal of the cladding to make his first tools — little metal toothed saws to cut metal to make more tools. The process of cutting metal wasn't unknown — the foot-manacles from escaped prisoners had been painstakingly cut in the same way. The metal from them was very valuable out here.

Somewhere down the line there would be a forge, welding and metal cutting. The first 'products' were small knives, and they were quickly sold – which Briz handled. "We gotta pay wages, Gus."

That was true. And there were certainly willing buyers. He was glad of having plenty of labor to do the tasks he could have done with a plasma cutter in seconds, and an ordinary angle grinder in a minute or two. But out here everything had value — even the metal fragments and the dust being reused into making grinding materials.

His experiments in making a simple wet-cell battery were hampered at first by finding suitable acids and porous pots — he felt somewhat like he was re-inventing history – knowing what the reactions were, what was needed, and... being stuck without the materials on a tangled drift of skyfrond. The frustrating thing was knowing that so much he needed and could use was easily and cheaply available, back on Azure, and even the Cloud-castles and the Plate were treasure houses full of short-cuts... compared to where he was, building everything from scratch.

It wasn't, he discovered, the only problem the stationers faced. In fact, on the scale of things, not even a serious issue. Big Bruce came rushing into the workshop they'd built, "Look mate, can yer lend me yer lads? Got a Zell harvester spotted heading for round paddock. Gotta move the jumbuck. Lot of jumping to bloody get there. It's up and we're down."

"Of course!" said Augustus. "Briz and I will come and give a hand."

Big Bruce shook his head. "Thanks, but no. Gunna be tricky jumps. Upwards. We're going to kite up."

They used big kites of fine woven Jumbuck wool to lift the Jack and Jilleroos up to a level from where they could jump. A gust could fling the rider off like a rag-doll, or make them dive and twirl. Accidents happened. There wasn't much in the way of medical treatment out here.

When everyone had left, Augustus said to Briz, "I think we need to build a flier."

"Bit of an ask, Mister Gus. We can't even take this one apart," Briz said looking at him, askance.

"There are slightly less demanding forms of wings. Those bladder-plants – they grow in different shapes and sizes, don't they?"

"Too right," said Briz. "But the little ones are only good for kids to play with. They starts off curved and pretty flat, until they fill out."

"We might need those. We're going to need to buy some good Jumbuck weave, and some jumbuck wool cords." Jumbuck wool was remarkable stuff, with long fine strands, which produced a fabric more like silk than wool, and made remarkably strong cord. It could also be doped with some of the plant-gum to make a waterproof fabric, which was used to seal the roofs of the station. A family with a few Jumbuck and a paddock of skyfrond could, with the knowledge

174

of the generations spent living out here, come up with much of what was needed to live a reasonable life.

By the time the crew returned, tired, bruised and with one splinted suspected broken leg, Augustus had done the drawings for a simple inflated-cell parachute. A little more work would be needed to design a paraglider-lifting airfoil. It was met with more doubt, but also more understanding than he'd expected. The concept of a parachute was familiar enough. They didn't get used much, because the jump-bubble was similar. So was the idea of a balloon. Those were used, but the problem was that the wind could carry you – sometimes at the same speed and direction as the paddock, and sometimes not. They understood that concept – but the concept of a wing and directional flight was unfamiliar.

A few days later, when the prototype was ready, and Augustus took if for ground handling testing, half the population of the district had somehow heard about it and came to watch. The canopy inflated well but the paddocks were not easy to run on. And Augustus wasn't too sure he was ready for a jump over the edge yet. So, he compromised with a tethered balloon for a take-off point. The canopy was held open by woven withy. A shonk carcass did for a 'pilot'.

Augustus shortly learned several important things.

Firstly, that dead shonk make terrible pilots.

Secondly, when the paraglider collapsed into a spiral and the shonk crashed through the roof of the station he found out what 'copping a serve' meant. The women who had been watching certainly gave him one. Briz laughed until he couldn't stand, which in the end proved for the best as everyone started to laugh too, as Augustus kept apologizing and promised to repair the damage.

The third lesson, however, was the most valuable. Big Bruce came up to him and said "Well, Gus, what are yer planning to do now?"

Augustus was terribly embarrassed by the failure. In a way, he wasn't really used to failing, at least not publicly. It wasn't the Azure way. Winning was all important, and so was success. TMI tested all their prototypes in secret, and released them when they worked well. But here that wasn't an option. He could walk away. There were many other projects to take on. But a streak of obstinacy made him say: "Try again."

Big Bruce slapped him on the back. "Yer a proper little battler, Gus. We wasn't too sure of you, mate. But good on yer. Now, let's go and have a beer."

And somehow, Augustus found he'd moved from being an outsider, quite respected for his exploits among the Thrymi, to being, suddenly, with two words in the face of failure, one of them. It felt good. Or maybe that was the beer. But he did realize that this was the key to how the outbacker society worked. They got knocked down – by the Thrymi hunting them, shooting their stock, taking them as slaves. The Zell harvesters, cutting the upper surfaces of the skyfrond could, destroy all the hard work that a station had put in to creating paddocks of suitable grazing – and destroy a tame herd. Weather and storms could break your work of a generation in half an hour. If these people didn't get up and start again, every time they got knocked down... they'd just die. On Azure, being the winner was the apogee of the social structure. On Sybil III winners were... relatively common (by their standards, anyway) but unlikely to stay that way, unless they got up every time they got knocked down, and tried again. Giving up was for dead people, or those from the Big Syd. To call someone 'a battler' – someone struggling their way up against the odds, was a compliment, a term of respect, and of endearment.

The more Augustus thought about it, the more he thought he could come to like it. Or perhaps that was the beer.

He awoke, with a somewhat sore head, and a lot of determination. He needed that, in the following few weeks. He wondered often how they managed to measure time – the clouds and moving with the skydrift on the air currents made day and night uncertain periods. He found that out when the station drifted into the darkness of Sybil's night. Sybil had a roughly eight day rotation, but Skyfrond drifts rode the air currents, keeping in the sun as much as possible.

When they did enter the night though, the skyfrond drifts slipped down into the clouds, and well below them. The air was as thick as treacle, and the darkness oppressive and apparently danger-ous. The plants had a strategy that got them through it, but it was no pleasure... how long it went on for was hard to say, but the human circadian rhythm kept ticking along.

The shelter Augustus and his workers had built around the aircar they were dismembering, became very popular in that time. The station burned little hydrogen flares, a trick the locals had learned, keeping a trickle of flammable gas coming from a carefully prepared plant-stem. It did for cooking, and did for light. But Augustus's little generator hooked up to one of the aircar's lights did much better. There was a steady supply of people willing to crank the handle on the simple generator, taking delight in the light. And in that light, work on the second paraglider went on steadily. By the time the Station started to rise to greet the sunlight, the work was mostly done. It was of somewhat different construction to the first, with thin bladders from the floatplant full of hydrogen for struts and the double layer of fabric held open for the air to provide the ram-effect – making the entire main canopy into a curved airfoil, that couldn't fold, with ram-air filled outer 'wings' that could fold – but it would not stop it being a parachute if they did.

And this time... he was going to fly it.

Not everyone was happy about that idea.

Briz tried giving him a thousand words about this crazy idea. There was no getting through to the drongo when he'd made up his bloody mind, she thought, crossly. There was just no need for this. They were making a fortune, and she was getting fat. Well, filling out a bit. Not as much as Mister Gus. He had muscles on muscles on muscles, and a great big red beard too. He was still blinder than blind Freddy with the Sheilas. All things considered that might be a good thing. Although a fair number of the Stationers looked at her like they was thinking what they didn't ask. That was outbackers for yer. Any one on the Big Syd would have, cast nasturtiums at least. She'd never understood that. What were nasturtiums? And why did they throw them? But here on the Station... they were kind of prudish. Didn't talk about sex. And unless yer slipped off private like to a far corner of a paddock or had your own quarters, like Big Bruce and his missus, everyone had to know who was rooting who, or even moving in that direction.

Mister Gus just about slept where he fell over, working. She'd chuck a jumbuck blanket over him and lie down somewhere close enough to deal with anyone who tried to sneak up... but they didn't. Outbackers. Just weird.

The slaves had hated him for working too hard. Here they cheered him on, and his crew were fiercely proud of him and tried to keep up. She'd had to do the same. She shook her head at herself. What was wrong with her, doing hard yakka, when yer could get some other drongo to do it?

She wasn't convinced this contraption was going to fly. Or that it even ever could. But... she just couldn't think how to stop him trying. She'd fallen asleep desperately trying to think of a way to nobble him into not doing so. Maybe toss it over the edge... but he'd just build another. The best she could come up with was to try it herself and prove it didn't work. But that could kill her. Well... yer had to do what yer had to do.

She was trying to lug the wing out of the workshop when Jase – Big Bruce's son, came in, yawning. "What yer doin'?" he asked, looking at her.

"I'm takin' a walk. What does it bloody look like?"

"It looks like yer taking the boss's toy with yer," he said. "Why?"

"'cause I'm gunna try it before he wakes up. I don't want him getting killed," snapped Briz.

Jase nodded. "Good-o. I'll give you a hand."

"What?" Briz stared at him, incredulous.

"It's bin worrying me. And Lindsey. And Ted. Didn't know how ter stop him. But I reckon I should try it instead."

"No yer bloody won't. Big Bruce will kill me. And Mister Gus for letting yer."

They were still arguing – carrying the wing to the balloon-platform they'd been rigging before tea, when the other two of the outbackers who Mister Gus had originally employed... well, she had, but for him, came along too. Then it was a four-way argument. She was winning, 'cause, well, she bloody well was going to. But... it was strange. They were worrying about her. And Mister Gus. It was bleeding odd to find they all felt that way about the mad drongo. She was winning. But Jase wasn't Big Bruce's son for nothing. "All right then, you do it. But not from high like the boss was planning. Do it from about a cable up. That way yer got half a chance. I jumped that far."

"And broke yer ankle," said his sister.

"Yeah. But I lived. And it was just a bad landing."

Briz knew how long a cable was – about two and a half stories. Maybe three. Well, she'd jumped that before. And lived too. "Lemme get into the harness, and yer can haul me up."

So, they did. It looked pretty high. No point in waiting... the canopy was open above her because of the ribs of balloon. She pulled the release tabs, bending her knees for the fall.

Which didn't happen. She gently glided downwards, as easily and effortlessly as a Yester-feather. It was a long glide – about ten, maybe twelve cables. The most difficult part was actually staying down – an errant gust nearly lifted her off her feet, and pulled her over backwards – fortunately, the rest of the workshop crew had arrived at the run. So had half the people from the station. That was when Briz got her next shock. "Hush. Shut up. We was just testing it before the boss woke up. Didn't want him ter kill himself," said Jase.

And a positive storm of 'shh!' and 'quiet' and fingers on lips broke out. It seemed that the stationers all felt much the same way about keeping Gus alive. It was very odd to find herself an insider, not, as she'd spent her life being, an outsider, in this conspiracy. And to be something of a hero. After they'd carried the wing back to the shop, she found herself propelled back to the station – where they all wanted to know how it felt, worked, and all manner of detail she couldn't give, because she'd been too scared to remember much. " Aw. I just did it. It worked ok."

"And if it hadn't?" asked Big Bruce.

"I told the crew to chuck it, and me, if I was dead, over the edge," said Briz.

Big Bruce looked at her. "Yer'll do," was all he said.

Briz understood enough about how the outbackers felt about the Big Syd, to realize this was praising her to the sky, comparatively. It sort of worked turn-about, too. She hadn't had much respect for bloody outbackers before this lot.

The other thing that came out of this was Lindsey, walking back across to the makeshift shed, looking at her and saying: "Yer a girl, ain't yer?" There was no way you could make a mistake about Lindsey. Her boobs were already way too big.

Briz looked warily at Big Bruce's daughter. Could she shut her up?

"Don't worry. I ain't goin' to tell no-one."

"It's my business," said Briz, gruffly. "Don't you say nothink to the boss, see. Or else."

"He doesn't know? We wondered if he was pretending."

"Nah. Blind as blind Freddy about some things." She sniffed, feeling a bit like she might blub, for no good reason. "He's too bleeding good for this world. So, I need to look after him, see. Or some bastard's gonna hurt him... or rob him, or, or something."

"He'll be all right here. Dad's a good bloke." She sniggered: "Mum says she won't let him be nothing else."

Briz nodded. "We got lucky. Could have ended up with some crook bastard finding us."

"There's always a few. But they don't last too well out here.

People just go jumpabout if they don't like yer. There's always somewhere else to go."

"Yeah. Not like the Big Syd."

"I always wanted to see that. I mean, Dad says it's a hell-hole. But it's got to be a bit livelier than this is, at times?"

"Oh, it's lively at times," said Briz, laughing. "Most times. But... it ain't all good, yer'd find out pretty quick. We ever get near enough, I'll show you the place, 'cause otherwise yer gonna be skun."

By this time they'd got back to the workshop-shed, and met Gus coming out of it, stretching, heading for a wash. Briz wasn't sure that doing that so often was healthy, but he was regular about it. It was sort of funny to see enough of the others on the station taking it up... to make Big Bruce moan about how much water they used. Gus waved cheerfully at them. "Time for the test soon. I must admit I'm a bit nervous. I don't know how it will go."

"Aw, yer'll be fine," said Briz, cheerfully.

"Well, it's never been done before. I'm not sure..."

Lindsey nodded. "No worries, Boss, we know yer can do it."

Briz thought she said it like she'd been living in the Big Syd all her life.

CHAPTER

FIFTEEN

Augustus, having washed and exchanged cheery 'G'days' with most of the station, it seemed, and having broken his fast, outbacker style with a huge bowl of porridge, a couple of slices of massas damper, with the yeasty, salty preserve that he was getting quite used to, a slab of shonk and a mess of scrambled Yester-egg. Despite all that he still had butterflies in his stomach. He would have thought there would be no room for them. What if it didn't work? What if he crashed straight down like the shonk had? It was less likely now, but still possible. What if, worst of all, he let them down? Didn't try again. Well. One thing was for absolutely certain, he wouldn't do that. But he was sweating, a little. And they all seemed so supremely confident that it would work, this time. He wished he had that much faith in himself, or their certainty. But... he was a Thistlewood. He put a brave face on it. The beard helped. No-one could see his face under that lot.

His crew had the paraglider ready and waiting for him. So... he had to step up and go. Keeping calm. When he had the harness on, he turned to Briz, and said, awkwardly: "Briz, there is some danger in this. Just in case something goes wrong... my wallet and watch are under my blanket. I want you to have them, as well as the aircar, for what it is worth. You can use it to pay off the crew. I've spoken to Big Bruce about it. And, um, there's a letter for my father and my brother Charlie, if you ever get back to the plate."

The little face pinched a bit. Briz sniffed. "Yer'll be fine," the lad said tersely, in a gruff voice, turning away. "Haul him up," said Briz.

So, they did. As he got higher the Bernoulli effect saw the wind-speed increase and ram the wing into full opening. He'd set the height at six cables, and even now he could feel the lift off the airfoil on the harness. The biggest danger was collapsing the canopy by hitting one of the balloon-stays. He'd done his best to minimize that danger, putting the stays out at a steep angle and the balloon well above the launch point, but it was still a risk, and knowing it made his mouth dry. He was a long way up. Then it occurred to him: he was a really long way up, before he left the shed on the station. Everywhere was a long way up, here. With that thought in mind he steeled himself, and pulled the release. The paraglider – and him – dropped away.

Fortunately, it did not drop like a stone or a falling shonk through a station roof, as he had expected it might, but in a glide, twitched by the wind. He experimented carefully with the left wing-cables, and was rewarded by a gentle turn. Now to make an equally gentle landing, without breaking anything this time. He could still remember the pain of that broken ankle. He scanned the surface of the paddock looking for as flat a landing place as possible. That was something he should have thought of before he started. The station paddock was developed as much as possible for the feeding and handling of jumbuck – whose choice of skyfrond-types was the type of fine-leafed stuff that grew on the edges of the tangles of skyfrond. It flourished on anything near vertical. So, the outbackers built their espaliered tiers all over the upper surfaces in parallel rows. They used the massas vine to twist into 'trees' whose vertical sides were then seeded with jumbuck's favorite food which only grew on the near vertical edges -- oatweed. The fruits of the massas and most of the leaf-matter was borne on the top, meaning the station effectively had a starch harvest from the tops, and grazing for the jumbuck between.

It was a very admirable bit of agriculture – if difficult to land on – especially as his gentle turn had him now flying at a right angle across the tops of the massas, away from the open area they kept for mustering, where the launch-balloon had been tethered. He turned more, swinging his glide in an arc – hoping he had enough height. A few moments later he realized he had plenty of height – he had flown right over the edge of the paddock. If he kept curving that way he'd crash into the side of the skyfrond tangle. So, he pulled in the other way – perhaps a bit too urgently which sent him away from the paddock-edge, but descending more rapidly than he planned. He opened up the outer 'wings as widely as possible, and reduced the angle of descent and looked around the clouds for another paddock. He just had to keep flying, he'd find one – provided he did not fall too low. The skyfrond drifted where it would, but being carried in the same air-movement tended to keep 'paddocks' relatively close for surprisingly long times. The stationers actually winched them closer occasionally. Doing his best to keep calm, Augustus kept his glide angle as slight as he could and peered about the cloud for any possible landing.

He was rewarded by the sight of the reddish-green of a paddock off to his right. He curved slowly and gently towards it. It took him a few seconds to realize that either the skyfrond paddock was descending, or he was rising. It seemed the paddocks were natural thermal generators, perhaps the process of splitting hydrogen... He wondered briefly how far this paddock was from Big Bruce's Home paddock, when he realized that was a balloon above the paddock – his launch balloon. He'd lost his sense of direction in the concentration, and plainly was rising on a thermal from Sybil's hot interior. Along with the enormous relief, there was real temptation to continue to rise and fly. It was, now that he felt a little more in control and secure, a wonderful feeling. But this was, after all, a test flight, not a mere joyride, and he still had to manage to land. But he could go up a little more...

So, he did, to perhaps three times the height of the launch balloon, catching a little turbulence as he flew above the skyfrond – but nothing dire, pulling the wing cables in slightly to begin his slow, circling descent, aiming for the mustering field, and wishing the balloon and its tethers were less in the way. The tethers worried him, being not that easy to see. But in a series of wide loops, he made his way downwards towards the upturned faces of the waiting outbackers. He was really getting the hang of the wing now, and managed to pull both wings in at the last to give him a feather-light landing.

The canopy rather spoiled that by drifting down on him, as he stood there, beaming.

But they had that off him quick enough. Besides, it weighed very little. Briz was the first to get to him. The lad's eyes were very wide. "Yer never do that again without me!" he yelled, and turned abruptly away.

The poor lad must have felt he missed an adventure – or perhaps was worried he was going to be left behind, if Augustus flew off.

"Don't worry, Briz. I'm not going to abandon you. I need you. It's a lot of fun, though."

"Yer got kangaroos loose in yer top paddock," said Briz gruffly wiping his eyes and nose on his shirt sleeve. By this time, they were totally surrounded by the entire station's worth of outbackers, down to the youngest babe in arms, all talking at the same time, and all, it seemed, wanting to thump him on the back.

By the time a few hours – and quite a lot of beer, had passed and been passed – everyone on the station wanted one, or at least wanted to try it. The possibility of flying up and even of larger directional flights than they could manage on their bubbles and cloak arrangement – to say nothing of the less unpleasant landings had vast appeal. Augustus tried to break them of that illusion, pointing out he'd broken his ankle the first time, and people got killed. He'd also pointed out that actually, it wasn't quite what he'd expected or planned – finding the thermal or landing well. And that he'd nearly lost the home paddock. No-one seemed to listen.

But he found out the next day that indeed, Big Bruce, at least, had. "We'll have you above the cloud soon. That'll be the time for practicing, eh? Low jumps, maybe two cables with a nice clear track to the muster-field. And no reason the lads can't take a jump-swag along."

A couple of other things soon became clear. Firstly, Briz wasn't just saying that he was taking the lad with him. Briz meant it. And what Briz meant, it seemed would happen.

And secondly, everyone wanted a paraglider. No matter that Augustus explained that there had to be equally vicious down-drafts and winds as well as up-drafts, or that it was actually rather dangerous.

"See," said Big Bruce, smiling, "We know all that. Dinkum, we really do. But it's not more dangerous than what we do – but it's got a lot more range and more steering and yer can get out of trouble easier, or at least as well as yer can now."

The desire was there – making them was going to be a bit more difficult. The reason, simply put, was the availability of woven jumbuck wool. The fleece was an all purpose material out here – providing everything from cord to clothing, to, when sealed with the sticky sap of one of the skyfronds, the roofs and buckets and bowls of the outbackers. Making cloth and thread and ropes with it was what occupied all the spare time of most stationers, particularly after their main meal (called 'tea' for some reason), when everyone was sitting around, before sleep. Yarns came with yarn and songs too. There was nothing to read and nowhere to go, so this produced useful materials, tradable and usable.

The downside of this was that it was slow and the volume took time. Mostly, time was something outbackers had. The station life was a fairly relentless amount of work – much of which had to keep being redone or maintained. Life out here was – barring the dangers, and relative isolation -- not unpleasant, but it was hard, with little spare labor for extra goods. When there were extra hands – most outbackers would strike out on their own and find themselves a partner and a few tame jumbuck and build their own station. They were a fiercely independent people, conditioned into the idea of doing this by the culture they lived in, from the day they were born. Those who failed could usually find somewhere to feed them and shelter them for a bit of work. One of the children would inevitably stay on the station, and take it over in time, apparently.

It worked, plainly. But it didn't provide for a lot of spare woven jumbuck fleece, immediately available, for making a whole lot more paragliders. It appeared that Briz had bought just about all there was to be had. Augustus blinked a bit, finding this out. Briz, it seemed, had simply taken over the commercial side of his enterprises – a side he hadn't even known existed. He had it seemed, twenty-three jumbuck, in agistment with Big Bruce's flocks. Big Bruce was apparently also doing well with extra livestock, and talking about sending some of the children off with a start of their own... except, right now, no-one wanted to go. It was too interesting and exciting here, right now. They wanted to see what happened – and besides, quite a few of them were doing rather well with small metal objects that would make their lives better – or be tradable for extra jumbuck or whatever else they wanted.

That was all very well, but he needed more fine sap-sealed cloth.

Briz saw to it. The lad was a talented barterer – and, it seemed, as good at managing money as great great grandmother Thistlewood had apparently been – back when the first settlers had included a brilliant young engineer, who was, family history said, as financially inept as he was technically brilliant. Augustus had always had a soft spot for the stories of great great grandad. The Thistlewoods – who all seemed – beside Augustus, to have inherited financial acumen from his bride, fondly regarded him as something of a family buffoon. Augustus had grown up around stories of his cluelessness, and failed to get anything from them but a certain sympathy for the man who bought the barren Marden Hills because they looked splendid. The fact that they turned out to be a mineral treasure-house, was no part of his plan. Fortunately, his young bride had taken it in her stride and made money out of his crazy starts. It meant Great Great had been able to spend a lot of money on machinery and tools that were the foundation of TMI – and that his bride kept the family to a habit of strict economy out of necessity, because her dear husband would spend any spare cash on the next project.

A lovely, frugal bride to make his projects all turn out financial successes, to fund the next project might be beyond him, but at least Briz dealt with the day-to-day side of financing this, that Augustus had had no idea where to even start with.

It was... different, especially after the flight, to find that several of the stationer women regarded the prospect of becoming his bride – if not a frugal one, with interest. Augustus didn't know quite what to make of it. Briz, however, was having none of it. "Them slags don't even know how to read. And they counts on their fingers," Briz pronounced loftily. "They ain't good enough for you, Mister Gus."

"Besides, I think arriving back on Azure with a Sybil outbacker wife would be rather cruel to her, as well as a shock to my family," said Augustus, with a smile.

"A WIFE? Bleeding heck. I thought yer just wanted to root 'em," said Briz.

By now Augustus had worked out that piece of argot. He blushed. "Outbackers tend to think of marriage, and we Thistlewoods do too, rather. Anyway, I would never marry someone I didn't love and didn't love me."

"Holy Dooley!" said Briz, "Yer don't want much, do yer? Now, I've sent messages out that yer wants to buy some cloth – if the price is right."

"How did you send a message? And we can't really fuss about the price."

Briz lifted his delicate-boned sharp face to the sky. Closed the bright blue eyes. Shook his head. "Yer tell them the price don't matter, yer going to get skun. And yer won't be able to buy enough." The boy was, compared to the outbackers, the size of a fifteen-year old – but good plentiful food was the norm out here, and Augustus knew that was not true of Briz's growing years, by the comments he made. Augustus wonderd exactly how old the beardless lad was – it was hard to tell. The lad might catch up a bit out here, thought Augustus. He was never going to be big, muscular and rugged, like the men out here tended to be. His face and expressions were rather feminine, if anything. "Hadn't yer spotted the smokes? They signal with those. Only works real well on top of the clouds, but word gets about. It's how they avoid the Thrymi and the Zell. 'course it don't always work 'cause the bastards sneak around in the clouds – and the Thrymi will sometimes go looking for smokes to hunt slaves."

"Ah yes. That's something else I need to work on. Radio. And one day, when I get back to Azure I'm going to have to talk my family into bringing political pressure to bear about the enslavement of humans by these aliens."

"Huh. These outbackers say people from the Big Syd are all bloody slaves to them. And in some ways, I think they're bloody too right. Yer at least don't have to do what nobody says out here. I mean yer got nothing, but they can't push yer around. And yer eat all right, and pretty much do what yer want... although what they seem to want is all pretty hard yakka. And they don't show what they got. How is anyone supposed to know Big Bruce is a big cheese?"

"They all know Big Bruce," said Augustus. "I suppose he doesn't have to show anyone."

"Or care what they think, 'cause it means nothing to him what they think, according to Tige. Now, we're gunna need some extra people to sew and yer need to check me math on how much material we need for every paraglider."

Briz's math was as precise as his handwriting. His spelling was atrocious, but his writing was neat and with each letter perfectly formed. And he learned fast. Briz had rapidly moved from being able to add and subtract – especially money, to division and multiplication, as if they were the easiest and most obvious things in the world.

The outbackers... could count. Add and subtract... sort of. Most of them. But they could neither read nor write. Everything was passed on orally while the weaving and processing of jumbuck fleece or the grinding of the massas was done. It made for good memories... and a lot of teaching.

On complimenting him on the careful calculations and lists that Briz had made for the production of paragliders, Briz gave him a wry smile. "Outbackers get cheated like them little bushpigs. I reckon a talleyman could make some good coin out here. Mind you, a crook one could rip them blind."

Augustus sighed. "Yet another job to take on. Briz, there's a million years work for a million of me, let alone that I am supposed to get back to Azure...when I can. I said I was going for a year."

"Yer think yer going to get back?" asked Briz.

"I think so. Look, we can see the space-craft come in from a long way off, and the paraglider will make covering distances quite possible. It may take a few years, I admit. But if the outbackers could signal what they see – well, it becomes a more plausible equation. I will see you settled back home, eventually. I think I might take one of those Thrymi guns with me and visit a few people and teach them the error of their ways. I was a little naïve when I arrived, but I have had time to think things through and understand them a bit better now."

There was slight silence at that. "Don't you want to go back, Briz?" asked Augustus. "I must admit I enjoy it out here more, myself. There's more space and I find it easier to get on with the people, even if those on the Trading Plate are more like the people in the cities of Azure. I mean, they're not that like them, but they're mostly city dwellers. I suppose there are people like this on Azure too, but I never really met them. You have to admit the food is good out here."

"Huh," said Briz, dismissively. "What's a mystery bag if yer know exactly what it has got in it, and all the things in it, it's supposed to have? Anyways, I made a start on getting them to learn to read and write, and do numbers. I told 'em yer won't be employing no low-class drongos who can't."

"What?"

"Yer want them to read and write and do math, don't yer?" asked Briz.

"Of course I do. I was hoping to encourage..."

"Yer'd be begging them, and because they're short of entertainment out here, likely a few might have let yer try and teach them," said Briz, sardonically. "I got them begging me. Paying too. And pleased to be doing it and working their butts off to learn. See, some of them will come and work for us. Yer was saying how difficult it was that you couldn't write down instructions or measurements. And others won't be up to bleeding scratch. But they'll teach, 'cause it is what they can do."

It was remarkable just how well that worked.

CHAPTER

SIXTEEN

Back on Azure, the two security men from TMI had literally been whisked, on their return, from the disembarkment ramp of the starship, to Marden house.

They did not want to have to go to the Thistlewood's home. No-one went there unless things were beyond serious. These were two men who wished they had some other news. The other six of the team were still scouring the Big Syd. Still getting stonewalled, and still getting no response from the radio-transmitter that should have given them a signal, if Augustus Thistlewood – or at least his shoe, was anywhere on the Trading Plate.

The news was received in stoical silence. Eventually Charlie's father said: "So just what happened to him, gentlemen? He's my son. I need to know."

The older of the two security men shook his head. "We don't actually know sir. But... I am afraid the biggest likelihood is that he's been killed and his body and shoes pitched over the edge of the Plate. There is nothing else on the planet. If it had just been some low-level killer... we've put out substantial rewards for information. For his clothes, even. They don't throw anything away there, while there is use to be got out of it, as you can imagine. That lot would sell-out their own mothers for a reward. We've got nothing. Someone... possibly the various gangs, have put the frighteners up them, badly – but then the gangs would sell each other out. But the gangs are in thrall to the aliens. Possibly the aliens believe that Admiral Halberd's threat to... destroy them, if a single Azure citizen was killed, to be real."

"Our present government is too gutless to do anything that effective," said grandfather angrily.

"But we are not the government," said Charlie's father, and then checked and looked at the two men. "Thank you, gentlemen. That will be all for right now. I will want some more information from you later. The housekeeper will see you made comfortable until then."

"Just one question before you go," said grandmother, stopping them in their tracks. "This local guide of Augustus's, this 'Briz'. Did you locate her?"

"No ma'am. It's as if she dropped off the edge of the earth..." he realized what he said and shut his mouth and retreated.

When the door had closed, more to say something than anything else, Charlie said: "I suppose the girl might be an easier lead."

His grandmother sighed. "Maybe. But she's also the only chance I see of a great-grandchild from Augustus. Not my choice for him, but at least... something."

"I was wondering when we'd get around to nagging me about getting married and having children," said Charlie, almost relieved to have the familiar, but upset enough to say things he wouldn't normally. "Look, grandmother. My share of the family business made Augustus and I... have a very hard time finding a partner. We hide in plain sight. No-one knows who we are. I'm just an engineer, whose name happens to be Thistlewood, and I work at TMI, like a lot of other people, some of whom also have the surname Thistlewood. An aircar makes my coming home to Marden very anonymous. But – short of never telling the girl who I am... sooner or later she'd have to come and meet you, and deal with being part of this family. And I haven't found the right girl to cope with that. It's not for lack of trying. I might be better off with a street thief from Sybil III who wouldn't know or care."

Grandmother glared at him. Father however ignored this. "I need to know exactly what happened to my boy," he said, heavily. "And I am going there to find out, by force, if need be. Charlie. Those ex-special services men..."

"Got them in training under Templeton. I thought we might, just possibly, be dealing with a kidnapping. We've got a mock-up of the Bondi Boyz headquarters, aerial pictures of the same, as much background and what experts I have been able to muster in the desert down at Tarkastad. I'm ready to go, immediately."

"Good boy," said his father. "Except you're not going. I am. And we'll take a few more days to prepare this. It's... not likely that time makes any difference now. How many men have you got?"

"Thirty-eight. But I should go, father. He's my little brother..."

"And I am his father. And thirty-eight is not enough. Fortunately, grandfather and I have another two hundred..."

"How are you going to bring in that many? The biggest ship that can land there is a c-class freighter..." said Charlie, recognizing the tone, and knowing arguing was futile.

"We will have to strategize accordingly. I don't want all these rats to run and hole up. And the embassy staff are frankly useless for this. We need a reason to bring in a decent force. Normally I'd say start a new industry. It's not as if TMI isn't looking for a direction to expand... But no one is going to believe we're there for business."

"The hotel," said grandmother. "Buy it, and send a team in to remodel it."

"Perfect. And we can sit the bulk of our men on standby in orbit. They can come in fast, if need be, or in stages, if not."

A few days later, Charlie was sitting talking to his father in the spaceport grounds, near where an unobtrusive freight hauler was loading a cargo into a C-class freighter. "They were remarkably keen to offload the Hyaton when our agents approached them. I gather it has proved expensive and difficult to run and to staff, and not profitable. Of course, they don't know TMI bought it. We didn't want it leaking back to the various criminals on that pest-hole."

"It's not really about the money, father."

His father gave a wry smile. "True. One gets too used to thinking in profit and loss terms. Anyway, if it does leak...TMI has been looking for new ventures for some time, but we wanted interesting engineering challenges. Building there will provide those. Not that we plan to stay that long."

"As long as it takes," said Charlie. "But not too long, or grandfather will come looking for you, and grandmother will drive me mad. And take care, and see whoever did whatever to my brother... repaid in kind. With interest."

"Your grandmother is coming with me. She's been going through Augustus's letters, and wants to see the place he died, and the people he died for. And to search for this girl she's convinced herself about."

Charlie and his grandfather saw them off the next day. Three C-class freighters had already left, as well as a small preliminary team on the Star of Space. All the research said no-one on the Plate on Sybil cared what cargo came in, except to see if they could steal it, but the security team's job was to make sure they didn't.

Charlie dearly wished he was going too.

CHAPTER
SEVENTEEN

Augustus didn't quite know how the tandem rig had ended up being at the top of the priority list, but somehow it had. Big Bruce's station now had six extra sheds, and a lot of people cutting and sewing... very, very precisely, which frankly wasn't something you'd think came naturally to the rough and ready outbackers. It didn't have to. It came naturally to Briz... or, via the lad's training to be a forger. That revelation had been something of a shock to Augustus, but he'd become a little more inured to shocks out here. And looking back, there was something to be said for the harsh things he'd been told about the occupants of the Trading Plate.

The outbackers could not have been keener to have a paraglider, or, it seemed, to be one of the team making them. "They all figure they'll learn and go and make them, themselves," explained Briz. She seemed a bit affronted by this.

"Oh good!" said Augustus.

"'s our business," said Briz crossly.

"We can make more businesses. The paraglider will help them to open up their society. Trade, exchange ideas..."

"And walk off with ours," said Briz, proprietorially. "But I've got them believing the writing and numbers is a kind of magic yer have to have, to make 'em work."

"That's... sort of true," admitted Augustus.

"Too right, Mister Gus." Most of them called him that now. "I got them showing up for a class every morning. I figured yer'd be pleased."

"I am."

"I got some cakes organized for you to teach them division tomorrow. They're not as dumb as those slags back on the Big Syd." Briz paused. "I always thought the outbackers were dumb, back there. They was mostly doing the hard yakka jobs, and getting robbed. But here they comes up with some ideas even I don't think of."

"I suppose staying alive out here does... um, kill off anyone who is too stupid, and favors the ingenious," he paused. "And not the criminal. You've taken over the business side, Briz. I'm... grateful. I don't have any talent for it. But I won't have anyone cheated. This isn't the Big Syd."

"Too right it ain't," said Briz, cheerfully. "But yer don't have to worry, Mr Gus. I'm giving them a fair go... just like they gives to us. Because they can still chuck us over the edge, and anyway, it's no fun ripping them off. Like stealing a snotblock from a toddler."

Augustus wasn't that reassured that Briz merely held off larceny because it was unsporting. "They trust us. I don't want to lose that. If we breach their trust..."

"Yeah, yer want to save that for the day yer really need it. That way they won't see it coming."

Augustus had the feeling that might be the nearest to morality he'd manage with Briz. It might not be the approach he would have taken, but he was pragmatic enough to accept that it was working, and that people were learning and eager to learn. And... Briz seemed to find the money to employ them, and rather than being resentful, the outbackers seemed to relish it. Briz seemed to be getting on better with them too. The lad had taken up with Big Bruce's daughter, Lindsey, who was one of the brighter apprentices he had. He'd semi-jokingly asked if they were courting or working at one stage. They had both laughed until they were unable to stand. He hadn't entirely got Sybil humor yet. It was long on Jumbuck jokes.

The tandem rig proved good for introducing customers – and all the workers, to the paraglider. Only Briz seemed quite relaxed about it. He had a touching level of faith in Augustus and his inventions and took to the gentle first glide like he'd done it before. Others were nervous. The others, however, were very keen on moving to solo flying. Briz showed no interest. "Tandem is good. That way I can keep an eye on yer."

Progress was far more rapid than Augustus expected, possibly because the outbackers had grown up around jumpabout, and using air currents and their cloaks to steer. There was a ladder and a soft landing that even toddlers practiced and played in. It wasn't long before some of his early pupils were doing better than he was – and his skills had improved. Theirs were remarkable, cheerfully launching off the edge of the paddock and staying up in the air for hours. Yes, there had been a few dramas, yes, he kept warning them that real disaster was inevitable... and they kept telling him they expected it. It was less dangerous than jumping with a gas-bag and a cloak-wing. He kept explaining that those were short flights. It was the time that made it risky. "We know, Gus," said Big Bruce, taking delivery of his own paraglider. "Thing is, dangerous or not, it means we can do a lot of things we couldn't, or at least lets us have a fair crack at it. It'll get me jumbuck moved and give us some chance to get away from those Thrymi bastards if they're hunting us, or our stock. They're having problems from one of the bastards about thirty mile away. They've only got one aircar, and so they're hunting people's jumbuck, because they're easier. Yer can't make us a few more of their guns, can yer?"

"I can't even make human firearms yet," said Augustus. "I've been working on it."

He had. Somewhat reluctantly, because the sociology lecturers had been so averse to them – but, firstly, it had become plain that they really had little idea what the reality was out here, and secondly it was a tool the outbackers really needed, let alone for any defense against the slaving, murderous Thrymi, or the Zell harvesters that destroyed their laboriously improved paddocks. The outbackers wasted little – not even urine – feeding the aerial plants nutrients the plants otherwise had to gather from the volcanic dust from the planet far below. Urine could provide nitrates – but it was still a long step to even simple black powder. And he had so much that needed to be built, and so little to do it with. Part of one shed was a laboratory where his various experiments were tried – and part of it was the store in which he was trying to accumulate what he might need. It was all very well knowing that in theory he could make a diode by doping silicon – but he had to obtain things like phosphorous and arsenic... and silicon.

Bootstrapping a civilization was hard. The outbackers had solved many problems by sheer ingenuity, by working with the materials they had, and by working around problems – but a few extra things could make life a lot simpler and easier out here. It was just annoying that so much of his knowledge rested on being able to access a few small, cheap components... cheap and easily available back on Azure. Glass, for instance, would help a great deal – but even assuming he could use the hydrogen burners to get up to temperature, he had nothing – except the metal from the aircar to make molds out of. And then there was the issue of materials to melt. Silica sand might be easy to come by... somewhere else. Blowing glass too could give him useful objects – but first he needed molten glass.

The current success had been producing small mirrors out of metal from the aircar. These, it appeared had three major points of desirability. Firstly, they were much better for looking at your reflection in than a whitebait swirling panflower pool, as one could hold it up instead of bending over a pool, and they didn't dry out. Secondly, if one was up in the sunlight, they could be used to signal over quite a long distance, and finally, as they were acute triangles, the lower point sharpened and encased in a little sheath, they were a useful small blade. Augustus's idea behind making them had been to provide a signaling method, but he had to admit vanity was a large driver in the sales Briz was so pleased about. You took victories where you could. People were using them to flash messages, using a variant of their smoke-signaling codes. The only down side of this was that he was going to run out of aircar hull soon, and the internal parts were going to be a lot harder to cut.

Still, the effects of his work out here were tangible. So, he had to admit, were the effects on his body and clothing. Thistlewood clothing – as dictated by his grandmother, and rebelled against by Charlie – was durable and hard-wearing. But it wasn't perpetual. It was also not designed to cope with the fact that he'd put on a lot of pounds since landing on the plate, mostly on his chest and shoulders, but even his thighs had been rubbing on his once loose trouser-legs. By now, only his dire-bull hide brogues were holding up, and even they were scuffed and worn. He wore a Jumbuck-wool checked shirt and singlet, and the same shonk-hide shorts as everyone else otherwise. He'd got used to them, and they were better suited to the huge amount of labor that a pre-industrial society – even an ingenious and adaptive one – required for day to day survival. He wondered how his former fellow sociology students would fare here. Innate honesty forced him to admit that even the Augustus who had come to Sybil III would have struggled, before being enslaved and forced to toughen up.

Days passed, more paragliders, mirrors, knives and experiments were made. It was in some ways idyllic, although he yearned for more tools and materials. The drudgery of working as a slave in the Thrymi cloudcastle had been long, rather dull work, and a stolen bit of fascinating interest. This, at least, was interesting all the time, even if it was just as tiring. There was an enormous satisfaction to walking out of the workshop into the hot sun of above-cloud and seeing – across the distant cloud tops, paragliders. You could see a long way from up here. His work was spreading. No matter what else happened, outbackers would have paragliders and even more freedom of move-ment. So too was reading and numeracy. It was a status symbol, to be able to write and figure, and getting a job in the workshop got the lads and lasses a lot of respect and interest from possible mates... Augustus didn't care what reason they had for it, it was spreading and had benefits far beyond that status, even if they didn't think so.

There were still many mysteries to unravel. Why did the skydrift paddocks accumulate? What happened when a rising paddock hit a sinking one? The underside of each paddock was effectively cone-shaped – as he had now seen on his flights.

Of course, anything idyllic was bound to hit a reality check.

The problem arose from the Thrymi cloudcastle with its single aircar – which Augustus suspected had to be the very one they'd escaped from. It was making up for its lack of hunting aircars by targeting human skydrift paddocks. And it was moving much closer to Big Bruce's station. The outbackers had little choice but to flee its path, and to move as many of their jumbuck as possible away from the path of the hunter. "We can't move what is left of the aircar. Yer better hide it as best yer can," said Big Bruce, pragmatically. "We're taking down the station and our sheds – the crook bastards burn them just for sport. You better do the same, mate. And yer jumbuck are flying with mine. So yer crew better come and help shift and scatter them. At least we can use paragliders to do it."

"Do we have no alternative?" asked Augustus, reluctant to pack up and interrupt so much work.

"No," said Briz, bluntly. "At least we got paragliders. The upside is we can move off easier. The downside is not getting their bloody prey will leave them Thrymi slimebags spewing and nastier than usual, but hopefully not with us, and they'll move on, looking for something to take it out on."

It was part of the way of life for outbackers: If you didn't like it, or were threatened, you moved. The planet was big enough to get away from problems, at least most of the time. It was... alien to the way the

Thistlewoods dealt with problems, which was to solve them, one way or the other, Augustus thought, irritated, his busy mind working on ways to get rid of at least this one pest. But, well, in Rome, eat spaghetti. So, he got busy working on packing up and hiding, and getting his crew to help with the scatter – and, with the mirrors and paragliders, to keep track of the oncoming Thrymi.

It was with this, finally, that things went catastrophically wrong. A paraglider came in, far too fast for a safe landing, aiming straight for the half-dismantled roof of the station. At the last minute, Ted – one of Augustus's crew of apprentices pulled up and flared the wings, landing hard. "They got Jase! The bastards got Jase!" he screamed.

Jase was Big Bruce's second son, his older boy having left with a girl and a dozen Jumbuck to set up a station of his own, before Augustus's arrival. Running to join the crowd surrounding the boy, Augustus heard the story. "It's closer than we thought, down in the cloud layer. We thought we caught a glimpse of it through a gap in the cloud, and went down to have a look. The aircar came out of the cloud. Jase never had a chance."

"Did they kill him?" asked Big Bruce.

Ted shook his head. "Netted him, with one of those net harpoons of theirs."

There was a silence. Big Bruce put his arm around his wife. Slavery – the imprisonment aspect particularly, Augustus had realized was viewed as a slow form of dying by the outbackers.

That could be why he said: "I am going to get him back."

They all – even Briz, looked at him as if he'd gone completely mad.

"Yer can't do that, Gus," said Big Bruce. "It's the Thrymi who've got him."

"And they had me. Once. They might have to have me again," said Augustus.

"They'll kill yer, Gus," said Big Bruce.

Augustus shrugged. "That could happen. Ted, how far off is the skycastle, and exactly which direction?"

"Don't be a bloody drongo, Mister Gus," said Briz. "Yer can't just attack a skycastle. Not even with the Thrymi weapons we got from the aircar. They'll blow you apart with the guns they used to shoot the aircar with."

"I'm not going to fly up and attack them. I want to land on the turret we woke up in, and use the lift. If they're down in cloud there is a chance I can do it without being seen. Once I am in there, I can break him out."

Briz sighed and shook his head. "We'll take them Thrymi guns, and a few spare knives, and a couple of lengths of rope. And a piece of that net you was going to use to hide the rest of the aircar."

"We? I can't risk anyone else."

"Yer got no choice, Mister Gus," said Briz firmly. "Come on. Let's get goin'."

"He's my apprentice, my responsibility, Briz. You're reasonably safe here."

"Yeah. Now let's get goin'," Briz said, taking him by the arm, and turning him toward the partly dismantled workshop. "We want to sneak up on 'em in the clouds. While they thinks they're sneaking up on us hiding down there, we'll sneak up on them."

"I really think you ought to stay behind."

"Yer really thinks a lot of things," said Briz, gruffly. "And some of them is wrong."

Looking back, Augustus suddenly realized at least half of the Outbackers and all of his crew were following along, except for the ones who were arguing behind them... and a few with small children. Several of them were already rigging paragliders. "Where are you all going?" asked Augustus.

"Where we bloody feel like," said Tiger, grinning at him. "I said to them, yer was as daft as a brush. But they wouldn't believe me. Yer gunna let me have a knife on tick?"

"Why not?" said Briz. "Yer either good for it or yer dead, or we all are."

"Or bleeding both," said Lindsey. "Yer gunna tell him?" she asked, gesturing at Augustus.

"Nah. Just confuse 'im," said Briz, picking up a spare knife. "Yer better let me carry the guns, Gus, as yer gunna be needing yer hands for flying."

Augustus had time to wonder what he was not being told after they'd launched into the sky, seeking a cloud-castle. He knew it was an insane attempt. He wished that the sky behind him was not scattered with every outbacker on the station that had a paraglider, carrying their puny little weapons. The paragliders – compared to the aircar – were dead slow and un-manoeverable. The Thyrmi castle's guns could blow them all to smithereens. Well, hopefully they'd shoot at him first, and the others would sheer off in the clouds and drifting paddocks. That of course was all very well, but he had young Briz along.

The only positive he could think of was the cloud-cover. But surely they would use radar or some sort of mass-detector? On the other hand, humans were no bigger than shonks and smaller than Herbeen which could be flying about anyway. Still, he was very nervous about this, as far below he spotted a turret rising from the cloud, and began descending towards it.

It would have been nice to have that radar himself. When he did see the cloudcastle they were smack on a collision course – and he had to sheer off – and instead of a sneak in the back door they did half a circuit of the wall before coming to the hanging turret. They were a bit high and the target was moving – he had to drop hard... and skidded over the edge of the walkway between turrets, the collapsing wing going over the other side, and catching the wind and dragging them up again, and towards the turret's lower door. Both he and Briz, the latter impeded with rope and net and tied-on guns, grabbed at the sill as the re-opening wing tried to drag them over. Fortunately, before it could drag them right off,

Augustus realized what was happening and managed to collapse the wing and pull it towards themselves – pulling them up and it under them. At that moment Lindsey landed on top of the canopy, neatly collapsing it and pulling her own down with skill. "Can't you drongos fly?" she said with a grin. They hastily hauled the 'chutes to the door – which opened easily enough. Looking out, Augustus saw Sam – the best flier among the apprentices, riding his 'shute neatly parallel to the skybridge-walkway between the turrets. "Yer want to span that net, to make landing easier?" he said.

So, hastily, they did. With two ropes firmly tied across the skybridge and the net quickly attached, the next ones in had an easier time of it. One missed and had to desperately correct the wing below, but more outbackers were coming in.

Augustus was not disposed to wait. He showed Lindsey how the elevator worked, left her in charge, and took himself down into the engine room with a Thyrmi gun and Briz at his side, equally ready. It was the same Skycastle. And it hadn't changed down there. It occurred to him that he could probably destroy the entire castle from here. It was the most important place in the whole structure – and it was neglected and unguarded. He said as much to Briz.

"See, Mister Gus, that's your problem. Yer expect them to think like you do, and they don't. We're just lucky they expects you to think like they does, and yer don't."

"You're a treasure, Briz," said Augustus, smiling despite the situation. "I don't know why you put up with me."

Briz looked at him oddly. Almost as if he was going to say something. The lad shook his head. "Me neither. So, what do we do now?"

That question was answered by the turret elevator opening and disgorging an awed but nervous group of outbackers, holding their little weapons at the ready, very relieved to see him, plainly torn between naked terror and amazement at their audacity – and its success.

So far, of course.

And they all wanted to know just what they did next. This was a little awkward when he wasn't that sure himself.

His original plan had been to wait until the outbacker slaves were locked in, the Big Syd slaves had knocked off, and then try to somehow break open the outbacker dormitory and, using the tandem paraglider, flee with Jase, giving the others at least a chance to make a break for it. But now... that needed to be re-assessed. He didn't have a space on his paraglider, and he had a lot of extra people – sixteen... about as many, including him and Briz as the Thrymi population of the cloud-castle. The big difference was of course that the Thrymi loved to kill, and were fast and deadly at it – and armed. The only thing that the outbackers had on their side was surprise and, if you could call it an advantage, the fact that they were bluntly terrified of the Thrymi. That might stop them going off half-cocked. "Let's, carefully, scout the launch deck. Look, this whole thing can be destroyed, but that'll kill whoever does it, and whoever is still in the cloud-castle. I'll show you in case it all goes wrong." He did, and when he'd done, Briz came along: "S' all clear on launch deck. The aircar is back. All the others look like they're still wrecked. They've carried the catch out of it already." Briz paused. "Including Jase. I could hear him yelling."

"I gotta go up," said Big Bruce, who Augustus hadn't realized was even there. "That's me boy up there. Yer wouldn't like to lend me one of them guns I suppose?"

A moment of epiphany broke over Augustus. The aircar had had the long-guns stored in them. The Thrymi had side-arms and knives... but there might be more guns for the taking. "I'm going up too. But first we'll see if we can get more guns. Briz... guns in the aircars?"

Briz slapped his head. "Of course. "Yer. Sammy and Piggy. Come with me. Mister Gus, you explain how they works, 'cause they won't have no practice time."

Fortunately, the alien weapons were quite simple to operate, although Augustus had not yet spent the time to try and work out how they worked – or how many times they could be fired. He just knew how to work them, so he showed them, before Briz and the helpers returned with armfuls of Thrymi weaponry, guns and knives, and handed them out. "Yer got one less of the bastards to get, Gus. One of them came down to fetch something. Sam shot him."

"With the gun?"

Sam shook his head. "Put me arrow through his eye. Briz pronged him with her knife. Good throw." There was a sort of incredulity there. The Thrymi, much hated, were something you feared, not killed, like shooting yesters.

"I reckon most of the bastards is up there on the work-deck, watching Jase get beaten," said Briz. "They like that."

Augustus took a deep breath, taking a hard decision. "Big Bruce. You take everyone but Briz and I and... two others. Jim. Kelly. You creep up the ramp and start shooting. Stay low, they have no cover to rush you with. Don't try any heroics, don't try and rush them. But give us the slow count of thirty. No matter if they're hitting Jase. They don't kill new slaves, just try to beat the resistance out of them. And they like to do it slowly."

Big Bruce nodded. "What are you going to do, Gus?"

"Going to go up the main elevator. Someone must still be at the controls up there. If we can get above them we can shoot them from above and behind. They'll be between us – and with luck, not know who to attack."

Big Bruce nodded. Swallowed. Reached out his hand to squeeze Augustus's shoulder. "Good luck, Gus. If any of us get away it will be one hell of a song, across the outback. Yer a fair dinkum battler, mate."

"You too... cobber."

That raised a smile as they set off in their various directions.

As expected, the large elevator took them up to the top of the center turret... where the cloudcastle's control panels were. And one bored Thyrmi sat idly surveying the various screens.

The one thing you could not say about Thrymi was that they

were slow to react. He turned as the doors creaked open, plainly startled by the main elevator opening. By the state of it, it didn't get used that often. Both Augustus and Kelly fired at the leaping Thrymi, his sidearm already coming up and firing. One of them hit the Thrymi in the shoulder, knocking him sideways and down. His face a snarl of rage and pain, the Thrymi tried to transfer his weapon to his still-functioning hand. Briz's thrown knife – the heavy hilted Thrymi one from the aircar, went into his chest. He clawed at that before Augustus managed to shoot him again, through the head. Kelly clutched a burned arm, dropping the Thrymi gun. Augustus could only be glad there had only been one Thrymi up there. Looking around hastily, he spotted a stairwell, and a door leading to the catwalks that the Thrymi so loved, around the central turret, and above the enclosed area that was the work-deck, about five stories below. The stair had a door, with a sturdy bolt – obviously intended to defend this area. Jim was trying to render first aid – and Briz had checked out the catwalk door. "There's shooting. Yer can't see them without going out."

Augustus bolted the stair-door. Looking at the cloudcastle's controls, they had a familiar similarity to the aircar – a similar triangular wheel and series of levers. "Briz. Drive it! Frighten them!" he ran to the door to the catwalk.

From that vantage point he could see the work deck below – and realized he was an easy target for anyone shooting from any of the flying buttresses. But it couldn't be helped. He squeezed off a shot, firing on the Thrymi down below – and then lost his footing and nearly joined the fight four stories down, as the castle lurched and the floor pitched thirty degrees. Then it dropped beneath him. He managed to grab the rail, but lost the gun, which fell hitting the inside of the outer wall and bounced onto a screaming slave who tumbled beneath the impact. The slave wasn't the only one screaming. It seemed everyone down below was. Augustus felt at least he had company.

Jim clawed the door open, and Augustus pulled himself toward it, as the castle lurched the other way, and shot upwards. And then it went into a spiral in the opposite direction, as he pulled himself inside.

"Yer better drive this thing," yelled Briz. "I ain't getting it."

"You guard the elevators! And chuck that dead Thrymi down on them. They're going to try to get up here, for sure!" said Augustus. "And hold tight when you can. I'm going to shake this thing around." There was no point in crashing the cloud-castle with all of them on board, no matter what else happened. Briz hadn't tried for any gradual disturbances – she thrust levers all the way, and then the opposite way.

The cloudcastle's screens were flashing puce shades of violet and yellow, various alarms were sounding... and Augustus set about firstly correcting the spiral and then working on the controls. Fortunately, the lights on the panels with each lever gave him a clue – violet through green-yellow. Yellow was bad. So was violet – but they were a balance of controls. Even with Augustus first trying to stabilize then control the stability of the floor it was more like being at sea than anything else.

"We chucked him down. Got one of them. Nearly got Big Bruce. Them's fighting below on the work-deck. Don't look like many Thrymi shooting."

"A few is enough. They're bound to come up here to try and get control. I hope Bruce has the sense to get out while they can."

"I pulled all the elevators up here," said Briz. "I got Kelly poking her fingers in the holes that call them up, keeping 'em here and open."

"They'll have to come by the stairs or the aerial catwalks from the flying turrets."

"Jim is watching them," said Briz. "I'm on the stair-door."

There was the sudden shrieking crack of one of the Thrymi guns. "Got 'im," said Jim. "And he took his mate behind him with him!"

That, thought Augustus, made a definite four... Out of what had been seventeen, when he had been a slave in the cloudcastle. The odds – even if the work-deck attack had accounted for some, were still bad. One Thrymi, was, he had to admit, more than a match for most humans. Probably three untrained humans. And the numbers had been about equal, before it started.

"Jim, can you see the work-deck?" asked Augustus, trying to think what to do.

"I'll crawl out a bit," said Jim. A few moments later he said. "Can't see anyone. No shooting from them Thrymi handguns."

Augustus felt the pit of his stomach sink. "Going to rock the castle about a bit. It's all I can think of." So, he did.

It had a reward in its way. From below, through the doorway that Jim had ajar to fire through came the sound of a stentorian bellow. "Gus! Can't yer bloody drive this thing properly?"

Never had Big Bruce's voice sounded so good.

Just then an aircar appeared on the bottom edge of Augustus's vision, and then vanished, diving down. "That's torn it. Some of them are in the aircar. They'll strafe us and I don't know how to shoot back."

"I don't think so," said Briz with a savage grin. "When we was up fetching the guns I tied one of them harpoon cables around what yer was showing me is the cable to the battery terminal. Remember, yer was explaining how like Azure batteries they was. Anyway they got about four cables outside before it pulls tight. Unless they broke it off or cut it."

"They're burning through the door!" yelled Kelly. Briz fired at it, and a shrieking ricochet screamed past her and buried itself into one of the sybaritic loungers that were scattered around the command and control deck. Leaving the controls, Augustus stuck Kelly's Thrymi gun into the melting hole and fired. It did not ricochet – or at least not back up here. So, he repeated it several times, until the gun stopped firing.

Big Bruce yelled from below: "We're comin' up. Don't shoot us."

"Tell them to come up the main elevator," said Augustus. "Briz, shoot through the hole if you hear anything."

"Well, I don't hear nothing so far, except some sort of yowling noise."

"We'll need to let the main elevator go down, Kelly."

She nodded, still wincing in pain, but at least, it seemed, able to function. "Better be ready to shoot if the wrong 'uns come up," said Briz.

Jim kept watch on the catwalk, and Briz and Kelly took up positions behind the loungers. Kelly had the hand-weapon from the Thrymi they'd killed in the control room, Briz had the thrymi long-gun and a knife out... but the elevator disgorged a group of outbackers. Not quite as many as had arrived in the cloud-castle – but a lot... and with a battered-looking Jase among them. He had a Thrymi handgun and very wild eyes – and a very bloody back.

"Are there any of our people below?" asked Augustus, doing a quick count.

"Too right. We got some hurt, and we've lost two – but we also got a lot extra."

"Extra?"

"We got some outbacker slaves joining us. They wanted to run, but now they want to kill the bastards. Yer really did turn everything upside down with that wild driving of yours. We was in trouble. And then that made them panic."

"We need to do a head-count. We can't have got all of them. There were seventeen."

A lot of counting on fingers went on. "We got four – two got suckered to come looking down the ramp. When we come up the ramp they was behind the prisoners and slaves. No way to get a clean shot at them. Tige fooled 'em. Called out there was an injured herbeen that had killed one of the 'masters' down below. The crew was in a bit of a hurry, started shooting early. Got two – the rest of them run behind the slaves to start shooting from there – pushing them towards us. It looked really ugly. Then the place started swaying and rocking and spinning. And they come apart. Before that they was... gunna win even if it was just seven of them left. But when the castle did that, they panicked. Four come running for the ramp – not like they was trying to get to us, but through us. We blew two away, wounded the others. The other was heading for a back door – so we came running. That was bit of a mistake, 'cause then they started fighting with us. We'd have been dead then, only they kept falling over. Not used to keeping their feet when things move under them, I guess. Not like us. Still, it was ugly. Then a Thrymi body come down and took out one of them, just before he got me. That seemed to take the heart out of them again. Three of 'em got to the door – one of the injured we thought was dead. We cut throats to make damn sure after that. Next thing we hear the flier taking off below – run back and there's three of them was crammed in it... they fly out and then there was a hell of a 'twang' noise. Someone run down the ramp looked over the edge and saw the flier falling straight down."

"That still leaves a few unaccounted for," said Augustus, worriedly. "I am not sure how many tried to come up the stairwell. And the elevators could deliver some more here."

"We'll have to do a careful search," said Big Bruce. "Them bastards will kill us if we give 'em half a chance. So, we aren't going to give 'em that, are we, cobber? And can yer fly this thing a bit less like a drunken shonk breaking up a brewery?"

"No! There must be some kind of autopilot, but we've over-ridden that and I have to work out how to get back to it. It may take me a while. You may have to get used to it."

"Well I suppose it makes them Thrymi feel even crooker than us," said Big Bruce. "But them Big Syd slaves, Briz. They're a bunch of whinging Poms."

Augustus wasn't sure quite what it meant, but he was sure that it wasn't polite.

While they searched the Thrymi Skycastle from top to bottom, and sideways, twice over, Augustus carefully experimented with the controls – in the process discovering some of the skycastle's arsenal. His conclusion, before he eventually found the stabilzers – was that the fact Briz had not sent the Skycastle to a catastrophic crash was miraculous. No wonder the Thrymi had panicked.

The search turned up one Thrymi – in the stairwell, dying. That, Augustus gathered, was something they helped her do. It was not, frankly, surprising. The outbackers hated the Thrymi. They had been enslaved, tortured, and hunted by them – and had never had a chance to even the score before. Even now they seemed hardly able to believe it had happened.

The search took a long time, because the castle was large, with a labarynthine array of rooms. Each flying buttress had whole suites – most of them dusty and empty. At one time something like a hundred to a hundred and fifty Thrymi must have lived here. The place, however, was a long way into rack and ruin, with everything from non-functioning lights to corroded and crudely shut off pipes. There were some twenty-eight non-functional air-cars, twelve of which Augustus had shorted the batteries of. It was not a big fix, but even that had not been done.

The Outbackers might be almost stunned by the technology and sheer wealth of it all – coming from a metal-less society. Augustus was more aghast than stunned at the state of the place. Plainly, repairs and maintenance had simply not been undertaken for what looked like centuries. The Thrymi who had built this were not the Thrymi who lived out their existence in it, hunting.

It was some hours later, when Big Bruce brought some roasted meat up to him on the upper deck where he was still puzzling over the controls, that the question was raised: "So what do we do now, Gus? Can yer take this back to the Station? Yer seem to have the hang of flying it, now."

"Well... I'm not sure where the station is," admitted Augustus. "We could go up and look for it."

"Yer'll frighten them to death. They probably reckon yer dead already," said Briz. "Reckon we go up a bit, and get the crew to fetch their paragliders, and they can fly and find them, and break the news that this ain't a Thrymi cloudcastle no more. It's Mister Gus's cloudcastle."

"Er. It's not mine..."

"Too right it is," said Briz, firmly. "Yer flying it, ain't yer? No one else can. No one else understands how all this works."

"I don't really."

"Better than anyone else," said Big Bruce.

"And all this was your daft idea," said Briz, firmly. "Without you they'd all be hiding like potomaroos from a hungry yester. Would have been the smart thing to do, too."

Big Bruce laughed. "Yer right. But next time, yer won't be. We're gunna sort these feral bastards out. Now we know we can."

"We were lucky and they didn't expect it," said Augustus. "Once they do..."

"So, Mister Gus is going to teach yer how to do it right, so they don't find out," said Briz.

There was a long silence. And then Augustus nodded. "Yes. That's what I'm going to do."

CHAPTER

EIGHTEEN

Charlie hated being stuck on Azure, not knowing how the search for his brother's killers was going. Father was nothing if not thorough... but his grandmother... he wondered quite if the people of Sybil had any idea what was about to hit them. Augustus had been six when their mother had died. He'd been eleven. Grandmother had mothered both of them, through the time when his father was trying to cope, and then burying himself in electronics. Charlie had a clue that being motherly was not his grandmother's strong suite. Not that she had the least idea of how to show it, but there was no doubt that inside that chilly exterior, Augustus had been very precious to her.

He put some time into reading up as much as he could about Sybil III and its former convict population, and the two remnant alien populations. There wasn't a lot to read. There was more archeological work than studies on the living.

And that was all he could do except go to work -- which he somewhat enjoyed, fortunately, and waiting, which he didn't. He felt faintly guilty that he hadn't done more to get Augustus out and about and having a real life. He'd been entirely too busy with his own double life, which might have been better than Augustus's, but still hadn't worked out too well. He had a slew of 'friends' – but most of them had now moved past the University party stage and were developing lives and relationships that sometimes went a bit further than beer and company.

It was lucky the waiting didn't last too long.

The call came in, midmorning. It was his father. "Get home, Charlie. Right now."

"What..."

"I'll talk at home," said his father and hung up.

So, Charlie went to his boss and said he had to leave, right now. The harassed-looking woman scowled and said: "Just finish the drawings and you can go. Production is waiting."

"Fire me," said Charlie, and walked out.

He was on his way out of the door before her jaw hit the floor, and on his way back to Marden a few moments later.

His father actually landed a few minutes after him. He'd called from orbit. "Firstly," he said as Charlie and grandfather met him at the aircar. "Augustus may well be alive."

"We'll tear the place apart if need be," said Charlie. "It's only a few square miles to search."

"It's a lot more than that," said his father. "A lot more."

"He was taken offworld? Kidnapped and taken to another planet?" asked grandfather.

"No. He was kidnapped and sold into slavery, but..."

"By who? And why have you come home?" asked grandfather. "Ransom..."

"Those he is... or definitely was, sold as a slave to, had no idea who he was, or even that he came from Azure. So far even the idea of ransom hasn't been mentioned."

"It's time to look into liberating some slaves," said Charlie. "But I imagine there is a problem, or you wouldn't be here. Where is grandmother, by the way?"

A trace of a smile flitted across his father's face. "Back at the hotel. I think she is enjoying the challenge. But yes, there is a problem. Augustus was sold to the Thrymi, one of the alien species who control about half of that pest-hole."

"And our dear government has an absolute moratorium on touching one little hair on their alien heads," said Charlie.

"I don't think we plan to tell them," said his grandfather grimly. "We need to know as much as we can about these aliens. Try to work out exactly where they are holding the boy. It's a small area. We can focus a lot of resources on it."

"It gets... more complicated," explained his father. "I might have just tried brute force extraction, or even buying him... but the aliens have a number of what the locals call 'cloud-castles' – small anti-grav plates with dwellings on them. Leftovers from the time when the place was a meeting spot for very rich traders. Augustus was sold onto one of those. Apparently, they go on long hunting trips – and this particular cloud-castle hasn't come back. So possibly Augustus is out there somewhere. He'd be very far out of range of the transmitter in his boot-heel."

"What are they hunting for?" asked grandfather. "I thought the place had no surface humans or anyone else could reach... or survive. That it was just a small antigravity plate sitting in the exosphere."

"It's an unusual world. A gas dwarf. And a puff-planet, you know, with a lot of dust flung up from pyroclastic events on the core, but a relatively low density," said Charlie. "I gather there is some floating vegetation in the upper cloud layer where the atmosphere is breathable. There was some mention of flying animals in the book I read on it."

"Correct, that's what they're hunting," said his father. "We know almost nothing about most of the planet, and it is a very large area to search."

"On the other hand, I gather they do return," said his grandfather.

Charlie's father nodded. "Yes, they come back to the trading-plate. Our men have set up a system to check if the transmitter comes in range. But the bad news is these Thrymi are known to be brutal and cruel masters. They are always buying new slaves. One imagines that means that a lot of them die. We need to track him down fast, and intervene hard."

"Agreed," said grandfather. "So, I assume you have ideas, and have come to discuss ways and means, son?"

"Yes, we need to deploy several satellites to find all of these 'cloud-castles'. Then we need to work out a way of transmitter-hunting. Then we're going to have to get a strike-team ready. We know very little of what they're capable of or what weapons they have or how they work. And we have to do it without our government – or any other government with an embassy there, finding out. I hope my son is alive, but this is going to be difficult, to say nothing of expensive."

"It could pay for itself quite handsomely," said Charlie, with a wicked glint in his eye, "If we get our hands on some of that technology. We've been looking for new engineering projects to explore. Our anti-gravity experiments haven't produced much yet, let alone a system which has to have operated and survived a long time."

"Which neither of the alien groups allows us to see, nor has any government been prepared to push to explore. Interference in alien affairs is utterly forbidden," said his father. "There is some small logic in it – technologically they were both ahead of humanity, and while their empires seem to have destroyed each other, either or both may yet survive and resurge, and be ready to punish humans."

"At which point we won't be able to respond on equal terms," said his grandfather.

"Yes," said his father. "And frankly, the little I have learned of the Thrymi, is that all they respect is overwhelming force. When Admiral Halberd administered a warning... well, he got into trouble when he got home, but no-one told the aliens, and I gather things improved a great deal for the people there, as well as the safety of visiting humans."

"We're going to need a few experts on these aliens," said grandfather. "Charlie... and we'd better get you transferred out of that design shop, to see to that."

"I think I may have just been fired," said Charlie, grinning.

"What? I'll see to that," said his grandfather.

"Oh, I would probably have done the same thing, in her position. Leave it be. We've got work to do. Finding an expert who won't hamstring us if they have the least idea what we're planning to do is going to be tricky. They're bound to have tenure and want to stay in the good graces of their Academic Institutions. I owe Augustus. I am looking forward to this." It was only half-sarcastic, as he was, except for the part about finding what he assumed would be a crusty archaeologist. He already had an idea who the leading experts were, from his reading.

"So, tell us just how you got this information, quite so quickly," said his grandfather. "Had the embassy got anywhere?"

"Useless chair-warmers," said his father. "No, that was all mother's doing. She read what our agents reported, and sent messages to the various capos, that we were re-developing the hotel, and looking for local partners to operate some aspects of it. Naturally, every one of the local thugs came in, like flies to dung. We knew it was the 'Bondi Boyz' Capo we were after. So, when he came in, he never left. He sang mightily and loudly. It seems that Augustus had managed to trash a number of criminal enterprises in the short time he was there. I mean, having been there, I understand why. I just find myself stunned that he managed to make them all co-operate in getting rid of him. They were, it seems, genuinely afraid of him. I was rather proud of my boy."

"It doesn't seem that these Thrymi were similarly concerned," said grandfather dryly.

"Actually, no. What reduced the Bondi boyz Capo to a nervous wreck was my mother saying she would take the matter up with the Thrymi. They're likely to kill him slowly and painfully for making Azure take an interest in their affairs. They still take Admiral Halberd's threat very seriously."

"I don't suppose that actually taking the matter up with them might get him returned?"

"We've done some investigation. There were problems with the Thrymi prior to that. Two Sinopese tried snooping the antigrav repulsors and got caught before they got in. The Thrymi tortured the one fellow to death, and dumped the body on the street in front of the embassy. The Sinopese sent their Ambassador to demand explanation and release of the other one. The Thrymi said they knew nothing of either, but they would happily come and destroy the Sinopese embassy if any more impertinent questions were asked. The Ambassador insisted... and yes, the Thrymi came down and killed four of the embassy guards, and chased the Sinopese through the streets and into a space-ship. They didn't come back until three years after the Admiral gave the aliens a show of force." His father scowled. "I've had informal talks with the ambassador. Unless we produce Augustus's body and clear unequivocal evidence, they're going to accept that it was done without Thrymi knowledge, and outside their influence."

"We shall see," said grandfather.

"We shall ignore them. Mother is taking steps."

"Oh," said grandfather. "Well. That's dealt with then."

Over the next two days, while satellites were being organized – a business TMI was heavily involved with anyway – Charlie found that he'd been entirely wrong about being fired, and the Thrymi expert. His boss called him a few minutes later. "Charlie. I need to talk to you."

"I think you need to fire me."

"I thought about it. Once I got over being angry... I realized that if you were ready to walk out on a TMI job for whatever the reason was, it must have been, well, something you needed to do very, very badly. No-one quits."

That was true. TMI took the best people, paid well, and if you wanted to be in mechanical industry, they were the best. "It was very urgent, Sandra."

"And you're an exceptional engineer. Look, I am sorry. When can you be back? I need to fill in leave forms."

"I... look, I'm busy with something really important. I'm not sure how long it is going to take."

"I don't want to pry, but can I help? TMI looks after its people. We have a discretionary fund. Mrs Thistlewood herself runs it. She's an old dragon, but really very supportive. I'll send a message..."

"Uh. Sandra. I'm actually on TMI business. Urgent business... for the old dragon, herself. And you should have fired me."

There was a silence. Then she said: "Thistlewood. You're related to the owners?"

"In a manner of speaking," said Charlie. "There is a family connection, sort of. I was asked to come quickly, so I did. Just forget about it, Sandra. Fire me."

"The company is full of rumors right now. Something is going on. Security guys being pulled suddenly..."

"Sandra. Just fire me and forget about it."

"I'm damned if I will. You're on leave for the next three months. Do whatever you have to do."

"Better make it six. And send a note to the old dragon saying you have given me leave to attend to family affairs."

Tracking down Dr. Aljon, the author of the Thrymi section in the book on Sybil's plate proved easy enough. He lived in the capital. Charlie decided it was best done in person. This was too close to family business, and too close to what could be overstepping the law to make it official. Aljon had in his opinion, written the best of the little he'd been able to find about the Thrymi. Neutral, factual and not – as some of the others did -- kowtowing to the 'superior' alien culture. He'd been in the History faculty of the local college when it had been written.

Dr Aljon did not appear to be an adjunct of the College any more – Charlie called the Xeno-archeology department to be told, rather frostily, that no, Dr Aljon did not work there. So, he took himself to the street number he'd wrung out of the publisher. It proved to be a bakery. He went in, wondering if it was the wrong address, or if the archeologist had moved. The plump, neat-bearded man behind the counter smiled and asked him how he could help.

"I'm probably at the wrong place. I was searching for Dr Aljon... but the patisserie is remarkable looking. I'll have to sample some of that. And those eclairs look good."

"I'm Fred Aljon," said the man. "I don't wear the Doctor label these days. Not much call for it in the baking trade. The eclairs are very good."

"You're the expert on the Thrymi on Sybil?" asked Charlie, trying to hide his surprise.

The man snorted: "As much of an expert as a man who can't go there can be."

"Would you like to?" asked Charlie.

"I can't. They won't grant me a visa," said the man, tersely, anger in his voice.

"Ah," said Charlie.

"Anyway, I am a baker now. What can I sell you?"

"Hmm. We need to talk," said Charlie.

"And I need to make a living. The rent is due," said the archeologist-turned-baker dryly.

"How much for a day of your time, Dr Aljon? My employers will pay you a number of months of rent for consulting you, about the Thrymi on Sybil."

The man looked suspicious. "The kind of business that comes out of Sybil III, I want nothing to do with. Get out."

"I have nothing to do with the thugs and rogues on Sybil III," said Charlie, exerting every effort to look and sound sincere and good, and wishing he'd left this to the professionals. "I work for TMI, an engineering company here on Azure. But those self-same rogues have attacked our interests. We need to understand the Thrymi to deal with the situation. I've read the chapters you wrote in 'Sybil III, a History'. I was very impressed, and so are the heads of TMI. We are very keen to consult with you, and will pay you appropriately."

The man paused. "You're not serious."

"I was never more serious in my life. Name your price. I can make a deposit, right now. And all we want is a little of your time and expertise."

"A visa and a ticket to Sybil III," said the man, derisively.

"Done. And we'll pay you appropriately. TMI does not short-change people. We hire the best, and I think you are that."

"You're really from Thistlewood Mechanical Industries? I don't believe this. I have a cousin who works for them."

"Which unit?" asked Charlie.

"Plastics and automotive, in Sellarfield."

Charlie smiled in relief. "Please, Dr Aljon, can you call him now, and ask him to press nine on his 'phone, which will allow him to call numbers within the unit, and patch you through. Ask him to get you Sandra Charia, the Chief Engineer of the heavy vehicle section. Tell her Charlie Thistlewood would like her to verify who he is, and ask her to describe me."

"I don't like to call Porky at work."

"Porky Josephs is your cousin?"

"Yes," said Aljon, doubtfully.

"He's a friend of mine. We play squash together. Call him, please. He won't mind. Get him to describe me, and put you through to Sandra."

A few minutes later Dr Fred Aljon came out of the back room he'd gone into to call from. He was smiling and shaking his head. "If you were one of my pastries, I'd have said 'too much cream'. Your Chief Engineer practically begged me to help you. You are who you say you are, it seems. Are you actually related to the Thistlewoods, the owners?"

"Somewhat," said Charlie. "But then all the Thistlewoods are related somewhere down the line. But yes, I am acting on their authority. And I mean every word I have said. We've got a problem on Sybil III, and we need to understand it as best we can. We're not used to dealing with that sort of thing."

"Neither was I. Look, I'm willing to talk to you, and tell you what I can. But... well, those thugs cost me my job in academia. I have rent to pay, a shop to keep open, and a family to feed. This evening, maybe?"

"Tell you what," said Charlie, "Why don't we make it a special day for the Plastics and Automotive unit, and get you a day off to come and talk? Do you have anyone who does deliveries for you? Otherwise I can get someone."

"Yes... we have an arrangement with one of my neighbors, for when I've done office party catering. He has a little truck."

"Good. Please give him a call. I will buy what stock you have, and I'll arrange for the unit to receive it. I'll give Sandra a heads-up."

Fred Aljon looked at him, doubtfully. "I am wondering if I've eaten something hallucinogenic."

"Not unless you baked it," said Charlie, cheerfully. "And I hope not. There are some friends of mine in that unit."

A half an hour later, the shop shut for the day, Charlie and his new friend set off for Marden. Charlie – who was good at getting people to talk, got the story of why Dr Aljon was now a baker. He'd finally got the money for a trip to the Antigrav plate on Sybil, to get to see living Thrymi and their society, having been to various ruins elsewhere. And then he'd made a mistake. He'd found one of the locals was dealing directly with the Thrymi, venturing into their mansions... and he'd attempted to bribe him to take him for a closer look. Next thing an undersecretary from the Embassy had showed up with four marines, and escorted him from the Hyaton to a locked compound in the Embassy grounds and then loaded him onto the first available ship. On his return, a few weeks later, he found his teaching contract and post had been abruptly terminated. One of his friends in the department found out that a large grant had been tied to that happening. The grant came from a close friend of Mister Camelthrob-Princhbut – the very same undersecretary who had seen to his expulsion.

So: he'd turned to his hobby, patisserie, to make a living. It was easier as a hobby than a livelihood, but at least it had been that.

"You'll be pleased to know he's been arrested. But he is also involved in the problem we have. So is the Capo of a gang that call themselves the 'Bondi boyz'."

"That was who I asked to get me a closer look," said Fred.

By the time they got to Marden, Charlie had established that the archaeologist was all in favor of finding out how Thrymi technology worked, and was of the opinion that the Thrymi were a murderous culture who would have done their level best to destroy humanity, as they had several other intelligent species.

By the next day Dr. Fred Aljon was an employee of TMI, his bakery regretfully up for sale. On the other hand, Charlie was in prime favor not only for providing a knowledgeable expert, but also a welcome stream of pastries, cakes and things grandmother probably would have utterly forbidden, but that the three men enjoyed greatly.

A week later, three heavily laden freighters had set off for Sybil. Buying heavy military equipment drew notice from various authorities. But when your company was the producer, it was a little simpler. Some of it was materials for the new hotel development there, due for trans-shipment as and when it was needed onto the smaller C-class freighters. They'd remain in orbit in the mean-time... along with an array of small satellites, mapping and surveying... their instrumentation set on the metals that were to be found in Thrymi cloud-castles. When they were pinpointed there were drop-probes – small, sacrificial craft, designed to get within the transmission radius, see if they got a signal and transmit that back into space, before falling into the gravity well. They were small, and quite cheap – which was just as well, because mapping had identified over five hundred Thrymi sky-castles, scattered across Sybil's exosphere. They'd mapped somewhat more of what seemed likely to be Zell cloud-castles. They were tracked, anyway, even if they were of less relevance.

Down on the anti-gravity plate, Dr Fred Aljon was officially the new pastry chef for the hotel, once it finished its upgrade. Unofficially, he had a team of what could only be called spies, snooping the Thrymi compound with everything from tiny drones to deep penetrating radar. He was a happy man, especially when he discovered that Mrs Thistlewood particularly liked light-as-air macarons.

Charlie, down there too, was learning a little more about the local populace and, just incidentally, what his little brother had been up to. Admittedly he had a rather robust escort of ten security men – which made some of the exploration difficult. Still, as grandmother had explained, in her best tones, that as they knew where all of the capos lived, any theft or injury to her staff would result in consequences for at least one of them. She could be quite terrifying, and they just did not know what to make of her. Charlie, very carefully, didn't know what had happened to the first few who had tested the limits of her patience. The testing had stopped. Grandmother was keeping herself busy overseeing construction – which included an aircar bay. The Thrymi or Zell might well have objected to that, just as they had to the botanical and zoological aircar expeditions that some previous Azure ambassador had apparently seen fit to pursue. If they had been told about it, that is.

CHAPTER

NINETEEN

I t had been harder to find the home paddock than Augustus had thought. A few of the precious paragliders had been lost in the process, and, indeed, one turned uptattered and battered on a paddock some time later. But they had found the station, and by the time that he'd steered the captured Thrymi cloud-castle there, it wasn't just his crew or people from Big Bruce's paddock waiting. The news was spreading as far as the paragliders could fly.

The party had already started when the cloudcastle slid up to the edge of the paddock. It had been a very drunken one -- not destructively so, which would have been worrying, seeing as Augustus already had plans for the cloud-castle – but awed, a little frightened still... but triumphant. "When the Thrymi get to hear about this, they'll come hunting," said Big Bruce.

"We'll just have to avoid telling the bastards," said Briz.

"Well, the story is too good to keep down, Brizzy," said Big Bruce. "Yer got a place in song forever, I reckon. Everyone who was there, has."

"Reckon they'll make up most of it," said Briz, cheerfully.

"Well, they have to make us look good somehow," said Lindsey. "Not like yer was in such a hurry to get there that yer fell off the side of the skybridge."

Everyone laughed. It was a happy, shared laughter, full of everything they'd been through. And, as the celebration wore on, Augustus realized he'd had to accept more beer than he'd ever had in his life. He'd also been clapped on the back, and kissed and hugged, far more times than he had ever in his life. And offered more beer. He was glad that he had the cloud-castle in safe hands... and now he just wanted to lie down somewhere. He smiled beatifically at all of them. Wasn't this just great...! Just great! He'd have another beer...

"Time for him to lie down before he falls down," said Briz.

With one of the apprentices on either side, they led him past several places he thought looked good to lie down. Every single one of his crew seemed to be there to wave and cheer him on the way past. Then he was into the elevator, and up to what must have been the boss-Thrymi's domain – a suite of rooms of sybaritic comfort. "I can't shleep here!" he slurred slightly.

"Briz said to put yer in that bed!" The larger of the two apprentices said firmly.

"And yer don't argue with Briz," one of the crowd that seemed to have come to see him into bed, informed him.

He nodded. "My guide. Seen me through a lot."

He lay down. Someone pulled his boots off – before being shooed out.

A few moments later the light was turned off, and the door closed. Distantly, outside, he heard Briz say: "Now bugger off, all of you."

That made him smile. All was right with the world. Briz was taking care of it. It was odd being in complete darkness and alone.

Some little time later he realized it might be dark in here, but he wasn't alone. He started to say something to the person who seemed to be taking off his clothes... but they put a finger across his lips.

Then they took his singlet off and snuggled up against him. They didn't seem to be wearing anything either, as they folded into his arms and kissed him in the darkness.

I t was a strange thing, Briz realized, to find somehow she'd wandered into being a bloody hero. It was not like it had been her plan, or that she hadn't thought people who did that sort of thing had kangaroos loose in their top paddock. Yer kept yer head down, brains switched on, and stayed alive. She understood people well enough to know that even if the Thrymi turned up in a mob tomorrow, and killed all of them, the story just wouldn't die. And the outbackers had somehow changed forever. They were going to try and kill Thrymi from now on.

That... could get ugly, fast. They'd been lucky and simply totally unexpected. No one attacked the Thrymi. Ever. So, the Thrymi had not expected to be attacked. She still knew just how close it had come to all going wrong. If Mister Gus and her had not escaped – and caused such un-thinkable damage to the aircars, the five Thrymi involved would have been alive and not killed by their own – having been disgraced. The slaves from the Big Syd had filled that piece of the story in. Just five more might easily have swayed the balance.

She'd tried to tell them. And then she realized: they knew. It just didn't matter. What they hadn't known was that they could ever win. That, in a fight between Thrymi and humans... Thrymi could lose. That changed everything.

Most of the time Thrymi would win. They'd hunt outbackers... only, she was starting to get some idea of just how big the outback was, and just how many humans might be scattered across it. It wasn't full by any means. But there were a lot more people out here than she'd ever imagined, when she'd been living in the Big Syd. If anyone had asked her, then, she'd have said maybe a few thousand,

231

tops. But Mr Gus said that it was more likely to be... a few million. Million! She couldn't quite get her head around that figure. She was getting more and more used to numbers but that was just hard to see in her head. At least ten times the population of the Big Syd, he'd said... Sure enough, if it took ten of them to get every Thrymi, they'd still run out of Thrymi before they ran out of outbackers.

But she still didn't want to be one of the ones killed. And she really, really didn't want Gus to be one of them. They'd want to kill him, most of all, if they ever found out. And that wasn't going to happen while she was able to stop it, if she had to kill every one of them, and herself, first.

It was... hard to work out what had happened to her head, and where the hell she'd stopped being Briz for Briz and the devil take anyone else... to now. The old Briz would have laughed at her and called her a stupid drongo.

But she wasn't that person any more. He was hers, and she was going to keep him. Safe if possible, and at least with her if not.

Which was why she'd made up her mind to do what she was going to do. Mind you, she was as pissed as a newt, because the idea scared her, even if, for the first time ever, she actually wanted to.

Mind you, it had been Lindsey's fault too. It was... strange. Briz had never HAD anyone she could trust. That she could talk to. And who could actually tell her that if she didn't hurry up and root him, someone else was sure to.

That was not going to happen. Her first step was to make sure he actually had a place to sleep. He'd got so used to just lying down in the workshop when he was too tired to function. She'd cover him up, and go to sleep herself, somewhere quite close. She should have taken her chances in the crashed aircar... but well, too late.

She'd made plans instead to get a little privacy, and a little darkness. That wasn't always easy out here. The treated sheets of jumbuck-weave kept water out, but were thin enough to let filtered light through. The cloud-castle, though, had solid walls and shutters and artificial lights. And she wanted Gus to have an absolute claim on it. Squatter's rights. He was going to need it for what he wanted to do. It didn't seem to even dawn on him that it made him rich beyond any outbacker's wildest dreams. It didn't matter to him. He'd probably already figured out ways to spend that. He'd be needing more.

It had, however, dawned on all of them that a cloud-castle captured by humans was going to be a target for any Thrymi that ever found out about it. They'd look to make an example of such uppity humans.

The castle was hidden, short term, as best as they could make it – snugged between three paddocks, down in the heavy cloud, and seeing as how Gus had figured how to make it stay stable and in position, staying put. They might be partying – but there were lookouts posted, others flying guard.

Be that as it may, their crew were firmly staying in the castle. Then there'd been the issue of the surviving Big Syd slaves. They weren't grateful to be rescued. They were terrified. During the fight... some of them had fought against the outbackers. Several of those had died, then and there. Most had fled into their quarters and barricaded themselves in.

The outbackers had taken the attitude that if they wanted to be in there, they could stay there. Briz was much less sure. She knew them, much better than outbackers did. In a way... they'd rather be Thrymi slaves than out here in the outback.

She'd thought that way herself, once.

Now she had something else to think about. And oddly, she'd found that the entire crew was in on her plan, and were pleased about it and determined to help her make it happen. That was just... well, she didn't know how to deal with it!

But... it did make it hard to back off, when they'd pushed her in and closed the door. She was pretty sure the entire bunch were listening outside. And she really wasn't sure about this. Even if she'd had a few beers to get her courage up.

It was dark in there. Her courage almost deserted her, when she found the bed, and he didn't move when she sat down on it. Perhaps he was already asleep... but then he stirred and touched her... so she followed through with her plan. It couldn't be too bad, surely? She was a lot older now.

She did want him, but she was scared. Only...

And then, folded in his arms, kissing him as she'd wanted to, she wasn't scared any more. And then she wasn't thinking much.

Later, very much later, with the slight pre-waking movements of her lover, a lover that she'd slept a sleep of deep contentment snuggled up to, she slipped away to her cold pallet in the next room. Under its covers she pulled on her clothes in haste, tucking her hair up inside her hooded cap, and decided she'd bind her breasts down, later. They didn't want to be bound down, right now.

Augustus, half-awake reached out... only to find that there was no-one there. He recollected with remarkable clarity that there definitely had been someone right there. He could recall the curves and...and other details vividly, despite having something of a headache this morning. The bedding was still warm where they'd been, he realized. He lay still, hoping they come back. He needed to know... well, it hadn't been something he'd set out to do, but he'd been a very enthusiastic participant. So had she. She just... hadn't wanted to talk.

It took him a while to get find a light, and get dressed, and go out, to find Briz nonchalantly having a mug of the small-beer that provided the safest alternative to water here. He looked rather guiltily at the lad. "Er. Been here long?" he asked.

"Long enough," said Briz, looking at him with a wry smile on the small elfin face. "Party is over, I reckon. People finding their way to their own beds. Yer have a good time?"

Augustus blushed. Briz looked at his face and laughed.

"Yeah, I know yer been rooting some bushpig in there," said Briz.

234

"And I'll keep it quiet. Unless yer want me to go away and don't need me any more."

"Briz!" exclaimed Augustus, shocked. "I couldn't do without you. You make all this work. I can make things, but I can't organize things. And... besides, who would I talk to? Bounce ideas off... and who would laugh at me? One day I hope to get you back to the Plate, and, although I don't want to think of leaving, I'll go back to Azure, because... because my family would expect it."

"And this girl yer rooting. What yer gonna do with her?" asked Briz, casually.

"Take her with me of course, if she'll come. I'd like to talk about marriage, it would be the right thing..."

Briz sighed. "Yer do have kangaroos loose in yer top paddock. It was her bleeding idea, wasn't it? And I've heard all about this bloody family of yours. They don't want no little bushpig from the Big Syd..."

"Then they'd either have to get used to it, or I'll do without them," he said, firmly. "I'll be free to come back here. But whatever happens, Briz, I'm going to see to it that you're looked after. I've come to understand a lot that that foolish young man Augustus StJohn Thistlewood blundered into on his way to here. I wouldn't have got this far without you. You could have left me to it. You're loyal, brave, trustworthy, and you've become a true friend. I hadn't had any of those before I came here. If you'd come to Azure, I'd like to see to your education, and I would somehow get you into TMI, so we can work together. Because... well, it is selfish but I've never been happier than I have been here. And I'm not blind enough not to know that you make it happen, lad."

Briz had been looking down. Now he looked up. There were tears in his eyes. "Yer as daft as a brush," he said abruptly and turned and walked off hastily.

"Briz?" he called.

"Leave me alone. I gotta think," said Briz, not turning back.

A little later Augustus saw the lad talking to Lindsey. Well, it was good that he had someone to talk to.

235

B riz knew she'd nearly given it away with the bit about the Big Syd. He'd messed with her head, with his soft talk.

She wasn't loyal, or trustworthy, or brave. She was Briz the gutter rat, thief, pickpocket and scared of anyone who could catch her – which was why she made sure they didn't, she would nick your last penny, and only looked out for one person, and that was herself. Only... Gus thought she was all those things. But he did need her... more than some dumb bushpig to root. He didn't even know he had three hundred and four jumbuck. Oh, he knew some existed, and he had people looking after them. He was kind and... friendly to them. They treated him like he was a Capo... nah. That was wrong. Nobody liked Capos. This lot... it wasn't the money, it was that they'd follow him to hell. Most of them had, in a way. A Thrymi cloud-castle was that.

And frankly, she didn't give a damn if she never got back to the Big Syd. The nearest she'd ever come to planning her life ahead was when she'd taken Gus his suitcase back.

"So: how was it?" demanded Lindsey.

"Yeah. Um. All right," said Briz evasively.

"Just all right?"

"Well, if yer must bloody know, yer stickybeak, it was... great. Bloody fantastic. Happy now?" said Briz, sticking her tongue out and feeling herself blush, and her nipples tighten, just thinking about it.

Lindsey grinned. "By the noise you two were making I'd have called yer a bloody liar otherwise. So, how did he react to finding out you weren't a boy?"

"He doesn't know, and I haven't told him."

"What? I mean... I just saw you run off from talking to him."

"That was something different. He still don't know I'm a girl. He don't know who it was. And if you tell him... I'll... I'll never speak to you again!"

Lindsey laughed. "You're even sounding more like a girl, Brizzy. You'd have threatened to kill me, once."

"I'll do that too. He mustn't know," she said, fiercely.

"Yer gonna have to tell him eventually," said Lindsey.

"Yeah. Just not yet. The time ain't right."

"It's never gonna be right, Brizzy."

"You don't understand, Lins. I'm so messed up. He thinks I'm loyal, brave and trustworthy..."

"Well, yer are. Yer were the first to go with him when he wanted to go and try and rescue me brother. And I'd trust yer with me life."

Briz rolled her eyes. "Yer even more daft than he is. I didn't do it because I'm any of that. I'm a gutter rat from the Big Syd. I set out to steal him blind..."

"So why did you do it, then?" asked Lindsey with a wry smile.

"I dunno," said Briz, shrugging. She did sort of know, but she wasn't ready to say it yet.

"You're in love with him," said Lindsey, helping her out.

Briz shrugged again. "I don't even know what that means, Lindsey. I'm just so... so messed up right now."

She got a hug. "Yeah. We can see that. But he will try to find out, Brizzy. You should tell him."

"He wants to bloody marry the slag that was rooting him," said Briz, not able to contain it.

"Oh, Brizzy I'm so happy for you..."

"You nong," said Briz, crossly. "He wants to marry her because he thinks it's the right thing to do. Because that's... what he is."

"But you love him, don't yer?"

"Yeah," said Briz reluctantly. "But it's not me he wants to marry. I'm his friend. He trusts me."

"But, Briz, it is you."

"Yeah. But he don't know that. He wants to marry some other girl, the one he's rooting with."

And Briz embarrassed herself by bursting into tears again.

It took a while to regain control. And then to tell Lindsey that he wanted to take his bride back to Azure. And her. That idea horrified Lindsey, for entirely different reasons to it terrifying Briz. The outbackers thought Gus was theirs. And they wanted to keep him. And oddly, they wanted to keep her too. Later, enough of them came and told her so, as Lindsey had plainly gasbagged. Well, she'd told her not to tell Gus. Not anyone else. It was kind of hard to be angry when they were all so plainly on her side. Jase even told her that her blood was worth bottling. Coming from an Outbacker about someone from the Big Syd... yeah well, it was easier for them to love Gus. They did.

And so did she. Even if he was a drongo that made her want to cry and laugh. At the same time sometimes.

That evening Gus took himself up to his room. He wasn't falling asleep on the desk. He wasn't being led up there in a befuddled state by his apprentices. He was actually willingly going to bed.

"I suppose you think yer bushpig is comin' back," said Briz, derisively. "Yer got a fat chance."

"No," said Augustus, "I wouldn't really expect that. It was the heat of the moment, I suppose. It's her choice of course, and I might... hope it happens. But I am pretty sure it won't. Besides... I am a little troubled by all of this. I'd... not want someone getting into a relationship for... um, purely physical reasons. Not that I've ever been much to look at. But I'd want them to at least like me."

"Yer a drongo, Mister," said Briz, thinking briefly of the skinny pale bloke that had got off the Star of Space and comparing him to the tanned, bearded, muscular man looking at her. "Anyway, no one's gonna come and crawl into yer bed. Stop getting yer hopes and anything else up."

"Would you stop them, Briz?" he asked.

"Nah," she said. "Anyone that daft deserves yer, Gus. But there won't be no-one."

"I know. She just... seemed to like me. In the way she whispered my name..." there was a sort of wistfulness there.

Briz snorted. She was quite proud of that.

But a little later she crept into the room and into his arms.

And for a while she was not confused or worried about how to work it all out. She was just happy to be held, kissed and caressed... and the rest was very good too, even if they were both learning.

The hardest thing was to slip away to her pallet before he woke up.

CHAPTER

TWENTY

The cloud-castle, Augustus decided, if it had been listed as real estate back on Azure, would have been called 'A good little fixer-upper' and taking the photographs to make it look good enough to sell it to anyone, would have been... a challenge.

With the eyes of an owner, the place was a mess, with a list of urgent repairs as long as his arm and less urgent ones, maybe twice that long. The slaves had cleaned the quarters the Thrymi had occupied. But the rest were simply neglected – some, by the looks of the dust, for centuries. The machinery – his first concern, needed cleaning, lubrication, and repair. The Thrymi seemed as untechnically minded as they'd forced their slaves to be. Some of the repairs were just elementary. Even the outbackers looked at blocked pipes and snapped shafts with incredulity. Rooms had been abandoned because a light-globe needed changing. They found a few of the alien globes in a dusty store-cupboard – but more would be needed.

The best find, however, was the Thrymi armory. Not only were there racks of the gauss-gun long arms, but there were various heavier weapons too – and a stack of damaged and broken ones, some of which Augustus could see how to repair, just by looking at them.

The cloud-castle's main weaponry – mounted in the flying buttresses, was well used. It was also not all in working condition. In two cases simply the alien equivalent of a fuse – which was still a fuse, just of somewhat different design, needed changing on the lower deck. Like the aircars, there was a lot of repair work to be done, and a lot of learning. Some of it was self-evident, some of it he was going to have to work out. There were generations of maintenance and repairs left undone, everywhere. Plainly the cloud-castle was old, and, at this rate, simply would fail for the lack of a drop of oil, someday. Much of it appeared to be designed for non-skilled use, and that was just as well, as the Thrymi plainly had little understanding of their own ancestors' technology.

Fortunately, Augustus found he had a growing horde of willing workers. Polishing and fixing were a labor of love to them. Some of them were soaking up mechanical principle like sponges. Living out here tended to select for practicality and ingenuity, Augustus reflected, and they'd had generations of it, honing their culture and genetics. Give an outbacker nothing at all except a piece of skyfrond, he'd turn it into a living and a home. Anyone who couldn't, died. For some reason it brought to mind the sociology class, which made him laugh. Reality was a long, long way from their texts. He had to admit very few of them, if any, would survive out here, let alone flourish.

"What's so funny?" asked Briz.

"Just thinking back. The Augustus who landed on the Big Syd would have had a hard time with this."

"He'd have done all right," said Briz. "Got it all wrong, but he was a bloke who'd dive into a sewer thinking it was a bath, and come up smelling like the ladies down at the Red-Hot Pussy Club. Me... I'm not too sure how I would have done, if yer had dropped me out here. Like them Big Syd slaves probably," she said with some disgust. "Worse than whinging Poms, they are."

They were, Augustus admitted, a problem. They wanted one

thing in life: to get back to the Big Syd. And even if he could do it for them, Augustus knew that would spell disaster – because word would get back to the Thrymi that one cloudcastle was in human hands, as fast as the former slaves could blab. The Capos would hear, and they'd tell their alien masters. The outbackers might all know – but they were not going to tell the Thrymi something that would get them tortured for more information – and would result in the Thrymi going hunting outbackers. That too, Augustus feared, would happen eventually – but the longer they could put that off for – the more prepared they'd be.

He had already discovered several things to change the situation. The one was the fuses for the ionization guns. Those were in the heavily armored lower section of the cloud-castle. That was the deck inside the main keep where the slaves had processed the carcasses. He could have disabled much of their weaponry at any time.

It was slightly more complicated to get to, but following and mapping the cloud-castle's steering controls – from behind the consoles on the bridge-deck, all behind undo-able inspection panels, which had plainly not been opened in centuries, led back down to a master-panel and regulating computer in a small armored room down on the engine-room deck. The cloud-castle could be driven as well from down there as from the bridge – and it over-rode the bridge. It even had screens to let you see in all directions – except three were no longer functioning on this cloud-castle. There was a testing circuit, which put the castle into a loop, circling, tilting and rising and falling. It frightened half the apprentices witless when he tested it – and they'd expected it and he'd explained it... If a prisoner – or even a single attacker, could get there, the Thrymi would prob-ably be in a hurry to leave, rather than fight. Disabling the alarms was something he already had an idea of, and now, able to look at the circuits, he could also show the outbackers just what needed bridging. Fortunately, using the controls was plainly intended to be possible without much real skill or experience – as long as you did not – as they had, over-ride the computer-driven compensators.

Between Briz and himself – Briz to provide discipline and himself, instruction, he concluded, they had trained up a number of the apprentices who could now, in a pinch, fly the cloud-castle without disaster.

Where to find these controls and fuses, what they looked like, and how to use them, had become a priority teaching task – that, and how to fire the gauss long-arms accurately. The latter was so popular, he was able to use perfect knowledge of the rest as a requirement. A gauss-gun needed recharge, which limited their use – and value outside the cloud-castle. That didn't stop a lot of outbackers wanting one. "It's a last resort," said Big Bruce – one of the lucky few. "Look, if yer being chased by a Thrymi aircar, and yer got five shots – or none, which are yer gonna choose, Gus?"

That was a rather solid argument, and one he wished he'd paid more attention to, later.

Still it was something of a halcyon time, busy and exciting... and very pleasant to go to bed in the evenings. He'd tried... probing gently with Briz, who plainly knew who it was, to find out who his secretive lover could be. Briz had put him sternly in his place. "If she don't want yer to know, then yer mind yer own business, see. Her choice, the silly baggage, but it's still what she wants. Count yerself lucky yer don't have to listen to her talk. She's got a foul mouth and she talks as much as me."

"Er. Of course, I'll respect her wishes. Um. Does she say anything about me?"

"Nothing sensible," said Briz dismissively. "Yer hoping she thinks yer the best lover what ever got born?"

Augustus blushed. "Well, no. Actually, I wanted to know what she thought of me. As a person. Every time I try to talk she puts her finger across my lips."

"She loves yer, yer drongo. Otherwise she wouldn't be daft enough to come back. And she thinks yer wonderful in the sack. I gather. She didn't actually say. But she was walking funny," said Briz, laughing.

Augustus felt himself blush right to the roots of his hair, and was left without a word to say. He hastily found something else to do. Fortunately, there was so much to choose from. He had a dozen projects he was working on, and there were a lot that were underway – some, even, that he hadn't started himself. The cloud-castle had a lot of space inside – and as one of the perks of working for Augustus was that you got to sleep in the former Thrymi quarters, quite full of people. That seemed like a good idea when they were first thinking about defense... now, well, it meant that some projects had had to expand onto the paddock.

Producing paragliders was still a main function, and from what Briz said, still their most popular product. It had, he was told, begun to change the way people farmed the paddocks. But it was just one of the forms of merchandise that were going out in increasing volumes – an enterprise Briz seemed to have taken over as if it was as natural as breathing. Some of them made use of the materials available only in the cloudcastle – but most used the machinery, the tools and Augustus's increasingly stretched knowledge. They ranged from combs – known well enough, but hard and time-consuming to produce – and easier, better and stronger with a metal saw blade, to soap, which all – from Briz to the plants that got the soapy water, had benefited from at least as far as smell was concerned. "I want to help people, Briz," he said as Briz gleefully recounted the trades over a meal after work.

"Yer think having yer own comb don't help?" asked Briz, who never let his hair out of his hood. "Lot of these girls only had a yester backbone to comb their hair with."

"You know what I mean," said Augustus, sternly. "I am not here to profiteer. I'm here to help with things that make their lives easier and better."

Briz sighed. "Look, Gus. Yer are. But we need jumbuck wool to make the Paragliders. We need tucker to feed ourselves with. Yer give someone a mirror – and its very nice. They gives yer a jumbuck for it, and it's worth a jumbuck. Yer come and work here, yer gets paid, and

245

fed. Where do yer think that comes from? They come jumpabout from miles and miles across the horizon to work here. Yer think they gonna do that if they go hungry?"

"True, that would not be fair," agreed Augustus. "But I don't want any gouging, hear me?"

"Aw. Yer heard any complaints?"

It was true, too. He hadn't. He hadn't had anyone leave, either. And he wanted to put in an hour or two on translating the manuals. He hadn't got far, but the diagrams helped. He'd been able to put English words to certain groups of symbols as a result. That still left a lot of mysterious symbols. He was not yet sure how the Thrymi language worked, or if this was a phonic alphabet or an ideograph system. He had got something of value out of Anthropolgy after all: he knew what those were.

It was... restful sitting there with a beer – because it was beer or water that might well have little fish in it -- and piles of notes, while Briz taught in the background.

Briz's teaching was... colorful. But the students were eager and the math accurate. There were several small texts to help with read-ing... once Augustus had corrected some of the spelling (at least of the words he understood) and grammar, Briz's precise neat hand-writing was being painstakingly copied, and were circulating wider and wider.

People read the simple stories of the Big Syd which Briz wrote with wide-eyed amazement and eagerness. Scarcity and novelty were a fine sauce. A printing press had been on his list – but he discovered Briz had been experimenting at making a simple Linocut-press with some of the plastic from the cloud-castle – and when that worked badly had then settled on some blocks of hardened sap from one of the varieties of skyfrond. Ink he'd helped with – burned bones and a gelatinous solvent that dried well – but, while there were pictures, there was also text, carefully cut into the plates. He was somewhat taken aback that the skills – and precise writing - were the result of Briz having been apprenticed to a forger, but comforted himself a little that it was being put to a better use. Briz didn't help that, by describing the demand as a license to print money, anyway.

He had, so far, amassed a series of logical probabilities about how the Thrymi devices worked. He'd taken apart broken Thrymi burners and gauss-guns, and now understood their alien workings – and fixed and improved both. He'd repaired nine of the remaining aircars. He'd worked out how and where the missile-launches worked from – and found that they had only seven missiles in stock – but space for several hundred. The Thrymi navigation systems were still baffling him, although he had managed to fathom their radar system. Still, his grasp of the alien treasures they'd captured remained on a par with Briz's flying of the cloud-castle: Shaky and with a distinct possibility of disaster.

It was still better than his knowledge about who was sharing his bed every night. So far all he had on that was they were not large, were definitely female and had long straight black hair. She'd left a strand behind. Straight black hair was rare on the Station, and he was steadily eliminating the possibilities.

He'd tried asking Briz again, fishing for clues, a few days later. It was not a great success. Briz had shrugged. "She'd tell yer if she ever wants yer to know. Yer might be just a passing fancy. Or yer might get sick of her. Yer could tell her to go away, if yer was."

"I don't think I am that kind," said Augustus, stiffly.

"It's not kindness we're talking about. It's rooting."

He felt himself blush again to Briz's obvious enjoyment. "Look," he said. "It's, um, just that ah, these things have... consequences. Pregnancy."

Briz looked, for the first time, startled, but said nothing.

"I'd like to do what is honorable and what is right." said Augustus. "It's... it may not be how you do things here on Sybill, but my family...

"You ain't rooting your family. Anyway, that's her business. Babies have nothing to do with men," Briz informed him.

He'd seen Briz, tough exterior forgotten, holding one of the babies in the station. "Well, they don't happen without us," he said. "And... well after mother died, my father did his best."

"Yeah. Well, I don't even know who my father was," said Briz, "Stop being a stickybeak. She'll tell yer if she wants to."

"I'm just thinking of the future," said Augustus.

"Yeah? Well, we might all be dead by then," said Briz, walking off.

Which might be true too. The one thing he was fairly sure of was that Briz must approve, somewhat, of the woman. Briz had moved from being a guide, to a mentor, to virtually running the entire place. And to being the one person in the entire place who would... both support him to the hilt, and tell him when he was off track. And – maybe because Briz had a slightly wider world background, he could follow Augustus's ideas, when others looked blank. The lad had tried exceptionally hard to learn as much as possible too. He'd been lucky in his guide.

He just had to hope that he was lucky in love too.

'The future'!? Briz had been carefully living in the present. It was just too complicated to think beyond that. Her feelings were a mess, for a hard-headed girl from the Big Syd. She was terrified of what he'd do and say when he found out. 'What was honorable. What was right.' Dingo's kidneys. She wanted neither of those. She just wanted to be wanted... for her. How stupid could she get? Yer always traded for advantage, to do yourself best. But... she didn't want to. If... and with him she never doubted it, somehow, they got back to the Big Syd, and he went back to Azure... taking her with him to his family? They terrified her. She had heard enough of how they lived to realize that they were rich. So rich yer didn't have to flaunt it. And she was a girl out of the gutter, came from nothing, who didn't even know who her father was. They would never ever accept her.

And he was very fond of them – especially his brother, who he often seemed to think would do things better than he did.

She wanted the present to stay. She didn't care if she never saw the Big Syd again. What had it given her, but survival? She was living better out here anyway... and she had friends. Friends? She hadn't even known what that meant, before. It was like respect. She had that too... now. And it wasn't just his reflection. They respected her, as her.

And if she did get pregnant? Suddenly, she realized that she wanted nothing more in the world. She wanted his child. No matter what happened, she'd still have that. She could stay here, even if he went away. She was, she thought wryly, a rich woman now. Even without counting what they were paid for paragliders and the other things, which were... sort of his. She managed the money – which was jumbuck – out here. She was surprised to find that not only was she good at managing that, but that her little stories were enormously popular. Oh, sure, someone else could start producing them tomorrow – but they'd have to catch up. And she could teach. She was surprised to discover that, and surprised that she enjoyed it. And even more surprised that her pupils regarded her like some kind of demigod. Respected... and yes, weird, they liked her. It was deeper than like... she'd seen one of them punch someone because they'd dared to say something... slightly impolite, but true, about her.

Of course, that wasn't quite the same as the way they looked up to Gus. He was a legend, already. Lucky he didn't have to live up to it – they just made it up, as he went on being himself. Blinder than blind Freddy. And just... better than the hero they made him out to be. He was that, but... but just because he was him, not that he set off to be heroic. They wanted a legend. She just wanted the man.

She felt like crying, which wasn't like her at all.

The mechanical and even the electrical side were proceeding well, Augustus thought to himself as he walked down into the old engine room of the cloud-castle. Its former owners would barely have recognized it. Clean, with racks of tools, and no mysterious smells of too-hot oil – it still smelled of warm oil, but that was like perfume to him – and to the outbackers working down there. He'd made a lot of progress tracing and understanding what the various systems did, although he wished he could read the alien script. He understood how some worked. The power-system and anti-gravity generator were somewhat more elusive. But they required something he was struggling with: the electronics. It wasn't as if he did not have a good grasp of the subject... it was just the lack of equipment to test what he had, let alone manufacture what he did not. There were racks of boxes of alien components. He could work out, roughly, what some were. But he'd never thought of operating where even something as basic as a voltmeter... he couldn't identify yet.

It was holding him back on what he considered his next big project: a radio system that the outbackers could use. The downside, of course, would be that it would make their presence obvious to the Thrymi, and also the Zell. The latter were, he gathered, less to be feared than the Thrymi. They did not actively hunt people, merely moving along paddocks and mechanically cutting the massas-pods. You could be within touching distance of the harvesters – and be left alone. They still destroyed a well-tended paddock, and any animals picked up by the harvesters.

He could easily enough make a simple static burst generator and use that to send a Morse code SOS. But who would receive it? And who would come looking? He was distracted and thinking about it in the cheerful hubbub that the ex-Thrymi cloud-castle had become – it was a place of talk, and oddly, music, these days. He'd been mildly taken aback when he'd come out onto the main deck to find a woman playing a peculiar stringed instrument to the people sewing paragliders. But it turned out she'd been hired by Briz... and productivity had gone up. "It's why they like working here, see," explained Briz. "They does it when they're shearing Jumbuck, and Lindsey told me it means yer get good teams. Seems to work."

"Uh. Mr Gus," said someone at his elbow.

It was Jase, Big Bruce's eldest still-at-home son. He looked both troubled, tense and determined. Augustus knew Briz had him working outdoors at something. He really didn't like coming into the cloud-castle. His back was badly scarred from the savage beating he'd taken, but he'd physically recovered well. "Jase," said Augustus smiling at him. "What can I do for you, young man?" Nobody called him Mister... barring Briz, and even that was 'sometimes', these days. And the young man was twisting his hat to pieces.

"Dad said I had to tell you, Mister Gus."

By now Augustus was expecting the worst. He looked around for Briz, to see he hadn't been hurt. Briz was just sauntering closer, and appeared fine. What then? Approaching Thrymi? Some of his people had offended Big Bruce? "What is it, Jase?"

"Mister... I'm going to leave. Going jumpabout," said Jase in a rush, looking as if he'd just confessed to something heinous, and not something that was just a fact of life with outbackers. "I'm... getting married. Katy and me, we... wants a station of our own."

"Congratulations, Jase," said Augustus, giving him a manly pat on the back. "She's a fine girl!" She was, a big strapping lass – the way they seemed to like them out here -- cheerful and good with her hands.

"You... you don't mind? Everyone says I am crazy to leave. And... well, I owe yer my life, Mister Gus." He sighed. "It's this bloody place. I... I don't want to be near it. Dad says he'll give me ten jumbuck to start... and I got Katy and me both paragliders. There's a few empty paddocks off sun-side, I heard."

"Of course I will be sad to see you go, Jase, but it's absolutely the right thing to do. We'll have to come up with a wedding gift for you two," said Augustus. "Briz? What do you think would be suitable?"

"Well," said Briz. "I think it's too late for them eyeglasses yer was talking about, Gus," It was said with a broad beam. "Not for you, Jase, for Katy. But I got another idea. Yer don't hate working for Mister Gus, do yer?"

Jase looked at her, startled. "Of course bloody not, yer drongo. He's... he's...bloody champ. Not like yer, Brizzy. Yer a pain in the arse." As it was also said with a broad smile. Outbackers tended abuse those they liked- but only to their face, and be polite to those they didn't, Augustus had noticed. It was all in the way it was said.

"Yeah. I have ter be," said Briz, cheerfully. "It's me job. Now, I was thinkin' about a job we need doing – but not here. Make yer yer own boss – something yer can't see me being able to do with these slackers. Now, I need to talk to Gus about this business idea..."

"If you think it is a good idea, Briz, it's good enough for me," said Augustus. "I'm not much good at business."

"Yer telling me," said Briz. "Now, look. We'll need to talk this over with Big Bruce, but he was givin' me words about havin' too many jumbuck of ours here. Way too many. So, here's me proposal: Yer get a couple of youngsters what also want to go jumpabout to be yer jackaroos, we provides paragliders for 'em, and yer take two hundred of our jumbuck, find some new paddocks, and yer get a cut of the young 'uns and the fleeces..."

It was a tough negotiation, with, in the end, both Jase and Briz allied against him, fighting their way to having the TMI mark on half the Jumbuck and fleeces, when he'd thought ten percent excessive. "But how am I gonna get them to you, Gus?" asked Jase. "See, we'll have to move a bit, to find grazing for two hundred and ten."

"Well," said Augustus, who would cheerfully have given Jase the entire flock, and was only deterred from it by a sharp shake of the head from Briz. It was true, it would set a precedent for future marriages. "You'll just have to keep track of the numbers and find grazing until I find a way. "Communication and transport out here are what I want to work on, and this will give Briz a reason to chase me along. Paragliders are going to change being an outback grazier, but we need more."

"Already changing, Gus," said Jase, comfortable on his own ground – farming. "Dad's running twice the number he had before, and there's jackeroos takin' young stuff from the wild ones, penning them, marking the young 'uns. Gunna mean outbackers spread out a bit more."

"Katy does good with the writing and numbers. You get her to keep track," said Briz. "Yer no good when yer run out of fingers and toes, yer bastard."

Jase just grinned. "Reckon she'll have little 'uns to count. Too busy to keep track o' yer jumbuck, Brizzy. Hope you and Gus are in that position soon."

Briz shot Jase a fulminating look. "I trust yer with me life, and me Jumbuck, but not yer bloody big mouth, Jase. Now shut up... about this, see. I don't want... everyone to know."

"I suppose they would all want something similar," said Augustus rather puzzled by the exchange.

"Too right," said Briz. "And I need people yer can trust."

"Sorry Brizzy," said Jase, humbly. "I was just... Okay, I am shutting my mouth and going to find Katy and talk to her... If that's all right with yer?"

"Of course," said Augustus. "And please give her my congratulations. I'm very happy for you. Of course, if she doesn't want you to take this partnership..."

"She'll love it," said Jase. "Leaving yer, after what you done, was upsetting her. A lot. She bent me ear about it enough."

"Get her to give yer a slap across the chops from me," said Briz, generous as ever.

"I will," promised Jase, grinning.

It was quite a party. Big Bruce was delighted with the outcome. His son was starting off well – even as part-owner – better than many stationers ever got to, and he was clearing some of the excess stock from the area, and his family bonds with Gus were tight, as he felt they ought to be. Jase's mother was less delighted, understandably. She'd lost her son, once, and somehow got him back. She wasn't ready to let go again. Yes, it was the norm on the stations and often as not, unless luck intervened, you'd never see or hear from your children again. Occasionally a smoke might carry word, but it wasn't likely, let alone sure. Conditions out here made families very tightly bound – in the certainty that this was something that could end tomorrow – either from weather or Thrymi or Zell, or just having to move to have a place of your own, which might never bring you back again.

Augustus got a window into this, stopping to talk to her at the wedding feast. He also got a window into a side of Briz he hadn't really seen much of. The mother of the bride and the mother of the groom had both been having a quiet cry together – this was not surprising because Katy was Big Bruce's head stockman's daughter, and the two women were firm friends, working together, feeding the station hands. "Yer've given them a big start, and we're ever so grateful," said Katy's mother, tremulously.

"And they gotter move to a place of their own, sometime," added Jase's mother. "But it's always hard to see them go. So sad knowing yer might never see them again." And she started crying afresh.

Augustus didn't know quite what to say. But Briz did: "Yer haven't thought this through, have yer?" Briz said bracingly, giving her a little shake. "See, thems half of our jumbuck. He even give Jase one of them Thrymi guns. Yer think Mister Gus is gunna send them off and never see them again? Yer think I'd let him do that?"

They both looked at Briz oddly. And then at Augustus.

"It don't make a lot of sense," said Jase's mother, cautiously, drying her eyes. "Of course, them new paragliders make travelling easier, but still."

"Tell 'em what yer told me," said Briz, prodding him in the ribs. "About that 'radio' thing yer working on."

"Ah," he faced explaining a very alien concept to two women who could make a home out of nothing but what they found on a wild paddock, but who had absolutely no grasp of physics or electronics. "Well it's a way of sending a signal... um, like the smokes or the mirror-flashes... but really long distances can be done. Thousands of miles. And you can relay them, even automatically. So, on Azure you can talk to someone ten thousand miles away, just like they were standing in the same room."

"Oh, it'd be great to hear their voices again. I'd love to hear how me Shirleen is doing," said Katy's mother, looking like she'd start crying again.

"Well, that's not all," said Briz, "Explain about the triangulation thing."

"It just means we can work out where a radio signal is coming from if we've got two receivers. It's finding someone out here that's the hard thing. And then I want to work on transport. The paragliders are a good first step... but one day I hope that you can be able to visit them, and then come home. It'll take a while but those are two of the things I'm working on," said Gus.

"And he has to, otherwise he can't fetch his share of the Jumbuck. So, I'll keep him at it, said Briz.

"Brizzy, his blood's worth bottling. And so is yours," announced Jase's mother, looking as if someone had just handed her a treasure.

"I can't promise to succeed," said Augustus uncomfortably. "And it will take some time. Years."

"Better than never," said Jase's mother.

"No one believed yer'd succeed in taking a Thrymi cloud-castle either. But people still followed yer, and yer did it. Jase is free, alive and getting married to me daughter Katy today because of that. I didn't believe yer would do that. I'm not making that mistake again," said Katy's mum.

"That was luck and not good judgement," said Augustus, shaking his head. "Look, if the Thrymi find out what happened, they're going to destroy us."

"Best the kids are away then," said Jase's mother, somehow forgetting that she was upset about them leaving.

A little later when Augustus was walking back to the cloudcastle to his room, and hopefully some company in it, he commented to

Briz who was walking next to him. "I don't know that I like to sell them dreams, Briz. Or you to sell them dreams."

Briz was silent for a bit and said: "Yer wrong, Gus. Out here, they just had their pride, see. Nothing much else. Little hopes, like a paddock or two of their own. Now yer giving them the chance to have big hopes. Dreams they didn't even think of before. That they couldn't think of. Maybe they don't work out, but outbackers, they pick 'emselves up and do it again. If yer don't know yer beaten, then maybe yer not."

"That's very thoughtful and insightful, Briz."

"I guess I know someone who don't know when he's beaten, and it's making me have dreams too," said Briz in a quiet voice.

"May I know who the lucky person is, Briz? Lindsey?"

That got a burst of laughter. "Yer a drongo, Mister Gus. It's what we like about yer." And Briz tucked an arm into the crook of Augustus's arm – a gesture very un-Briz-like. "Let me get yer tucked safely into yer little bed, so I'm free to chase after me own dreams, even if they're daft. At least they're big. Bigger than I ever dreamed in the Big Syd."

"Ah Briz. Anytime you need to go off chasing them... you've got my blessing and support. Anything I can do to help. I'll miss you, but I want you to be happy."

There was a longer silence. "I ain't doing too bad, Gus," said Briz. "Now hop into yer bed and close yer eyes and hope something nice happens to yer. That girl has no bloody taste. She keeps coming back for more."

TWENTY-ONE

"Sir! We've got it! We got a pingback from the transmitter," said the caller from the orbiting freighter, not waiting for any routine politeness.

"Fantastic!" said Charlie. "I'll call the others! You have a position and you're tracking I imagine?"

"Oh yes, Sir. We're not going to lose this one. It is about a thousand five-hundred miles off your position. Seems to be moving relatively slowly."

Going with the news to his grandmother, Charlie weighed it up. That was beyond the range of the aircars. It was of course, much closer than it could have been. And... well, that was the transmitter. Good news, after all this time, but it only meant Augustus's shoe had been found there. Not that he was alive and wearing it.

He found his grandmother contemplating the clouds, sipping tea and eating one of Dr Aljon's delicate little pieces of patisserie. She looked faintly guilty about it. "I have never sampled such things before, but Frederic looked so hurt when I said I wouldn't try it, as he had made it especially for me."

"He's good, isn't he? News, grandmother. They found the signal from the tracker in Augustus's shoe."

"Thank heavens! What needs to be done?" she asked getting to her feet. Charlie realized suddenly how small his grandmother was. She was just so forceful he forgot that she barely came up to his shoulder.

"We'll need a council of war on this. Us, for a start, Templeton, the security fellow. He'll be glad of a chance to plan real action. He reckons the local gangs are the worst bunch of larcenous rogues in all human space, but he's a fighter, not a chaser after petty criminals... Look, grandmother, there is no guarantee that Augustus is alive. We just have a trace on the shoe. It's a long way off, too. There are a fair number of logistical and military preparations that need to be made."

"They may well be simpler than the intractable problems of this hotel," said his grandmother. "It seems that the Hyaton chain had every reason to be glad to sell. Their staffing costs -- as they flew all their staff in, and that of importing everything, are exorbitant."

"The local food is not bad," said Charlie. "A bit strange at times, but surely that could be part of the experience for tourists?"

"I was unaware there was local food to be bought. I do suppose they have to eat something, and they could hardly afford to buy imported food at those prices," said his grandmother, doubtfully.

"Talk to Fred. He introduced me to some of it. He's been using the flour-substitute in his baking. When he was here doing his research he could barely afford the hotel, and certainly not the meals. So, he had to learn. It apparently comes from the floating plants, and the meat from flying animals that the Thrymi hunt and sell."

"That man has been a very valuable find," said his grandmother. "I trust you will invite him to our meeting."

"I have to," said Charlie. "He's our expert on the Thrymi, after all. Besides, I like him."

The meeting consisted of Charlie, his grandmother, Mark Templeton, ex-special services, and now head of hotel security (officially) his father, via a link from one of the freighters, Mel Su, who was the logistics head, and Dr. Aljon.

His father let Charlie know he was not alone in wondering if that was just Augustus's shoe, without his brother. "We've modified and dropped in another ten probes. Between them we can map any movements of the tracker. If he's confined in any area, we'll know exactly where it is soon enough."

Dr. Aljon produced some excellent petit fours and detailed plans of the external and even some internal structure of the typical Thrymi cloud-castle. "They vary somewhat, but the general ground-plan appears similar, regardless of the size." He smiled. "Every xeno-archeologist should have a team of industrial agents to help them." He – or the team – had been very thorough. They had the numbers of Thrymi on all the cloud-castles that had come in – which ranged from twelve to over fifty, with a median around twenty-three. They also had a little detail on the Thrymi weaponry. "They like a burner of some sort – an energy discharge, which takes some time to kill, but is painful, as a personal weapon. It stops them killing each other quite so often, I was told. They have various forms of gauss-weapons firing projectiles, as well as an ionization discharge weapon. We think there may be some missiles or rocketry, but that is anecdotal. They are said to be very fast and brutally effective in combat – but once again that is largely anecdotal. It's hard to gather information from the locals who tend to be in awe of them. We've had some luck in some of the bars favored by the stevedores. They tend to be what the locals call 'outbackers'."

Charlie had come across the term and wanted to ask about it, but discussion moved on to the logistical problems of taking a force in an aircar, or several aircars, some 1500 miles there and then back – and how to arm them and how any attack could be undertaken. The hotel project had allowed six aircars with considerable armoring to be brought, quietly, in pieces, and assembled. The downside was that they had a range of just over a thousand two hundred miles – which meant they would have to either carry less arms and men and extra fuel tanks, or refuel in flight. A combination of these seemed best, but it would reduce their ability to use all the craft. And any attack seemed risky, anyway.

"The two things we do have in our favor is that, when away from the plate, the cloud-castles we've been tracking seem to generally stay above the clouds. They dip within the cloud and floating vegetation – we've now got that separated out in our mapping – it's a three-dimensional issue with the vegetation. And the other factor is their ionization weapons, from observation, have a range of around three miles. Missiles would be different, but they're a finite resource. Very few of the cloud-castles come closer than that three-mile limit from any other castle. So: hidden down in the cloud and floating vegetation rafts – it appears it forms aggregations, we'd be able to get within four miles of them."

"Comfortable range for a small, non-metallic drone."

"The one of the only two exceptions to the rule of the cloud-castle spending most of its time above the cloud," said Charlie's father, "Happens to be the cloud-castle we detected the signal from. It appears embedded in this floating plant – except when the vegetation raft rises above the clouds. It drops down, then and remains below the raft – but in the cloud-cover."

"So," asked Charlie... "If we dropped a parachutist onto that vegetation raft... would they fall through it or...could they sit there and wait?"

There was a silence. Then Dr Aljon said: "Well, the outbackers do live on it. Maybe we can ask them?"

"An excellent suggestion, Fredric," said grandmother. "And get some idea of what, exactly, life is like out there. How this hunting works, and what the Thrymi do out there."

"Do we have any parachutes?" asked ex-Sergeant-Major Templeton. "I have a number of men with the training and experience."

"No," said Charlie's father. "But we are quite well set up out here. I can see to them being manufactured quite fast. And thanks to the need for fabrics for the hotel, we have an automated programmable cutter-stitcher."

"It's whether this stuff will support a landing sir. It's a pretty ugly end, otherwise. A long way down."

"We'll test all of this thoroughly first," said Charlie, firmly. "None of our people are jumping to certain death."

"We take our chances, Mr Thistlewood," said the big man. "You pay well, and look after our families. That's more than the army did."

"We still prefer not to have to look after families and to leave that to you," said grandmother, flintily. "So, we will take as few chances as possible. But yes, we do look after our own. That's what we are. And that is why we're doing this."

It was some hours later that two new developments took place, which up-ended a few of Charlie's ideas. A few of everyone's ideas, really. First up was Fred Aljon, who brought with him a burly man, sporting a puglist's nose and curly hair. "Charlie," said Fred – they were very much on first name terms. "Can I introduce you to this gentleman? I think it is quite important, and I hope of value to both him and you. Bill, I'd like you to meet my mate Charlie. Bill is an outbacker."

"Too right I am," said Bill, sticking his hand out. "And bloody sick of this place. Fred says yer might get me out of here, if I gives yer some gen about it."

Charlie took his hand, shook it firmly. "Of course," he said, trusting Fred Aljon. "Where would you like to go? To Azure?"

"Bloody hell, no! I want to get back to the outback. It's difficult from here. Them bloody Zell keep most of the skyfrond well away from the Big Syd. There's always twenty blokes too many for any bit that comes drifting in. And a good chance them Zell will blast it to ash under you."

"Well, we're hoping to take an aircar out from here..."

"Give me a ride and I'm yer man," said Bill eagerly. Then he looked askance at Charlie. "Yer wouldn't happen to be some relation of that bloke what the Capo's are tryin' to keep everyone shut up about? Got a look of him about yer, and he was from Azure too."

Something in the tone said to Charlie that 'Capos' were not popular with this Bill. He produced a picture of Augustus. Bill nodded and grinned. "I was in the Queen's Legs, when he broke the place up. Man, that was quite a blue." Then he looked wary. "Yer not going to rat on me, are yer? Word's out we ain't to talk about it."

"Absolutely not," Charlie said evenly. "That's my brother. I'm here looking for him."

The big man winced. "I reckon they done him in, mate," he said quietly. "He vanished. Probably minced into a mystery bag by them Bondi Boyz. They're the crookest bunch of all these bastards."

"We think he may be alive, in the outback."

"Oh, he'll be right then. Look, it's not like here. This lot would skin their own bleeding mother. Outbackers ain't like that. I know," he said ruefully. "They skun me."

"He was sold – by the Bondi-Boyz – to the Thrymi on a skycastle."

Bill pulled a face, shook his head. "He's dead, mate. Look, I could lie to yer, and get me lift out to the skyfrond, but he's yer brother. Them Thrymi are evil bastards. If he's out on a cloud-castle yer'll never find him, and yer can't fight 'em."

"Bill, the one thing you can be sure of, is we'll get you your ride off the plate," said Charlie, his heart sinking somewhat. "We keep our bargains."

"He was a bloody legend, yer brother. Yer should be proud of him," said Bill. "Remember him for that. But you can't find anything out there."

"We've tracked him – or at least pin-pointed the cloud-castle..." His phone vibrated. It was his father. "Sorry, I have a call. Fred. Can you get Bill a drink, something to eat – and reassure him that TMI always keeps their agreements."

The call was news of the second development. "Charlie, the tracker is moving around anyway."

"Well, that's good news! Got some triangulation on where so we can plan on the possible strategy, Dad?"

"Well, not really. We've used seventy probes... He's moving around a fair bit – top to bottom of the structure. But here's the really interesting part, Charlie. He's not always IN it. He's out on the vegetation. Up to three miles from the cloud-castle... or," he said with sudden caution. "His boot-heel is."

"If we could tag him three miles out, snatch and run, we'd be out of range of some of the Thrymi weaponry," said Charlie, thoughtfully.

"Yes. And we're fitting stealth cloaking to the aircars. We just need more information about exactly what goes on, on these floating plants. Fascinating things."

"I've got just the man. Fred's got us an outbacker."

"Man's a treasure," said his father, his mouth twisting into a smile. "He's even got my mother trying new food."

Charlie tracked the Xeno-archeologist and the outbacker down. It wasn't hard, Fred gravitated towards the kitchens at the drop of a hat, and had rather taken over part of them. The outbacker was looking a little bemused, but he was sitting with a beer in one hand and was tentatively sampling a slice of quiche.

He looked up at Charlie. "Yer've left me feeling a bit of a stunned mullet, mate. I could have put it kinder. Fred says yer whole family is out looking for him. And that yer have a bigger spread than the Big Syd."

"A little bigger yes," admitted Charlie. "That was my father. The tracker signal – there's a tracker on my brother's heel – is moving around. So, either he or his shoe is attached to something alive. And – here's the part that I need input about from you, Bill. The tracker has been picked up out on the floating vegetation. What you call the 'skyfrond'. We'd like to know a bit more about that."

The outbacker looked at him in puzzlement. "Thrymi don't let their slaves outside. Maybe to butcher something big like a skywhale?"

"A what...? I see we're going to have to talk. A lot. I'll need some of that beer too, Fred. And I'd better call Templeton and Su."

Soon they were taking notes about matters as diverse as 'jumpabout' to yesters, herbeen and skywhales, from how the outbackers lived, to what they knew of the Thrymi slave-conditions from the few outbacker slaves who had escaped.

Charlie asked about his home and how they could get him back to it. The man paused. Then said, tersely: "Can't really happen, mate. I've no idea where they are. I could jumpabout for the rest of me life and never have a chance. Paddocks move around with the wind. They'll make out. Me missus will have found someone else by now. She was a good sheila."

"So, why did you come here?" asked Mel Su.

"Didn't have much choice. Got picked up by a Zell harvester."

They all looked at him. "So: the Zell. We haven't really investigated them... can you explain?"

The outbacker shrugged. "They harvest massas. So do we. We run our jumbuck there too. And I was too slow to get out the way." He sighed. "Anyone they pick up, they drop off here. If yer don't work yer don't eat, but the Zell aren't nasty like them Thrymi. Just say we don't belong out there. I was bloody born out there! I don't belong here!"

"But they transport people back here if they find them out there... if someone wanted to come back here?"

Bill snorted. "Some kids might. But yer don't want to get taken by the Zell. They gives yer the snip, see."

They looked at him blankly. He looked a little embarrassed. "Look, when they catches yer, they dope yer up, put you in this machine and it fixes yer."

"Fixes?" asked Mel, trying to see why this was a problem.

"Yeah, fixes yer so yer can't have no more kids."

"They neuter their prisoners?"

Bill nodded.

It took a while to tease the entire matter out. Bill assumed they knew and understood what any one on the Big Syd – or in the outback knew about the Zell and life here. In essence, any outbackers caught by the Zell were neutered – male and females, and were kept prisoners on the Zell cloud-castle, and then released back on the plate, when the cloud-castle next came back there.

"So: basically, they treat humans rather like stray cats or dogs."

"Dunno what those are, but I'm glad I had a couple of kids before they picked me up," said Bill.

"Would the Zell be in any way prepared to aid us?" asked Mel Su.

"Don't do much to help anyone but themselves," said Bill, shaking his head. "They say anything that ain't a Zell is not really worth anything. They believe they're superior, see. Because they don't eat meat, they say."

"I dated a girl like that once," admitted Charlie. "Not the sharpest pencil in the box, but she thought she was better than everyone else because she was a vegan."

"What's a vegan?" asked Bill.

They explained and he looked even more puzzled. "I don't think we got those, outback. I mean, mostly there is lots of food, but if things get tight yer eat what yer can get."

"It's complicated," said Charlie, tactfully. "Anyway – I gather the Zell and Thrymi do fight..."

"Only long range. The Zell stay away from the Thrymi. They're not fighters."

Relaying this to his grandmother when they had their 'evening' meal – daylight might be perpetual on the Anti-gravity plate, but people still followed a circadian rhythm -- he saw how her hands stiffened on the knife and fork. "To think I thought these 'Thrymi' the worst. I just have to hope these 'Zell' do not find Augustus. And it is high time you got married, Charlie. When will the rescue mission be ready?"

"We're just waiting on components for the aircars that somehow got miss-shipped. Azure is a long way off to correct errors in loading manifests."

TWENTY-TWO

I t was a few weeks later that, as they were eating breakfast – as they occasionally did, by invitation, with Big Bruce and the Station family, news came in via the mirrors that a Zell cloud-castle was harvesting off to the sun-side. "It doesn't look a problem. It's the same one come through round-paddock just when you came here," said Big Bruce. "One comes along every few years. Bloody pain in the arse. Mind you, we'll go over and help them shift their stock and stuff. Much easier with the paragliders."

"Is it wise to let them see the paragliders?" Augustus asked.

"Aw, it's Zell. They don't do nothing except harvest massas pods. 'Course they take anyone who gets in their way, and yer don't want to do that, 'cause they geld yer, but if yer twenty paces away they leave yer alone. Yer should go have a look."

"Well we might do that. I am curious, and they're far enough from our cloudcastle to be no threat. What do you think Briz?"

"I think I'm gonna throw up," said Briz, and left the table in a rush.

Augustus started to his feet. Big Bruce's wife put a restraining hand on his shoulder. "Leave Brizzy alone."

"But he doesn't seem well. I... I don't have much medical knowledge but the Blue men trained me in first aid...

"Trust me," said Big Bruce's wife. "Briz don't need yer right now. It's perfectly natural. Happens to quite a few of us. Sometimes in the morning, and, when yer get used to that, in the afternoon instead or as well, just to mess with yer."

"Is it something in the diet? I've been fine."

"You would be," said Big Bruce's wife with a tolerant smile. "It'll come out of its own accord. Now, why don't yer go and look at the Zell cloudcastle, and leave Brizzy in peace?"

A little later Augustus, still somewhat worried, went in search of Briz. Briz was asleep on the pallet in the front room of Augustus's suite of rooms, exactly where he was most mornings – except he wasn't usually asleep. The poor lad would never be large, but had got a little plumper than he used to be. Well, about that sharp little face anyway. He had lashes that the girls in the teams envied. The rest of Briz was kept in baggy ragged clothing. Augustus had moved to working in the local clothes, made by the stationers out of Jumbuck fleece. Briz stuck with his Big Syd clothes, and had somehow contrived to add more – but equally baggy.

Briz, with reflexes honed from living on the Big Syd, woke up as he stood there, a hand going to his pocket, reaching for the small knife Augustus knew was always there. He carried one himself these days – and several of the odd three-sided screwdrivers that the Thrymi castle required, along with several pairs of pliers and various other useful things, all in pouches made of Shonk-neck leather that someone had made for him.

"It's just me," said Augustus reassuringly. "I just came to see if you were all right."

Briz did look a bit pale, as he tucked an errant strand of jet-black hair back into his hood. "Yeah. I was just... feeling a bit crook. I'm fine now. Are we gunna fly out and look at that Zell harvester?"

"Not if you're feeling crook," said Augustus, by now completely at home with the local meaning of the word. "Maybe you should just take it easy, Briz?"

"I'll do that when I'm bleeding dead," said Briz, sounding far more like himself. "Let's go." He put a slim-fingered hand on Augustus's forearm. "But, when I get back, um, you and me got to talk."

"Any time Briz. Right now, if you like. Is something wrong?"

"I'll tell yer, when we get back. Come on. I just want to enjoy this flight."

Normally you had to put a cork in Briz to shut the lad up, but he was being oddly silent right now.

Preparations for the mission were reaching an end point back at the former Hotel Hyaton. The aircars were assembled. They were large thirty-seaters, partly stripped out to take military equipment and also the medevac units. Research too continued apace. This was perhaps what Special Services troops did: fight enormous odds, deep inside enemy territory – but even with mock-ups of the inside of Thrymi cloud-castles – this was a fight in territory that none of them had ever experienced. Talking about the 'paddocks' as Bill called the aggregated masses of floating vegetation, Templeton asked if a parachutist could land on them.

"A what?" asked Bill. "Oh, you mean one of them fliers. Yeah, I reckon. I seen a Thrymi flier land on a paddock to untangle a harpoon cable. It sunk a bit."

They all stared at him. "You mean... land an aircar on the floating vegetation?"

Bill shrugged. "We live on them. Whole families, sheds, the lot. Why don't yer go and try it?"

It was such a practical answer that they all wondered why no-one had thought of it. "The Thrymi or Zell might put a stop to the expedition we plan, if we test the fliers before they leave," said Mel Su, eventually.

"Cloud and full cloaking," suggested Templeton.

"Worth trying, I reckon," said Charlie.

So, after talking it over with Charlie's father and grandmother – an additional distraction was arranged – an aborted landing by one of the freighters --two of the cloaked aircars slipped out into the cloud, dropping steeply, like discarded rubbish. One only had one crewman and a pilot. The other, lifting gear. The mission, to settle the first and have its crewman get out. If the aircar fell through, the pilot would attempt to re-start. If need be, the crewman could be winched to safety. If the outbacker was to be believed, people walked about on the stuff, all the time. The aircar proceeded some fifty miles out, keeping in the cloud, avoiding the vegetation masses – and on a path that would keep it away from the cloud-castles that the TMI ships above had located and were tracking.

In some ways it worked perfectly, and in another it didn't. The craft set down, and did not fall, not immediately. The crewman got out. He did not fall immediately either, as the assembled TMI rescue-crew listened in to his reporting on the tight-beam transmitted to the orbiting freighter, and then back down to the 'construction site' on the anti-grav platform.

"It's a bit springy, and somewhat awkward to walk on..."

There was a sudden burst of noise, which included at least some obscenity... And then a loud thump. "OW!"

The pilot cut in. "Uh. He's um, under attack! Some woman has just punched him on the nose."

"What's happening?" demanded Templeton.

"He has fallen down, she's yelling at him and hitting him with a basket every time he tries to stand up," said the pilot in a tone of horrified fascination.

"What action can you take?" asked Templeton.

"Uh. I've locked the doors," said the pilot. "She's, uh, quite angry. We... we appear to have blown her washing away."

There was a moment of stunned silence in the command room.

Then Charlie said: "You'd better go and help him, Henry. Apologize to the lady. Promise to pay for her washing."

"I'm a flier, not a negotiator," protested the pilot, nervously. "If I was any good at talking to women I'd be married, not sitting out here. What do I pay her?"

"That's a good question. I'm not sure they'll take Azure dollars, for all they're keen on them here. I'll ask Bill. Take a headset so we can tell you."

Bill had to stop laughing first. "Oh, she'll want at least a jumbuck for that," he said with a broad smile. "Tell the sheila yer don't know what she's so upset about."

"Don't!" warned several voices.

Bill beamed. "Yer a bunch of wet blankets. Look, offer her anything metal. If yer got a knife, she'll probably want to root both of yer."

They discovered a number of things during that expedition. Firstly, flying in the clouds was a risky pastime, because avoiding drifting sky-frond – little bits of it, and large masses of it, was a constant hazard once you got away from the plate. Secondly, it was perfectly possible to land safely and to walk on the drifts – as long as you chose your landing spots carefully, avoiding laundry. Thirdly the cost of a load of washing was one penknife and a wristwatch, after which you got coy inquiries about your marital state, and fourthly, the plant matter liked the metal of the aircar as much as the outbacker liked the metal of a knife. It had clung and involved some engine strain and ripping noises. Some of the plant had come back with it. That was quite useful, firstly they all got to look at it, and secondly got to test a plasticized paint that would allow for the aircar to land without needing to be cut free.

"I think a cargo of suitable trading goods might be a wise idea," said grandmother, with a sniff. "Seeing as your pilots are not able to tell a landing site from a washing-line. Perhaps an external loud-speaker so your pilots can communicate without risking their lives. And I suspect you will need a medical kit."

"Trading goods are a great idea. So is the speaker – but there actually is an external one for warning people not to approach until the fans shut down. We've got a medic with each squad, and a full medevac unit for each aircar. The ones TMI have been making for remote disaster relief. Everything from whole blood to sticking plaster," said Charlie, pleased to at least be ahead on that issue.

"Well," she said dryly, "If you can get them back here, we have an excellent hospital wing, which just happens to be fully staffed and operational, and have a top cardio-thoracic surgeon and an expert on respiratory medicine on the staff. Not that I suspect your grandfather's hand in any of that. At all."

"Taking care of you, is he?" said Charlie with a grin.

"I wish he wouldn't, but it does seem that there is scanty medical treatment available here. That part of the hotel is already running and already making money."

That was her only objection, except to the idea of Charlie going along with the rescue flight. On this, however, Charlie was adamant. He didn't fight it. That wasn't Charlie's way, and he was aboard the aircar, quietly but definitively, before either his father or grandmother realized. The plan had evolved somewhat to involve new long-range fuel tanks on all of the aircars, so the halfway-plan could be passed over. Two aircars remained, that could fly them more fuel if needed, while they sat on a drifting plant mass and waited. It was going to take six hours to get into proximity, taking it at a fuel-saving slow pace. Bill had agreed to go with them up to that point, to help with any contact with the locals, provided they avoided their laundry. Bill had a stash of goods from his time working on the Anti-grav plate – and now from his new employers – that he seemed confident would make him a wealthy man, and a popular one, even if there would be no more children for him.

The six hour flight seemed to be a long time.

During the flight Charlie had a lecture from his grandmother, and a worried consultation with his father. "Look, Charlie. I understand. But... the military men we recruited, this is what they're good at, this is their field of expertise, this is the job they have to do. They can't do it well if they're trying, principally, to keep you alive. Because they will be."

"I promise I'll leave the close stuff to them Father. I've been told my place. Templeton told me he'd tie me up if he had to. I'm staying in the back-up aircar. We're stopping seven miles off on whatever plant-drift we can find. We have anti-missile missiles, we've got a rocket-booster, we're out of range of their ionization weapons..."

"I will still worry. And your grandmother worries more. She wants to be there too."

"I'll take as much care as possible," said Charlie.

"I've got probes ready to drop. We've got hi-res lenses focused on the areas – the cloud is a problem, of course. We're also getting something strange in those visuals. I'll send you a picture so you can show them to your outbacker. It may give us a clue what the Thrymi are up to."

But Bill also had no idea what the odd rectangles on the images were. Some Thrymi devilry, no doubt.

"We wondered if they were some kind of animal, which they could have stopped to hunt. We've spotted them in a radius around the Thrymi castle we get the pingback from, with occasional ones up to a hundred and fifty miles away, but most of them within thirty to fifty away, and the highest occurrence within ten. Some are quite colorful."

"The Herbeen get real colorful when they're mating. Yer don't want to be anywhere near 'em, then. Never do, but then even less," said Bill, unhelpfully. "But them ain't Herbeen."

It was a little later in the flight that Charlie's father called in again. "Charlie. We've got a situation emerging. There's a Zell Cloud-castle about twenty miles off from the Thrymi one. Tracking says your brother's transmitter is heading for it. He appears to be with or near those rectangles I sent you a picture of."

As this had come through the main speaker system, so

Templeton heard it, and came across to Charlie. "What are these rectangles, Boss?" he asked.

"We don't know. I showed Bill, but he doesn't either. Here's the picture." He showed the screen to Templeton, who peered at it, with his mouth opening, shaking his head. "I'm sorry, it's not very good resolution..." said Charlie.

"Good enough," said Templeton. "That's a parachute. Or rather, a paraglider wing. You can see the cells. Has your brother ever done any paragliding?"

"Once. He broke his ankle."

Templeton scratched his jaw, thoughtfully. "I reckon he's doing it again, if you ask me. Better ask how long it's going to take that 'rectangle' – at present rate of travel – to get to that Zell castle. Your brother doesn't have a Thrymi problem. I reckon we've prepared for the wrong situation. I reckon he has a Zell problem, and that could make your grandmother very unhappy." He leaned forward to the pilot. "Hey Chalkie, screw fuel economy, give us the best speed you can get out of this bus. And tell the others." Then he turned back to Charlie. "Sorry, Boss. Military habits. Is that all right?"

"Out here, you're in charge," said Charlie. "I thought that was understood. And I think you might want to get Bill to talk about Zell cloud-castles and Zell in a fight, if you think that's what's coming. It would be like my brother to somehow be out there, paragliding."

"I thought he was the quiet academic one of the family?" said Templeton.

"He is. But he has this odd streak, every now and again. It's a shame we don't have the same depth of knowledge about the Zell that we do about the Thrymi."

"The Thrymi expert – Aljon, did tell me he'd talked with Bill. The internal structure of the castles is much the same as the Thrymi arrangement as far as Bill saw. A flight deck equivalent where the harvest comes in, and the same 'keep' and courtyard above that. The courtyard is roofed though. And apparently the material it is constructed out of is weirdly transparent from the inside."

CHAPTER

TWENTY-THREE

I t was all the fault of the betraying fold of cloud. If it had not been for that they would have seen the Zell flier before it was far too late. As it was, one moment they were flying along slowly, looking at the mechanism of the rotating line of the massas-pod harvester from a safe distance, and next there was a stubby-nosed Zell flier racing towards them from the rear. Briz managed to get one shot off with the Thrymi gauss-gun before the enveloping purse of net snatched them out of their dive, and in a wild swing ripped them skywards in the enfolding net bag, as it was winched in toward the flier – which was arcing bac to the Zell cloud-castle. There was no way to bring the Thrymi gauss-gun to bear, and even if they could have, the fall might well have killed them anyway. That wasn't stopping Briz slashing at the tough net – the wing was a collapsed tangle in with them, so getting free of the net would not help. The flier zipped inside the Zell-flight deck, just as Briz got the second strand of net to part, and the net was dropped into a cage of metal bars against the outer wall, which, except for a metal box attached to it was darkly transparent. A roof of bars slid almost entirely across, and the purse-rope of the net pulled, freeing them into the cage, as the net dragged through the tiny gap and it closed, leaving them sprawled on the metal floor on the torn paraglider.

"Bloody hell!" yelled Briz. "We got to get out of here!" Briz grabbed the bars desperately. August pulled the harness release on the paraglider, allowing him to stand up and shakenly survey the scene.

"Gus! We gotta get out of here!" shrieked Briz in naked panic.

"We'll get out, somehow," said Augustus, looking at the cage. "We did before."

"You don't understand! The first thing they'll do is sterilize us! And I'm bloody pregnant!"

Not even being slung around in a net-bag had shaken Augustus that much. He just stared at Briz for a moment, uncomprehending. Then a strange metallic voice sounded from a speaker in the wall. "Remove all your integument coverings and any objects you are carrying, and place them in the hopper on the wall. They will be returned to you when we release you at your place of origin. You have a short time to do this voluntarily, before you are tranquilized for your treatment. Anything you still have not put in the hopper will be disposed of and you will not get back. Be assured that the procedure will be painless, as you will be anesthetized. Recovery is good and any pain is of short duration. You will be well treated. We wish to question you about the flying device."

But even as the Zell was speaking, Augustus had taken out his refurbished Thrymi burner, and having decided the door hinge would be the weakest spot was cutting it with the hottest part of the plasma. "Get yours too. Work on the same hinge. Why didn't you tell me! I didn't even know you were a girl."

"That's why, you nong," said Briz, getting her burner onto the same spot.

The hinge 'spanged' and dribbled hot metal. Augustus kicked the door-frame and it bent out.

"Lie down! Hold the bars and we can push with our feet," said Briz. They did and the cage door lock creaked and snapped, leaving the door hanging by one hinge. "We can get out," said Augustus. "The wing is a wreck. Bring the gun."

Briz grabbed the gun and slid through the gap. Augustus had to squeeze through, leaving the buttons on his shirt behind. As he pulled free, metal shutters slid down from the roof, and closed off the cage – where they could – the broken door impeded them somewhat. A pale vapor trickled out. "Gas!" shouted Briz. "We gotta go. Where to, Gus?"

The flight-deck doors were closed, and they were separated from the stubby flier in a large empty room with some ominous-looking machinery with what could only be some kind of operating table attached to it, and several trolleys. A closed door at the far side seemed the only option. They ran to it. It did not open. But Augustus saw something oddly familiar about it – the same narrow holes that served for door and elevator mechanisms on the Thrymi cloud-castle. He pushed his fingers into them, hoping this was not a trap. He could smell the gas. "Hold your breath."

Briz nodded. And the door opened.

It too was an elevator. And the directional pattern of its controls was identical to the Thrymi one – except for being lower and set into the transparent material of the outer wall. Briz plainly recognized it too. "Which way?" he... she asked reaching for the holes.

"Down."

The door slid closed behind them, and Augustus asked: "Um. Who is the father?"

In answer Briz pulled her hood and cap off, pulled loose a pin and a cascade of fine long black straight hair fell down over her shoulders. "Who do you bloody think, you drongo. Too hard to cut it out here," she said, as it framed her face, and the elevator stopped. Augustus barely noticed the stop. She pushed him at the opening door. "Go on!"

"Briz...I love you!"

"No yer don't. But get us out of here anyway, Mister Gus, please?"

Looking past her, he could see this was indeed the engine-room of the Zell cloud-castle. And, looking at the structures he was as sure as any engineer ever could be, that, no matter how different the outer facing of the Zell cloud-castle might look – the engines were designed by the same engineers, maybe even built in the same factory. The only real difference was the transparent walls through which they could see the sky. It was... less neglected than the Thrymi one had been, but it too had a layer of dust. Dust, surprisingly was a fact of life on Sybil – somewhere far below its turbulent core threw up vast quantities of it. It provided cloud-nuclei and that ended up on the skyfrond, and that in turn used a lot of it... but some blew off again, and settled elsewhere or formed more cloud nuclei. The dust in the Thrymi engine room had spoken of many years, if not centuries. This merely spoke of months or maybe a year or two. There had been no way out to the outside of the Thrymi engine room, and he doubted this would be any different. "Control room. Over there!"

As they rushed across to it, a klaxon horn sounded an eerie wail. "I think they've figured we've got away."

"They'll be searching for us soon. Do yer think we should be stuck in the control room? It's got no way out."

"I was just going to cut off the weapons firing mechanism, and set it spinning and rocking, and leave them to come down and fix it while we try to steal an air-car again."

"Charlie, Charlie! Are you receiving me Charlie?"

"Loud and clear, Papa. What's up?"

"The tracker is now inside the Zell castle. We have pictures of a small craft coming out and intersecting with the approximate path of the paraglider. There was some cloud..." he sighed. "Your grandmother is not going to take this well. Please take exceptional care, Charlie."

"Will do. What's our intersection time, father?"

"Fifty-seven minutes if all the trajectories remain the same."

"We may need a few minutes to formulate an attack when we get close," said Charlie.

"We're tracking. If anything changes we'll inform you."

After a tense wait of slightly more than fifteen minutes, of keeping quiet while the ex-military discussed their business exactly as the ex-military always did in extremis – reverting to type, another call came in. "Charlie. Something very strange is happening down there. The Zell castle is no longer proceeding linearly but has started a tight circle around one spot. We're sending the new co-ordinates directly to the pilots."

"Bill," said Charlie. "Know any reason why a Zell cloud-castle should fly in small circles?"

The outbacker shook his head. "No. They'll sometimes do two sweeps of a paddock if it is too wide."

I n the bowels of the Zell Cloudcastle engine-room, going into the control-room, Augustus was even more certain that whatever differences in the external appearance of their cloud-castles were, the chassis, as it were, of Zell and Thrymi Cloud-castles came from the same design. He and Briz knew exactly which of the alien controls did exactly what. "Do weapons. I'll disable the bridge and get the ship on that rotation mode," panted Augustus. He had thought about the mode since discovering it on the Thrymi cloud-castle. It must be a testing pattern, keeping the ship circling, and putting it through a series of tilts, spins, and rapid rises and falls. It would test the machine's computational correction and, as they knew from experience, the stomachs of any passengers.

He was just finishing the settings, when he heard an ominous, loud click. The massive, thick, heavy reinforced door, which they'd left open... had closed. Briz, always quicker to react, rushed to it and tried to pull it open. The one on the Thrymi cloud-castle had been as easy and responsive as this had, coming in.

It did not move, not even when she swore at it.

Augustus rushed over to join her as the cloud-castle gave its first turning lurch, nearly knocking both of them off their feet. "There must be an emergency opening control!"

But neither of them could find anything in the rocking, swaying control room that would open that door. They were very thoroughly trapped. "Can we burn our way out?" asked Briz, pulling out her Thrymi burner.

Augustus shook his head. "Mine is just about out of charge from doing those other hinges. There must be a way... this must be a security lockdown."

"What's that mean?"

"It means that – unless I am wrong, the various doors all lock, and you need some kind of special pass or reset to open them. We're... stuck. I'm sorry, Briz." He felt desperately that he'd let her down. His mind was a tumult of emotions, that he really didn't know how to cope with. He hung his head, and shook it.

She put an arm around him, and he looked down into her bright blue eyes. "If I got to be stuck, Gus... I'm sorry too."

"Whatever for, Briz? You usually get me out of trouble. I should have looked after you better..."

"Sorry I tricked yer. About being a boy. And... then I didn't know how to tell you."

"You don't have to be sorry, Briz," said Augustus. "I'd never have hired you if I had known you were a girl. I'm not much good at even talking to girls. And then I would never have known you. And... I think you're the best thing that ever happened to me."

"I'm an ugly little slag who took advantage of yer when you was drunk."

He looked down at her, still holding on as the castle gyrated. "I don't think you're ugly. You have beautiful eyes, and wonderful hair..."

"And crooked teeth and small tits."

"They felt just the right size to me. And I can't say I care if your teeth are skew. And I might have been drunk that first night, but so were you. And you came back the second night, and neither of us were drunk. And I still think you're the best thing that ever happened to me."

"Yer say all the right things," said Briz burrowing into him. "Are we ever gonna get out of here, Gus? What's gonna happen?"

"I don't know," he admitted. "We have air from outside through that vent, we have water in that tank in the corner, so short term we're all right. But... well I will have to try to work out how to get us out. And we don't know what is going on out there."

"Got plenty of screens to show us."

It hadn't even occurred to Augustus to look. The view could make you quite dizzy even if the movement didn't.

"Charlie. One of the techs just had a look at the original Thrymi cloud-castle. It's on the move too."

"Is it heading toward the Zell cloud-castle?"

"Yes. It's not flying too straight or particularly fast. We're running estimates... Ah, it should precede you there by about five minutes. That's to the same site as the other cloud-castle, presuming it doesn't stop and fire at it from a distance. I gather they usually engage hostility at about two miles. The other thing... those paragliders. We've counted ninety-three so far. They all seem to be making their way toward the Zell cloud-castle, allowing for the fact that they're catching thermals to gain height."

"Templeton here, Mr Thistlewood. Are they all coming from the same place?"

"No, there are some from as far off as sixty miles out. You'll get there well before those. But a lot came from the Thrymi cloud-castle and that area."

"I'd say your boy has stirred up a real hornet's nest."

There was a moment's silence. "Ah. Mr Templeton," said Charlie's father, "Augustus... I am very fond of him, but he couldn't stir up a cup of tea, let alone a hornet's nest. This can't have anything to do with him, except by accident."

"Well, Mr Thistlewood, it looks like a very lively accident," said Templeton.

"Yes. I... I don't want to interfere in your plans but I think you might have to just see what is going on before rushing in." He sighed. "It is possibly too late anyway. Not, to be realistic, that Augustus ever showed any obvious interest in the fairer sex, let alone fathering children. And at least I gather they are unlikely to have killed him."

After the transmission ended, Templeton looked at Charlie. "Charlie... we're going to transfer you to the back-up craft. Now. No arguments. Sorry. Air transfer is a pain but I think it necessary."

Charlie shrugged. "I suppose so. But... my father is right. Augustus, he's my brother... but he couldn't organize a drinking party in a brewery. He's quite timid, quiet, very idealistic, and not terribly practical. Not much good at anything physical either."

"He's still got a lot going on," said Mark Templeton. "I don't know exactly what, and we have to be careful."

Charlie had little choice but to go along with it. He and Bill transferred. Just after his transfer he saw the first of the paragliders. Scope-vision showed it clearly. It was a human flying it.

"Well, I'll be damned," said Bill, rubbing his eyes and staring again. "That's a new way to go jumpabout."

"Is that an outbacker, Bill?" asked Charlie.

"He's dressed like one," said Bill. "But I never seen a thing like that before. I wants one!"

"We'd better let Templeton know. We can patch Bill through on the external speakers if we need to talk to them."

They were closing on the Zell cloud-castle now, with it visible on the horizon. The pilot focused telescopic view on it. "It's jumping around like a flea in a fit," he commented. "And there's a bunch of those paragliders closing on it."

T rapped down in the control room, Briz was glad she'd thrown up most of breakfast. Gus was checking alien screws, seeing if he could open the back of whatever drove the closing and locking of the control room door. She was watching the screens. They'd found a group of Zell on them. They hadn't deserted the cloud-castle, as Gus had hoped they might. Instead they seemed to be struggling their way down to the Engine room.

Gus had just freed a large panel exposing wiring, when on one of the tilt-and swirls, Briz looked at one of the screens showing the outside, and saw a bunch of paragliders. "Gus! Gus! Our mob are here! Paragliders! Can we stop the rocking and whirling so they can land?"

He nodded and pulled his way across to the odd-shaped seat and began work on the controls, bringing the gyrations to a halt. He hugged her. "Looks like the cavalry have come. I wish I could tell them where the Zell are and where we are. Problem is there are a lot of locked doors between them and us. I'm just amazed they got here so fast."

"There was another paraglider about a mile off when we got took. They'd have seen it. Must have flashed a mirror-message. I'm gonna drown them in beer," said Briz, hugging him back. "Of course, we're still stuck in here, and they're out there."

283

CHAPTER
TWENTY-FOUR

The TMI aircars – with the exception of Charlie and the backup aircar – which was seven miles behind -- were barely three miles out, keeping low, just on the cloud-tops, keeping the Zell cloud-castle between them and the Thrymi. "Coming in range of the energy weapons, Mark," said Chalk, the pilot.

"You know the drill," said Templeton. "Swing off while Alpha does a probe. We'll see if our cloaking works on them." He was peering through the magnifier. "Those paragliders are landing on the towers!"

"Message from the freighter, the Zell has stopped circling and is now stationary."

"Nothing has fired on us yet," said Alpha. "We're at one point two. What now?"

"We're coming in. Be ready to provide cover. Chalk... we're going for that central tower. Drop and run. Positions boys." His men bunched at the two cargo hatches."

He heard Charlie through his headset. "Chalk. External speaker, broadcast 'Outbackers, Friendly!'"

Fifteen seconds later he and his men dropped onto the tower

roof, rifles ready. There was a startled looking paraglider-pilot there, pulling free of his harness. He had what Templeton recognized as some kind of weapon in his hand, that was not helping him shed the harness. Templetom brought his own Ultima 37 up to bear. And the paraglider flier looked at the aircar – which, naturally enough had the company logo on the side. "TMI!" shouted the paraglider-flier, in obvious delight. With shock Mark Templeton realized he'd been about to shoot a woman. "TMI" he yelled back. She gave him a huge thumbs up. "Gimme a hand. I don't want to lose me wing."

"Don't shoot," said Templeton into his throatmike. "They're friendly. Broadcast the word 'TMI' and stand off, Chalk. Tell the others to come running."

Moments later he was helping a buxom young woman with a very alien weapon unhook her harness. She plainly knew where she was going – there was an open hatch with a burned off handle. Attached to it were a good dozen harnesses and a washing-line of collapsed paragliders. She hooked hers up and dropped in. He did too. "Where are you going?" he asked. They were in a long corridor – transparent and terrifyingly like walking on air.

"These bastards have got the Boss and Briz," said the woman. "I'm going to kill the bastards."

The name 'Briz registered – his throat mike was open to the aircars and Charlie suddenly spoke up in a yell they must have all regretted in their earpieces. "Briz. That's the kid who was with my brother!"

The voice plainly startled the woman. "Who is that? That you Gus?"

"We're from TMI. We're looking for Augustus Thistlewood III."

"Augus... yer mean Gus. Yer not taking him away." It wasn't a question. The alien rifle had come up.

"Tell her we're here to help him," said Charlie.

"We've come to help him," said Mark Templeton hoping his men would do what had to be done. "TMI," he said, because that had seemed a magical phrase.

It seemed to work this time too. "Yeah. We all work for TMI. Come on." Then as they advanced down the passage. "Yer not taking him away."

"We're just here to help," repeated Mark Templeton. He was a soldier. He'd leave this to Charlie to sort out. That was what young Thistlewood did well. "Do you know where they are?"

She nodded. "The Boss is down in the control room, I reckon. Might be some Zell in the way." They arrived at another burned open door and went through onto what was plainly the bridge. It was deserted. She ran across to the wall and poked her fingers into some holes.

"Down the stairwell," yelled someone. "Elevator is bust. We need more burners."

Down the stairwell they went, Templeton posting two men to hold the bridge and guard the exit. He'd noted that these outbackers seemed very familiar with the Zell castle, and elevators... that didn't gel with primitive farmers living on patches of floating vegetation. They weren't soldiers – but they were plainly tough – and exceptional paraglider pilots.

There were another seven outbackers at the next level, trying to break down the next door. He was in time to see one of them slap the barrel of one of the alien rifles down. "Bloody ricochet will kill us, yer stupid bastard. "Lindsey, you got a fresh burner... Who are you lot?"

"TMI," said Templeton.

"They say they've come to help the boss," said the girl. "Here's me burner, Brent."

The alien handgun did weaken the door, and determined kicks took them through. "Fan out," said Templeton – as they'd arrived at another atrium, with several passages off it.

His men did. The outbackers, and there were more coming in behind them, didn't. They plainly knew where to go to. "Bloody door is locked. Burners!"

"We have some small charges. We can get you through there," said Templeton, as one of them tried a plainly near powerless hand-weapon. Meanwhile the earpiece informed him that the passage was clear, but all the doors off it were locked. He stationed a few more men on watch here, as his team sapper quickly placed some C4 and got them to back off. In the background he heard Charlie being told that the Thrymi castle was coming alongside – that every tower seemed to have humans on them – and that it had guns trained on the air-cars – as well as some pointed at the Zell cloud-castle.

"Don't start anything," said Charlie.

That was fairly sound advice seeing as they were still in this crazy alien semi-see-through structure, and were a long, long way up and even further from the relative safety of the Hotel Hyaton.

The door blew open and they went down another stairwell, with steps not designed for human stride length or human feet.

Down in the control room they could see the screens and do little else. Stopping the gyrations had certainly helped friends to land, Augustus realized – and... some other people. External vision showed the aircars, complete with TMI Logos on the sides.

"What's them?" asked Briz.

"Human aircars – thirty-seaters by the looks of it. I don't know how they done it, but it looks like my family have tracked me down."

"They're not taking yer away!" said Briz, heartbreak in her voice.

"I'm not going anywhere without you, Briz." Augustus said, bracingly. "Not now, not ever. If you don't want to come with me, this is where I'll stay."

She looked at him and shook her head. "They'll take yer."

"No, they bloody well won't," said Augustus. "Not that I don't want you to meet my brother...except that he might steal you from me. But if they can find me and come out here once, they can twice."

"I'm scared to meet yer family... Oh oh," she pointed at the screen. "Look the bloody Zell are coming through."

The absence of wild gyrations had allowed both the outbackers and the TMI men to land – but it had also allowed the Zell to move more easily. They'd got down as far as the engine room. And, looking at the devices they carried, they were armed. And, plainly, they had some way of opening the locked doors. There were about seven of them. He and Briz had one Thrymi Gauss-gun with four more charges, and an exhausted burner, and one with a little more charge.

It was Briz who spotted the obvious. There was a straight, old-fashioned bar that could be slid into heavy solid brackets on either side of the door. While the bar and brackets held, the door could not be opened. They pushed it into place... just as the door clicked loudly. The screens showed the Zell trying to drag the door open. Then they retreated a little, and aimed their weapons.

"Quick! That panel. Let's get down!" yelled Briz grabbing for it and covering them, just before something hit the door a hammer-blow.

Augustus reached for the Thyrmi gun just as the Zell tried a second blast of concerted fire.

One of the brackets shattered, with most of the shrapnel going into the roof – but one piece pierced the panel-shield, went straight through it... and hit Briz in the upper chest. It knocked her backwards, sprawling, reaching a hand to clutch at the metal fragment. She screamed and so did Augustus.

He looked down in horror. Blood was welling through her clothing. "Love you," she said, her blue eyes wide and her voice fading. "Behind..." The first Zell was pushing the door away. Augustus was too angry and too distressed to think or be afraid. He just shot the Zell at point-blank range. Two of them were knocked backwards and he charged at the others, firing, and then when the gun failed to fire, swinging it like a club, bringing down one of the now fleeing Zell. They'd dropped their strange weapons, and one was frantically unlocking a door. Augustus felled that one, but the other three crammed through the now open door.

He ran back to Briz, who was lying on the floor, her eyes closed, gasping. His first instinct was to pull the knife-like piece of shrapnel out of her chest, but that long-ago seeming Blue Men first aid course stopped him. He used his knife to cut away the cloth of Briz's baggy shirt exposing her chest and the wound. It had hit her in the upper right of her chest, and the wound bled and bubbled. He didn't know what to do. This was beyond his first aid... But those were TMI craft out there. Maybe... he picked her up, cradling her in his arms, and ran to pick up the Zell door-opening device. With it in hand he headed for the entry the Zell had arrived at minutes before. Just before he got there, there was a muffled explosion from the other side of the door, and it fell in. He stepped over it and through into the smokiness beyond.

"You," shouted Augustus at the first armed man he encountered. "Who are you? Are you from the aircars?"

The burly man in camouflage and battle armor looked at him, straightened up, and half-raised his hand to salute. Afterwards he said the last time he'd heard that sort of voice had been from his Colonel. "Templeton, Sir. We're looking for Augustus Thistlewood"

"That's me," snapped Augustus. "What medical support have you got? I need it now!"

"We've got a medic and a medevac kit on the aircar, Sir."

"Well, lead me there," snapped Augustus. "Jump to it, man!"

It had been many years since the former Sergeant-Major had been told to jump to it. But he didn't hesitate for an instant. Nor did he attempt to help the bearded, bloody, bulgingly muscular man carry his burden. Instead he said, via the throat-mike: "Beta, come running. Got him, he's OK but we need the medevac ready. Boys, I need an escort, and I need a landing place blown open."

By the time they got up there, part of the roof to the central courtyard was down, and an aircar was cautiously dropping in. Several armed men kept wary watch. Others were getting ropes onto the remaining bits of roof to pull them out of the way.

Augustus – and his escort, approached the opening cargo-hatch with its stretcher and crewman hastily pulling its straps out of the way. He'd seen his brother there. He'd even spoken to him, he thought. It was unimportant. His entire focus was on Briz. He put her down onto the stretcher. The medic checked her airway, and was feeling for a pulse as the stretcher unit swung back into the aircar with both of them. "What injuries?" asked the medic, "Besides that one?" He pointed at the piece of jagged metal protruding from her chest.

The medic had shears out and was cutting away the rest of her clothing around the wound, before Augustus could reply. "I don't know. She was knocked backwards by that." The medic nodded, looking at the bloody, bubbling wound. "Stand clear please Sir. Let me do my job. I'll tell you if I need assistance. Do you know if she has any pre-existing conditions or allergies or taking any medications? Do you know when she last ate?"

"She's pregnant. I don't know of anything else. I don't think so. And she threw up after breakfast – a good few hours ago. I'm sorry, I don't know exactly. Three or four."

The medic nodded, and went on with what he was doing, calmly, efficiently and paying attention only to his patient.

CHAPTER

TWENTY-FIVE

"Excuse me, Sir," said a man with pilot's tabs who had come back to them. "There's a bunch of outbackers out there. They're armed and it looks like it'll turn nasty any minute. Also, all the guns on the Thrymi cloud-castle are now aimed at us. They want you, Sir. They're not listening to Charlie. We're mid-transfer of fuel. We can't lift yet."

The medic looked up. "Go, please. You're in the way right now. Come back in five minutes when I have everything set up and the patient stabilized."

So, Augustus went. It was indeed looking fairly nasty, with the TMI security men forming a solid cordon – and more paragliders arriving by the minute. When they saw him emerge onto the top of the aircar steps, an enormous cheer went up. Augustus stopped there, and held up his hands for silence. "It's all right. Briz is badly hurt, and they're," his voice cracked slightly, "just busy trying to save her life. We need to take her to a hospital in the Big Syd."

"We can't let them take you two away," said Lindsey from the front of the outbacker crowd.

Augustus looked calmly at Lindsey. "I have to do this, Lindsey. I promise I'll be back as soon as I can. I always do what I say, or I'll bloody die trying. You know that. You all know that. As soon as the fuel is transferred, I'm taking Briz to get the best healing help I can. They can, maybe, keep her alive. She'll die if she stays, so I am not staying. This lot," – he pointed at the flier that was having its tanks pumped across. "Probably doesn't have the fuel to get anywhere. They'll stay here, and while they are here I can find you easily. I'll trust you lot to look after them."

He looked at the outbackers. "Tommy. You're to see the Thrymi castle gets back to Big Bruce's Station. Krya, you're to keep this crew from TMI here to help you." He turned to Templeton. "I want forty of your men left here. Pick them now. Two aircars, one to go with each cloud-castle, twenty men in each. You're to do a room-to-room search of the building and arrest the surviving Zell. There are a couple in the engine room store. Take them alive if possible, dead if they resist. And hear me: You're under Kyra's command. She knows the local conditions and local dangers. Heaven help you if you step one micron out of line, because I am coming back. She'll fly this cloud-castle back to Big Bruce's round paddock, well away from the other. We'll be in radio contact. You'll see that the structure is guarded, and keep a weather eye for any other cloud-castles. We don't know if the Zell got a message off. If there is a Zell rescue attempt, contrive a bomb, put it in the engine room and abandon the castle. Is that clear? I want no unnecessary loss of life, but on the other hand I want as much of the new Zell gear for TMI. See to it, Kyra." He paused. "Lindsey. I'm asking this because you're Briz's friend. Will you come back with us? I'll bring you back here, myself. I... just don't know how long it's all going to take." There was the first crack in his demeanor. "She may die. She may lose our baby. I want her to have a friend along."

Lindsey paused for a moment and then nodded. "Right-o. I'm with yer, with yer both, Gus. Tommy, you'll tell mum and dad?"

"I'm right here," said Big Bruce, pushing his way through. "Like I'd let me mate Gus get taken by these bastards without doing as much as he did for me son! And yer go ahead, girl. Yer come back when yer can. Gus is one of us, and we stand by our own." He hugged his daughter, and turned to the crowd and roared: "Now get on with it. Yer heard the man."

"Refuel is done, Sir. We're ready to roll," said the pilot.

In an odd imitation of Big Bruce, the TMI security head bellowed at his crew – who as they were wearing throat mikes and ear-pieces clutched their ears... "You heard the man. I need the team from Delta and Theta here. Alpha team will be going back as soon as fuel from Theta is transferred. Alpha team medic get across to Beta. Alpha, you're there to provide defense and run interference if there is any trouble. Johnson, you're in charge." Then he muttered. "Timid. Quiet. Not practical. Can't organize..."

Augustus didn't care. He had turned and gone back to the medevac unit. "How is she?" he demanded of the medic, who had an array of monitors and probes attached to Briz. The protruding piece of metal was still there, but was stabilized with towel-rolls and strapping.

"Blood oxygen level has come up nicely, I have an IV line in. Blood-pressure has stabilized and come up a little which is good. The machine is blood-typing and we'll be able to replace a few losses."

"Is she going to be all right?" Augustus looked at Briz's pallid little face, his voice held very even.

The medic looked at him, over the top of his glasses. "Things are improving, Sir. We don't know what other internal damage was done. We've got her on a trans-hypnotic which is safe for pregnant mothers, because she's in pain and was distressed and moving. She's got at least one broken rib and probably needs a chest drain, as well as that piece of shrapnel out. I've seen people with worse fine, and less, die. It's other damage we don't know about, as we don't know where that piece of shrapnel extends to, and if it has done any arterial damage on the way. So long as there is no other damage or complications, she's got a good chance. But we won't know if it is all, for some time."

"And... the baby?" asked Augustus.

"The mother's body tends to protect that at all costs, Sir. Even at the expense of the mother's own well-being. Pete from Alpha-team is better at ultrasound than I am, and we'll be looking for free air or blood in the abdomen anyway. If she has a full-ish bladder we may pick up a fetal heartbeat. How many weeks pregnant is she?"

"I don't know. I didn't even know she was pregnant until earlier today."

Another medic came back to the casevac unit. "Pilot says strap in guys. We're on our way."

"Sir," said the first medic. "Tell him we want him to provide a stable platform, no high speed manoevers. He'll listen to you."

So, Augustus went and did as he was told.

Charlie had had an interesting time of it, so far. Augustus... he hadn't even recognized the bearded, bare-chested, blood-covered muscular man carrying a woman in his arms, being escorted by Templeton and three others, who were having some trouble keeping up, when they'd run up to the open hatch for the medevac unit. They'd got his burden onto a stretcher and into the unit, before the bearded man had looked away for the first time from the girl he'd carried, and said: "Hello Charlie."

It had taken his brain a few moments to process the voice. "Augustus? It can't be..."

His brother had nodded. "It's me. Charlie, we need to get this thing headed for a hospital as soon and as fast as possible. I've got to stay with her. Make it happen, please, big brother."

And with that he'd followed the stretcher in.

It had been over to Charlie to speak to the pilot. The pilot nodded. "Charlie... we could just about halve our flight time if we transfer fuel from one of the other aircars. Full tanks we'd have enough to do the run at full power. Even if we have to abandon one of the aircars, or come back for it. They were planning to spend time hiding out here anyway."

"Good man. Make it happen. Two craft. And you're due an even bigger bonus for that. I must get onto my father."

He patched through to the freighter in space above them. He wasted no time. "Got him, Dad."

"Wonderful! Let me speak to him please."

"He's on board. But he's with the medics..."

"How badly is he hurt!?"

"He's fine. He came running to the air-car. He was carrying a badly injured woman. He's barely spoken to me, yet."

"Oh. Is she going to be all right?"

"I don't know, father. I was just telling you the news. Augustus wants us to head for a hospital as soon as possible."

"I can't see why that's not immediately, once we have our people out."

"I'll see to it."

"Good. I will contact your grandmother. We'll be in touch about a course in order to avoid any incidents."

A few minutes later, Charlie was talking to Mark Templeton, getting all the men back up from inside the Zell cloud-castle, and discussing what could be done, with the possibility of abandoning one of the aircars, and cramming everyone into the others, when the pilot came out. "Got your father on the radio again."

So, Charlie had run back in.

"Charlie. Your grandmother wants to know if the girl's name is 'Briz'? She's being very insistent and wants to know now. Go and find out. And give Augustus my love. Her's too."

Charlie had gone to where his almost unrecognizable brother

was anxiously watching the medic working on the girl. She was definitely a girl. The medic had cut away her clothing to dress the wound. She had an oxygen mask on, and he was hooking up a blood-pressure monitor. There was a fair amount of blood and a large piece of metal sticking out of her chest. Charlie had never seen anything like that before. He didn't mind if he didn't again. But he had to touch Augustus, before his brother stopped watching. "What is it, Charlie? When can we go? We've got to keep her alive, brother."

"We're just transferring fuel. It'll take a few minutes, but it means we can fly a lot faster. grandmother wants to know if this is Briz. She and dad send their love, by the way. They've been worried, you know."

Augustus sketched the shadow of a smile. "I couldn't really let you know I was fine, Charlie. Yes, that's my Briz. The love of my life. And... she's carrying our child. I hope. I... I can't cope if she dies, Charlie."

"Then we'll just have to do our best to see that that doesn't happen, Augustus," said Charlie, battling to deal with all this. Fortunately, his brother was already looking back at the girl.

Charlie went back to pass it all on to his father. His father snorted. "Your grandmother will be telling me 'I told you so', shortly. Is the girl going to be all right? What's she like?"

"Father, she's on a stretcher with a piece of metal sticking out of her chest. Other than injured and the fact that Augustus seems utterly distraught about it, I can't tell you anything about her."

"Ah. Well, we'll get the hospital unit ready. Once things settle down, you can patch one of the medics through to the Doctors there so they know what is going on. How's Augustus looking, besides being upset?"

"You won't recognize him. He's got a massive red beard, and he's tanned and muscled like a dire-bull. About all that hasn't changed is his voice."

"I hate to ask... but given what the Zell do... is he... entire? Grandmother wants to know."

"I didn't ask and didn't look. But he says the girl is carrying his child. He hopes."

"What!"

"I don't know either. I assume that he means he hopes she hasn't lost it rather than he hopes she's pregnant. Father, I have to go. There is stuff to organize, and it looks like there's a mob of these outbackers..."

He'd not been getting anywhere fast, dealing with them.

Then his little brother had come along and taken over, sorted everything out and made people jump to it. Augustus had... changed a lot, thought Charlie with a smile. Those people had been cheering as if he was some kind of video-star.

The outbacker girl who had come out of the crowd, uneasy-looking, into the aircar, had looked about, trying to work out quite what to do. Charlie, in a brief moment of gallantry had beckoned her to come and sit next to him. It would be a good chance to find out, second hand, what Augustus had been up to. And perhaps he could find out more about Augustus's girl before grandmother gave him the inquisition about her. Besides, she was nice looking – even if she was at least as tall as he was, and fairly broad-shouldered. She needed the shoulders to carry the frontage, but, thought Charlie, she was still statuesque. She had a fresh, open, friendly face, with freckles on her cheeks and nose to go with her slightly carroty, wavy hair. She sat down, resting a workmanlike alien rifle on her knees.

"I could put that in the overhead locker for you," said Charlie, obligingly.

She shook her head, and smiled at him. It came complete with a dimple. "Yer never know when I might need to shoot one of yer bastards," she said cheerfully. Charlie decided she would probably do it too. She looked at him, askance. "Yer sound a bit like our Gus. Yer related?"

Working out that 'Gus' was Augustus, Charlie nodded. "I'm his brother," he said.

She looked him over with a beaming smile. "Never! Are you

Charlie, then? He talks about yer. But I reckoned yer be ten foot tall and could wrestle a shonk to its knees with one hand."

"Yes. I'm Charlie. I'm not too sure about shonk wrestling though. And you are?"

She gave a peal of cheerful laughter, which gave her even more dimples. "Yer better come and harden up with us a bit. Start small, with jumbuck wrestling." She stuck out a hand. "I'm Lindsey. Big Bruce's daughter," she said with a wry twitch to her smile. "I'm one of Gus's apprentices. Brizzy is me best friend. Is she gonna be all right?"

"They're doing their best, they've got good equipment and they're both very qualified paramedics, so we hope so," said Charlie.

"What's a paramedic? Do they parachute?"

And thus began Charlie's education of Lindsey, and, contrairiwise, her education of him. He hadn't realized that he had so much to learn: about the outback, about his brother and what he'd been doing, or, after a while, he realized, about women who had not grown up in Azure's wealthy and... comfortable society. The women he'd had much to do with had never dealt with death, the destruction of all they had, home-childbirths, inimical aliens, unpredictable weather, wild animals, or... the vast tyranny of distance that was the core to her life and the way relationships and families worked out here. He learned something of his brother's girl, a great deal about his brother's exploits. He was somewhat taken aback by the naked hero worship 'Gus' got – and yet, the outbacker's tolerant amusement for his ineptitiudes, which they were all well aware of, it seemed. "Aw, he couldn't find his own head, if Brizzy wasn't there to find it for him," she informed him. She had a surprising and sharp grasp of mechanical matters and the function of Thrymi devices, and how airfoils worked - especially when Charlie put two and two together, and realized that much of her knowledge had to have come via his brother – and his brother hadn't been there that long.

Part way through the flight, that brother came down the aisle, looking, Charlie thought, exhausted... but not quite as close to despair. "Thought I'd come and tell you, Lindsey, she's doing okay so far. And the best news of all, they got a fetal heartbeat. I could see the baby on the scan."

"Can I come and talk to her?" asked Lindsey, trying to get up and forgetting her seatbelt. "Ow. I need the dunny so bad."

That actually drew a laugh out of Augustus. "Charlie hasn't been looking after you. Better take her down and show her, Charlie. She won't have met a flush toilet before. You can come and see Briz, but she's not awake. They're keeping her under sedation for now. The medic assures me that this generation of drugs is fine for pregnant women."

Lindsey laughed. "So, she finally told yer, did she, Gus? Yer a real drongo, yer know. She even talked to me mum about it. So how do yer feel about her being yer girl, and you being a dad?"

He smiled, a smile Charlie could see went all the way, not just the mouth, but the eyes, and the heart. "If I wasn't so worried about her, I'd say I was the happiest and luckiest man alive, Lindsey. Now, Charlie will show you where the dunny is – that's a toilet, Charlie, and I'll bet he hasn't given you any tucker either."

"I could murder some tea and a beer," said Lindsey. "They looking after you, Gus? Yer look all in, mate."

"They brought me something. Charlie, tea is a meal. And beer means beer. Come down when you're ready. I'm getting back to her. I can't do much, but I can sit there."

Charlie was left to explain the working of the toilet (which she thought bizarre, and wasteful – because in the outback all wastes went to helping the 'paddock' grow) and the hand-basin – whose taps were quite different to Thrymi ones, and introducing her to pre-packaged meals, and bottled beer, which he was surprised to find on board. She smelled it. "Are you pulling a raw prawn over me? Does this come out of the bottom end of a Jumbuck?" she asked, raising an eyebrow.

"A raw prawn?" he asked.

"A trick. A joke."

"Oh. No. Look, I'll have one too."

That did convince her, but she was not sold on the taste. Hops, Charlie suspected, had no part in outbacker beer. He found some fruit juice that she said was much more drinkable, but rather sweet. An offer of water got a look of blank incomprehension. He gathered one didn't drink water out there.

They went back to see Briz. And then Charlie escorted her back to her seat, and offered her a tissue. "What's that for?" she asked.

"To wipe your eyes and blow your nose," explained Charlie.

She looked at the tissue doubtfully, and then tried it. "Thank you," she said. "how do yer dry it out?" she asked flattening it carefully.

"You don't. We throw them away."

"Bit of a waste, isn't it? Sorry. I didn't mean to cry. I'm just not used to seeing Brizzy like that. She doesn't normally stay still for an instant."

"I am sure she'll be fine," said Charlie injecting as much confidence into his voice as he could.

She smiled at Charlie. "Yer nice. Poor Brizzy was in a state about Gus's family. She reckoned yer would never let him be with her. That she wasn't going to be good enough for yer."

Charlie was somewhat taken aback by this. He was even more taken aback to be told that Briz had hoped that they would never get back to the Big Syd, and had wanted to stay in the outback – at least partly because she didn't think Augustus's family would approve. He was storing all of this up for both his father and, especially, his grandmother. He made some comment about being surprised by his brother's acumen in selling paragliders, and got a merry peal of laughter from Lindsey. "Gus? Yer kidding. He's the smartest bloke in the outback when it comes to making things, but he'd give everything away. He's got no sense. Nah, that's all Briz. She makes it all work. Me mum says it's just like our family. She looks after the

Jumbuck and Dad spends em. Gus'd never have a brass razzoo for his next project. Brizzy sees everyone gets tucker, everyone gets paid, and yer brother's got about nine hundred jumbuck, about half agisted and half on shares."

A few more delicate questions and Charlie worked out that his brother – and Briz, were by outbacker standards, very wealthy, by their own endeavor. And it came down to his brother's ability, and this girl's management. There was no doubt that Lindsey was very partisan, but whatever went on in the relationship, it did seem not just to be one of predation – which, reading the reports of his brother's short time on the Plate, it had seemed it might be. He'd have to wait and see.

It made the flight go very quickly, compared with the flight out. He almost regretted the end of it, and decided that he'd have to make a plan to see how she was getting on, before he went home to Azure. They strapped in, prepared for potential trouble, coming in to the plate, but it seemed that too was un-necessary.

The hospital nurses, orderlies and doctors were all on hand when they landed, and his brother and the girl were whisked away. Charlie realized that looking after the outbacker-girl wouldn't end quite yet. He had to admit that she was better value than a lot of the girls he'd dated, and plainly absolutely fascinated by the world they'd brought her to. Her reactions were a delight to observe – and her commentary priceless, if not always polite. His grandmother had gone to see Augustus, and his father would only be landing in an hour. Charlie, sensibly, stayed within the confines of the Hyaton, not trusting his ability to keep her safe from larceny outside – or stopping her from shooting anyone that tried it. He actually rather wanted to examine the Thrymi gauss-gun, but judged asking would be unwise.

He also discovered the single thing that fascinated her more than any other. It was a glossy, printed brochure. Mostly people preferred these on screen – but the old front desk still had some for other destinations.

He realized, rapidly, that it wasn't just the pictures... which she was fascinated by, but the text. He got this pretty fast because she asked him to explain a word. "Brizzy has been teaching us to read. But these are longer words."

Charllie paused. The level of literacy on the Plate was, they'd discovered, very low. It occurred to him that it was almost certainly much lower in the outback. From Lindsey he found out about the reading, writing and numerical skills required to enter the service of the local part of TMI. He hadn't known the company had a local arm – because it hadn't, before his brother and this girl took the liberty of creating it. So: this Briz was numerate and literate... well, that couldn't hurt. It didn't hurt his opinion of Lindsey either, even if she was more interested in reading a travel brochure than talking to him. "Take it with you," he said. "You can read it later. I'll probably have to go off and talk to my grandmother and father soon. Actually, let's go to the housekeeper and arrange a room for you, and, um, any other things you need."

"Ooh! Are you sure I can take it with me? I'll take great care of it until I give it back" said Lindsey, handling it as if it were a precious relic.

Charlie did another quick mental re-assessment. She'd probably never seen glossy pictures or printing before. "It's yours."

"You trying to root me?" she asked, looking at him sideways.

Charlie worked that out a lot faster than his brother had. He had more experience. He grinned. "Well, I would say it was worth trying a lot harder than that! Seriously, we make them to give away. To anybody. Not just... people we're trying to root."

"Yer as crazy as Gus," said Lindsey, plainly unable to process such prodigal behavior. "It must run in the family."

"I think," said Charlie, "that from what I have heard, that's a compliment." He wondered briefly if maybe, he should collect a lot of brochures for her, but instead they found the housekeeper and one of the staff took them to show Lindsey her room.

At this point, another one of the staff tracked him down and informed him that his father was here and looking for him, so he left her and the brochure there, promising to come back soon.

C harlie was escorted back to his father and grandmother, and then, coming in just behind him, Augustus. His brother was looking exhausted, but had a happy smile on his face. "Looking at you, I take it the news is good," said Charlie.

Augustus nodded. "Very good. I can't thank you enough, Charlie. Papa. Grandmother. They say she's going to be fine. The shrapnel was not particularly deep – just went in far enough to puncture the chest, and let air into the pleural space, and collapse the lung. There was a bit of bleeding, but it has stopped. They have taken the shrapnel out, and put a chest drain in. And the baby is fine."

Charlie realized there were tears coming out of his brother's eyes. They were not an expressive family, but Augustus was hugging all of them. Then, suddenly alarmed, he exclaimed: "Charlie. Where is Lindsey? You can't let her out onto the Big Syd on her own. Big Bruce would kill me."

Charlie burst out laughing. "I think she'd kill them. Relax. She's in her room, safe and sound, with something much more interesting than the city bars."

"What?" asked Augustus, curiously.

"A glossy travel brochure. She likes the pictures, but it's got text," explained Charlie.

Augustus beamed. "She likes to read. I'm going to take a lot of books out there, when I go back."

He was tired. But Charlie noticed the look between his father and grandmother. "Time for that later," he said, easily. "I assume that your girl is still going to be recovering from anaesthesia for a while?"

"Yes. They wouldn't normally give an anaesthetic for this, but medevac transhypnotic is going to take a while to wear off. They promised to page me as soon as she even started stirring. I don't want her waking up in an unfamiliar place without me. But they said it would be about an hour. I want to be back in half of that."

"Well, looking at you, I'd say go and wash, eat, and catnap at her bed, because you won't sleep anywhere else. We can all talk later," said Charlie, firmly. "I'll tell Lindsey. And keep her out of trouble."

His brother smiled broadly. "Thanks Charlie. I can't tell you how much I've missed your ability to organize things..."

"Yes," said Charlie, thinking of his brother dealing with the mob of outbackers. "Now, off you go. Let's just call someone to see you to your room."

"It's next door," said his grandmother. "I'll see him there."

"All right," said Charlie. "But let him rest, grandmother. Come back here and question me instead."

She did. Charlie kept his calm under fire well. After a while he said: "Look, I know this isn't exactly what you planned or expected. But... he's alive. I gather either the Zell didn't geld him, or at least he has a child."

"They didn't do anything to him," his father replied. "I got that from the medic on the aircar. They got away just in time."

"And frankly, he's done us proud out here. He's given Thistlewood Mechanical Industries a whole new unit."

"What?" said his father, as they both gaped at him.

"With over a hundred employees, and not one, but two, working alien antigravity generators – and quite a bit of other technology, I would bet. He's also built a viable and very profitable local business."

"I barely recognized him when he came in here with that beard," said his father dryly, "But Charlie, Augustus is my son. Your brother. We love him, but we know he's got the business sense of a rutabaga. grandfather despaired of..."

"Yes. But from what I've heard great-grandfather was just as bad."

"Your great-grandmother, however," said grandmother, frostily, "was a brilliant business-woman. She, more than anyone else, built TMI up from a minor engineering works, to what we are today."

"And Augustus has found himself someone to do likewise," said Charlie. "Great-grandma was a pretty rough diamond, from what you've said, grandmother. Give this girl a chance. By the sounds of it she kept him alive more than once. And don't bully her, or you'll lose Augustus as well. And that great-grandchild you wanted. Now, I'm going to fetch Lindsey. She can tell you a lot more about Briz than I can, and quite a lot about Augustus that will amaze you."

TWENTY-SIX

Briz knew she was dead. Only she'd expected to feel better when you were dead. She opened one eye. Dead. For sure. It was all white and pale blue, like nowhere she'd ever seen.

There was a vague awareness that someone was holding her hand. "Briz?"

"Gus. Are you dead too?" she asked, blearily, happy in a way, wishing her mouth was not so dry when she was no longer alive to drink. At least they were together.

"Neither of us are dead, dearest," he said, and she looked up into the face that was beaming down on her.

Conciousness slipped away for a while, but then she came to with a start reaching for her knife. A hand restrained her. Gently. "It's all right Briz. You're going to be fine. I promise," said Gus.

"Me knife... them Zell bastards. They'll kill me baby."

"We got away, Briz. And the baby is fine. I promise. Just lie still. I'm here to look after you." His voice was so calm and his face, so happy, that she relaxed, a little. "I love you Briz."

"If yer love me, give me something to drink."

He held a glass to her lips. "Just a sip."

She had that, and a little spilled on her chin. He wiped it away, and smiled at her. Her brain was working a little better now. This was a bed she was in. Her chest was still sore. She squinted down at it to look at the piece of metal. Her clothes were gone. So was the metal. She didn't like the feel of that part of her, or the clothes she was wearing... but she liked the fact that Gus was looking at her like that. "Bloody water," she muttered. "If you really loved me you'd give me beer."

That got him to laugh. She shouldn't have tried to join in that because it hurt a lot. Then there were other people in white coats fussing around with her. She was sore, felt rotten, but... she was alive, and so was he. And so was her baby. They brought Lindsey in, a little later, after she'd dozed a bit. That was comforting, even if they both ended up crying. Lindsey was with someone who looked oddly familiar.

When they'd left she asked Gus who he was.

He clicked his tongue. "Tch. I'm so tired I am not thinking straight. Of course, you don't know him. That's my brother, Charlie. He came looking for us, just in time. I should have introduced you. But I am so used to assuming everything I know, you know."

The pieces slowly came together. They were back in the Big Syd. This was inside the Hyaton, where she'd never been. And Gus was back with his family, where she could never go. She didn't say anything. She felt too sick and weak to do anything. But she desperately wished to be back in Big Bruce's paddock with Gus. Or anywhere but here.

Later, they brought food. She'd always wanted to sample the expensive food in the Hyaton. If it was like this, she hadn't missed much. The woman who brought it said she should move around as much as possible, to help her lung re-inflate. She also said, very respectfully, to Gus, that he should go and get some sleep, and that they would look after the young lady for him.

Young lady? Well, Gus just shook his head. He did look all in. "Yer better rest," she told him.

"Time enough for that when I'm dead," he said.

"How can yer make me laugh? It bloody hurts."

"I'm not going to leave you again, Brizzy. I thought I might lose you."

"Honest, this sick and sore is making me behave like a girl," she said, sniffling, as he leaned over and kissed her.

"I know you are," he said. "You can't fool me again."

"But yer do need sleep sometime. Come and lie next to me."

"I think they might throw me out if I did that. Hello. We have visitors again."

It was Lindsey, and Gus's brother Charlie again. He was smiling at her. And he did look a lot like that lost drongo she'd picked up. "I suspected you would still be here," he said. "So, I have the ward-sister bringing another bed in here for you. And we'll sit and talk to Briz, and keep an eye on her for you. You can trust Lindsey even if you don't trust me."

"Charlie, I wish I could organize everyone like you do. Now, I need to introduce you properly. Briz, this is my big brother Charlie. His name is Charles Anson Roberto Thistlewood the fourth, but everyone calls him Charlie."

"Everyone calls yer Gus," said Briz. "And yer so can organize. Yer just don't."

"I can see I'm going to really like my sister-in-law," said Charlie, stepping forward and holding out his hand.

"You're supposed to shake it, Briz," said Gus, his shoulders shaking. "But spit on your hand first, Charlie. That's the way they do it around here, brother."

Fortunately, two orderlies pushed another bed in at that point, because laughing at Charlie's face hurt Briz's chest again.

"They're pulling a raw prawn on yer, Charlie," said Lindsey, plainly on very good terms with him. "Yer supposed to kiss 'em. With a bit of tongue. Especially outbacker men."

Charlie grinned. "I can see why you lot have done my brother so much good. Now, you can show me how it is done...Gus. With Briz. And then lie down and sleep before you fall down."

He did. And that... made it all less problematic. After a while she had to admit that Charlie did too. He was very relaxed, and plainly trying to be friendly and kind. He was very like Gus – just not as blind as blind Freddy as to what was going on.

Lindsey was bubbling over, though. "Brizzy, yer won't believe it, but I just spoke to mum and dad. Gus's father organized it, with that radio thing Gus was talking about. They called them to the aircar, and I spoke to them and we talked and it was just like they was right next to me!"

They talked. Briz utterly forbade either of them to go out into the Big Syd without her...Lindsey took her for an expedition to what they had for a dunny, here. She was glad to have someone there to show her. Somewhere down the line she fell asleep. When she woke up Gus was sitting next to her again, with a new shirt, and breakfast. He was looking better, and she was feeling that way. The future still looked murky, but the present wasn't too bad. Until she had the breakfast and then felt sick. Throwing up with a chest-drain and a re-inflating lung was bloody awful and very painful, even if they said it had something called a catheter dripping local anesthetic into her next to the wound. The wound part made sense.

Charlie and Lindsey came back later. "Company so Gus can sleep. He won't leave yer alone," said Lindsey. "But he can trust the two of us."

"He needs a break," said Charlie, looking at his brother. "Go on. The staff diner is open already, and go and ask for Dr Fred Aljon. He wants to talk about the Thrymi. I think you need to meet him and see if he'll go back with you. You need him, but he has a family."

Barely minutes after he'd left, someone from housekeeping came up to call Lindsey for a fitting for some clothes that had been arranged for her.

When she was gone Charlie smiled. "Right. Briz, we need to talk."

She looked at him suspiciously. "You organized that. I know. I ain't good enough for your brother and your family. Yer want to try and give me money to go away."

"No," said Charlie, cheerfully. "I don't know if Augustus is good enough for you..."

"He's the best man in the bloody world," She said, firing to his defense, immediately. "Me, I'm..."

"The person who kept him alive," interrupted Charlie, "And went into certain death, just because he was going. And I also think that my little brother is one of the best men alive, but you have to admit he needs looking after, at times. I think you're the right person to do that. Actually, I think you're the only person who can. Lindsey told me that you're very afraid my family will take him away."

She nodded, warily.

"I want you to know I am on your side," he said gently. "And I want you to help me to keep you both together, here. Well, on this planet anyway. Probably where you were, just with a lot of extra kit and defenses. You've got to admit, living out there suits him, and has been good for him."

Briz looked at him through narrowed eyes. "Why are yer doing this?"

Charlie sighed. "Because he's my little brother. When our mother was killed... he was with her, in the aircar. My father... just pulled back into his work. He was never the same after that. I mean, he looked after us, but... he looked like Augustus when he thought you might die. Part of my little brother shut down then, too. Grand-mother did her best, but, well, I was twelve. I had to be his mother and father, sort of. Augustus, he always was a bit obsessive... it's a problem in our family. They don't really get jokes. They don't really get people. They do their duty, they do what is right. But they don't bind easily to individuals. Augustus cared for the world, thought it right to help it, but not actual people. In you, especially, but also the outbackers... he's found people he cares about. And I have never seen him as happy as when he told us you were going to be all right."

313

"Yer very like him, yer know," said Briz, sniffling. "Smart. But different."

Charlie shrugged. "He's the genius of the family. I'm just the organizer. Like you."

"Yeah, but yer nicer than me. And yer watch yer step with me friend, or I'll come and sort yer out, I don't care who you are."

Charlie actually looked startled. "She'd shoot me if I tried anything."

"Uh huh," said Briz. "Now, what do you want, mister smooth talking?"

"I want to prime you on dealing with my... and your Gus's grand-mother and father."

"I don't want ter see them. Or them to see me," said Briz, reflex-ively. Everything she'd been through, the last while, said these people were more powerful than Capos... by a long way.

"You don't have to. But it would help my brother... and me. And you have a few secret weapons."

"Like what?" asked Briz wondering if he knew about her little knife under the pillow.

"In more or less order, me, your friend Lindsey, who spent a couple of hours talking to them already, Augustus... sorry Gus. I like that. And, finally, that baby. My grandmother has been banking on it. Between us, we're going to swing this."

She wanted to believe him. But she hadn't grown up in the Big Syd by trusting anyone. "And yer gets to take over yer brother's share of yer family business?" Actually, she could live with that. In the outback she could do well enough for both of them.

He shook his head, grinning. "You're the perfect match for my brother. He trusts everything, you're suspicious of everything. Look, I can prove it to you if need be, but the way TMI works is that the chil-dren inherit different units. The oldest child goes on being TMI. The others rename, and go their own way. Half our competitors were once part of TMI. Some don't succeed, and in some cases don't go on with the same line of business. But the family likes to experiment, so we do a lot of things. The answer to me is that Augustus should, when he and I eventually inherit, get the Sybil III Unit, as well as whatever else he gets, and run and build it now. From what I can work out, that's really something you made happen, and, because I inherited the business side of the family brains, I'll tell you what they don't see yet -- it's the unit with the biggest growth potential. You – and my brother – can do that. I probably couldn't. I'd be lost out there. Au...Gus has them jumping when he gives orders."

She had to smile. "Most of the time, he doesn't give orders. He doesn't even notice what people are doing. But he does give orders pretty wick when he has to. And they'll follow him to hell. Yer got a deal." She spat on her hand and held it out.

Charlie paused for a second and did the same, and shook her hand, both smiling and shaking his head.

C harlie looked at the slight young woman – still pale with her long black hair, and bright blue eyes, and at the mischievous tweak just in the corner of her mouth. He was good at reading people. He'd rather expected her to be mercenary, given her background, if she had any idea how much TMI was worth. What he hadn't expected was that she didn't even seem interested in looking after herself. She was mercenary... when it came to looking after Augustus. That was confirmed in his mind when Augustus came in, and Charlie saw the look in her eyes, and the involuntary lift of a hand reaching for him. He came and kissed her. "Doctors are coming to check on you," he said.

Charlie made his way to his grandmother and his father. Both were, inevitably, busy working. It was as much part of them as breathing. They both looked up from desks and screens with just a little bit of 'why aren't you working' in their eyes. He was used to that by now. In a sense, he was working, the way oil worked. "Do you know when Augustus will be coming up again?" asked his father.

"You said for us to leave this to you, but we need to schedule flights back to Azure."

"I suppose we can leave any time," said Charlie. "Augustus will be here for another three days until his girl is ready to leave hospital."

"We might as well all travel together," said his grandmother. "I will be quite sad to leave this project. Despite the problems I have quite enjoyed it. A few more days and I hope I will minimize our losses when we sell."

Charlie shook his head. "A couple of things you need to accept. Firstly, Augustus and the girl are staying here."

"Here? In this cess-pit? Surely, he's got over that philanthropy nonsense by now, after what it led him through?" snapped his grandmother. "Besides, the child cannot be born here. When is it due?"

"Oh, I think he's over the philanthropy," said Charlie, crossing his fingers behind his back. "And he's not going to stay here. Although I wouldn't put it past him to clean out this cess-pit. And far from a losing proposition, this hotel is going to look like the smartest purchase that TMI ever made."

"You're talking in riddles again, Charlie."

"This is going to be TMI's new unit, and I think our most profitable and probably the biggest. And Augustus is going to run it. Because he's the only one who can."

"You've said this before, Charlie. And I accept we're excited about the anti-grav technology, but... there's no land. There's no industry, no materials, nothing we need, well, other than some alien technology that could be valuable if we can replicate it. What has it got?"

"A massive market," said Charlie, cheerfully.

"It's tiny and barely worth it. A couple of hundred thousand people in a shanty town, corrupt to the core, and with nothing of value. Even the tourism value is small."

"Oh, this place," said Charlie. "I agree. But that's not what we're talking about. I've been talking to our satellite boys, and getting them to monitor heat points. I'm estimating 50 million people out there, and they're still so scattered the average is less than 0.01 per square mile. It's never going to support a huge population per square mile like Azure can, but there's a lot of square miles. They've got generations of space to grow."

"Fifty million!"

"An aircar lands on a random patch of floating plant and hits someone's washing-line, Papa. Work out the odds."

"No matter how many people there are, they have nothing to buy anything with," his grandmother said.

For an answer, Charlie stuck his hand in his pocket, and pulled out a piece of cloth, and handed it to her. "That's Jumbuck wool. It is strong, light, wicks and thermo-regulates better than anything else we've got – I've had some of our people here testing it. It's going to be worth a mint – and you can't really farm it anywhere else. And Fred reckons the flour-substitute harvested from the floating plants is better than wheat-flour. It's what he's been baking your various treats with, grandmother, remember, I told you. Interstellar transport is cheap compared even to sea-transport. No gravity, lots of volume... It's getting in and out of the gravity well that is expensive. With a working anti-grav system, that becomes very do-able. We can mine the various asteroids and even run factories in orbit. But we can't easily grow crops there or farm animals. There are half a dozen worlds crying out for cheaper carbohydrates, and protein. Did I mention that the meat from those Jumbuck is very tasty? And that's before we get onto the value of plants that can split hydrogen, and store it, or the other technology we can scavenge and learn from and build on."

There was a long silence. Then his father spoke: "Yes... but, Charlie. Augustus. He... he can be brilliant. Academically. But he's not capable..."

"Oh, he can be if he has to. It's there in him, and being out here has brought it out. I saw that, first-hand. Templeton says he made him and his men jump around like raw recruits. But he won't have to. I've just been down talking to Augustus's girl. He's done well for us."

They both looked at him. "I have done some research on her background," said his father, stiffly. "It's a bit unfortunate. We know so little about her, not even her age, but what we do know is not good. But that bouncy young woman you brought in to meet us did indicate she had been quite heroic in his service."

"There is the issue of the child of course," said grandmother. "But I dare say I've raised two, at Marden, I will raise a third if need be."

"Briz is nineteen going on seventy," said Charlie, calmly, not pointing out how that information had been derived. The calculation was derived from the start of Briz's menses and who the Azure ambassador had been at the time, information via Lindsey, whose mother, as the midwife to the station, had asked the questions. "And she's been through hellfire, growing up. None of us would have survived it. She should be the last thing that we want in the family – but somehow, she's come out as exactly what we need. I don't know if it was my brother, circumstances, or genetics that just needed a chance, or all of that together. She's saved Augustus's life at great risk to herself several times, and she is quite painfully loyal, to the point of taking my dear brother's faults as virtues. She loves him, grandmother. And he loves her, Papa, as much as you loved our mother. It'd break him to lose her, and it's made him to have her. She's... scared of you taking him away. Go down, meet her, talk to her. Talk business, to her. You'll be impressed. She's... like you said about great-grandmother, a rough diamond. But she's a diamond."

B riz was still nervous when Charlie herded in Gus's father and grandmother into the hospital room, and introduced them. She promptly forgot just about everything Charlie had told her. Gus's father looked – and dressed – very like Gus when he arrived on the Big Syd. His grandmother, quite without meaning to, impressed Briz far more. She'd got some idea of just how rich and powerful this family actually were. And it finally got to her: when you were that rich and powerful… you didn't have to flaunt it, with a diamond in your tooth. 'Cause you didn't have to care who knew. You just were. And then she spoke. Briz stared open-mouthed. And then said: "So that's where he gets it from. Yer sound just like Gus when he wants people to do exactly what he tells them to do."

Charlie laughed. "You have got it in one, Brizzy. She tells us all what to do."

"I do not," said the old woman. "Now, be quiet and get me a chair, Charlie. I wish to make Augustus's young lady's acquaintance."

"You've just proved Briz right, mother," said Gus's father. Maybe because he looked like Gus, or maybe because he was smiling at her –and Gus, who was standing with a hand on her not-sore shoulder, giving it a very gentle squeeze, she took to him. "I like yer," she informed him.

He blinked. "Um. The feeling is mutual, my dear. I owe you a great debt for looking after my boy."

"He needed it," said Briz. "But he don't need it no more. He can look after himelf these days."

"I do still need you to look after me, Brizzy," said Gus, "And I always will. I was a real drongo when I came here."

"I brought the family down to meet you, and talk about your future," said Charlie, keeping things going.

"We," said Gus, squeezing her shoulder gently again. "Are going back to the outback. To Big Bruce's station. I promised I'd return, and Thistlewood's keep their word."

"He does sound just like you, grandmother," said Charlie.

"We hope you will open a new unit there," said Gus's father. "There is lots of potential, exciting potential here, as Charlie has been telling us. We do need to talk about logistics, materials, what we can do and what needs doing. About the business side. I believe you have some projects going?"

Briz hadn't been looking forward to this, no matter what Charlie said. She also had not been looking forward to spending an enforced four days in this place. She was taken aback to find the next few days flew, and were full and exciting. There was so much to plan, and, well, it was natural as breathing – which hurt less, day by day.

FINALE

"It annoys me, Charlie," said his grandmother, dourly. "When I have to admit you are right. She will do very well for Gus... goodness me. I have caught that from her. Augustus. And this has done him a great deal of good. I am amazed to see him participating in planning business matters."

"He's only doing it to please her," said Charlie. "But he can if he has to."

"She is remarkably astute, considering, and her handwriting is a joy compared to yours, even if her spelling is interesting. But she's very quick to learn. Doesn't make a mistake twice, which is more than I can say about your father. I will be staying on here for a few more months to finish setting up this establishment. We will be sourcing our staff from among the outbackers, and food from them too. You may arrange for grandfather to come and join me, and we shall make a trip out to Augustus's unit."

Privately, Charlie suspected that getting the new hotel up and running might go on for quite a long time... maybe even, how many months did Brizzy have left? He'd have to get back to Azure himself.

There was a lot of organizing to do. A lot of things that needed shipping less than obtrusively. His grandfather, who was an old pirate at heart, would approve. Charlie was slightly less sure, and saw the need for caution. Augustus wanted missiles, or the materials for them. That was easy enough, in some ways. His brother had the knowledge, given some materials and something he could make into a guidance system, to do that all on his own. It was what those blood-thirsty women were cheerfully discussing doing with them – which was to take out every Thrymi or Zell cloudcastle. It was worrying enough as to what might happen when the news of the two Cloud-castles in TMI affiliate hands leaked. "Our government might... get quite upset if it was widely known we'd taken these alien structures by force," he'd said. "Let alone taking any more. We don't want to stir coals."

Lindsey snorted derisively. "We don't give a potamaroo's arse, Charlie. Yer got to remember the Thrymi hunt us for sport. They've killed plenty of outbackers. They were torturing me brother and would have killed him, when Gus bust up their party and took the castle. Even the Zell took outbackers from their homes and families and neutered 'em and left them to die stuck in the Big Syd, never to see their families again, for doing nothing to them. This world is our place. They can shove their 'upset' where the sun don't shine."

His brother made peace. "I think the answer – when the question is asked, is we didn't take them. The outbackers did. And, for the record, seeing as I have been there, both as a student, and then as a slave and as a prisoner... I think the assumption, largely coming out of academia, that other cultures are superior to ours, and that we have to walk around them on tip-toe, is absolute nonsense. Briz and I were Thrymi slaves. Whatever their culture might have been, it's intolerable now. And, I'll tell you this from experience: if there is one thing the Thrymi respect, it is superior force. That's how their whole society works. Besides... if Fred is right, and it makes sense, both the Thrymi and Zell must have ousted others. The system of five holes in the machinery suits neither the three-fingered Zell, nor the seven fingered Thrymi. Yet both aliens have the same system."

"Yer say Admiral Halberd got trouble back home, but he's a hero in the Big Syd," said Briz. "Anyway. Someone said the size of the embassy depends on the population and the Azure embassy here is only that big a building because the Sinopese or Roptor bastards might have been bigger otherwise, and now the government want to cut staff because of the mess with Pinchbutt. Well, I never met one of those useless embassy jokers who wouldn't like to have a bigger patch... which they gets if they has an embassy for fifty million outbackers, not just the Big Syd. So long as they stay here, and stay out of the outback, who cares... But if they're gunna kiss Thrymi and Zell butt, we'll kick the lot of them out. Yer couldn't unite outbackers on anything, except that, hey Lindsey?"

"Too right," agreed Lindsey.

"Think of it this way," said Augustus. "They're really defensive weaponry, unless we take the cloud-castles we've got, looking. And with hook-ups to the satellite network you set up, we will know where the other cloud-castles are. They don't have that advantage, and unless they mob us, we can avoid fights, and will. We have too much work to do, and too much at stake to start fights. But if they step on us, we're going to bite back. I'm not having my people, my wife and my child defenseless. One way or another, we'll do this. So, we might as well do it the easy way. You'll work out the best methods to not make this into an issue, Charlie. We'll work out a way of 'landing' ships out there, so they won't know about it here, for years, likely. Do it quietly: It's what you're good at. We're not going on the warpath. But we're going to have our people there, we're going to have Azure TMI engineers and scientists and teachers, and even Fred and his wife and kids there. We need them safe. So: let's leave you to sort out details on that. Now, there are a lot of communication and transport issues to sort out. Let's talk about radio components again."

"That's where the money will be," said Briz.

"And that's what will change people's lives," said Augustus.

They were both right, Charlie thought. One couldn't go without the other. He was a little envious: Augustus would be busy building and changing a whole world, and he'd be left to keep TMI functioning on Azure. But he'd be back. Quite soon in fact. grandmother had decided she was introducing Azure Thistlewood traditions to Sybil III outbacker marriages, which were not up to her ideas of formality and pomp. He wasn't sure how that would work out, but, well, it was better than trying to get Brizzy or Gus back to Azure. Fortunately, Lindsey had played the tradition card with saying the wedding was the bride's family's business, and Big Bruce and her mother had said as Brizzy didn't have any parents, they were standing in.

And his sister-in-law to be had buttonholed him to say that when he came back, he'd better bring a crate of travel brochures.

He'd been a little embarrassed. She'd remembered that and relayed it to Briz, had she? "Er. Look, Brizzy...it's not that I don't like her. I do. A lot. She's just so different to any girls back on Azure. But... I gather it's not something casual, here."

"Yer a drongo," said Briz cheerfully. "Yer never heard of whale-snot? Probably not, but they wouldn't collect it if no one used it."

"Yes... but, well, if I was serious... I couldn't live out there, Briz. And it's all she knows." She was a pretty woman, bordering on beautiful in the new clothes she was delighted to have, but still.

The corner of Briz's mouth tweaked up. "Except for what she read in a travel brochure. And can quote. Look, she's already talking about how hard it will be to go back... and here I can't wait to go back. She's talking about taking a job in the hotel with yer grandmother. If yer don't show up with them brochures, pretty soon, yer can bet someone else will. She likes you, but she's a farmer's daughter. Practical like that."

"I had no idea she even liked me much." He said, for the first time weighing up the fact that this was a girl who knew exactly who and what he was, that he would never have to explain his family to, because she knew them, and, it seemed didn't give a damn who they were – and, oddly, they all seemed to like her.

Briz chuckled. "Let you look at her gauss-gun, didn't she? Near as an invitation to the sack as yer gonna get."

"Oh," said Charlie, reviewing the fact that Lindsey was due to fly back with Briz and Gus, and he was leaving in a few hours. "Thank you."

"Just payin' back me friend for some advice she gave me," said Briz, with that quirk to the side of her mouth. "Bloody good advice it proved to be, too."

Augustus sat at a table in what had once been the Marvel Room, and would probably soon be again, but right now the only diners were Briz and himself. There was a distant vista of clouds, and at the moment, no cloud-castles, jumbuck or skyfrond. Just the young woman he had sat down to dine with. "Yer looking at me, Gus," said Briz, slightly uncomfortably.

"I love looking at you," said Augustus, not stopping.

"I don't feel right in these clothes," said the slim young woman, with long, lustrous black hair framing an elfin, slightly pale face, her bright blue eyes sharp and never quite still. She was dressed, probably for the first time in her life, in skirts and a blouse. Certainly for the first time in her life in ones that cost quite so much, or were cut quite so well.

"There wasn't much left of your old ones," said Augustus, still enjoying looking at her. "But we can get you some more, as soon as we're back home."

Briz gave him her characteristic one-sided smile. "Home. The bloody outback. Beyond the black stump. Yer know... I can't bloody wait. I don't belong in the Big Syd any more, Gus. Anyway. I got a present for yer." She reached down into a bag one of the security men

325

had carried in for her, and handed him a book. A book he recognized. A tome on Philanthropy and Uplift, by Belcher.

He burst out laughing, looking at it. "Where in heaven...?"

"I nicked it from yer. Never got to give it back. I had some of the security blokes go fetch it. One of them got his pocket picked," she said derisively.

"Oh Briz... I don't think I need Belcher any more. I've got you. Besides, those experts have no real idea of how to uplift massas. It's hard yakka."

"Too right. But that hasn't stopped yer, yer drongo." It was said with a smile and a hand reaching for his, squeezing it, hard.

"It was a very stupid young man that came here, Briz," he admitted.

"If yer hadn't been, yer would have stayed away from me," she said, with a laugh that hardly hurt at all. "Now, yer promised to shout me some good tucker, if I came with yer on this 'date' thing. What's for tea? I'm famished."

"Curried jumbuck tripe, from the Black Stump. That was sort of our first date, if you think about it. We'll go there again, soon. And for a butcher and a pie floater. You might find it a bit dull, though. Grandmother has put the frighteners up the Capos. I believe the Bondi Boyz no longer exist. But jumbuck tripe does."

She laughed until tears came out of her eyes. "I was still winding yer up a bit. Thought yer'd throw up."

"I worked it out. Later. But you enjoyed it. So, I arranged it. I'd like to have taken you there, but the Doctor looked like he was going to have a fit. Because I love you, Briz, and I wanted to remember that green young man, and the urchin that took me in hand."

She looked at him, blinking tears again. This was making her into a sook. "I love yer too, Gus, even when yer a drongo. Maybe even more when yer are. I'm just not used to saying it much. But I'm working on it."

"I don't think I'm going to change. And we're going to build a future here, for us, and for our children."

"Yer want more than one?" she asked with an almost straight face.

"Too right, I do."

"Oh, good-o," she said, her eyes full of promise, smiling back at him.

-oo-

REQUEST FROM THE AUTHOR

Psst. I have a favor to ask. The best form of advertising is word of mouth. That's especially true when it comes to books. Friends and family trust reviews and suggestions for books that come from people they know.

That is especially true in this digital age. If you enjoyed this book, do me a favor. Spread the word. Tell people on your various social media accounts. Leave a review. If you're a blogger, write a post about it. All that does help. Besides, it is the one way we, as authors, know you really enjoyed our work.

Thanks!

ABOUT THE AUTHOR

Find something unusual and which people of common sense would have avoided like the plague, and most likely I've somehow blundered into it. I was a conscript soldier in Medical Corps in South Africa. When I got out of that I (after seven years of study) ended up as an ichthyologist and fisheries scientist. I was a research scientist for the commercial shark fishery for some years, before going fish-farming, and from that somehow falling into writing, mostly because author is easier to spell than ichthyologist. I did a bunch of equally bizarre jobs along the way, including being the relief chef and a group of luxury ecotourism lodges. With all this we lived in the hottest part of the country, the coldest (at 6000 feet) the wettest, and everything, between, before emigrating to Australia and moving to a remote island in the roaring forties. I grew up in a hunting, fishing, diving and rock-climbing family, and still do all of them, as well as trying to farm for at least self-sufficiency. I am one of the volunteer ambulance officers on the island, providing the only service we have, and put a lot of hours into that. I'm long and happily married, and have two grown up sons, and severe lack of grandchildren to teach to fish and shoot, and cause mayhem, but I believe this is being remedied. Other than that, I write and read a lot of books. I think it helps that I have done some of what I write about.

BOOKS BY DAVE FREER

MORNINGSTAR

A MANKIND WITCH

STARDOGS

CHANGELING'S ISLAND

TOM

Dragon series

DRAGON'S RING

DOG AND DRAGON

Coalfired Cuttlefish series

CUTTLEFISH

THE STEAM-MOLE

JOY COMETH WITH THE MOURNING

For younger readers (10-13):

WITHOUT A TRACE

Co-authored Novels

RBV series

RATS, BATS & VATS (with Eric Flint)

THE RATS, THE BATS AND THE UGLY (with Eric Flint)

Pyramid series

PYRAMID SCHEME (with Eric Flint)

PYRAMID POWER (with Eric Flint)

SLOW TRAIN TO ARCTURUS (with Eric Flint)

Karres sequels

THE WIZARD OF KARRES (with Eric Flint and Mercedes Lackey)

THE SORCERESS OF KARRES (with Eric Flint)

THE SHAMAN OF KARRES (with Eric Flint)

Heirs of Alexandra series

SHADOW OF THE LION (with Eric Flint and Mercedes Lackey)

A MANKIND WITCH (relisted because it the second book in the series)

THIS ROUGH MAGIC (with Eric Flint and Mercedes Lackey)

MUCH FALL OF BLOOD (with Eric Flint and Mercedes Lackey)

BURDENS OF THE DEAD (with Eric Flint)

ALL THE PLAGUES OF HELL (with Eric Flint)

Shorter works

SOOT AND CASSANDRA

THE ROAD TO DUNDEE

RED FIDDLER (with Eric Flint)

PIRATES OF THE SUARA SEA (with Eric Flint)

Bolg, PI stories

BOLG, PI: THE VAMPIRE BRIDE

BOLG, PI: WOLFY LADIES

BOLG, PI: AWAY WITH THE FAIRIES

BOLG, PI: THE BOLG AND THE BEAUTIFUL

RBV Universe stories